RAZORBLADE TEARS

ALSO BY S. A. COSBY

Blacktop Wasteland
My Darkest Prayer

RAZORBLADE
TEARS

S. A. COSBY

FLATIRON
BOOKS
NEW YORK

RAZORBLADE TEARS. Copyright © 2021 by Shawn A. Cosby. All rights reserved. Printed in the United States of America. For information, address Flatiron Books, 120 Broadway, New York, NY 10271.

www.flatironbooks.com

Designed by Donna Sinisgalli Noetzel

Library of Congress Cataloging-in-Publication Data

Names: Cosby, S. A., author.
Title: Razorblade tears / S. A. Cosby.
Description: First edition. | New York, NY : Flatiron Books, 2021. |
Identifiers: LCCN 2021004762 | ISBN 9781250252708 (hardcover) |
ISBN 9781250252722 (ebook)
Subjects: GSAFD: Suspense fiction.
Classification: LCC PS3603.O7988 R39 2021 | DDC 813/.6—dc23
LC record available at https://lccn.loc.gov/2021004762

Our books may be purchased in bulk for promotional, educational, or business use. Please contact your local bookseller or the Macmillan Corporate and Premium Sales Department at 1-800-221-7945, extension 5442, or by email at MacmillanSpecialMarkets@macmillan.com.

First Edition: 2021

10 9 8 7 6 5 4 3 2

To my mother, Joyce A. Cosby,
who gave me two very important gifts:
determination and curiosity

My drops of tears I'll turn to sparks of fire.

—WILLIAM SHAKESPEARE, *HENRY VIII*

RAZORBLADE TEARS

ONE

ke tried to remember a time when men with badges coming to his door early in the morning brought anything other than heartache and misery, but try as he might, nothing came to mind.

The two men stood side by side on the small concrete landing of his front step with their hands on their belts near their badges and their guns. The morning sun made the badges glimmer like gold nuggets. The two cops were a study in contrast. One was a tall but wiry Asian man. He was all sharp angles and hard edges. The other, a florid-faced white man, was built like a powerlifter with a massive head sitting atop a wide neck. They both wore white dress shirts with clip-on ties. The powerlifter had sweat stains spreading down from his armpits that vaguely resembled maps of England and Ireland respectively.

Ike's queasy stomach began to do somersaults. He was fifteen years removed from Coldwater State Penitentiary. He had bucked the recidivism statistics ever since he'd walked out of that festering wound. Not so much as a speeding ticket in all those years. Yet here he was with his tongue dry and the back of his throat burning as the two cops stared down at him. It was bad enough being a Black man in the good ol' US of A and talking to the cops. You always felt like you were on the edge of some imaginary precipice during any interaction with an officer of the law. If you were an ex-con, it felt like the precipice was covered in bacon grease.

"Yes?" Ike said.

"Sir, I'm Detective LaPlata. This is my partner, Detective Rob-bins. May we come in?"

"What for?" Ike asked. LaPlata sighed. It came out low and long like the bottom note in a blues song. Ike tensed. LaPlata glanced at Robbins. Robbins shrugged. LaPlata's head dipped down, then he raised it again. Ike had learned to pick up on body language when he was inside. There was no aggression in their stances. At least not any more than what most cops exuded on a normal twelve-hour shift. The way LaPlata's head had dropped was almost . . . sad.

"Do you have a son named Isiah Randolph?" he said finally.

That was when he knew. He knew it like he knew when a fight was about to break out in the yard. Like he knew when a crackhead was going to try to stab him for a bag back in the day. Like he knew, just knew in his gut, that his homeboy Luther had seen his last sunset that night he'd gone home with that girl from the Satellite Bar.

It was like a sixth sense. A preternatural ability to sense a trag-edy seconds before it became a reality.

"What's happened to my son, Detective LaPlata?" Ike asked, al-ready knowing the answer. Knowing it in his bones. Knowing his life would never be the same.

TWO

I t was a beautiful day for a funeral.

Snow white clouds rolled across an azure sky. Despite it being the first week of April the air was still crisp and cool. Of course, since this was Virginia, it could be raining buckets in the next ten minutes, then hot as the devil's backside an hour later.

A sage-green tent covered the remaining mourners and two caskets. The minister grabbed a handful of dirt from the pile that sat just outside the tent. The pile was covered by a weathered artificial grass rug. He moved to the head of the caskets.

"Earth to earth. Ashes to ashes. Dust to dust." The minister's voice echoed through the cemetery as he sprinkled dirt on both caskets. He skipped the part about the general resurrection and the last days. The funeral director stepped forward. He was a short chubby man with a charcoal complexion that matched his suit. Despite the mild conditions, his face was slick with sweat. It was as if his body were responding to the calendar and not the thermometer.

"This concludes the services for Derek Jenkins and Isiah Randolph. The family thanks you for your attendance. You may go in peace," he said. His voice didn't have the same theatricality as the minister's. It barely carried beyond the tent.

Ike Randolph let go of his wife's hand. She slumped against him. Ike stared down at his hands. His empty hands. Hands that had held his boy when he was barely ten minutes old. The hands that had shown him how to tie his shoes. The hands that had rubbed salve on his chest when he'd had the flu. That had waved goodbye to him in court with shackles tight around his wrists. Rough callused hands that he hid in his pockets when Isiah's husband had offered to shake them.

Ike dropped his chin to his chest.

The little girl sitting in her lap played with Mya's braids. Ike looked at the girl. Skin the color of honey with hair to match. Arianna had just turned three the week before her parents died. Did she have any inkling of what was happening? When Mya had told her that her daddies were asleep, she seemed to accept it without too much trouble. He envied the elasticity of her mind. She could wrap her head around this in a way that he couldn't.

"Ike, that's our boy in there. That's our baby," Mya wailed. He flinched when she spoke. It was like hearing a rabbit scream in a trap. Ike heard the folding chairs squeak and whine as people rose and headed to the parking lot. He felt hands flutter against his back and shoulders. Words of encouragement were mumbled with half-hearted sincerity. It wasn't that folks didn't care. It was that they knew those words did little to soothe the wound in his soul. Speaking those platitudes and clichéd homilies seemed disingenuous, but what else could they do? It was what you did when someone died. It was as axiomatic as bringing a casserole to the repast.

The crowd was thin, and it didn't take long for the chairs to empty. In less than five minutes the only people in the cemetery were Ike, Mya, Arianna, the gravediggers, and a man Ike vaguely recognized as Derek's father. A lot of Ike's family hadn't shown up for the service. As far as he could tell, only a few of Derek's people had bothered to attend. Most of the mourners were Isiah and Derek's friends. Ike noticed Derek's family members. They stood out among the bearded hipsters and androgynous ladies that made up Derek and Isiah's social circle. Lean wiry men and women with hard flinty eyes and sun-worn faces. They wore blue collars around their red necks. As the sermon neared the thirty-minute mark, he'd watched their faces begin to bloom with crimson. That was when the minister mentioned how no sin was unforgivable. Even abominable sins could be forgiven by a benevolent God.

Arianna pulled one of Mya's braids.

"Stop it, girl!" Mya said. It came out sharp. Arianna was silent for a moment. Ike knew what was coming next. That pregnant pause was the prelude to the waterworks. Isiah used to do the same thing.

Arianna began to howl. Her screams pierced the quiet contemplativeness of the funeral and rang in Ike's ears. Mya tried to soothe her. She apologized and brushed her forehead. Arianna took a deep breath, then began to scream louder.

"Take her to the car. I'll be there in a minute," Ike said.

"Ike, I ain't going nowhere. Not yet," Mya snapped. Ike stood.

"Please Mya. Take her to the car. Just give me a few minutes, then I'll come and watch her and you can come back," Ike said. His voice almost cracked. Mya stood. She pulled Arianna close to her chest.

"You say what you gotta say." She turned and headed for the car. Arianna's cries withered to whimpers as they walked away. Ike put his hand on the black casket with the gold trim. His boy was in there. His son was in this rectangular container. Packed and preserved like some cured meat. The breeze picked up, making the tassels hanging from the edge of the tent flap like the wings of a dying bird. Derek was in the silver casket with the black trim. Isiah was being buried next to his husband. They'd died together and now they'd rest together.

Derek's father rose from his seat. He was a lean and weathered piece of work with a shock of shoulder-length salt-and-pepper hair. He walked up to the foot of the caskets and stood next to Ike. The gravediggers busied themselves with shovel inspections as they waited for these two men, the last of the mourners, to leave. The lean man scratched at his chin. A gray shadow of a beard covered the bottom half of his face. He coughed, cleared his throat, then coughed again. When he got that under control, he turned toward Ike.

"Buddy Lee Jenkins. Derek's father. I don't think we ever officially met," Buddy Lee said. He held out his hand.

"Ike Randolph." He took Buddy Lee's hand and pumped it up and down twice, then let it go. They stood at the foot of the coffins, silent as stones. Buddy Lee coughed again.

"Was you at the wedding reception?" Buddy Lee asked. Ike shook his head.

"Me neither," Buddy Lee said.

"I think I saw you at their girl's birthday party last year," Ike said.

"Yeah, I was there but I didn't stay long." Buddy Lee sucked his teeth as he adjusted his sport coat. "Derek was ashamed of me. Can't say I much blame him," Buddy Lee said. Ike didn't know how to respond, so he didn't.

"I just wanna thank you and your wife for getting everything straight. I couldn't afford to put them away this nice. And Derek's mama couldn't be bothered," Buddy Lee said.

"Wasn't us. They had things already taken care of. They'd set up some kind of prepaid funeral package. We just had to sign some papers," Ike said.

"Man. Was you setting up funeral arrangements at twenty-seven? I know I sure wasn't. Hell, I couldn't set up a fucking paper route at twenty-seven," Buddy Lee said. Ike ran his hand over his son's casket. Whatever moment he had imagined having was ruined now.

"That tat on your hand, that's Black God's ink, ain't it?" Buddy Lee asked. Ike studied his hands. The indistinct drawings of a lion with two scimitars above its head on his right hand and the word RIOT on his left had been his silent companions since his second year in Coldwater State Penitentiary.

Ike put his hands in his pockets.

"That was a long time ago," Ike said. Buddy Lee sucked his teeth again.

"Where'd you do your time? I did a nickel at Red Onion. Some hard fellas out that way. Met a few BG boys out there."

"I don't mean no harm, but it ain't really something I like to talk about," Ike said.

"Well, I don't mean no harm, but if you don't like talking about it, why don't you get the tat covered up? Shit, from what I hear, they can do that in an hour," Buddy Lee said. Ike took his hands out of his pockets. He looked down at the black lion on his hand. The lion was standing on a crude map of the state.

"Just because I don't wanna talk about it doesn't mean I want to forget about it. It reminds me of why I don't ever wanna go back," Ike said. "I'm gonna leave you with your boy now." He turned and started to walk away.

"You ain't gotta go. It's too late for me and him," Buddy Lee said. "Too late for you and your boy, too." Ike stopped. He half turned back toward Buddy Lee.

"What you mean by that?" Ike asked. Buddy Lee ignored the question.

"When he was fourteen, I caught Derek kissing another boy down by the creek in the woods behind our trailer. Took off my belt and beat him like a runaway . . . like he stole something. I called him names. Told him he was a pervert. I whupped him till his legs was covered with welts. He cried and cried. Saying he was sorry. He didn't know why he was like that. You never got into it with your boy like that? Never? I dunno, maybe you was a better daddy than I was," Buddy Lee said. Ike adjusted his jaw.

"Why we talking about this?" Ike said. Buddy Lee shrugged.

"If I could just talk to Derek for five minutes, you know what I'd say? 'I don't give a damn who you fucking. Not one bit.' What you think you'd say to your boy?" Buddy Lee said. Ike stared at him. Stared through him. He noticed tears clinging to the corners of the man's eyes, but they didn't fall. Ike ground his teeth so hard he thought his molars might crack.

"I'm going," Ike said. He stomped toward his car.

"You think they gonna catch who did it?" Buddy Lee shouted after him. Ike picked up his pace. When he reached the car, the minister was just leaving the parking lot. Ike watched as he creeped by in a jet-black BMW. Rev. J. T. Johnson's profile was sharp enough to slice cheese. He never turned his head or acknowledged Ike and Mya at all.

Ike jogged down the driveway. He caught the minister before he turned onto the highway. Ike tapped on his window. Rev. Johnson lowered the glass. Ike dropped to his haunches and extended his hand into the car.

"I guess I should thank you for preaching my son's funeral," Ike said. Rev. Johnson grasped Ike's hand and pumped it up and down a few times.

"No need to thank me, Ike," Rev. Johnson said. His deep rich baritone rumbled out of his chest like a freight train on greased tracks. He tried to pull his hand away but Ike gripped it tight.

"I'm supposed to thank you but I just can't." He gripped Rev. Johnson's hand tighter. The minister winced. "I just gotta ask you, why did you preach the funeral?"

Rev. Johnson frowned. "Ike, Mya asked—"

"I know Mya asked you to do it. What I'm asking you is why did you do it? Because I can tell you didn't want to," Ike said. He tightened his grip on Johnson's hand.

"Ike, my hand . . ."

"You kept talking about abominable sin. Over and over. You thought my son was an abomination?" Ike asked.

"Ike, I never said that."

"You didn't have to say it. I might just cut grass for a living but I know an insult when I hear it. You think my son was some kind of monster and you made sure everybody at his funeral knew it. My boy was less than five feet away from you, and you couldn't shut the fuck up about how his sins were forgivable. His abominable sins."

"Ike, please . . ." Rev. Johnson said. A line of cars was forming behind the good minister's BMW.

"You didn't say nothing about him being a reporter. Or that he graduated top of his class at VCU. You didn't talk about him winning the state basketball championship in high school. You just kept talking about abominations. I don't know what you thought he was, but he was just . . ." Ike paused. The word caught in his throat like a chicken bone.

"Please let go of my hand," Rev. Johnson gasped.

"My son wasn't no fucking abomination!" Ike said. His voice was as cold as a mountain stream flowing over river rocks. He gripped Rev. Johnson's hand tighter. He felt metacarpals grinding to powder. Rev. Johnson groaned.

"Ike, let him go!" Mya said. Ike turned his head to the right. His wife was standing outside their car. The line behind them was ten deep. Ike released Rev. Johnson's hand. The minister spun tires as he rocketed onto the highway. Ike marveled at how fast the German engineering carried Rev. Johnson away.

Ike walked back to his car. Mya got in the passenger seat as he slid in the driver's side. She crossed her arms over her narrow chest and leaned her head against the window.

"What was all that about?" she asked. Ike turned the key in the ignition and put the car in gear.

"You heard what he was saying in his sermon. You know what he was saying about Isiah," Ike said. Mya sighed.

"Like you haven't said worse. But now that he's dead you want to defend him?" Mya asked. Ike gripped the steering wheel.

"I loved him. I did. Just as much as you," Ike said between clenched teeth.

"Really? Where was this love when he was getting picked on morning, noon, and night in school? Oh, that's right, you were locked up. He needed your love then. Not now that he's in the ground," Mya said. Tears rolled down her face. Ike worked his jaw up and down like he was biting the tension between them.

"That's why I taught him how to fight when I came home," Ike said.

"Well, that's what you know best, ain't it?" Mya asked. Ike clenched his teeth.

"Do you want to go back over there and—" Ike started to say.

"Just take us home," Mya sobbed.

He stepped on the gas and pulled out of the cemetery parking lot.

THREE

B uddy Lee sat straight up in his bed. Someone was banging on the door of his trailer so hard it felt like the whole structure was shaking. He checked the clock sitting on the milk crate that served as his nightstand. It was six o'clock. The funeral had ended at 2 P.M. Buddy Lee had stopped off at the Piggly Wiggly and picked up a case of beer. He'd crushed the last can around 4:30. Then he had flopped on his bed and passed out cold.

The banging at his door erupted again. It was cops. It had to be cops. No one banged on your door that hard except Johnny Law. Buddy Lee rubbed his eyes.

Run.

The thought flashed in his mind like an LED sign. The impulse was so strong he was standing up and taking two steps toward the back door before he realized what he was doing. He took a deep breath.

Run.

The thought pulsed in his head even though he was ten years out of Red Onion. Even though he only had a jar of moonshine in the cabinet and two joints in his truck. Even though he'd basically kept his nose clean since he'd started driving for Kitchener Seafood three years ago. Well, he didn't have to worry too much about keeping his nose clean anymore since Ricky Kitchener had fired him instead of giving him a week of bereavement time.

Buddy Lee cracked his knuckles and walked to the front door.

The temperature had skyrocketed since he'd passed out, so he flicked on the AC unit before he opened the door.

A short squat man was standing on the four cinder blocks that made up Buddy Lee's front step. His balding head was ringed by rust-colored patches of hair on the sides and in the back of his skull. His white T-shirt sported a week's worth of stains. They spelled out his eating habits like indistinct hieroglyphics.

"Hey Artie," Buddy Lee said

"Your rent's a week late, Jenkins," Artie said. Buddy Lee burped and he thought all twenty-four beers in the case were going to make a surprise appearance in his mouth. Buddy Lee closed his eyes and tried to conjure up a calendar in his head. Was it the fifteenth already? Time had taken on a strange inconsequential quality since the cops had shown him a picture of Derek's face with the top of his head blacked out.

Buddy Lee opened his eyes.

"Artie, you know my son died, right? The funeral was today."

"I heard, but that don't change the fact the rent is due. I'm sorry about your boy, I really am, but this ain't the first time you been late. I done let you slide a few times but I gotta have it by tomorrow or we gonna have to have another kind of conversation," Artie said. His tiny rat eyes sat in his head dull and brown like old pennies.

Buddy Lee leaned against the ragged doorframe. He crossed his wiry arms.

"Yeah, I can tell you've really fell on hard times here, Artie. How in the world you gonna keep up your fantastic wardrobe?" Buddy Lee said.

"You can joke me all you want, Jenkins, but if I don't have full payment tomorrow, which includes the lot fee and the rent for the trailer, I'll—" Artie said, but Buddy Lee stepped down onto the first cinder block. Artie hadn't expected the move. He took an awkward step backward and nearly tumbled to the ground.

"You'll what? What you gonna do? Call the cops? Go down to

the courthouse and get a warrant to kick me out of this broke-down-ass trailer? Lord have mercy, what in the world will I do without this fucking mansion that got a toilet that ain't flushed right since 'ninety-four?"

"Ain't no free ride here Buddy Lee! This ain't one of them Section 8 setups. You want that, you can go over to Wyndam Hills and hang out with the other welfare cases. I knew I should've never rented to no ex-con. My wife told me but I didn't listen. Every time I try to give somebody a break they screw me," Artie said. Spittle sparked from his lips.

"Well, somebody gotta screw you since your wife gave up on getting you to take a bath more than once month," Buddy Lee said. Artie flinched like he'd been slapped.

"Fuck you, Buddy Lee; I got a glandular condition. You know, you ain't nothing but trash. Been trash just like all them Jenkins. That's why your son was a—" Artie didn't get to finish the statement. Buddy Lee had closed the distance between them in one and a half steps. A jackknife, its brown wooden handle smooth and slick from years of use, was pressed blade first against Artie's belly. Buddy Lee balled up a wad of Artie's T-shirt and put his mouth close to the shorter man's ear.

"That's why my son was a what? Go on. Say it. Say it so I can slit you from nuts to neck. Split you open like a killing hog and let your guts fall out like we cooking chitterlings for Sunday dinner," Buddy Lee said.

"I . . . I . . . just want the rent," Artie wheezed.

"What you want is to come over here while my boy ain't even cold in the ground and swing your dick around like you the cock of the walk. All the time I been here I done let you talk your shit because I didn't want no trouble. But I buried my boy today and now I ain't really got a goddamn thing to lose, So, go ahead. Say it. SAY IT!" Buddy Lee said. His chest heaved as his breath came in rapid bursts.

"I'm sorry about Derek. Jesus Christ, I'm so fucking sorry. Please let me go. I'm so damn sorry," Artie said. From his armpits a fetid odor wafted up that made Buddy Lee's eyes water. At least that's what he told himself. With the mention of his boy's name, the rattlesnake in his heart that Artie had poked slithered back down into its hole. The fight flowed out of him like water pouring through a sieve. Artie was a mean-spirited, unhygienic son of a bitch but he didn't kill Derek. He was just another asshole that didn't understand who or what Derek was. That was something he and Buddy Lee had in common.

"Go back to your fucking house, Artie," Buddy Lee said. He let go of the man's shirt and put his knife back in his pocket. Artie scuttled backward and sideways. When he felt there was enough distance between him and Buddy Lee, he stopped and flicked him off.

"That's your ass, Jenkins! I'm calling the cops. You ain't gonna have to worry about the rent now. You gonna be sleeping in a jail cell tonight."

"Go away, Artie," Buddy Lee said. It came out flat and listless, all the bravado gone. Artie blinked hard. The sudden de-escalation confused him. Buddy Lee turned his back on him and went into his trailer. The AC hadn't so much conditioned the air as suggested it might want to cool down.

He sprawled across his sofa. The duct tape on the armrest snagged a few of the hairs on his forearm. He fished around in his back pocket and grabbed his wallet. Behind his driver license was a small wrinkled photo. Buddy Lee pulled the photo out by the corner using his thumb and forefinger. It was a picture of him and a one-year-old Derek. He held the boy in the crook of his arm as they sat in an aluminum lawn chair. Buddy Lee was shirtless in the picture. His hair was down to his shoulders and black as an ace of spades. Derek was wearing a Superman shirt and a diaper.

Buddy Lee wondered what the young fella in the picture would think of the old man he'd become. That fella was full of gunpowder and gasoline. If he looked really close, he could see a small mouse under his right eye. A souvenir he'd acquired collecting a debt for Chuly Pettigrew. The man in that picture was wild and dangerous. Always down for a fight and up to no good. If Artie had spoken ill of Derek in front of that man, he would have waited until dark and then cut his throat for him. Watched him bleed out all over the gravel before taking him somewhere dark and desolate. Knocked out his teeth and cut off his hands and buried him in a shallow grave covered in about fifty pounds of pulverized lime. Then the man in that picture would have gone home, made love to his woman, and not lost a minute's sleep.

Derek was different. Whatever rot that lived in the roots of the Jenkins family tree had bypassed Derek. His son was so full of positive potential it made him glow like a shooting star from the day he was born. He had accomplished more in his twenty-seven years than most of the entire Jenkins bloodline had in a generation. Buddy Lee's hand began to shake. The photo fell from his fingers as the tremors worsened, working their way through his hand. The photo floated to the floor. Buddy Lee put his head in his hands and waited for the tears to come. His throat burned. His stomach was doing cartwheels. His eyes felt like they wanted to burst. Still no tears came.

"My boy. My sweet boy," he muttered over and over as he rocked back and forth.

FOUR

Ike sat in the living room sipping on some rum on the rocks. He'd changed out of his suit and was wearing a white tank top and jeans. Despite the ice, the rum burned as it went down his throat. Mya and Arianna were taking a nap. In the kitchen, containers full of chicken, ham, and mac and cheese were spread across every available surface. A few of Isiah and Derek's friends had brought vegetarian barbecue. Whatever the hell that was.

Ike brought the rum to his head and finished it in one huge gulp. He winced but kept it down. He considered getting another one, then changed his mind. Getting drunk wasn't going to make things easier. He needed to feel this pain. Keep it fresh in his heart. He deserved it. In the back of his mind he'd always thought that he and Isiah would come to an understanding. He just assumed time would thaw the glacier between them and they would both experience an epiphany of sorts. Isiah would finally understand how hard it was for his father to accept his lifestyle. In turn, Ike would be able to accept that his son was gay. But time was a river made of quicksilver. It slipped through his grasp even as it enveloped him. Twenty became forty. Winter became spring, and before he knew it he was an old man burying his son and wondering where in the hell that river had taken him.

Ike held the empty glass to his forehead. He should have walked across that goddamn glacier instead of waiting for it to melt. Sat down with Isiah and tried to explain how he felt. Tell him he felt like he had failed as a father. Isiah, being Isiah, would have told him that his sexuality had nothing to do with Ike's shitty parenting skills. Maybe they both would have laughed. Maybe that would have broken the ice.

He let out a sigh. That was a nice fantasy.

Ike sat his empty glass on the coffee table. He sat back in the recliner and closed his eyes. The recliner had been a gift to himself. A place to rest his weary bones after ferrying bags of peat moss and mulch all day long.

Ike's cell phone vibrated in his pocket. He checked the number. It was one of the detectives who were supposed to be working Isiah's case.

"Hello," Ike said.

"Hello, Mr. Randolph, this is Detective LaPlata. How are you holding up?"

"I just buried my son," Ike said.

LaPlata paused.

"I'm sorry, Mr. Randolph. We are doing everything we can to find the people who did this. To that end, would it be okay if we came by and talked to you and your wife? We are trying to see if any of Isiah and Derek's friends or associates have reached out to you. We're having a hard time getting them to talk to us," LaPlata said.

"Well, you're cops. A lot of people don't like talking to cops even when they're innocent," Ike said. LaPlata sighed.

"We're just trying find a lead here, Mr. Randolph. So far, we can't find anyone who has a bad word to say 'bout your son or his boyfriend."

"They were . . . they were married," Ike said. More awkward silence clogged the line.

"I'm sorry about that. We talked to your son's employer. Did you know he had a death threat sent to him earlier this year?"

"I didn't know that. Me and Isiah . . . we weren't as close as we could've been, so I don't think there's anything I'm gonna be able to help you with," Ike said.

"What about your wife, Mr. Randolph?"

"This isn't really a good time to talk to her," Ike said.

"Mr. Randolph, I know this is hard but—"

"Do you? Did somebody shoot your son in the head, then stand over him and empty a clip into his face?" Ike said. The phone creaked in his hand as his grip tightened.

"No, but—"

"I have to go, Mr. LaPlata," Ike said. He hit the END button and put the phone on the coffee table next to the empty glass.

He walked over to the cheap pressboard entertainment center that housed their television and dozens of framed photographs. Isiah kneeling with one hand on a basketball in his gold-and-blue Red Hill County High School uniform. A picture of preteen Isiah pinning Mya when she graduated from nursing school. A picture of Isiah, Mya, and Ike the day Isiah graduated from college. Mya stood between them. A demilitarized zone to keep them from arguing. That came later. At the cookout they had for Isiah getting his journalism degree. It was supposed to be a day to remember. It had been, but for all the wrong reasons. Ike picked up the graduation picture and ran his thick callused fingers across the glass before putting it back on the top of the entertainment center.

Ike walked through the kitchen and out the back door. He headed for his shed. He opened the door, stepped inside, and flicked on the light. The air was filled with the scent of fuel and iron. The shed was large. Forty by forty with a skylight and a vent. On one side of the structure a collection of tools and yard equipment were stored with military precision. Two leaf blowers and two weed trimmers hung on hooks and gleamed like showroom models. Rakes and shovels were stacked next to each other like rifles in an armory. A push mower and an edger sat next to each other without a trace of grass or dirt anywhere. Suspended on the right side of the shed in the corner behind motes of dust was a heavy bag. The lonely light hanging from the ceiling cast odd shadows against the wall behind the bag. Ike went over to it and began bouncing on the balls of his feet. He bobbed and feinted, then started peppering the bag with punches. Quick one-two combinations, feeling the sting of the weathered leather against his bare knuckles.

Growing up, Isiah had been a natural athlete. When he worked the heavy bag, his movements were powerful and fluid. His footwork was exceptional. His head movement was elusive.

When Ike was released, boxing was the only thing Isiah enjoyed doing with him. They didn't have to talk when they wrapped their fists and worked over the weathered cowhide. Ike had wanted him to enter the Golden Gloves or join an AAU team. He had hoped boxing would be the thing that would bridge the gap between them. But Isiah refused to fight. Ike pressed and pushed him but he wouldn't budge. He was as stubborn as any other fourteen-year-old kid. Finally, Ike had pushed one too many times, and Isiah had cut to the heart of the matter.

"I'm not like you. I don't like hurting people."

That was it. They'd never gone into the shed together again. Ike unleashed a flurry of elbow strikes. He jumped backward, tucked his chin into his chest, then fired off a series of rights and lefts in a staccato rhythm. The steady beat of his knuckles smashing against the taut surface of the bag reverberated throughout the shed.

Ike always pushed Isiah too hard and Isiah pushed right back. Mya said they were so much alike Ike should have given birth to him. Their last conversation, a few months ago, had been a verbal shoving match that ended with a slammed door. Isiah had come over to tell his mother he and Derek were getting married. Mya had hugged him. Ike had gone into the kitchen and poured a drink. After a few more kisses from his mother, Isiah had followed him.

"You don't approve?" Isiah had said. Ike had gulped his rum and sat the glass on the edge of the counter.

"It's not my place to approve or disapprove. Not anymore. But you know this ain't just about you. Y'all got that little girl now," Ike had said.

"Your granddaughter. Her name is Arianna and she's your granddaughter," Isiah had said. A vein in the furrow of his forehead began to pulse. Ike crossed his arms.

"Look, I stopped trying to tell you what to do a long time ago. But that little girl, she gonna have it hard enough already. She's half Black. Her mama was somebody you paid to carry her, and she got two gay daddies. So now what? You gonna make her a flower girl in your wedding? Y'all gonna rent out the Jefferson Hotel and make a big production out of it? And in a couple of years you gonna walk into her kindergarten class and all the other little kids can ask her which one is the mommy. Did you or Derek ever stop and think about that?" Ike had said.

"That's the first thing that comes to your mind when I tell you I'm marrying the love of my life? Not congratulations. Not even an insincere 'I'm happy for you.' But what people might think. What people might say. News flash, Isaac, I've dealt with what people have to say ever since I had to explain that my father was a jailbird. I guess you'd rather we said our vows in a shack in the woods at midnight. I don't know if you are aware of this, but not everyone thinks the way you do. Not everyone is disgusted by their children. And the people that do think like you? Well, they'll all be dead soon enough," Isiah had said. Ike didn't remember picking up the glass. He didn't remember hurling it against the wall. He just remembered Isiah turning on his heel and slamming the door on his way out.

Three months later his son and his husband were dead. Shot multiple times in the front of a fancy wine store in downtown Richmond. Once his son and his husband were down, the shooters had double-tapped them both. The sign of a professional. Ike wondered if the last image Isiah had of his father was a glass shattering against a kitchen cabinet.

Ike started to scream. It didn't build in his chest first then erupt.

It came out fully formed in one long savage howl. The heavy bag began to jerk and jump spasmodically. Technique was tossed aside in favor of animalistic instinct. The skin on his knuckles split and left red-hued Rorschach paintings on the bag. Droplets of sweat ran down his face and dripped into his eyes. Tears ran from his eyes and stung his cheeks. Tears for his son. Tears for his wife. Tears for the little girl they had to raise. Tears for who they were and what they all had lost. Each drop felt like it was slicing his face open like a razorblade.

FIVE

Buddy Lee checked his watch. It was five minutes to eight. The sign said that Randolph Lawn Maintenance opened at 8 A.M. Monday through Saturday. Ike should be rolling up any minute.

The AC in his truck wasn't much better than the AC in his trailer. The air blowing from the vents was tepid at best. The system needed a dose of Freon, but his electric bill was due this week. When it came down to having a working fridge at home or a working AC in his truck, the fridge was going to win every time.

Buddy Lee changed the station on his radio. Nobody played real country anymore. Just a bunch of baby-shit-soft male models singing about bumping and grinding over a steel guitar. A logging truck flew down the road past the gas station where Buddy Lee had parked his truck. Randolph Lawn Maintenance was housed in a single-story sheet-metal warehouse across the road from a Spee-Dee Mart and down the road from the Red Hill Florist. Buddy Lee resided in Charon County, which was about fifteen miles from Red Hill. Buddy Lee thought it was funny his son and Ike's son had grown up only twenty minutes apart but found each other in college. Life sends us down some strange roads on our way to our destiny.

He was about to go back in the gas station and get another cup of coffee when he saw a white dually truck pull up to the gate at Randolph Lawn Maintenance. The truck stopped, and Ike hopped out to open the gate. He rolled the chain-link gate out of the way and pulled into the parking lot. Buddy Lee watched him get out of the truck again and enter the building.

As he climbed out of his own ramshackle truck, he started coughing. He knew it was going to be bad. His esophagus felt like it was being pulled like saltwater taffy. His lungs strained to force oxygen into his bloodstream. Buddy Lee gripped the steering wheel so tight his knuckles went white. After sixty agonizing seconds the cough subsided. He spit a wad of phlegm on the ground and jogged across the two-lane highway that bisected the town.

The inside of the warehouse was as sparse as a military barracks. A worn coffee table sat to the right of the entrance buffeted on one side by a metal folding chair and a threadbare leather love seat on the other. An old-fashioned glass-faced drink machine sat against the left wall. Most of the slots in the machine were empty. The three that weren't had a plain blue can that said COLA on the front. On both walls there were numerous posters advertising a wide variety of lawn and garden products. All the posters either promised to kill your grass or make your grass grow. A few suggested they would execute insects with extreme prejudice. The back wall of the lobby had a security window in the center with a door on the left. Ike was standing near the security window. A big key ring dangled from one finger.

"Hey, Ike," Buddy Lee said. Ike put the key ring back in his pocket.

"Hey. Buddy Lee, right?" Ike asked. Buddy Lee nodded his head.

"Hey, you got a minute? I'd like to talk to you about something," he said.

"Yeah, I got a few. Can't talk long, though. I gotta get my guys out on the road," Ike said. He pulled the keys out again and opened the Masonite door. Buddy Lee followed him through the door to back of the warehouse. Pallets of fertilizer, granular herbicide, and pesticides were staged in lines that stretched ten deep all the way back to a wide roll-up door. Long sections of metal lawn edging were stacked against the back wall on the right side of the roll-up door. A small metal desk with a laptop and a Rolodex was positioned directly behind the security window. Behind the desk was a cubicle. Ike entered the cubicle and sat behind another metal desk. Buddy Lee sat in a weathered wooden chair positioned in front of the desk. The desk was as spartan as the lobby. It had a laptop, a pen holder, an in-box and an out-box, and nothing else. A short two-drawer filing cabinet sat next to his office chair.

"You ever thought of getting one of those, um, I don't know what you call it, but it's a bunch of metal balls hitting each other. Looks like a magic trick."

"No," Ike said. Buddy Lee stroked the scruff on his chin. The smell of sweat and cheap whiskey hung around him like a cloud.

"It's two months today," he said. Ike crossed his arms across his massive chest.

"Yeah, I know."

"How ya been? Since the funeral and all?" Buddy Lee asked.

Ike shrugged. "I don't know. Doing alright I guess."

"You heard anything from the cops?"

"They called me once. Ain't heard nothing since."

"Yeah, they called me once, too. Didn't seem like they had much in the way of leads," Buddy Lee said.

"I guess they working on it," Ike said. Buddy Lee ran his hands over his jeans.

"I've become a homebody in my old age. I go to work, then I go back to my trailer. In between I kill a few cold ones. That's about it. If I can help it, I don't have nothing to do with the cops. But this morning I got up at six and drove up to Richmond. I went by the police station and I asked for the detectives on the Derek Jenkins–Isiah Randolph murder case. Do you know what they told me?" Buddy Lee said. A quiver ran through his voice.

"No, I don't."

"Detective LaPlata said the case is currently inactive. No one knows anything, and if they do, they ain't talking," Buddy Lee said. He swallowed hard. "I don't know about you, but that don't sit right with me." Ike didn't respond. Buddy Lee rested his chin on his fist.

"I see him in my dreams. Derek. The back of his head is busted open. His brain is beating like a heart. There's blood running down his face."

"Stop."

Buddy Lee blinked his eyes. "Sorry. It's just I keep thinking about what the cop said. That their friends won't talk to them. I can't say I blame them. I think we both know it can be dangerous to talk to Johnny Law," Buddy Lee said.

"I ain't shocked it went inactive. They ain't making a priority out of two . . . out of two men like Isiah and Derek," Ike said. Buddy Lee nodded.

"Yeah. I wasn't never a fan of that gay shit, but I loved my boy. I didn't show it all the time, and I was gone a lot, but I swear I loved him with everything in me. I think you felt the same way about your boy. That's why I wanted to talk to you," Buddy Lee said.

"What did you want to talk about?" Ike asked. Buddy Lee took a deep breath. He'd been working on his pitch for a week, but now that he was about to say it out loud, he realized how crazy it was.

"Like I said, I don't blame people for not talking to the cops. But what if they didn't have to talk to the cops? What if they talked to us? Folks are liable to tell a couple of grieving fathers shit they wouldn't tell the police," Buddy Lee said. The words spilled out in one long continuous sentence. Ike cocked his head to the side.

"What, you want us to play some private-eye shit?" Ike said.

"There's a motherfucker walking around right now. He getting up in the morning and he eating him a big breakfast. Then he goes and does whatever the fuck he does during the day. Then he probably gets him a piece of ass at the end of the night. This motherfucker killed our children. He popped them full of holes like a piece of chicken wire. Then he stood over them and blew their fucking brains out. Now, I don't know about you, but I can't live with myself while that son of a bitch is on this side of the dirt," Buddy Lee said. His eyes were bugging from their sockets.

"Are you saying what I think you saying?" Ike asked. Buddy Lee licked his lips.

"You didn't get that BG tattoo by being a wannabe. That's shot-caller ink. And you don't get to be a shot caller unless you done put in some work. A lot of work by the looks of it. Now, I won't no shot caller but I've done my share of work, too," Buddy Lee said. Ike let out a chuckle.

"What's so funny?" Buddy Lee said.

"You should hear yourself. You sound like some cracker in an old hillbilly crime movie. Like you should be an extra in *Gator*. Look around here. I've got fourteen people that work for me, not including my receptionist, who's late again. I've got fifteen property-management contracts. I have a little girl in my house that I've gotta help raise because your son and my son made my wife her legal guardian. I've got responsibilities. I got people depending on me so they can put food on their tables. And you want me to what? Play some *Rolling Thunder* or *John Wick* shit with you? You're drunk, but I can't believe you're that drunk," Ike said. Buddy Lee rubbed his forefinger against his thumb. Ike could hear the calluses rasp as they slid against each other.

"So, you scared to get your hands dirty? Or you don't care that the man who killed our sons is walking around free?" Ike's face settled into a rigid mask. Under his desk his hands curled into fists.

"You think I don't care? I had to bury my only child in a closed casket service because the mortician couldn't put his face back together. My wife wakes up crying in the middle of the night screaming Isiah's name. I look at his daughter and realize she won't remember what his voice sounded like. I wake up every morning and I go to bed every night praying he didn't go from this world hating me. You see some tattoos and all the sudden you an expert on who the fuck I am? You don't know nothing about me, man. What, you thought you'd walk in here and get the big, scary-ass Black nigga to go kill some people for you?"

Buddy Lee could see the muscles in Ike's neck standing out in sharp relief like a 3D map. His pupils had narrowed to pinpricks. Buddy Lee leaned forward.

"Not some people. The bastards that killed Derek and Isiah. And I wasn't asking you to do it for me. We can get more than one gun," Buddy Lee said.

"Get the fuck out my office," Ike said. The words came out slow and brutal, like cinder blocks being dragged over asphalt. Buddy Lee didn't move. He and Ike locked eyes, and Buddy Lee felt the air between them change. It was charged like a thunderstorm was on the horizon. Buddy Lee dug around in his pocket until he found an old receipt. He grabbed one of Ike's pens. He scrawled his cell phone number on the back of the receipt. He folded it once before laying it on Ike's desk. He stood and walked to the door of the cubicle. He stopped and looked back at Ike.

"When you go to bed tonight and you're praying your boy didn't hate you, listen real close. You'll hear him asking why you didn't do something to make it right. When you ready to answer him, you give me a call. If you don't, then I guess you should cover that lion up with a big fat pussy," Buddy Lee said. He stomped out of the cubicle.

Ike heard the door chime go off as Buddy Lee left the building.

He brought his fists from under the desk. His breath was coming in short shallow bursts. Ike raised his arms and slammed his fists down on the desk. The pen holder jumped and skidded off the desk. Ike slammed his fists into the desk again and this time the laptop did a little jig.

That white boy had the nerve to sit there and tell him he didn't care about Isiah. He should have fed him his fucking teeth. Ike got up and walked out of the cubicle. He stood in the middle of the warehouse flexing his fingers, trying to work the stinging sensation out of his hands.

Did Buddy Lee really think he was the only one who was hurting? He didn't have a monopoly on grief. There wasn't a moment that went by he didn't think about Isiah. Every day it got a little bit harder and a little bit easier. Whenever the pain ebbed slightly he felt guilty. Like he was disrespecting Isiah's memory if he didn't feel an agonizing ache in his chest every single second. The days it got harder he sat in the shed and drank until he could hardly stand.

He should have jumped across his desk and snatched Buddy Lee's skinny ass up out of his chair. Pushed him up against the wall of his office and pressed his forearm across his throat. Ike could have told him how in his dreams he found the people who had blown off Isiah's face. He could have told Buddy Lee about how in those dreams he took those people some place nice and quiet. A place stocked with pliers and hammers and a blowtorch. Ike could have told him how in his dreams he introduced them to Riot Randolph. The OG with nine bodies on him, not including the one that had gotten him a manslaughter charge.

Ike massaged his temples. He hadn't been that man in a long time. Not since June 23, 2004. That was the day he'd left Coldwater State Penitentiary. Ike had walked through those gates and found strangers waiting for him. A wife that had taken company with other men. A son, more man than boy, who wouldn't look him in the eye. Strangers he loved who flinched at his touch.

He'd made up his mind the first night he was home. He was done. He was getting out of the life. As far as he was concerned, Riot had died in prison. Ike sacrificed him for his family. Just like Abraham had attempted to do to his namesake. At first no one in town wanted to believe it. The first couple of months he was home, crackheads would still sidle up to him asking if he was holding. For years the Red Hill Sheriff's Department made pulling him over and searching his car their favorite hobby. People in the grocery store alternately gave him a wide berth and the side-eye. He ignored them all. He kept his head down and his eyes on the prize. He started a lawn-care service with a rickety riding mower and a rusty sling blade. He didn't just work hard, he worked harder than anyone in five counties. By the time Isiah had graduated from college he'd paid off the house and the warehouse.

He learned how to control his temper. There was no such thing as nonviolent conflict resolution in the joint. You hit first, and you hit hard. If you didn't, you would find yourself washing another motherfucker's boxers. The first time he got cut off in traffic after being released had been tough. It had taken everything in him not to chase the guy down, drag him out his car, and curb-stomp him.

Buddy Lee had it all wrong. Ike wasn't afraid to get his hands dirty. He wasn't afraid to spill blood. He was afraid he wouldn't be able to stop.

Grayson raised his garage door. The heat was a living thing that reached out and touched him with a suffocating caress. An oily haze gave the neighborhood a sepia tone, like he was trapped in an old photograph. The afternoon sun cut through the exhaust from the diesel repair shop to the east and the smoke and steam from the sheet-metal plant to the west. Grayson threw one heavy leg over his bike. He slipped his helmet over his broad head. Long blond hair trailed from under the helmet and down his back. He was just about to fire up the Harley when Sara opened the door and hollered at him.

"Your cell phone is ringing. You know, the one in the nightstand you forbid me from touching," she crowed. Grayson pulled off his helmet.

"Bring it here."

"Oh, I can touch it now?"

"Bitch, bring me the goddamn phone," Grayson said. Sara opened her mouth, changed her mind, and disappeared into the house. When she returned she had Jericho on her hip and the phone in her free hand.

"Tell her she better not kiss you because she'll be eating my pussy," Sara said when she handed him the phone.

"Jesus, watch your fucking mouth in front of him," Grayson said.

"Like you don't say worse," Sara said.

"Go in the fucking house."

"Sure, keep treating me like crap. Maybe one day you'll come home and I'll be gone."

"You promise?" Grayson said. Sara flicked him off before going back in the house. Grayson grunted out a brief chuckle. They'd be hate-fucking later tonight. They played the same song and dance for the last five years. Neither one of them was going anywhere. And they both knew it.

Grayson opened the burner. He read the number and shook his shaggy head before answering it.

"Hello?"

"Hello. I suppose you know why I'm calling."

"I got a guess." The person on the other end of the line paused for a full minute.

"So, you haven't found her."

"It's been two months. I had guys looking for her all over the place. Even put some feelers out with some of the homeboys that buy hardware from us. That bitch is in the wind. After what happened to that reporter, she ain't saying boo to a cat. You got nothing to worry about," Grayson said. The person on the other end was quiet for nearly a minute this time. When they spoke again they articulated each word with a bestial intensity.

"I would like to ensure that she keeps her mouth shut. We're too close to let some whore ruin our plans."

"You really gonna go through with that shit, huh?" Grayson asked.

"It's time for a change. Our people are ready. We don't need her interfering with that. That's why I need you to find her. And green-light her."

"Hey, she ain't at that address you gave us. She ain't been to work since the reporter got popped. She's a ghost, man. You're good."

"Do you know how I've gotten to where I am? I'll give you a hint. It isn't because I don't pay attention to details. You and your club have been compensated to perform a task. That task isn't completed until the girl is taken care of as well. Do we really need to go down that road where I threaten you and your associates? Because I'd rather not do that. We've had a mutually beneficial relationship for many years. No need to put that in jeopardy. But I need that girl. Before the twenty-fourth."

Grayson clenched his jaw. He held the phone away from his face for a few moments. Two deep breaths later and he felt he was able to speak.

"I hear what you are saying. But we've known each other a long time. So you know I don't do threats. Let's get that straight. We'll keep looking for the girl because that's what we said we would do. But that relationship you was talking about? That goes both ways, motherfucker. Remember that," Grayson said.

"Duly noted. We can discuss the terms of that relationship at another time. Right now, I need you to take care of that slut."

"Uh-huh. And where do you suggest we look for her?"

The voice on the other end of the line was quiet for another full minute.

"That reporter. He should have some kind of notes about her. He was going to write a story about her and how she is connected to my aspirations, correct? There might be a clue to her whereabouts in his notes. Go to his house and look around."

Grayson laughed. It was a wet throaty sound that echoed through the garage.

"You really think he left some map on his computer that says 'Look here for a party slut?' Come on, man."

"Since you asked me for suggestions on how to find her, I'm going to assume you don't have any better ideas. And no, I'm not asking you to be cartographers. I'm asking you to be what we both know you are. Killers. I'll text you his address."

The line went dead. Grayson closed the phone and put it in his pocket.

"Fucking prick," he murmured before firing up his bike.

ke took a bite of his pancakes, then sipped his coffee. Mya sat across the kitchen table with a Newport dangling from her lip as she read the paper. The smoke floated around her head like a gray halo.

"What you and Arianna gonna do today?" Ike asked. Mya didn't look at him.

"I don't know. It's my last day off from the hospital so I wanted to do something nice with her, but I can't think of anything," she said. Ike sipped his coffee again. He thought about suggesting they go to Kings Dominion, but he didn't want Mya to snap at him again. Lately, any input he had about Arianna was met with disdain.

"I'm sure you'll think of something," he said. Mya knocked some ash off her cigarette into a teacup she was using as an ashtray.

"I don't know. I can't seem to get my brain to work." Ike didn't touch that one. Mya took a long drag off her cigarette. The tip glowed red like a dragon's eye until she exhaled.

"I don't think they are ever going to catch them," she said. Ike looked up from his pancakes. She had folded the paper and put it on the table. Her honey-brown eyes seared into him.

He let out a sigh, finished his coffee, and got up from the table. He'd lost what little appetite he had. He went to the sink and rinsed out his cup before putting it in the dishwasher.

"What?" Mya asked.

"What do you mean 'what'?"

"That's your 'something is bothering me' sigh. What is it?" Mya asked

Ike leaned against the counter.

"Derek's daddy came by the shop last week."

"What did he want?"

Ike sucked his teeth. "He told me the cops had marked Isiah's case 'inactive.'"

"I know. I talked to Detective LaPlata on Monday. It's been two months as of last week," Mya said. Ike closed his eyes. He hadn't talked to LaPlata since right after the funeral. He hadn't been out to the grave, either.

"Well, Derek's dad thinks we should go looking for them," Ike said.

"Are you?" Mya asked.

"What? Go looking for them? You know I can't do that."

"Why not?" Mya asked. Ike worked his jaw. He listened to the ligaments pop.

"You know why. I made you and Isiah a promise. If I go looking I might find them. And if I find them, I'll kill them," he said. The words came out plain and without much inflection. She'd known him since he was fifteen and she was thirteen. Mya knew he wasn't exaggerating.

Ike waited for her to say he couldn't do that. He stood there waiting for her to say let the cops handle it. He waited and waited. The ice maker kicked in, breaking the silence.

"I'm gonna go wake up Arianna," Mya said finally. She stubbed out her cigarette in the teacup. She rose from the table, then slipped up the stairs.

Ike watched her climb the stairs. Her steps seemed weighted down by a burden she obviously thought she was carrying alone. Maybe Mya was right. Maybe he didn't deserve to grieve Isiah. It didn't seem fair for a man to mourn someone abundantly that he had loved so miserly.

Ike grabbed his lunch container and was about to walk out the door when his cell phone vibrated in his pocket. He pulled it out and looked at the screen. He didn't immediately recognize the number, but it was his work phone so he answered.

"Hello."

"Hello Mr. Randolph, this is Kenneth D. Adner at Greenhill Memorial Cemetery."

"Yes," Ike said.

"Sir, I'm so sorry to have to tell you this, but we have a bit of a problem with your son's grave."

"The funeral home said everything was paid for. My son had set up a prearrangement," Ike said.

"No, sir, it's not about the payment. I'm afraid there's been some damage to your son's grave."

"What kind of damage?" Ike asked.

"Sir, I think you should come down to the cemetery. I don't think this is something we can discuss on the phone," Kenneth said.

Ike had expected to arrive at his son's grave (that phrase would never sound right to him) and see a large chunk missing from the headstone. He knew how pieces of gravel became ballistic projectiles when launched by the blade of a riding mower. That was why he had all his guys bonded and insured. Perhaps he would see a huge chunk of grass missing. The result of an overzealous groundskeeper testing out a brand-new weed trimmer. Ike worked in the dirt. He knew there were only so many ways to damage it.

He hadn't expected anything like this.

He and the manager were standing side by side at the foot of the grave. The manager was pale as the belly of a fish. His blond hair was slicked back with so much product a fly would break its neck trying to land on it. He was sweating despite the AC in the office being on arctic. That had been Ike's first indication that the issue with the grave was more extensive than he had first thought.

Ike walked over to the headstone. It was a double stone with both Isiah's and Derek's names carved into the black granite. Someone had cracked it in two. Probably with a sledgehammer. Once they had cracked it they had decorated it with their own views on homosexuality and interracial relationships.

DEAD FAGGOT NIGGER. DEAD NIGGER FAGGOT LOVER was sprayed on the two halves of the stone in neon-green spray paint. They had also sprayed it on the grass over each grave.

"I can't tell you how sorry I am about this, Mr. Randolph. Of course, we will replace the headstone. The grass will be a bit more difficult," Kenneth said.

"Dig it up and replace it with sod," Ike said. His voice sounded like a recording to him.

"Well, yes, I guess that is one solution," Kenneth said.

"I want the grass fixed today. Go ahead and move the stone now. My wife is supposed to be coming by today. I'll tell her one of your trucks ran into it."

"Yes sir, of course. I again want to sincerely apologize. Greenhill accepts full responsibility for this unfortunate event," Kenneth said. He tried to smile sympathetically. Ike caught his eyes and the smile died on his lips.

"Get the grass done today," Ike said. He started walking toward his truck. He left the manager and his golf cart at the grave. He felt strange. He was well acquainted with his rage. It lived inside him like a demon waiting for moments like these. Seeing the stone should have released it like a hungry beast freed from a cage. The familiar sensations associated with it weren't immediately present. His vision hadn't taken on a crimson sheen. His stomach wasn't doing yoga poses in his guts. Was this the numbness people talked about? That crippling feeling that took over your body when you were finally pushed beyond your limits.

Ike got in his truck and dialed his office.

"Randolph Lawn Care and Landscaping, Jazmine speaking. How may I help you?"

"Jazzy, go into my office. There's a receipt on my desk. On the back of it there's a telephone number. Text me that number."

"Okay. Good morning to you, too, boss."

"Get the number, Jazzy," Ike said.

"Alright. Hey, you okay? You don't sound—"

Ike ended the call.

Buddy Lee pulled into the parking lot of Sander's Grab and Go. He thought the name of the place didn't exactly match the actual layout. It was built like a Tastee Freez or a Dairy Queen. There was an order window and a pickup window, both with a plexiglass sliding door, but there were also a bunch of bright-red picnic tables littered across the front of the building. Buddy Lee figured the name kinda fit. You could grab your food, then go to a table.

Ike was sitting at one of the tables near the far end of the building. Buddy Lee put the truck in park and loped over. Ike was eating from a red-and-white-checkered paper container. He tore into a piece of fried fish, then took a sip of fountain drink.

"Hey," he said after washing down his food.

"I didn't think I'd be seeing you again," Buddy Lee said.

"Have a seat," Ike said. Buddy Lee hesitated, then took a seat. He picked up a plastic menu from the tabletop and started perusing it.

"What's good here? I'm so hungry my stomach is hitting my backbone," Buddy Lee said. Ike pulled out his phone and sat it on the table.

"The catfish is good. They got fried okra, too. Don't mess with the cornbread. It's hard as a brick," Ike said. He took another sip of his drink.

"If you invited me up here to apologize for telling me to get the fuck out your office, I accept. I don't think either one of us are in our right minds these days," Buddy Lee said without raising his head from the menu.

"I'm not apologizing," Ike said.

"Alright, this gonna be an awkward date then," Buddy Lee said.

Ike wiped his hands on a thin brown napkin. He leaned on his fore-arms.

"I need you to know everything I said the other day was true. About being responsible. I built my business from scratch. From nothing. I'm proud of that. I've worked hard every single day since I got out, to make a good life for my wife, for my son," Ike said. He paused. The laughter of a group of teenagers two tables away filled the space the pause had made.

"How you become a landscaper anyway? No offense, but you don't strike me as a flower lover," Buddy Lee said. His head was still buried in the menu.

Ike looked down at his hands. At his tattoo. Some white boys in a truck with a lift kit so high they probably needed a ladder to get in the damn thing and a Confederate flag decal in the back window rolled through the parking lot. They left a trail of black smoke in their wake.

"Took it up inside. They had classes on it. It got me out my cell. When they cut me loose I realized it'd give me space on the out-side. Nobody wants to make small talk when it a hundred degrees and you got a pole saw in your hands," Ike said. The Confederate boys parked their truck. They got out and walked to the order win-dow. One of them gave Ike a look, saw something in his eyes he didn't like, and quickly looked away.

"It got to where after a few years I started thinking it was why I was put here. You know how they say everybody good at some-thing, right? But planting flowers and trimming shrubs, that shit ain't what I'm here for. That's not what I'm good at. Not really," Ike said.

Buddy Lee raised his head.

"You didn't call me because the catfish here is so good, did you?" Buddy Lee asked. Ike pulled his phone out of his pocket and placed it on the table.

"When was the last time you were at the graves?"

Buddy Lee put the menu aside.

"Eh . . . I was planning on going this week, but work got crazy. I mean . . . shit, man, I haven't been since the funeral," Buddy Lee said. Ike touched his phone screen and slid it across the table. Buddy Lee closed his menu. He picked up the phone and stared at the screen.

"What the fuck is this?" he said.

"What it look like? The motherfuckers who killed our boys went and pissed all over their graves," Ike said. Buddy Lee slid the phone back toward Ike. He ran his tongue across his bottom lip.

"You think the punks who killed them did that?"

"Who else would do it? Isiah and Derek weren't famous. Nobody would know they were . . . different just by reading their headstones," Ike said. He drummed his fingers on the tabletop. Buddy Lee hunched forward and leaned across the table.

"Let me guess. Now you ready to do something about this," he said. Ike thought he heard the hint of sarcasm in his voice.

"I was all set to let the police handle this. Even though I knew they probably wouldn't find out who did it. I was willing to let those motherfuckers get away with it because the promise I had made to my wife and my son was more important than getting even. But then they had to go and fuck up his grave. And it was like I realized, what good is the promise if my son is dead and my wife looks at me like she wishes I was the one in the ground? It's like you said. That cracked-up headstone is my boy asking me what the fuck am I gonna do about this," Ike said.

He had closed his eyes. Isiah's face floated up from the depths of his memories. Isiah at four hours old. At seven when Ike had started his bid. At sixteen when he'd gotten his driver's license. At twenty-seven on the slab at the funeral home with most of his head blown away. He almost believed the line of bull he'd fed Buddy Lee. It would have been beautiful if Isiah had sent him a ghostly message from beyond. But Ike didn't believe in any fairy-tale paradise in the sky. His boy was dead. He would be dead longer than he had ever been alive. The truth was, deep down inside, Ike had always been afraid it would come to this. Maybe subconsciously he wanted a reason to break his oath. In that case the tombstone was just a convenient catalyst. An unexpected means to an end. After everything he'd said to Buddy Lee last week, he had to feed him that line of crap. Make him think he'd struggled with this decision.

"Hey, you preaching to the choir. When you wanna get started?" Buddy Lee said. His eyes shined like wet concrete. Ike opened his eyes.

"Just so we on the same page. If we gonna do this I need your head clear. You gonna have to cut back on the drinking until this is done," Ike said.

"Hey, don't worry, a few cold ones ain't gonna—"

Ike cut him off. "You're drunk right now and the sun's still up. I'm not going to war with somebody who can't hold their liquor."

Buddy Lee sat back in his chair.

"That bad, huh?"

"You smell like you slept in a mason jar full of shine," Ike said. Buddy Lee laughed.

"That sounds about right. Alright, I'll lay off the sauce." Buddy Lee had no idea how that was going to work, but he'd give it a try. For a little while.

"One more thing. I don't know what the boys was into, but it was bad enough somebody killed them over it. We start poking around this then things are probably gonna get nasty. Now, I know what you was saying the other day, but I want to make sure you understand what this is. Once we start, I'm prepared to do whatever it takes to find these sons of bitches. If I gotta hurt some people, then that's what I'll do. If I have to punch somebody's ticket, I'll do it. If I gotta crawl a hundred miles over broken glass just to get my hands on these motherfuckers, then that's what I'll do. I'm prepared to bleed. Are you?" Ike asked.

Buddy Lee leaned his head back and stared up at the sky. The clouds danced across the horizon, taking on vaguely familiar shapes. A horse, a dog, a car, a face with a crooked smile just like Derek's.

He lowered his head and locked eyes with Ike.

"Abso-fucking-lutely," he said.

EIGHT

Buddy Lee parked his truck next to Ike's in the parking lot of Ike's shop. He started to lock it, then stopped. If anyone stole it, they would just be taking on his troubles. Ike unlocked the passenger door and Buddy Lee climbed in the cab. Ike put the truck in gear and they backed up, turned around, and merged into traffic.

"My truck gonna be okay there? I don't want it to get in the way."

"It's fine. I told Jazzy it was cool."

"Where we headed?"

"I figured we would go to Isiah's job. The cops told me he got a death threat last year. I called my wife and she gave me the address. Good a place as any to start, I guess," Ike said.

Buddy Lee felt the old familiar twinge working its way up from his guts but he pushed it away. He wanted a drink. Hell, he needed a drink. They drove in silence for a few miles before Buddy Lee couldn't stand it anymore.

"Hey, can you play some music?"

Ike touched a button on the steering wheel with his thumb. The cab of the truck was filled with the angelic falsetto of the Reverend Al Green singing about the good times. Buddy Lee sat back in the passenger seat and drummed his thin fingers on his thigh.

"I don't suppose you're a fan of country, are you?" Buddy Lee asked.

Ike grunted. "Why, because I'm Black?"

Buddy Lee ran a hand through his wild locks. "Well, I mean, yeah. No offense or nothing. Just don't know many of your kind that are into country."

"You say 'your kind' again and I'm gonna throw you out this truck," Ike said. He didn't raise his voice or look at Buddy Lee.

At first Buddy Lee thought he might have misheard him. When he caught Ike's reflection in the rearview mirror he was confident he had indeed heard him correctly. "Sorry. I didn't mean nothing by it. Shit. Sometimes my mouth runs away from my head."

"When you or some other white boy says 'your kind' it's like I'm some fucking animal that you trying to put in a cage. I don't like that shit. So that's your one," Ike said.

"My one?"

"Your one. I'm gonna let it slide because, like you said, we both might be in a weird state of mind. But the next time you say something like that I'm going to chin-check you," Ike said.

"Hey, man, I said I'm sorry. I ain't gonna tell you no lie and say I got a lot of Black friends, because I don't. I know some boys that I'm cool with. But I don't think I could call any of them if I had to bury a body," Buddy Lee said. Ike gave him a quick glance before returning his attention to the road.

"I'm not a racist or nothing. Just don't know a lot of Black people," Buddy Lee stammered.

"I never said you was. You just another white boy that don't have to worry about people like me and the shit we go through," Ike said.

"Look man, the only color that really matters is green. Look at you. You got your own business. You ain't got a boss you gotta threaten to get some bereavement time. You got a nice house. I live in a shitty-ass trailer in an even shittier trailer park. You doing alright. Hell, you're doing way better than me. And you're pretty Black," Buddy Lee said. Ike gripped the steering wheel so tight his knuckles popped.

"You don't know how hard I had to work to just be doing alright.

You say you believe that shit about green being the only color that matters, right? So, let me ask you this: Would you switch places with me?"

"Do I get the truck? Because if I get the truck, hell yeah, I'll switch places with you," Buddy Lee said. He let out a low chuckle.

"Oh, you get the truck. But you also get pulled over four or five times a month because ain't no way your Black ass can afford a nice truck like this, right? You get the truck but you get followed around in the jewelry store because you know you probably fitting to rob the place, right? You can get the truck but you gotta deal with white ladies clutching their purses when you walk down the street because Fox News done told them you coming to steal their money and their virtue. You get the truck but then you gotta explain to some trigger-happy cop that no, Mr. Officer, you're not resisting arrest. You get the truck but then you also get two in the back of the head because you reached for your cell phone," Ike said. He glanced at Buddy Lee.

"So, you still wanna trade places?"

Buddy Lee swallowed hard and turned his head to toward the window, but he didn't say a word.

"That's what I thought. Green don't matter if it's in a Black hand," Ike said. They drove on with the dulcet sounds of D'Angelo having replaced the Good Reverend swimming through the cab.

Ike hit the interstate and headed for Richmond. Fifty minutes later he took the downtown exit and guided the truck through an off-ramp so sharp it could slice bread. He checked the rearview mirror and merged onto Blue Springs Drive. Traffic was a mess, but the dually bullied its way down the road. Ike hated driving in the city. The narrow streets made him feel like he was a rat in a maze.

The GPS said they were two hundred feet from their destination. Ike saw a plain brown five-story building up ahead on the right in the middle of a copse of oak trees. Richmond city planners were trapped between their affections for the natural scenery of Central Virginia and their lust for urban expansion. The R. C. Johnson Building sat at the nexus of those two competing sensibilities.

Ike pulled into the parking lot and shut off the truck. The engine let out a death rattle, then was silent. Ike hopped out and Buddy Lee followed him. The heavy glass doors of the office building squealed when they opened them. The lobby was a time capsule from the eighties. Alabaster models with electric neon lips stared at them from portraits on both walls. Chairs designed with strange geometry were scattered throughout the lobby area. A black pegboard with white letters served as the directory.

"*The Rainbow Review* is on the third floor," Ike said.

"Yeah, that sounds pretty gay," Buddy Lee said. Ike cut his eyes sideways at him.

"What?" Buddy Lee said. Ike shook his head and made a beeline for the elevator. Buddy Lee rolled his eyes and followed him.

The offices of *The Rainbow Review* were the smallest suites in the building. There were six desks crammed into a space meant for four. A huge personal computer and a laptop adorned each desk. Each desk was manned by a pair of intense-looking young men and women. Everyone was typing on keyboards or talking on their cell phones or doing both simultaneously. Buddy Lee and Ike walked up to the desk closest to the door. A redheaded bearded man and a dreadlocked Black woman had put their heads together and were conferring about an image on her tablet. The man raised his head.

"Do we need to move our cars again?"

"What?" Ike said.

"You guys are from the lawn-care company, right?" the bearded man asked. Ike sighed. He was still wearing his work gear. Randolph Lawn Maintenance was emblazoned over the pocket of the shirt.

"Can we do it a little later? We're kind of busy here," the woman with the dreadlocks said.

"Hey, Redbeard, we ain't the lawn crew," Buddy Lee said. That got Redbeard's attention.

"Excuse me?" Redbeard asked.

"You heard him," Ike said. Redbeard's face started to match his hair.

"Just what do you want?" he said.

"Are you the boss here?" Buddy Lee asked. The man ignored him, but the woman with the dreads responded.

"No, he isn't. I'm Amelia Watkins. I'm the managing editor. What can I do for you gentlemen?" Amelia said. She was studying their faces, but Buddy Lee noticed her left hand was under the desk.

"Before you pull that heater, we ain't here for no trouble," he said. Amelia pursed her lips.

"So you say. It's a dangerous time to be a journalist. Especially if you work for a nonprofit that focuses on the LGBTQ community," she said. Her voice was deep and vibrant. It made Buddy Lee think of a blues singer he'd heard in Austin years ago.

"I'm Ike Randolph. This here is Buddy Lee Jenkins," Ike said. Amelia stood and walked around her desk. She was nearly as tall as Ike, but slim and toned. Her dreads fell to the small of her back.

"You're Isiah's father."

"Yes, I am. And Buddy is Derek's father. Is there someplace we can talk?"

"Sure, let's go downstairs to the coffee shop."

Amelia took her coffee black and she drank it fast. Buddy Lee wished he had some whiskey to pour in his cup. Ike didn't get anything. Amelia crumpled the coffee cup and tossed it in the wastebasket four feet away. It swished through the air and into the wastebasket. Nothing but net.

"You play ball?" Ike asked.

"Isn't that just too clichéd? The lesbian plays basketball. But yeah, I like to play. I went to college on a scholarship."

"Isiah could ball," Ike said.

"Yeah, he had a wicked outside shot."

"I could never figure out how he could be that way and be so good at sports," Ike said.

Amelia laughed but it was bereft of mirth. "You think because he was gay he should have been knitting scarves?"

Ike drummed his fingers on the table. "I don't know. I never could . . . I didn't understand why he was like that. It caused problems between us."

"I know. He told me," Amelia said.

"He did?" Ike asked.

"We traded coming-out stories when he first came on board. You and my dad would have gotten along famously. You both think our sexuality is something that has to be explained. It isn't. It's just who we are. It wasn't Isiah being gay that caused problems between the two of you. It was how you dealt with it or didn't deal with it that caused the problems," Amelia said.

Ike blinked hard. "It . . . it wasn't that simple."

Amelia shrugged. "If you say so. At least you still spoke to Isiah. My dad hasn't talked to me since my junior year in high school," Amelia said.

"No offense, but we ain't here for a therapy session. We want to ask you about a death threat his boy got last year," Buddy Lee said. Ike stared daggers at him, but Buddy Lee just shrugged.

"Oh yes, the Blue Anarchists," Amelia said.

"The what?" Buddy Lee said.

"The Blue Anarchists. A bunch of extreme progressives who favor throwing bottles and Molotov cocktails over constructive discourse. I think they are just a bunch of overprivileged hipster assholes jumping on the next subversive bandwagon. Back when I was in school they would have been goths," Amelia said.

"Don't sound like you took them too serious." Ike said. Amelia opened her hands and shimmied her shoulders.

"They were pissed because Isiah wrote a piece calling them out on their transphobia and bullshit rhetoric. We all thought it was just them blowing off some steam, but we reported it anyway. Better safe than sorry," Amelia said.

"So you don't think they could have done it?" Buddy Lee asked.

"My gut says no, but who knows? People are crazy these days. We're working on a piece right now about Isiah and Derek and all the queer people who have been murdered so far this year."

"There's a lot of that going on?" Buddy Lee asked.

"Murders of gay and bisexual men are up four hundred percent since last year. It seems like somebody made hatred hip again," Amelia said.

"Where do these Blue Anarchists hang out?" Ike asked. Amelia motioned for the waitress. A young Asian woman brought her another cup.

"Their headquarters are a head shop in Glen Allen. I can give you the address. Listen, I'm pretty sure they're just a bunch of spoiled kids," Amelia said.

"How'd you get their address?" Ike asked.

"They mailed Isiah their threat. These kids are all about keeping it vintage," Amelia said.

"Well, we just want to talk to them. We're kinda looking into what happened to our boys. The cops seem to think the trail's gone cold. They say you and the rest of their friends won't talk to them. I can't say I blame you. I hate those fuckers," Buddy Lee said. Amelia squeezed herself. Ike noticed the striations in her arms and shoulders when she did. It wasn't an unappealing sight.

"It isn't that we won't talk to them. Speaking for myself, I don't know anything."

"Isiah didn't tell you about any kind of story he was working on?" Ike asked.

"No. Typically our stories aren't the kind that can get you killed. Being Black and gay usually does a pretty good job of that," Amelia said. Buddy Lee studied the ceiling tiles.

"Do you think it was a random hate crime?" Ike asked. Amelia sipped her coffee. She took a long time to answer.

"No. I don't know what it was about, but I don't think it was random," she said finally.

"Alright. I guess we better get that address."

"Hey, don't hurt those kids, okay?" Amelia asked. Ike cocked his head to the right.

"What makes you think we would hurt them?"

"I can see your tattoos," Amelia said.

"Well ma'am, you ain't got nothing to worry about. We just two old men asking questions about what happened to our boys. We're as harmless as a couple of old hound dogs sitting on a porch," Buddy Lee said. Amelia laughed. This time it filled her eyes with light.

"You are too much," she said.

"Darling, you have no idea," Buddy Lee said. Ike shook his head and let out a sigh.

NINE

ke started up the truck and backed out of his parking space. Buddy Lee studied the scrap of paper in his hand.

"You think that girl is all the way gay?" Buddy Lee asked.

"How the fuck am I supposed to know?" Ike said.

"Hey, I'm just wondering," Buddy Lee said. Ike slammed on the brakes.

"We out here trying to find out who killed our children, and you flirting with a lesbian. Are you taking this seriously? Are you really?" Ike said.

"Did you forget I'm the one who came to you? You think I ain't taking it seriously? I ain't you, Ike. I don't have nobody waiting for me back at my fancy two-bedroom trailer. Derek's mom left me a long time ago, and there ain't been nobody serious in my bed since. Just some good-time girls here and there. She turned her back on me and Derek and married some big-shot judge. So, excuse me if I ain't a fucking monk. But don't you ever ask me if I'm serious about this again. I mean that," Buddy Lee said.

"Fine," Ike said before putting the truck in gear.

The headquarters of the Blue Anarchists of RVA was located in a brand-new strip mall on Staples Mill Road. Ike parked the truck and shut it off.

"I think Amelia was right," Buddy Lee said.

"I'm sure she could tell you she pissed honey and lemonade, and you'd believe that, too," Ike said as they got out the truck. A sign above the door of the shop said TIME AND THYME UNIQUE GIFTS. The place smelled like incense and peppermint and something Ike couldn't put his finger on exactly. A mixture of hair grease and roses. The walls were covered with posters of bands and cartoon characters he didn't recognize. There were shelves and shelves of bongs, pipes, and cannabis accessories. The shop also had a few shelves dedicated to comic-book miniatures and collectibles. A raspy voice filtered through the store's sound system sang about a lost love and a winding sheet and dark skies.

Three narrow-looking white kids sat behind a glass display case that served as the sales counter. A bearded guy, a clean-shaven guy who was sporting a monocle, and a girl who looked like she had just stopped wearing light-up shoes a week ago.

"Can I help you?" she asked.

"I hope so. We want to talk to somebody from the Blue Anarchists," Ike said. The three kids exchanged furtive glances. Finally, the bearded kid stood up from his stool.

"We are all Blue Anarchists. I'm Bryce, this is Terry, and this is Madison. We aren't the only members, by the way. Our numbers are growing every day as more people wake up from the coma of forced patriotism and imperial subjugation," Bryce said. Buddy Lee thought he looked awfully proud of himself.

"You been practicing that for a while, ain't ya?" Buddy Lee said.

"It's our manifesto," Bryce said.

"I'm not here for your manifesto. I want to ask you about Isiah Randolph and Derek Jenkins," Ike said. He had his arms crossed over his chest.

"Who?" Terry, the one with the monocle, asked. Ike stepped forward. Bryce sat back down on his stool.

"Isiah Randolph. You sent him a death threat last year for a report on your pep club," Ike said. Bryce stood back up defiantly.

"Oh, you mean the guy who tried to ruin our reputation? It wasn't a death threat. It was a redress of grievances for his vitriolic comments," Bryce said.

"Jesus, you got any change for them ten-dollar words?" Buddy Lee asked.

"He's dead. He was my son and he's dead, and I wanna know whether or not your little punk-ass crew had anything to do with it," Ike said. A chime went off and a couple walked in the store. They must have felt something in the air, because they turned around and walked out.

"Look, I'm sorry your son is dead, but we didn't have anything to do with that. But I'm not surprised. He was just a tool of the corporate industrial complex. People are waking up, man. They aren't going to stand by and let the media lapdogs create a false narrative of what is going on in the world. Get woke, man," Bryce said. Ike cocked his head to the left. Buddy Lee watched his hands clench and unclench like bear traps opening and closing.

"What did you say about my son?" Ike asked. Bryce ran his tongue over his upper lip.

"I'm just saying—"

Ike's arm shot out as quick as a cobra. He grabbed Bryce by his beard and in one brutal movement yanked his head down until his forehead slammed into the glass counter. Ike grabbed Bryce's right hand with his left and twisted Bryce's arm until it felt like it might snap. Terry jumped up off his stool, but Buddy Lee pulled out his jackknife and flicked the blade open.

"Slow your roll, Panama Jack," he said as he pointed the knife at Terry's chest.

Ike bent forward until his mouth was inches from Bryce's ear.

"I'm going to ask you some questions about what you know about my son. Every time I don't like an answer I'm gonna break one of your fingers," he said. Madison began to cry.

"Hush, baby girl. We ain't gonna hurt you. We just wanna ask some questions," Buddy Lee said as he flashed the girl a smile. She cried harder.

"Now, did you have anything to do with what happened to our boys?" Ike asked.

"Oh my God, I'm bleeding!" Bryce mumbled against the top of the display desk.

"I don't like that answer." Ike said. He grabbed Bryce's pinky with his left hand. Holding the younger man down with his right hand, he pulled on the pinky with a brutal backward motion. A wet snap. Madison slipped from her stool and quietly vomited on the floor.

"Let's try this again. Do you know who killed my boy?" Ike asked. He didn't recognize his own voice. He realized Ike Randolph was taking a back seat to the action. This was Riot speaking.

"Jesus, fuck no. We . . . just . . . we just wrote him a nasty letter," Bryce cried. Buddy Lee heard the pitter-patter of water hitting the laminated floor.

"Ike. I think he telling the truth. He just pissed himself," Buddy Lee said.

"You know how many suspect motherfuckers I've seen piss themselves when they got caught?" Ike said.

"Yeah, but man, look at him. He couldn't bust a grape in a fruit fight," Buddy Lee said. Ike did what Buddy Lee suggested. Blood had pooled around Bryce's forehead. It was also spilling across the countertop onto the floor. Ike could see one of his eyes. It rolled around in his socket like a ball bearing. Ike wanted to let him go, but Riot wanted to break a few more of his fingers on general principles. Amelia was right. These kids weren't killers. They were just a bunch of overly idealistic children. Somewhere a mother or a father was mildly disappointed in them. Ike took a deep breath and let it out through his teeth.

He pushed Bryce off the top of the display case. The young man fell into his stool before sliding to the floor clutching his right arm. Madison went to his side. Her mouth was stained with orange and red vomit. Ike took a step back from the counter.

"If I find out you lying, I'm coming back and breaking the rest of your fingers," Ike said. He turned his back on them and walked out of the shop.

"Y'all should probably keep this to yourself. Just saying. Might be healthier that way," Buddy Lee said. He folded the jackknife and put it in his back pocket.

Ike had the truck running when he hopped in. He had barely closed the passenger door before Ike was mashing the gas pedal to the floor and backing out of the strip mall's parking lot. He executed a three-point turn and crossed the grass-covered median. Once they were a few miles from the Time and Thyme, Buddy Lee let out a whoop.

"What the hell was that for?" Ike said.

"Shit, man, it feels good to be doing *something*. We not just sitting in the dark crying anymore. We doing something for our boys. For a minute I didn't feel like a piece-of-shit father," Buddy Lee said.

"We didn't find out anything. It was a waste of time," Ike said.

"Maybe. But it felt good slapping those punk asses around, didn't it? Shit, we did what their parents should've done a long time ago. Blue Fucking Anarchists. What the hell is that?" Buddy Lee said.

"You enjoyed that, didn't you?" Ike said.

"You didn't?" Buddy Lee said.

Ike didn't answer.

TEN

"I think that's it over there," Buddy Lee said. Ike pulled the truck up to the sidewalk and parallel-parked it with surprising ease.

"You know how to wheel this thing, don't you?" Buddy Lee asked.

"Part of the job," Ike said.

They got out of the truck and started walking down the sidewalk a few feet until they stopped in front of a building with a flashing LED sign in the door. The sign said ESSENTIAL EVENTS BAKERY.

"You sure this the place?" Ike asked.

"Yeah. Fairly sure. The last time I talked to Derek he mentioned he was up for a promotion at his job. I asked him where he worked. He didn't want to tell me at first. I guess he thought I'd come down here and embarrass him. Ask them to make me a titty cake or something."

"A titty cake?" Ike said.

"Told ya it's been a few lonely years," Buddy Lee said. Ike felt a smile trying to crawl across his face, but he pushed it away.

"Hey, before we go in here, I guess I should say thanks for having my back over there earlier," Ike said. Buddy Lee shrugged.

"I know you don't particularly like me. And to be honest you're kind of an asshole. But we in it to win it now," Buddy Lee said.

"Yeah, I guess so. You think they know anything about what happened?" Ike asked.

"Fuck if I know. But where else we gonna go?" Buddy Lee responded.

Essential Events Bakery was housed in a cavernous building with high ceilings and multiple skylights tinted a light green. It gave the interior a vibrant verdant hue. Ike could taste sugar in the air and smell bread baking. His mouth began to water like a Pavlovian dog's. Several tables were set up throughout the building with a multitude of displays. Six-tier wedding cakes, flower-shaped loaves of bread, cupcake towers, skewers of beef and chicken arranged in interlocking levels like a puzzle. There was a cornucopia of epicurean designs and delights. Buddy Lee walked up to one of the cakes and extended his finger.

"It's covered in polyurethane," a young man said. He was standing behind a counter with a cash register and more examples of the artistry Essential Events was capable of creating. Behind him a blackboard listed the daily specials in bright-red chalk.

"Damn that icing look good," Buddy Lee said. The young man smiled. He had a wide grin with huge teeth that were as white as his pale skin. His light-blond hair was tied up in a short bun on top of his head like a sumo wrestler's topknot.

"It is. But these are just for display. See anything you like?" The young man asked. Buddy Lee walked over to the counter. He smiled back at the man.

"Well, to be honest, we're not here to buy any cakes. I'm Buddy Lee Jenkins," Buddy Lee said as he held out his hand.

"I'm Brandon Painter," Brandon said as he shook Buddy Lee's hand. Buddy Lee had felt a firmer grip from his grandmother on her deathbed.

"Nice to meet you, Brandon. That big ol' bear back there is Ike Randolph."

"Are you guys looking for cake for a special occasion? Are we celebrating an anniversary?" Brandon said with a smile. Buddy Lee frowned.

"Say what?" he asked. Brandon smiled again.

"Hey, it's all good, man. We ain't like that baker in Colorado. We'll make a cake or set out a spread for anyone. You two make a nice couple," Brandon said. Buddy Lee glanced back over his shoulder at Ike. Ike glowered back at Buddy Lee.

"Nah, son, you got it mixed up. We ain't . . . like that. My son is . . . was Derek Jenkins. He was with Ike's son, Isiah," Buddy Lee said.

"Oh my God. You're Derek's dad. I don't know why I didn't put it together. Oh my God, I'm so sorry. We miss him so much," Brandon said. His voice cracked as he spoke.

"Yeah, so do I. Hey, so we're kinda looking into what happened. The cops seem to think things have gone cold. You know how that is, right? They couldn't find their ass with a flashlight and two hands. Did Derek say anything to you about anybody threatening him? Maybe some crazy disgruntled customer or something?" Buddy Lee asked.

"Uh, nah, he never said anything to me," Brandon said.

"How about something personal? Did he say he had beef with anybody? Maybe another caterer?"

"No way. This ain't like the mafia. No one kills anyone because they can make a better buttercream frosting."

"Well, did he say anything strange in the weeks before it happened?"

Brandon shook his head. "I don't really know anything."

"Yeah. Ya know, when the cops told us Derek and Isiah's friends wasn't talking, I didn't believe it. But here you are lying to my face," Buddy Lee said. Ike heard a hard edge in his tone. Like steel striking steel.

"What? I'm not lying. I don't know anything." Brandon said. His hands flopped around on the counter like dying trout.

"Yeah, you do. You know what a tell is, Brandon?"

"A tell?"

"It's something you do that tells me you're lying. Everybody got one, and everybody's is different. Now you? Yours is just a little thing. You wanna know what it is?" Buddy Lee asked. He walked closer to the counter and grabbed Brandon's convulsing hands.

"I've asked three times about Derek and what you know. And

all three times you tug at your earlobe before you answer. That's your tell, Brandon. It tells me you know something and you lying about it. Now, if you really miss Derek and you was really his friend, you'll tell me what you know," Buddy Lee said. Ike noticed the edge had gone out of his tone. Now he sounded comforting, like a priest. Or a good cop getting a confession.

"I told you I don't know anything," Brandon said. He snatched his hands away from Buddy Lee. "I think y'all should go. I got a lot to do, and the boss will be here soon."

Buddy Lee stepped back from the counter. He turned, brushed past Ike, and went to one of the display tables.

"You guys need to go," Brandon said. His hands started dancing again.

Buddy Lee stared back at Brandon. Using one hand he tipped the display table over. The six-tier model cake splattered across the floor. The chunks of chemically treated confection looked like huge pieces of candle wax.

"What the hell are you doing?!" Brandon wailed.

"You know something, Brandon. Tell me," Buddy Lee said. Brandon came from behind the counter. Ike stepped between him and Buddy Lee. He put his hand on the young man's chest and stopped his forward momentum cold. Ike could feel his heart fluttering in his chest like the wings of a hummingbird. Buddy Lee walked over to another table of displays. Using both hands this time, he flipped the table over. Six different styles of cupcakes spilled across the floor as the table clattered and the legs folded in on themselves.

"Jesus! Stop!" Brandon howled. Buddy Lee came striding over to him and grabbed him by the front of his T-shirt. Ike stepped back out of the way.

"You want me to start on you? You gonna look worse than them cakes if you don't tell me what you know. Just tell me what you know, Brandon. Help me. Help me make this fucking thing right," Buddy Lee said.

"I'm scared," Brandon said. He dropped his head until his chin was nearly touching Buddy Lee's hands. Buddy Lee let go of his shirt and put both hands on his shoulders.

"I know you are. I know. But what you tell me ain't going no-where."

Brandon mumbled something into his chest.

"What?" Buddy Lee asked.

"I said, Derek met a girl. Some girl at an event we did for some guy who had a recording studio. He told me the girl was seeing some guy who was a big deal. The guy was married and the girl wanted to tell the world what was going on. Derek was real upset about it. Said the guy was a major-league hypocrite and asshole. He said he was gonna get Isiah to publish her story. A couple of weeks later he was dead," Brandon said.

Ike felt like he'd been punched in the gut with a sledgehammer.

"Who was the girl?" Buddy Lee asked. Brandon shrugged.

"I don't know. He didn't say her name. He just said she was at the party and they started talking."

"Which party? Who threw it?" Ike asked. Brandon raised his head and looked at Ike with eyes as wide as a startled deer.

"I don't know. I just the run the counter. I don't go out on jobs. And Derek didn't say who; he just said what the guy did. That's all I know, I swear. When the cops came around I was too scared to say anything," Brandon said. His voice dropped to barely a whis-per. Buddy Lee clapped him on the face a few times.

"Okay. That's good, Brandon. That's real good," Buddy Lee said. He gestured toward the door with his head. Ike started to walk out.

"Brandon, if anybody ask, some kids came in, tore up the shop, and left. You got me?" Buddy Lee said.

"Yeah. Sure," Brandon said.

Ike merged back into traffic and headed for the interstate. The afternoon traffic was slow and steady. The light from the setting sun bounced off the parked cars that lined the sidewalk.

"That was pretty slick back there with that 'tell' thing. I never had a name for it. I mean, I know how to read the room. I can tell when somebody about to go off. You notice how they standing or where they put their hands. Shit like that. Was you on the grift, back in the day?" Ike said.

"I did a little bit of everything. My old man was on the grift. My uncles were outlaws. Only my mama tried to walk the straight and narrow. She was Jesus all day. I think what I learned from my daddy done come in handy more times than what my mama taught me," Buddy Lee said.

"It's almost six. What you think we should do? How we gonna find this girl?" Ike asked. Buddy Lee scratched at his chin.

"I was thinking about that as soon as he said it. What do you think about going by the boys' house? Take a look around. We might be able to find out who this guy was that owned the music studio," Buddy Lee said.

"Might find out who this girl was, too. Alright. I got Isiah's keys. Did they give you Derek's stuff at the funeral home?" Ike said. Buddy Lee bit at one of his fingernails. He didn't speak until Ike had hit the on-ramp.

"They tried to. I was in bad place at the wake. I didn't want it. I don't know, I guess I was kinda mad at Derek because he was dead. And if I didn't take his stuff, then it wasn't real. I was pretty drunk that day, too," Buddy Lee said. Ike let a breath whistle through his lips.

"Yeah. I know what you mean. It was like they weren't real. Laying there like mannequins. I think I killed a whole bottle of rum that night."

"Hey, there's only room on this team for one alcoholic," Buddy Lee said.

Ike's cell phone vibrated in his pocket. He pulled it out and checked the screen. It was Mya.

"Hey."

"Hey. Where you at? I called the shop and they said you weren't coming in today."

"Just had a few things to take care of. What's up?"

"I just left the cemetery. They said Isiah's headstone got damaged. Did they call you?" Ike checked his mirror and changed lanes.

"Yeah, I was gonna tell you when I got home. The guy said they gonna replace it."

"Jesus, what the fuck are they doing up there?" Mya asked.

"It was an accident. They gonna fix it."

"Arianna got down on her knees at the grave today. I asked her what she was doing. She said she was saying hi to her daddies," Mya said. Ike didn't say anything. He could feel the silence between them slowly strangling him.

"I nearly lost it, Ike. I wanted to lay on top of that grave and stay there all day," Mya said.

"It hurts," Ike said.

"And it ain't never gonna get any better, is it?" Mya asked.

"I don't know," Ike said. Mya's breathing got heavy. Her weeping began to fill his ears.

"I guess I'll see you when you get home," she said between sobs. The line went dead.

"Everything alright?" Buddy Lee asked.

"No," Ike said as he put the phone back in his pocket.

ELEVEN

Grayson pulled up to the clubhouse in a cloud of dust. The ride from the Southside to Sandston had been miserable. It felt like he'd been stuck in the armpit of a goddamn orangutan. He climbed off the bike and strapped his helmet to the handlebars.

The clubhouse was an old two-story farmhouse with a wraparound porch. Tommy "Big Boss" Harris, the club president before Grayson, who was now serving twenty to life, had built an enormous three-car garage behind the clubhouse for brothers to work on their rides, break in fresh tail, and handle club business. A row of bikes was parked off to the left of the main building. Muscular examples of American steel and ingenuity. Iron horses for the new outlaws.

Two brothers were hanging out on the porch. Dome, the vice president, was leaning against one of the columns that supported the roof of the porch. Gremlin, the club mechanic and sergeant at arms, was lounging in a leather recliner that was parked in the corner of the porch. The beat of a southern rock song exploded out the open front door. The smell of weed followed it, accompanied by a woman's high laugh.

When they saw Grayson approaching, Dome straightened up and Gremlin rose out of his seat.

"Hey, Grayson."

"What's up, brother?" Gremlin said.

"Them jigs been down yet?" Grayson asked. Dome and Gremlin exchanged furtive glances.

"Yeah, they came down. They didn't wanna buy the MAC-10s, though," Dome said.

"Why the fuck not?" Grayson asked.

Dome shifted his weight from one foot to the other. "They said their boss guy said they were too hot. Couldn't move them. Said you and the boss was gonna talk about it."

"And y'all just let him walk away like that?" Grayson asked.

Dome licked his lips. "Uh. I mean, he paid us for the rest of the stuff."

"Took all the handguns," Gremlin chimed in. Grayson put his left foot on the bottom step of the porch. He motioned for Dome to bend forward. The taller man hesitated, then did as he was asked. Grayson grabbed the hoop dangling from Dome's right ear and twisted it until the lobe looked like a piece of braided rope. Dome squealed as Grayson whispered in his ear.

"Don't you ever, as long as you got breath in your lungs, ever let somebody short us on a deal. They asked for MAC-10s, they take the MAC-10s. This ain't motherfucking Burger King. You got people out here thinking we soft-ass punks. What does that patch on your back say?" Grayson asked.

"Rare Breed!" Dome howled.

"You think we punks? You think we some gangbangers on the corner moving shit out the back of a broke-down Impala?" Grayson gave the hoop another quarter turn.

"NO!" Dome screamed.

"Don't you ever let anybody walk away from here with some of our money. You're supposed to be the fucking vice president. You better start acting like it," Grayson said.

"Okay, okay!" Dome wheezed.

"Find another customer for them MAC-10s." Grayson let go of Dome's ear. "Tell Andy and Oscar I want to talk to them at the table," Grayson said. He headed for the garage. Dome rubbed his ear. His fingers came away red.

"You need some alcohol or something?" Gremlin asked.

"Just go get the fucking prospects," Dome said.

Grayson was sitting at the head of the table when the prospects came shuffling in. A string of sickly yellow lights cast weak shadows throughout the garage and across the table. The club's emblem, a wolf's head covered in iron plating, was painted in the center of the table where the club voted on official business. Andy and Oscar stopped at the foot of the table. Grayson didn't ask them to sit.

"You both want your patches, don't ya?" Grayson asked. The two men nodded. Oscar nodded so hard his hair fell into his face. Andy was tall and lean like a sapling. Oscar was as wide as a walking refrigerator. Grayson thought they resembled the number 10. They both wore denim cuts with the chapter location on the bottom.

"I'm looking for a girl calls herself Tangerine. Been trying to find her for a few months. There was this punk-ass reporter who was talking to her until he got himself killed. I need y'all to go over to his place. You'll probably have to bust in. Look around, see if you can find anything about Tangerine. If you do find something, I'll speed up patching you in."

"We gotta break in the place?" Oscar asked.

"Did I fucking stutter? Did you not just hear me say you gonna have to break in the place? What the fuck is wrong with you?" Grayson said. He punctuated each sentence by slamming his fist into the table.

"Don't worry, we got it. We ain't gonna let you down," Andy said.

"You better not," Grayson said. He stood and extended his fist. Andy and Oscar extended theirs. The three men bumped knuckles.

"We make them bleed for the Breed," Andy said.

"We make them bleed for the Breed," Oscar said.

"Damn right you do," Grayson said.

TWELVE

Ike parallel-parked his truck between a bright-pink scooter and a car that was so small he could have probably picked it up with one hand. A streetlamp with a busted bulb towered over them.

"This my first time here," Buddy Lee said.

"I came here once for the housewarming. Right after it . . . happened, Mya was talking about us coming over and cleaning the place up. Two months later and all we did was talk," Ike said.

The housewarming. Another night that ended in yelling and slammed doors. He opened his door and Buddy Lee soon followed. Civilly engineered oak trees dotted the sidewalk at twenty-foot intervals. They chased the streetlamps down the sidewalk. Bike racks popped up every few feet like iron hedges. Ike and Buddy Lee walked side by side as they headed to the town house.

"Things up here done changed a lot," Ike said.

"Oh yeah?" Buddy Lee said.

"Back in the day there used to be this ol' boy who ran a lot of product through this part of town. I used to run with a crew back home who bought from him. When we used to ride through here to re-up, every other building was a crack house. Base heads wandering up and down the street like zombies. Offering to have their girl suck your dick for a ten-dollar rock. If times got really tight, they'd offer to do it themselves. I come through one time doing a favor for that ol' boy. Sprayed this whole street up with an AK, then carried my ass back to Red Hill."

"Who was you after?" Buddy Lee asked.

"I don't even remember. I think somebody was trying to push up on him. Or maybe they stepped on his homeboys' shoes over at the Satellite bar and he had me come through to correct them. I don't know. I did a lot of dumb shit back then for street cred. When I went inside I learned the hard way street cred don't mean shit," Ike said.

"I think I could give you a run for your money in the dumb-shit department. My last time around the mulberry bush I took a fall that wasn't mine to take," Buddy Lee said.

"For real?" Ike asked.

"Yeah. My brother, my half brother Deak, and me got picked up with a trunk full of ice. We was moving it for a fella named Chuly Pettigrew. Deak didn't have a record. Mine was long enough to wrap up a mummy. I wanted Deak to stay clean. He wasn't built for that kind of life. They would have eaten him alive inside. I did my best to make sure it was his first and last run. So I kept my mouth shut about Chuly, took the blame for Deak, and got three to five years. Did the full five. After I went away Deak went out west and got a job on a natural gas crew. Far as I know he's still there."

"Huh," Ike said.

"What?"

"You had a trunk full of meth and you only got five years? If you had looked like me, they would have put you under the jail for moving that much weight. I got friends who got three to five for holding weed. Weed," Ike said.

"I don't know about that," Buddy Lee mumbled.

"I do. This is the place," Ike said. He'd stopped in front of a two-story town house with slat-board siding stained a deep burgundy. The front steps were painted a sleepy cream color. A large black ceramic planter sat at the base of the steps. It was decorated with the initials IR & DJ. The letters were fat and wide and painted white. Like they had been drawn on by hand. Ike pulled the key out of his pocket and opened the door.

They stepped into a small foyer that was decorated in understated blues and whites. An umbrella container sat to their left next to a coatrack carved out of a large piece of what appeared to be driftwood. A lack of movement inside the house had allowed a pall to settle over the entire structure. The air had a stale, spoiled scent. A thin layer of dust covered most of the exposed surfaces. Death had laid his cold hand on this place and stilled its heart.

The living room continued the understated motif. A sectional couch dominated the space. A flat-screen TV was mounted on the wall facing the couch. To their right, pictures detailed various moments of Isiah and Derek's life together. Trips they had taken, parties they had attended. Quiet candid moments. Pictures of the two of them holding Arianna as a newborn. The three of them wearing paper pirate hats at a restaurant. A black-and-white picture of Arianna blowing on a dandelion. A picture of the three of them and Arianna holding a poster with the word "DEED" written on it in cartoonishly large letters. Derek and Isiah were grinning from ear to ear. Arianna appeared nonplussed.

The photos were a mosaic showing the evolution of their journey together.

"They look happy," Ike said.

"Yeah. They do," Buddy Lee said. He pointed at the picture of the comical deed.

"They must have paid the house off. Derek told me one day he was gonna have a house, not a trailer. Goddamn if he didn't do it," Buddy Lee said.

He clapped his hands hard. A crack echoed through the house.

"Where should we start?" Buddy Lee asked.

"I guess we should split up maybe? I'll go check the bedroom, and I think Isiah had an office in the back. I remember him saying they had closed in the back porch. You wanna check around in here?" Ike said.

"Yeah, that's cool. I'll just go through anything that has a drawer pull on it," Buddy Lee said.

"Alright. Holler if you find something," Ike said. He walked through the living room and down a short hall. Buddy Lee started with an end table that sat next to the sectional. It was full of junk mail and odds and ends. He moved on to a coffee table with two drawers on each end. He thought that was a strange design choice, but what did he know? He used milk crates for furniture. A multitude of remotes were in one drawer. The other drawer held a few magazines. Buddy Lee closed the drawer and studied the wall of pictures. He hadn't noticed an accent table that was sitting under the pictures. There were two tiny book-shaped picture frames sitting on the table. He picked one of them up and felt his chest heave. It was a copy of the picture he kept in his wallet. The other frame showed a young Black boy and a man that was a much younger Ike. The boy was on Ike's shoulders. Buddy Lee put the frame back on the table. Next to this picture was a photo he hadn't seen in over twenty years.

It was Christine and Derek. They were sitting on the steps of the trailer the three of them had shared before Buddy Lee got himself locked up the last time. Christine was as beautiful as a sunset. Auburn hair falling down her back like a waterfall. Big cornflower-blue eyes. That dimple in her chin that had driven him crazy all those years ago when they had first met. He'd asked her to dance at a bonfire and she had said no. Not in a cruel or haughty way. Just a simple, succinct, I-can't-be-bothered fashion. He'd gone and found a handful of wildflowers just inside the tree line. He returned to the log she and her friends had been sitting on and got down on one knee.

"Dance with me. Just one dance and I'll never bother you again for the rest of your life."

"Is that a promise?"

"Scout's honor."

"You don't look like much of a scout."

"And you look like the prettiest woman on God's green earth. C'mon, one dance. I won't even try and dip you."

She had laughed at that. A full, throaty laugh as bright and sweet as summer itself. They had danced. They had kissed. They had gone down a long dirt lane in his Camaro and found paradise under a harvest moon. For a few years it had been magic. But magic was just sleight of hand, and eventually the magician's assistant had seen every trick. By the time he'd done his second stint inside, Christine had seen enough. He didn't begrudge her moving on and marrying that rich prick. Hell, he would have divorced him, too. That was understandable. But the way she erased Derek from her life was just wrong. He knew he wasn't much of a father, but what kind of mother did that to her own child?

Buddy Lee removed the picture from the frame and put it in his back pocket. He moved on to the kitchen. Buddy Lee was overwhelmed by the sheer volume of equipment that was crammed into this space. The decor in here had an old-school Americana vibe. Black-and-white-checkered floors. Stainless-steel appliances. Black cabinets with granite countertops. Buddy Lee figured those countertops had to be granite to hold all the cooking utensils and machinery Derek had acquired over the years. Buddy Lee didn't know what half of this shit did, but he knew his son had probably mastered all of it. Derek had loved to cook ever since he'd first seen his grandmother stirring cake batter. Buddy Lee's cousin Sam had been a hell of a cook, too. Culinary skills ran in the Jenkins family. It had just leapfrogged over Buddy Lee and landed on Derek. Derek's affinity for cooking had never struck Buddy Lee as gay, per se. It was just something he was good at. Even when they argued—which wasn't often, because, if he was being honest, he didn't see Derek that much—he'd never thrown any shade at him for being a chef. Not that he deserved a medal for that. He'd said plenty of other shit that he regretted. It was just too bad it took Derek dying for him to realize it.

Buddy Lee went through the cabinets checking sugar dishes and saucepans with tops. He wasn't surprised when he found some weed. A lot of people hid their stash in the kitchen. He'd robbed enough houses to say it wasn't an anomaly. There was nothing in the drawers except knives, forks, and spoons. Buddy Lee put one hand on his hip and rubbed his forehead with the other.

What was he doing? This was a waste of time. It wasn't like he was going to find a notebook with the girl's name, the name of the person who killed his son, and an address where he could find them. What he should do is go back and talk to that kid at the caterer's. Squeeze the name of the guy who had the party out of him like an apple caught in a vise. Buddy Lee placed his hand on his forehead. The ice maker made a horrific sound before it dropped a load down the chute into the holding container. Buddy Lee thought it sounded like maracas. He took a step toward it. There was a notepad on the fridge attached with a magnet. Buddy Lee grabbed it. There was a doodle on the first page of the notepad. A fairly sophisticated drawing of a pair of shoes, then an arrow, then what he supposed was a piece of fruit followed by an exclamation point. At the bottom of the page there were a series of numbers, then a space and then another set of numbers and an exclamation point.

Buddy Lee studied the drawings. A part of him thought it was just what it looked like, a doodle. Maybe Isiah and Derek were joking around and one of them scrawled an amateur comic strip on their message pad. But his gut told him it was something more. The exclamation point made it seem important. Buddy Lee fanned the pad against his hand.

He tore the page off and put it in his front pocket. He trusted his gut but he didn't always listen to it. That's how he ended up taking two falls. He wasn't a genius but he learned from his mistakes. Most of the time.

Ike stood for a long time in the doorway of the first room he came to. This was Isiah and Derek's bedroom. This was where they slept together. Held each other through the night. Ike didn't get it. How could Isiah feel the same way about Derek that Ike felt about Mya? Ike shook his head. If Isiah were here he would tell him there was nothing to get. Love is love. But Isiah wasn't here. He was dead.

Ike stepped in the room and started to tear it apart. He pulled out the drawers in the nightstands and dumped them on the bed. They were filled with the usual hodgepodge of items that found their way into a nightstand. Fingernail file, eye drops, bandages, lube, and a huge collection of bar napkins. Ike picked up one. In the corner the word *Garland's* was printed in cursive. Almost all the napkins were from Garland's. Ike balled up the napkin and tossed it in the trash. He turned and went to the closet. There was a collection of hats on the top shelf. Baseball caps, fedoras, skullcaps, and a tam-o'-shanter. The closet was jam-packed with shirts and blazers hanging in color-coordinated order. Ike smiled. Isiah used to do the same thing with his sneakers as a kid. The smile faded.

Ike walked out of the bedroom and headed straight for Isiah's office. The room was just as organized as the closet. A slim bookcase in the far-left corner had all the editions arranged in alphabetical order by title. In the far-right corner was a tall filing cabinet. In the center of the room was a clear Lucite desk. A computer was in the middle of the desk. A landline phone sat next to it like a relic in a museum. There was a composition notebook next to the phone. Ike flipped through it. There were notes written in Isiah's precise handwriting. Most of it was gibberish to Ike. It was some sort of shorthand that only Isiah could decipher. The last entry was only one sentence.

"Does she know?"

Next to it Isiah had drawn a frowny face. Ike stared at the page. What the hell did that mean? Who was "she"? Was she the girl from the party? Was she someone else not connected with that girl at all? Ike put the notebook back on the desk. How did the police do this shit? He didn't know enough about Isiah's life to make sense of anything in it.

Ike pushed a button on the phone and pulled up the call log. He'd seen a detective do it in a movie once. He scrolled through the numbers without any firm idea of what he was trying to find. He didn't know Isiah's friends, so the numbers were just a collection of digits. No one had called since March 24. That was the night it happened. As he scrolled, something jumped out at him. The day before the boys were shot, one number called eight times in a row. Ike pushed another button on the phone and checked the messages. A robotic voice announced there were twelve messages.

Ike pressed PLAY.

The majority of the messages were fairly innocuous. He was sure the cops had already done this, but it didn't hurt to hear it for himself. The last message was left the day before the shooting. A breathless voice rumbled out of the speaker.

"Hey, it's me. I changed my mind. I don't want to talk about it. I'm sorry. I'm scared. Bye."

The machine cut itself off. Ike didn't recognize the voice, but he thought it sounded like a woman. She wasn't just scared. She sounded terrified. Ike checked the phone number. It had a local area code. Ike grabbed a pen and a scrap of paper off the desk and wrote the number down. As he was transcribing the number he couldn't help thinking, *What the hell had Derek gotten Isiah into?*

THIRTEEN

Andy pulled a screwdriver out of his pocket. He jammed it between the doorjamb and the lock. Oscar stood behind him, shielding him from the street with his bulk. Not that he really needed any shielding. There was hardly anybody on the street. A few stumbling lost souls who weren't worrying about anything but their next drink or hit. They'd parked three blocks away just in case some civic-minded neighbor decided to copy down Andy's license-plate number.

He gripped the doorknob and turned it as he forced the screwdriver into the jamb. To his surprise the knob turned with almost no effort.

"Shit, I think it was open," Andy said.

"Huh. Well, let's get this over with, I guess."

Andy paused. Why was the door unlocked anyway? Had they stumbled on somebody robbing the place? He wasn't sure of how you defined irony, but he thought that would be damn close. Andy touched the small of his back. The butt of a .357 Colt Python rested against his waistband. He'd gotten it from Grayson when they left the clubhouse. He didn't think they would need it, but if you stayed prepared you didn't have to get prepared. That was one of the only things his piece-of-shit mother had said that actually made sense.

"Yeah, let's do it," Andy said. It didn't matter why the door was unlocked. It didn't matter what might be on the other side of that door. All that mattered was getting what Grayson asked for so they could be made full members. Andy pulled the door open and stepped inside the house.

Buddy Lee leaned against the sink. His chest was as tight as virgin pussy. He tried to cough but he couldn't seem to get enough air into his lungs. He flicked on the faucet. He cupped his hands and caught some water. He splashed his face, took a deep breath, and finally coughed up some phlegm. He spit into the sink. The lightgreenish phlegm was stippled with red spots.

"Well, that ain't good," he murmured.

The front door opened.

Buddy Lee snapped his head up and whirled around until he was facing the living room. Two men had stepped inside the house. One of them was a tall drink of water with a spindly frame that could use a few pounds. The other one had bulk to spare. He could donate fifty pounds to his buddy and still be as wide as a tank.

They tiptoed into the room like a pair of skittish deer. Buddy Lee leaned back against the sink. He reached behind him and pulled the first thing his hand touched out of the drain basket. That happened to be a heavy decorative jelly jar. He gripped it behind his back with his right hand. They hadn't seen him yet. He could try sliding out the kitchen and down the hall. Probably wouldn't work but he could try it. Of course, if he did that he wouldn't be able to ask them what the hell they were doing in his son's house. He didn't think they were Jehovah's Witnesses.

"Hey there, fellas," Buddy Lee said from the kitchen. The two men stopped in their tracks.

"Hey," Andy said. He let his right hand slip into his back pocket.

"What y'all fellas doing walking up in my son's house without knocking? Y'all friends of his?"

Andy and Oscar exchanged a look. Buddy Lee had seen that look before. They were deciding which one of them were going to tell the lie. Andy smiled.

"Yeah, we're friends of his."

"You all must work with him at the newspaper," Buddy Lee said. Andy moved his hand closer to his gun.

"Yeah, that's it. We all work at the newspaper together," Andy said. Buddy Lee smiled back at Andy.

You a lying sack of shit, he thought.

Andy saw the smile crawl across Buddy Lee's face. He noticed it never reached his eyes.

Shit, he thought.

The house went quiet. Buddy Lee could hear the ticking of the clock above the sink. The hum of the traffic on the street. The sighs and groans of the house as it settled into a monolithic position for the foreseeable future.

The ice machine rattled again.

Andy reached for his gun.

Buddy Lee hurled the jelly jar at his head. It exploded against his right cheek. Buddy Lee was on the move as soon as he threw the jar. He slammed his whole body into Andy before Oscar even realized he was in the living room. Andy and Buddy Lee crashed into the coffee table. Despite their total body weight barely breaking the 250-pound barrier, the table collapsed under their bodies. Andy felt the gun biting into the skin just above the crack of his ass. He wanted to grab it, but the old man was trying his best to knock his teeth down his throat.

Buddy Lee punched Andy as hard as he could on the right side of his face. The kid tried to block his punches but to no avail. When Andy raised his hands to protect his eyes and forehead, Buddy Lee cracked him in the chin. When he inverted the position of his hands, his cheek bore the brunt of Buddy Lee's assault. The old man was as wiry as a spider monkey.

Buddy Lee suddenly felt like he was flying. Oscar had grabbed him around the waist like he was a bag of laundry. The big man squeezed Buddy Lee so hard he thought his nuts were going to pop. Buddy Lee opened and closed his mouth like a trout bouncing around on the floor of a jon boat. As Andy got up to one knee, Buddy Lee kicked him as hard as he could in the face. The younger man fell back into the ruin of the coffee table. Buddy Lee tucked his head forward, then snapped it backward. The sound of Oscar's nose breaking was music to his ears. The big man released him from his deadly embrace. Buddy Lee landed on his feet, then mule-kicked Oscar in the right shin.

Andy swung the Colt butt-first into the side of Buddy Lee's head. Stars exploded all around him as he dropped to all fours. He was vaguely aware his hand had landed in the razor-sharp remains of the table. Shards of glass sliced through his thick calluses and buried their way into his palms. His stomach convulsed but the contents of his belly stayed put. Oscar fell against the door clutching his shin.

Andy put the barrel of the Python against Buddy Lee's temple. Buddy Lee felt a trickle of blood run down his face and wind its way over his five-o'clock shadow. Andy's top lip was beginning to swell. His cheek was on fire. A cloudy film seemed to be covering his left eye. The old man had punted him in the face like he was kicking the winning field goal in the Super Bowl.

"Cut the cord off that TV and tie him up." Andy said. He spit a pinkish globule onto the floor. It was equal parts saliva and blood. Oscar grabbed his knife out of his pocket and limped over to the television. He tied Buddy Lee's hands behind his back. Oscar couldn't believe how fast the old man moved. He'd been a blur coming out of the kitchen. It was like watching the Flash.

"I think you broke one of my teeth, old man." Andy said. He probed his right molar with his tongue. The tooth wiggled against the intruding tongue.

"That ain't nothing compared to what I'm gonna do when I get loose," Buddy Lee said. Andy laughed. He pressed the barrel into Buddy Lee's head.

"You about two seconds from getting a hole in your fucking head.

But first I'm gonna ask you a couple of questions and you gonna give me some answers," Andy said.

"Hey, I mean this from the bottom of my heart. Fuck you," Buddy Lee said. Andy kicked him in the stomach. The few remaining wisps of air in his lungs rushed out of his mouth with a *whoosh!* Buddy Lee pitched forward. His face landed in a pile of crushed glass. A few slivers tried to find their way into his mouth. Andy grabbed him by his hair. He put his mouth close to Buddy Lee's ear.

"You miss your son? You gonna see him soon enough. But before that happens you gonna beg for a bullet," he said.

Andy kicked him again. This time his lunch did make a break for it. Stomach acid burned his throat as the vomit raced up his esophagus. It spilled over his lips like a waterfall.

"You better kill me," Buddy Lee gasped. Andy laughed.

"Ooh, I better kill you," he said. He spoke in a high-pitched nasally tone.

"Maybe we should ask him about the girl," Oscar offered. Andy stopped tittering.

"You know anything about the girl, old man?" Andy asked. He should have thought of that before Oscar suggested it. He was getting caught up in the moment and forgetting the task at hand.

"You better kill me or you going to regret ever crawling out of your mama's old chewed-up cunt," Buddy Lee said. Andy blinked rapidly a few times.

"My mama's cunt, huh? Say hi to your son for me," Andy said. He cocked the hammer on the Colt and pointed it at Buddy Lee's face. Buddy Lee felt like he was tumbling into the barrel like it was a bottomless mine shaft. Andy pressed the barrel against his cheek. Buddy Lee closed his eyes. He hoped he would see Derek, but he wasn't sure they were going to be spending eternity in the same place.

A deafening crash echoed from the back of the house.

"What the fuck was that? You got somebody here with you, old man? Oscar, go check it out," Andy said. Oscar licked on his bottom lip.

"I didn't bring a gun," he said.

"Tough titty. Now go check it out," Andy said. Oscar wiped his face, then studied his hand. Blood was smeared across his palm like Sanskrit.

"Yeah. Tough titty alright," he said. The big man lumbered down the hall like Godzilla. Had the light been on in the hall when they first entered? Oscar couldn't remember. It was off now. He flicked a switch on the wall and nothing happened. His breath came in quick irregular gulps. His nose was beyond fucked up. He couldn't even force air through it. He descended into the shadows.

"Did you kill my son?" Buddy Lee asked Andy. The stars had finally retreated and his vision had cleared. Andy had moved the gun out of his face. Instead it was hanging loosely by his leg.

"Shut up," Andy said.

"Who sent you?" Buddy Lee wheezed. He hadn't exerted himself like that in a long time. His heart felt sluggish in his chest. The back of his throat was so dry he thought if he coughed now gravel would pop out and clatter across the floor.

"Shut the fuck up," Andy said.

Oscar came to a door on the left side of the hall that was partly ajar. It was narrower than the other three doors he had already passed. This had to be the bathroom. Was someone hiding in the tub with a shotgun? He'd seen that in a movie once. The good guy had shot one of the bad guys when he was taking a piss. Oscar used two fingers and pushed the door open all the way. It was indeed the bathroom. A blue ambient light in the ceiling gave the room a ghostly glow. The blue light was built into the exhaust fan. The bathroom had a shower stall, a sink, and a pale-blue toilet. Or was that the effect of the blue LED light. Oscar frowned. The top of the toilet tank was missing. He heard the reservoir filling with water. Like someone had just flushed it. Oscar backed up into the hall. He heard glass crunching beneath his feet. He raised his head and squinted. There had once been a light fixture in the ceiling. One of those fancy pendant jobs. Now there was just a thin metal tube hanging down. Like someone had smashed it—

Oscar spun around just in time for Ike to shatter the top of the toilet tank over his head.

"You gonna wish you had killed me, boy," Buddy Lee rasped.

"You keep talking that shit like you somebody I ought to be afraid of. You ain't nothing but an old drunk that needs to shut his fucking mouth. Yeah, I can smell it coming off you. Just like my dad," Andy said. Buddy Lee heard the bravado in his voice and the uncertainty that was hiding just beneath the surface. A minute after Oscar had ventured down the darkened hall, the whole house shook. Something had hit the floor like a slab of granite.

Andy took an unconscious step toward the hall with his gun raised. Buddy Lee was on his knees when the kid stepped toward the hallway. Quick as a wink he dropped to his ass and used both feet to kick the kid in the side of his right knee. He thought he heard a snapping sound. Andy screamed and fell backward and to the left. When he hit the ground, the big pistol jumped out of his hand like the Gingerbread Man making a break for it. Andy clutched at his knee for the briefest of seconds before realizing he had lost his gun. He rolled onto his left side and stretched out his right hand for the Colt.

Ike came out of the shadows like the spirit of Nemesis in the flesh. He stomped on Andy's right hand, and Buddy Lee was positive he heard a crack that time. Andy screamed again as Ike picked him up off the ground by his shirt. Once he had him on his feet, Ike hit him with a ferocious uppercut. The younger man was lifted at least three inches into the air. He landed in a heap under the wall-mounted television. Ike glared at him for a moment before picking up the Colt and tucking it into his waistband. He went to Buddy

Lee and retrieved his jackknife from his back pocket. Ike cut him loose, then helped him to his feet.

"Glad you decided to join the party," Buddy Lee said.

"When I heard the commotion, I figured I'd hang back a minute. Sounded like more than one guy, so I tipped over the dresser to get their attention. Force them to split up. Besides, I figured you could handle yourself. No use losing the element of surprise," Ike said.

"Well, I'm glad you had all this confidence in me. But tell me this: What was you gonna do if they had blown my goddamn head off?" Buddy Lee asked.

"They didn't, so we don't have to find out," Ike said. Buddy Lee shook his head. He looked down at the crumpled form of the skinny kid.

"I told you you should've fucking killed me," Buddy Lee said.

"Did you really say that?" Ike asked.

Buddy Lee nodded. "I meant it, too."

FOURTEEN

Andy's eyelids fluttered. He had promised to make them bleed for the Breed. The tables, however, had been turned. He was bleeding, and it didn't seem like he was going to be allowed to stop anytime soon. He tried to raise his head but it felt like it was full of bricks.

Buddy Lee slapped the kid as hard as he could. He followed that up with a one-two combo to his ribs. He took a step back and leaned forward with his hands on his knees. A glob of sputum worked its way out of his lungs. He closed his mouth and walked over to the trash can near the second roll-up door in Ike's warehouse. He spit it into the small brown wastebasket. He didn't have to look at it to know it would have more of the faint red spots mixed in it.

"You alright?" Ike asked.

"Yeah, just out of fucking shape. Why don't you ask him?" Buddy Lee said. He walked over to a pallet of mulch and sat down on top of it. Ike went to his cubicle office and got his roller chair. He placed it right in front of the kid. Then he went to the tool rack. He came back with a tamper. It was a tool they used to even out the dirt when they planted a large tree or ran some sprinkler lines. A four-foot-long wooden handle with a flat black iron square at one end, it was a fairly simple piece of equipment. He placed the tamper between him and the kid before taking a seat in the roller chair.

The kid was in the wooden office chair. Ike had zip-tied his wrist to the arms of the chair. Once Buddy Lee had cleaned himself up, they had grabbed an area rug from Isiah's office and rolled the kid up inside it. The decision to take the kid wasn't something they had discussed. There was no need. It was obvious the kid and the big guy were somehow involved in what had happened to the boys.

The kid was about a hundred pounds lighter than his partner. In this case his partner had drawn the short straw, genetically speaking. So, they left the big guy sprawled across the hallway floor and carried the skinny kid out of the town house like a pair of late-night movers. They passed a few people as they walked to the truck. Most of them didn't look up from their cell phones long enough to notice two men carrying a vaguely human shaped rug down the sidewalk. If any of Isiah and Derek's neighbors had heard the ruckus, they didn't feel it was necessary to get involved. Apparently the neighborhood wasn't that gentrified yet.

Ike put his finger under the kid's chin. He raised his head until they were eye to eye.

"What's your name? You ain't got a license on you. That was smart," Ike said. Buddy Lee was shocked at how gentle his voice sounded. It was like he was about to tell the boy a bedtime story.

"Fuck you," Andy mumbled. Ike pulled his finger away. The boy's head dropped into his chest. Blood dripped from his mouth and his nose. The wound on his cheek was weeping like a broken-hearted bride. Ike place his hands on the end of the tamper's handle, then placed his chin on top of his hands.

"You smart. And you got heart, I'll give you that. But you got to know this ain't gonna end good for you, right? I mean, you break into the house that belonged to our sons. You try to kill my man over there. You know what that tells me? Either you killed our sons or you know who did," Ike said. Andy didn't strain against the zip ties. He used every ounce of his waning strength to raise his head.

"Who sent you to that house?" Ike asked.

Andy spit into Ike's face. His head dropped back down to his chest. The spittle landed on Ike's chin. He stood. He wiped his chin, then wiped his hand on his pants.

"Help me take off his boots," Ike said. Buddy Lee grabbed the kid's left foot and Ike grabbed the right. They pulled off his boots and tossed them next to the pellet lime. Ike grabbed the tamper. He moved behind Andy. He raised the tamper until the flat square head was parallel with his belt buckle. He brought it down with all his strength. The metal head striking the concrete floor created a cacophony inside the cavernous warehouse. Ike took a position near Andy's left arm. He slammed the tamper down again. Both Andy and Buddy Lee flinched. Ike moved around Andy like the hands of a clock, each time slamming the tamper down and sending a harsh report through the building.

"Who sent you, boy?" Ike said finally.

Andy flexed his wrists. The zip tie on his left hand was immovable. The one on his right, however, had the tiniest bit of play. The Black guy had looped it through a spindle, then around the armrest, then around his wrist. The spindle was loose. If he put his back into, he could probably break it. Then he could use the chair as a weapon and make a run for it. None of that would happen if this motherfucker smashed his toes.

"A guy sent us. He was looking for info on a girl," Andy said. Ike stopped moving.

"What guy?" Buddy Lee asked.

"I don't know. I mean I don't know his name. He just told us he was looking for a girl that was supposed to be talking to a reporter. He wanted info on where she might be," Andy said.

He took a deep breath, sending an ache through his chest that made him wince. Ike bent forward. His face was barely an inch from Andy's.

"You lying to me?" Ike asked.

"No. I swear."

"What was the girl's name?" Ike asked.

Andy sighed.

"Tangerine."

Buddy Lee pulled out the piece of paper. He stared at the drawing, then at the kid in the chair.

"I'll be damned," he said. Ike straightened. He went over to where Buddy Lee was leaning against the pallet of mulch. He left the tamper near Andy.

"What is it?"

Buddy Lee showed him the piece of paper.

"I took this off the fridge at the boys' place. I thought it was an orange, but I suppose it could be a tangerine. But I don't know what that building is," Buddy Lee said. Ike thought of the napkins he'd found at the house.

"You think it could be a bar? Maybe Isiah was going to meet this Tangerine girl at a place they hung out a lot?" Ike asked. Buddy Lee pushed off the pallet and turned his back to the kid. He dropped his voice to the bottom of his chest.

"What if she was supposed to meet them and then they got killed? Whoever killed them might be the one who hired Junior over there," Buddy Lee said.

"He might be the one the kid at the bakery was talking about," Ike whispered.

"That's what I was thinking."

"We should lean on him some more. I bet if I smash one of his toes he'll remember who hired him," Ike said.

Andy watched them as they turned their backs on him and huddled close.

"What if he don't give it up?" Buddy Lee asked.

"They always give it up," Ike said.

Andy raised his head. It was now or never. He strained against the right zip tie. He relaxed, then strained again, this time twisting his upper body and pulling his right arm toward the left.

Ike heard a snap a millisecond before he turned and took a chair to the head. The kid was swinging it like a club. His left wrist was still attached to the armrest. His bare feet hadn't made a sound on the cool concrete floor. Ike took the full brunt of his swing to the left side of his head. He went down to all fours like he was searching for grains of gold dust.

Andy shoved the chair at the thin white guy. The guy instinctively grabbed the chair legs, and Andy pushed him backward toward the pallet of mulch. Buddy Lee felt his feet slip on the concrete even as he gripped the chair by its legs. His chest rattled and his lungs begged for air. Was he passing out? He wasn't sure, but the next thing he knew, his ass was on the floor and his hands seemed to go numb. A coughing fit picked the absolute worst time to possess him. The kid pulled the chair out of Buddy Lee's hands and raised it above his head.

The shadow the chair cast over him was the shadow of death. Buddy Lee felt a desperate surge of adrenaline course through his veins. A huge wad of phlegm escaped his chest at last. Sweet oxygen filled his lungs like ambrosia. Buddy Lee grabbed his jackknife from his back pocket. As the kid swung the chair downward, Buddy Lee rose to one knee. In one smooth motion he flicked the blade out with his thumb and shoved the knife in the kid's belly up to the hilt. The hole in his belly took some of the power out of his swing. Buddy Lee raised his free arm and blocked the blow rather easily. He watched as the kid stumbled backward. He pulled himself off Buddy Lee's blade. A languid stream of crimson began to pour from the hole in Andy's gut.

Ike shook his head side to side like a hound dog killing a rat. He jumped to his feet and grabbed the tamper. As the kid stumbled back from Buddy Lee, Ike gripped the handle with a two-handed high choke grip. He swung the tamper like he was sending a pitch into the upper deck. The flat tempered iron connected with the back of the kid's head with a dull fleshy *thump*. The kid crumpled to the floor with the chair landing on his chest.

Ike stood over the kid.

His thin lips were quivering like the death throes of some strange woodland creature. The kid had hit him with the chair. He'd tried to kill Buddy Lee. He'd broken into Isiah's house. He'd spit in Ike's face. He had probably been lying about some guy hiring him. He probably knew who had killed Isiah. The kid's eyes rolled back in his head. Hell, he might have even been the one that wrecked the headstone.

"You motherfucker!" Ike screamed. He raised the tamper and slammed it down onto the kid's head. The skin around the eye socket split and bones beneath shifted. The kid looked like he was having a stroke. Ike raised the tamper again and brought it down with all his strength. His biceps and deltoids worked together with long practiced synchronicity. He'd done this same motion thousands of times. Hundreds of thousands of times. His wide forearms burned as he rammed the tamper into the kid's face again and again. He felt something wet splash against his face. Bits of bone and teeth flew up from the floor.

"You killed him, didn't you, motherfucker!" Ike howled. Buddy Lee stood and leaned back against the pallet. His lungs were on fire. The tamper moved up and down relentlessly. It sounded like Ike was leveling out a mud-filled hole.

"Ike," Buddy Lee said. The large man's arms continued to move the tamper like a piston.

"IKE!" Buddy Lee yelled. Ike froze. The head of the tamper was parallel with his chest. It was stained red like a painter's brush. Ike stared at the garden tool like he had never seen it before. A guttural groan escaped his lips as he tossed it aside. It clanged as it skittered across the floor. It left behind narrow red streaks. Ike dropped to his haunches, then to his ass.

Buddy Lee skirted around the kid's body and the rapidly expanding pool of blood that was quickly surrounding it. He eased himself down to the floor next to Ike.

"Guess we leaned on him too hard," Buddy Lee said.

"I . . . I didn't think he could get loose," Ike said.

"Well, what do we do now?" Buddy Lee asked. Ike wiped his face with his shirt. When he looked down at it he saw dark splotches. He let out a long deep breath.

"I got a wood chipper, a bucket loader, and a two-ton pile of manure out back," Ike said.

"I think that'll work. He was real piece of shit," Buddy Lee said. He'd tried to make the statement a joke, but neither one of them laughed.

FIFTEEN

Dome was five seconds away from busting a nut in the mouth of the brunette that had been crashing at the clubhouse since Saturday, when he heard the sound of metal smashing against metal. Reflexively he grabbed his .44 off the nightstand and popped his nut all in one movement. He pushed the girl's head away and pulled up his pants with one hand. The girl slid off the bed and hit the floor with all of her considerable ass.

"What the fuck?" she said.

"Shut up," Dome said. He took the steps two at a time as he flew down the stairs. Gremlin was already up and pointing a sawed-off shotgun at the door. Too Much pushed aside the plain brown curtain at the front window and peered outside. They called him Too Much because all the girls said he had too much dick for a guy who was just a frog's hair over five feet tall.

"It's Andy's grocery getter," Too Much said. His long brown hair fell in his face, and he pushed it aside with the back of his left hand. He had a .38 in his right. Dome opened the door and stepped out onto the porch. Andy's money-green LTD was parked on top of Keeper's bike. Keeper was in the garage working on a tat for Cheddar. He either didn't hear the commotion or didn't care enough to stop working on Cheddar's back piece. The parking lights on the LTD were still on, but the headlights were black pits like the eye sockets of a skull. The car's big block 405 engine was idling rough. It was like the rolling tank was trying to clear its throat. Dome let his .44 fall to his side as he stepped down onto the first step.

The driver's door flew open and rocked back and forth a few times. Dome pulled his gun up and aimed it at the driver's side. As soon as he did it he felt foolish. If somebody was planning on spraying them up they wouldn't have just parked there. Crashing into Keeper's bike was a shitty thing to do, but it wasn't the action of an assassin. Most likely Andy and Oscar had gotten lit instead of tossing the house. Grayson would be pissed.

Almost as if thinking his name had summoned him, Oscar emerged from the car.

"Holy shit," Dome muttered.

The big man's face was covered in so much blood Dome was surprised he hadn't bled to death. It was like he was wearing a mask made from his own plasma. Oscar took three halting steps toward the house.

"Hey, Dome," the prospect mumbled. Then, like a marionette whose strings had been snipped, he fell face-first onto the gravel-covered ground. Dome rushed to his side.

"You guys come on and give me a hand!" Dome yelled. Gremlin and Too Much sailed off the porch. It took all three of them to get Oscar on his feet. They carried/dragged him into the clubhouse. They dropped him on the leather couch in front of the television. Gremlin got some water and whiskey from the kitchen. He handed both to Dome. Dome tossed the whole bottle of water onto Oscar's head. His face seemed to melt like a candle as the blood was washed away by multiple rivulets. He blinked four or five times before his eyes focused on Dome. Dome put the bottle of whiskey to Oscar's lips and tilted his head back. Oscar coughed, wheezed, then coughed some more. He motioned for the bottle again and Dome poured another shot down his throat. Oscar nodded his head and held up his hand declining another drink.

"What the fuck happened to you, man?" Too Much asked. Oscar put his huge paw of a hand on his forehead.

"You ain't gonna fucking believe it," he said.

Once Oscar had recounted the entire evening, Dome called Grayson. The president answered on the second ring.

"This better be important," Grayson said.

"It is. Oscar's back."

"And?" Grayson said.

"And Andy's not with him. Oscar's head is busted wide the fuck open and he's covered in blood. His own blood," Dome said.

A hollow silence bloomed on the phone line until Grayson spoke again.

"Did he see who hit him?" Grayson said. His voice was deathly quiet.

"He didn't, but he says he and Andy got into it with an old dude that was in the house when they got there. He thinks the old dude was the father of one of the punks. He also said he saw a truck parked near the house. Truck said Randolph Lawn Maintenance on the side," Dome said.

"Randolph, huh?" Grayson asked.

"Yeah," Dome said. Another few seconds of silence.

"I'll be over there in twenty minutes. Call a church meeting. We gonna take care of business and deal with Father Knows Best," Grayson said.

The line went dead.

SIXTEEN

Buddy Lee parked his truck right in front of the 7-Eleven. He cut off the ignition and listened to the engine dieseling for a few minutes. Once the motor stopped coughing and sputtering, he got out and went into the store. The sun had just risen. A ragged patchwork of clouds hung low in the eastern sky like cotton candy.

A robotic chime sounded as he walked through the door. Buddy Lee slipped down the center aisle and made a beeline for the cooler in the back. He plucked two tallboys from the rack and headed for the counter. He had considered just going cold turkey until they were done with whatever the hell they were calling this mission they were on, but that was just ridiculous. He hadn't done that since the last time he was in the joint. He couldn't go down that road again. That route led to shakes and vomiting and bugs in his hair that no one else could see. He could cut back, but stopping altogether was as likely as seeing a monkey driving a goddamn Cadillac.

Buddy Lee put the two cans of beer on the counter and waited for the clerk to turn around. The small brown man was stocking the cigarettes while whistling a tune that teased Buddy Lee with its familiarity. When the man finally emptied the carton he was working on he turned and scanned Buddy Lee's beer.

"Buddy Lee. How are you, my friend? You look a bit unrested."

"Well, good fucking morning to you, too, Hamad," Buddy Lee said.

"I mean no harm, Buddy Lee. I am worried about you, my friend. You look like you have not slept a wink," Hamad said.

"You don't know the half of it, son," Buddy Lee said.

After he had stabbed the kid and Ike had caved his head in like an overripe melon, they had stripped him naked and fired up Ike's wood chipper. Ike had positioned the discharge chute directly onto the manure pile in the back lot of his warehouse. They used handsaws and machetes to break the kid down into manageable pieces. Once it was all done they pressure-washed the floor and the wood chipper. Buddy Lee had plopped down on the lime pallet and watched Ike mix up the manure pile with his economy-sized front-end loader. By the time they were done, it was two hours before sunrise. He supposed he should be shocked how fast his disposal skills resurfaced, but it was not really that much of a surprise. Chopping up your first body is disgusting. Your second is tiresome. When you're doing your fifteenth, it's all muscle memory.

"I know it is hard," Hamad said.

"Huh?"

"After the passing of your son. I know things are hard," Hamad said.

"Yeah, I haven't slept much since Derek . . . died," Buddy Lee said. He'd never get used to the way the words "Derek" and "died" felt in his mouth.

"Everything seems hard when one you love dies," Hamad said as he placed the beer in a brown paper bag.

"Mm-hmm," Buddy Lee said. He handed Hamad a ten-spot.

"You will get through this, Buddy Lee," Hamad said.

"I don't know if I want to get through it, Hamad. I feel like every minute I'm not grieving I'm letting my boy down," Buddy Lee said.

Hamad handed Buddy Lee his change.

"He wouldn't want you to grieve forever, my friend," Hamad said. A man and a woman came into the store laughing in that way that told Buddy Lee they were a couple, and a new one at that. Buddy Lee grabbed his bag.

"You sure about that?" Buddy Lee said.

The clouds had dispersed by the time he got to the cemetery. The headstones shimmered in the unrelenting sunlight. The temperature rose steadily, like a bottle rocket. In another hour it would be hotter than fresh-cooked fried chicken. Buddy Lee walked among the tombstones with a steady gait. He only stopped to cough twice before he neared Derek's and Isiah's graves. He came up around the red maple that overlooked his son's final resting place and stopped short.

"Christine," he said. His heart leapt up out of his chest and slapped the back of his throat. She was standing at the foot of the graves. Her honey-blond hair brushed the collar of her blue blazer. Those long legs he loved were wrapped in a sensible blue skirt that matched her blazer. Deep-set eyes the color of sapphires stared out at him from a heart-shaped face. How many times had he gazed into those eyes? Seen them change color like a mood ring. Darken with passion or sparkle with desire or glow blue hot with rage. She'd had some work done. Mostly around the eyes and her mouth. He didn't blame her. Why not? From what he'd heard, her husband could afford it. The surgeon had only shored up what the Almighty had given her. Christine Perkins Jenkins Culpepper was as beautiful a woman as he had ever had in his arms. A few doctored crow's feet couldn't change that. No matter how much Christine would have liked to pretend their eight-year marriage had never happened.

"Where is the headstone? The other family said they had a headstone," Christine said.

"It got damaged. What are you doing here? How did you even know where they were buried?" Buddy Lee asked. Christine pushed an errant blond lock out of her eyes.

"It was in the paper."

"I gotcha," Buddy Lee said.

"What happened to the stone?"

Buddy Lee cracked open one of the cans of beer and took a long swig.

"Somebody hit it with a sledgehammer and wrote a bunch of fucking nasty shit about gay people all over it," he said. A sharp intake of breath from Christine sent a whistle echoing through the graveyard.

"That's . . . unfortunate. Even though I didn't agree with Derek's lifestyle, there was no need for someone to perpetrate such a vile act of vandalism on his tombstone," Christine said. Buddy Lee took a step toward her and she took a step back. She glanced down and realized she was standing on either Derek's or Isiah's grave and stepped toward the right.

"Is that why you didn't come to the funeral? Because you didn't agree with his lifestyle? Or was it because Gerald Culpepper didn't let you?" Buddy Lee asked. Christine rubbed her nose and ran a hand through her hair.

"You wouldn't understand. A man in Gerald's position can't be seen coddling a stepson who engages in perverse activities."

"Oh, I understand. I understand you kicked our son out of your house right before the judge ran for Richmond City Council the first time. I understand our son was living on the street. Bouncing from house to house because you cared more about being the wife of some stuck-up, rich, first-family-of-Virginia asshole than being a mother to your child," Buddy Lee said. He felt the color rise in his face. Tremors moved through his body like a high tide coming into shore.

"Don't you stand there and get sanctimonious with me, William Lee Jenkins. You think you were Father of the Year? Our son dedicated himself to an immoral lifestyle. An abhorrent, sacrilegious life that neither my husband nor I could abide in our home. Yes, I made him leave but I never punched him in the face. I never slapped him to the ground. If you were so concerned about him, why didn't you take him in? Oh, that's right, you were behind bars, drinking toilet wine," Christine spat at him.

Buddy took another sip of his beer.

"Those fancy etiquette classes Culpepper had you take was good. But your accent's slipping. I can hear Red Hill County all up in your voice when you get mad. You ain't that far from the back seat of my Camaro after all," he said.

"I will not let you take my peace. I will not let you take my peace. I will not let you take my peace," Christine muttered. Buddy Lee thought she was talking to herself, not him. She glared straight ahead as she clenched her fist, digging her manicured red nails into the palms of her hands. Buddy Lee studied her eyes again. She'd had some work done, but there was something else there. A manic look he recognized from many a backwoods trailer party.

"Christine, are you high?" Buddy Lee asked. His question snapped her out of her affirmation.

"What?"

"Are you high? Because your pupils about as wide as the bottom of this can," Buddy Lee said.

"I have a prescription," Christine said.

"I'm sure you do. I bet you got a shit ton of them."

"I'm not going to stand here and be lectured by some white trash redneck ex-con," Christine said. She stomped her red-bottomed heels past him. He caught a whiff of her as she passed. Not her expensive perfume, but her. The fresh-scrubbed sweet scent of her. In an instant he was back in the aforementioned Camaro. His mouth against her neck. His nostrils full of the same raw fresh scent. This exchange was a microcosm of one half of their past relationship. They'd hit each other with one verbal haymaker after another. Searching for the soft and secret places to make the deepest cut in a way that only someone who has shared your bed more than once can do effectively. There would be no replay of the remaining half of their past relationship. Buddy Lee sipped his beer. That part was always the fun part.

"We was both shit parents. But at least I showed up to watch him go in the ground. You coming here now is more than a day late and way more than a dollar short," Buddy Lee yelled. He heard her stop in her tracks.

"Fuck you, Buddy Lee," she said without turning around.

"So much for peace," he mumbled.

He waited until he knew Christine was out of earshot. He walked up to the graves and knelt on one knee. He opened the other can of beer and poured the entire contents over Derek's grave.

"No offense, Isiah, but I didn't know what kind of beer you like. Derek was a Pabst man at one time. I gave him his first one when he was fifteen. This was before I went down for my last visit to the 'graybar hotel.' I thought it would make a man out of him. Stupid. I know that now," Buddy Lee said. He finished his own beer before crushing the can.

"I just wanted to tell you that me and Ike, we did something. We got one of them. I know it's not what you would want me to do. I think I'm finally starting to understand you could never be the kind of man I am and I couldn't be the kind of man you was," he said. He crushed Derek's can and put both cans back in the brown paper bag.

"I know if you was here you'd tell me to let it go. That it wasn't worth it. Then I'd have to steal one of your lines," Buddy Lee said. He rose to his feet and brushed the dirt from his jeans. His eyes burned but he was too tired to cry.

"This is who I am. I can't change. I don't want to, really. But for once I'm gonna put this devil inside me to good use."

SEVENTEEN

Ike opened his eyes. His lower back felt like it was filled with spun glass. He rose from his office chair and listened to his knees pop like rifle shots. His watch said it was a little after eight. He checked his phone. Mya had called a few times. She'd also sent him two terse texts. Both asked where he was and when he was coming home. The first one was longer than the second. The guys would be rolling in in a few minutes. Jazzy would be late as usual. They had seven jobs today from Queen County all the way to Williamsburg.

Ike walked around his desk to the spot where he'd killed the kid. A pressure washer and some bleach had cleaned up the blood nicely. He hadn't killed anyone in sixteen years. He hadn't had a fight in eleven years. Eleven years of walking the straight and narrow gone to shit in a matter of minutes. The two of them had slaughtered that kid like a pig and fed him to the wood chipper like a mama bird feeding a chick.

The two of them. Eleven years. One plus one was two. When he was inside he had read a book that said some numbers had a mystical significance in some religions. Not for the first time he considered all the weird knowledge you could acquire when there was nothing to do but lift, read, and fight.

Ike went out to the back lot of the warehouse. He grabbed the water hose attached to a hose reel near the back door and pulled it over to a smoldering barrel near the corner of the building. He soaked the ashes in the barrel until they stopped smoking. The kid's jeans and shirt had gone up like kindling. It had taken his boots a lot longer to burn down to barely recognizable lumps. He sprayed some water in his hand and splashed it on his face. He'd given Buddy Lee a big tough speech about spilling blood, but he hadn't expected it to happen this suddenly.

That was the thing about violence. When you went looking for it you definitely were going to find it. It just wouldn't be at a time of your own choosing. It jumped up and splattered your nice new boots before you were really ready. The thing is, if you chase it long enough, you realize you're never really ready for it. Shit happens and you either roll with it or you don't. Eventually you got used to it. When he was a kid he liked to think that made you hard. He hit the barrel with the hose again. After a few years inside he figured out that was bullshit. Human beings were wired to get used to just about anything. That didn't make you hard. It made you indoctrinated.

Ike pulled the hose over to the wood chipper. They'd aimed it at the manure pile as they dropped pieces of the kid into the inlet chute. Then Ike had gotten on the bulldozer and turned the manure over again and again. By the time the sun was coming up the kid was just fertilizer.

He dropped the hose and went back inside the shop and grabbed the bleach. He went back to the chipper and poured bleach in the inlet chute, then grabbed the hose and flushed water through the chipper and out the discharge chute. A chipper was a practical way to chop up a body, but it was a terrible way to get rid of evidence. Despite rinsing it out with Clorox, it was still covered in DNA that wasn't visible to the naked eye. Bits of bone and hair were probably imbedded in the gears and teeth inside the machine. The only thing he could do now was take it to the dump and toss it onto the ever-growing pile of rusted-out refrigerators, washing machines, and lawn mowers at the rear of the landfill. A thousand-dollar piece of equipment reduced to scrap. He couldn't even take it to the salvage yard and get some of his money back.

Ike finished with his cleanup job and rolled the chipper around to the side of the building. He'd get one of his guys to help him load it onto his truck later. He'd give them some story about it conking out on him and then casually never mention it again. He was a little disconcerted how easily he was able to slip back into Riot's habit of lying without compunction. But only a little.

He went back inside the shop and was making his way to the front door to unlock it when Jazzy came in thirty minutes early. Ike stopped and put his hands on his hips. He'd given her a key over a year ago but she'd never arrived early enough to use it.

"This must be the end-times, because you're actually here early," he said. Jazzy rolled her eyes.

"Marcus's car broke down so I had to take him to work at the window plant. It's right up the road from here. I ain't see no point in going home after I dropped him off, so here I am. I thought you'd be happy I was here all early and shit," Jazzy said.

"I am, I'm just recovering from the shock," Ike said. Jazzy rolled her eyes again and headed for her desk. Ike was about to follow her when he heard a thunderous roar come from the road. He stopped, turned, and looked out the door. A line of motorcycles, about five or six deep, were flying past the shop. They sounded like a pride of lions on the hunt.

EIGHTEEN

Buddy Lee parked his truck and slid out onto his unsteady legs. He closed the door and stumbled toward his trailer. He'd left the cemetery and headed to the nearest bar. A quiet little neighborhood spot called McCallan's. He started with beer, then moved to whiskey and finished with bourbon.

Sleep. He needed to sleep this off before he called Ike to talk about their next move. He stepped on the first cinder block but immediately lost his footing. He tumbled to the right, hit his trailer, then fell to the ground, landing on his ass. Buddy Lee rolled over onto his knees. As he tried to push himself up, all the air in his lungs evaporated. In its place a wad of phlegm the size of a lemon filled his chest. Buddy Lee's eyes bulged from their sockets as he tried to get enough breath in his lungs to cough.

Strong hands pounded against his back. The sharp strikes forced the ball of phlegm out of his throat. It spilled across the ground like a squashed toad. Buddy Lee felt himself being pulled to his feet.

"You alright?"

Buddy Lee nodded to his savior. A slim narrow-hipped woman with sharp rough-hewn features held his left arm in an ironlike grip. Her skin shined with a deep burnished tan born of hours under the high hot sun. Two long black pigtails interspersed with snow-white strands trailed down over her chest and fell almost to her waist.

"You a terrible liar, Buddy Lee," she said.

"Just lost my footing for a minute, Margo. No need to get ya panties in a bunch," Buddy Lee said. Margo let him go and wiped her hands on her jeans. Her white tank top had dark splotches covering it like it was a piece of modern art.

"I stopped wearing panties when Herb died. That was my second husband. He was a good man but, Lord, he was so uptight he squeaked when he walked," Margo said.

"Husband number three didn't mind you going commando?" Buddy Lee asked with a wink.

"Colton? Lord no. That man would've banged the crack of dawn if it would've stood still long enough. I wasn't shocked he died on top of a woman, I just always thought it would be me." Margo said. Buddy Lee chuckled. The chuckle became a laugh. The laugh became a cough. Margo patted him on the back. It was a strangely intimate gesture, and Buddy Lee found it comforted him more than he cared to admit. Finally, his cough subsided.

"You know, we've been neighbors for five years now. When I first came around here you had a Sam Elliott thing going on. Now you look like Sam Elliott's granddad."

"Gee thanks, Margo. Maybe I should go get a dog so you can kick it," Buddy Lee said. Margo shook her head a few times.

"That's not an insult. It's an observation. You drink too much and you don't eat enough. You look like you get an hour of sleep every couple of weeks. You need to get that cough checked out. Those are just facts. My first, he had a cough he wouldn't check out, then he checked out," Margo said. Buddy Lee wiped his mouth with the back of his hand. The world wasn't spinning but it was doing a little soft shoe. The bourbon and the beer were having a bar fight in his guts, and his stomach was threatening to kick both of them out. The last thing he needed to do was throw up in front of his well-meaning but nosy neighbor. It would probably be more red than brown, and that would just invite a lot of questions he wasn't in any kind of mood to answer.

"I told ya, I'm fine, Margo. Just been a long week. Hell, it's been a long year," Buddy Lee said. Margo's face softened just a bit.

"I know. I'm sorry about your boy. I've buried four husbands, but I don't know what I'd do if I had to see one of my girls go in the ground. It should be against the law for parents to see that shit," she said. Buddy Lee felt his eyes moisten without any warning.

"Yeah. Yeah it should. Well, I'm gonna go on inside now and go in a coma," Buddy Lee said.

"Alright. But you need anything, just holler. I'm out back in the garden."

"Didn't Artie tell you to dig that garden up?" Buddy Lee asked with a wink. Margo's lips curled up at the corners.

"Yeah, and I told him if I had to dig up my tomato garden I might be so depressed I might let it slip I'd seen him sneak into that Carson girl's trailer while his wife was at work at the nursing home."

Buddy Lee whistled.

"You drive a hard bargain, don't you?"

"Hey, he shouldn't be dipping his wick in that girl's wax. He ought to be glad I caught him instead of his wife or that Carson girl's boyfriend. I just can't for the life of me figure how she can stand the smell of him."

Buddy Lee laughed.

"Me neither. Well, like I said, I'm gonna get some sleep." Buddy Lee stepped up onto the cinder block and grabbed his doorknob.

"I'm making spaghetti tonight. Gonna use my big beef tomatoes for the sauce. You more than welcome to come over and get a plate," Margo said.

"You not gonna poison me like you did your husbands, are you?" Buddy Lee asked. Margo rolled her eyes.

"You're an ass, you know that?"

"That seems to have been the general consensus most of my life," Buddy Lee said. Margo grunted.

"The sauce probably be ready around seven. I know you miss your boy but you gotta eat. He wouldn't want you go to seed," Margo said. She strolled back across the driveway and disappeared around her trailer. Buddy Lee stared after her for a few moments.

Margo wasn't a bad-looking woman. He pegged her at fifty or fifty-five. A few years older than him but she was in way better shape. She worked down at the Lowe's as a lawn-and-garden specialist. For most of the five years they had been neighbors she'd had what she termed a "friend with some benefits," who sometimes spent the night. Buddy Lee had seen him through his kitchen window a few times. A big ol' hoss with a crew cut who drove an old Jeep Wagoneer with a faded MITT ROMNEY FOR PRESIDENT bumper sticker. Crew Cut hadn't been around much these past few months. He wondered if that had anything to do with Margo inviting him over for dinner?

"Get your head out of your ass. She was just being nice. That's all. That's all you gonna get nowadays," Buddy Lee murmured. He went inside his trailer and kicked off his boots before peeling off his shirt. The AC sounded like someone had tossed it in a washing machine. It clanged and wheezed asthmatically, but at least it seemed to be actually working today. The cool air made gooseflesh pop up all across his back and chest.

Buddy Lee's eyes had just closed as he sprawled across his couch, when someone began pounding on his door. He groaned as he sat up and his feet hit the floor.

"Damn it, Margo, I said I was fine," he mumbled as he opened the door.

Det. LaPlata was standing on his bottom cinder block. He was alone except for his shield and his gun.

"Mr. Jenkins, we need to talk," he said. He didn't ask if he could come in, but instead just stepped up into the trailer. Buddy Lee took a step back. LaPlata was giving him the long stare. Buddy Lee knew what that meant.

He had fucked up and LaPlata wasn't fucking around.

NINETEEN

Ike went over the work orders for the day while Jazzy clicked and clacked away at her computer, paying invoices and emailing clients their monthly bills. His crew would start trickling in within the hour. Soon the sounds of trucks loading up with mulch and planting soil and manure and fertilizer would be rumbling through the warehouse.

Ike tried not to think about the manure. Or more specifically, what was in the manure.

He heard the bell on the front door ring and then he heard Jazzy's sunny greeting. A few seconds later she popped her head around the corner of his cubicle.

"Ike, these guys asking for you," she said. Her eyes were wide and her breath was coming in ragged little bursts. Ike stood up from his desk.

"What's wrong?"

Jazzy spoke in a low voice.

"'Bout five bikers out here asking about you," she said. Ike sat up straight. It sounded like a bad joke. Five bikers walk into a landscaping office. . . . Ike rubbed his forehead. Last night he and Buddy Lee had run into a couple of boys that had that peckerwood look all over them. He'd busted one of them boys in the head, and he and Buddy Lee had killed the other. Now some bikers come strolling into his shop. The kid had said he had been hired to look for Tangerine. What if the bikers had been the ones that hired him? Ike had told Buddy Lee they weren't detectives, but you didn't have to be Easy Rawlins to put this together.

We should've took the other boy, too, Ike thought.

"Tell them I'll be out in a minute," he said.

"I can just tell 'em you ain't here," Jazzy said.

"No, that's okay. Let's see what they want," Ike said. He walked around his cubicle and headed for the lobby. As he was on his way he grabbed a machete off the wall.

Five men in leather vests and various degrees of hirsuteness were standing in the lobby. A couple of them were reading the advertisements on the walls. Two more were standing near the door. A big blond man with a wicked scar on his cheek that cut through his beard was leaning against the soda machine with his heavily tattooed arms crossed.

Ike placed the machete on the counter.

"Can I help you?" Ike asked.

The blond biker pushed himself off the soda machine. He glanced at the machete, then smiled at Ike. His teeth were crooked and he was missing matching incisors.

"Well, that depends. We looking for a friend of ours, and I think you might know where he is," the tall blond said. The pale scar on his face wound its way down to his chin like an EKG pattern. The vest he wore had a patch over the heart that said PRESIDENT. The other four men came up and stood next to him. The one to his left had a patch that said SERGEANT AT ARMS. He reached for the small of his back and pulled out a metal pipe. There was electrical tape around one end. The other three men pulled out their own homemade weapons. One had a chain with a padlock on the end. The other two had sawed-off pool cues with bright-green and red handles respectively. The one with the president patch leaned forward and put his hands on the counter. He was within an arm's length of the machete.

"I don't think you have any friends here," Ike said. He stared into the man's light-blue eyes. Behind him Jazzy continued to tap away at her computer.

Ike usually liked the way the shop smelled first thing in the morning. It was strange but it gave him a sense of tranquility. The scent of gasoline, oil, topsoil, even the goddamn manure. It all smelled of an honest day's work. Of hours spent beautifying someone's yard who wouldn't spit on you if you were on fire but had to pay you because they wouldn't or couldn't be bothered to put down their own mulch or fertilize their own flower gardens. Their disdain was inconsequential to Ike. Those countless shovelfuls of dirt had paid for his house. Those untold rolls of sod had put food on his table. Those endless wheelbarrows full of mulch had put Isiah through college. As long as the checks cleared, they could think whatever they wanted.

But there was another scent that floated under the pungent odor of refined petroleum and pulverized lime. A bitter metallic fragrance that reminded you of pennies and old batteries. Did that smell register with the bikers? He'd cleaned up for hours, but it seemed like that coppery aroma had soaked into the walls.

"What? You telling me we ain't friends?" the blond man said. Ike curled his fingers around the handle of the machete. He let his eyes linger on the blond man for a long time.

"Not even a little bit," he said finally. The man nodded as if that was the answer he expected. He straightened and turned to his sergeant at arms.

"Fuck this shit up."

As Dome raised his pipe to smash the complimentary candy dish on the counter, Ike's left hand shot out like a tiger's paw. He grabbed Grayson by his right arm. He snatched him forward and at the same time pulled downward until his head bounced against the countertop. Dome froze with his pipe raised above his head as Ike placed the edge of the machete against the side of Grayson's neck. The big man started to struggle until Ike pressed the edge of the machete into the soft flesh below his ear.

"Back the fuck up or I'll cut off his goddamn head," Ike said. Dome didn't move. The pipe was vibrating like a tuning fork. The other three bikers were similarly paralyzed.

"What the fuck are you waiting for? Get this motherfucker!" Grayson said. Ike sucked his teeth. He felt like the room was rapidly shrinking by the foot, then by inches. His heart was fluttering in his chest. Once upon a time, he had found himself in a situation much like this one. It had not gone well for him. Not well at all.

Ike bit down on the inside of his bottom lip and gripped the handle of the machete tighter. He couldn't let his face betray one ounce of the fear that was slowly working its way up his spine. You let an animal know you're afraid of it and it loses all respect for you. If it doesn't respect you, it has no qualms about ripping your belly open and showing you what your stomach looks like. Men might walk on two legs but they were the most vicious animals of all. Especially when they thought they had a numbers advantage. If these biker boys caught one whiff of weakness, they'd be on him like a pack of wild dogs.

Dome swallowed hard. He took a halting step toward Grayson and Ike.

Ike pulled the blade backward across the blond man's neck. A needle-thin ribbon of blood appeared as if by magic. It slipped over Grayson's throat like quicksilver and spilled onto the counter.

"This thing sharp enough to shave with. I'll cut his throat to the bone before you get around that corner. Believe that," Ike said.

"Jesus Christ, Dome, rush this nigger. It's five against one for fuck's sake!" Grayson said. It came out somewhat muffled, but Ike heard the word "nigger" loud and clear.

Grayson tried to push himself up off the counter again. Ike applied more pressure to the blade. It bit deeper into his thick neck. He stopped struggling.

"Them is some good odds, boy," Dome said. The shock of seeing

Grayson thoroughly overwhelmed was wearing off. Ike watched as the other three bikers seemed to shake off their own malaise and began to advance as well. He'd have to take out the president first, then move on to the one called Dome. Ike caught his gaze as he moved toward the end of the counter. If you had blinked you would have missed it, but for a split second Dome hesitated. There was murder in Ike's eyes, as pure and as potent as corn liquor.

"How about five against a .38? What do you think about them odds?" Jazzy said. Ike chanced a glance to his left and saw his receptionist pointing a small chrome-plated pistol at the biker holding the pipe. He stopped in his tracks.

"You ain't gonna shoot nobody. A pretty little thing like you ain't got it—" Dome started to say, but then Jazzy fired into the ceiling and he closed his mouth with an audible *plop*. The echo from the shot reverberated through the building and bounced off the exposed girders above their heads.

Ike tried to hire a lot of ex-cons for his crews. He knew the value of a second chance, and he also knew how hard it was to get a job when your employment history had ten-to-fifteen-year gaps. But for once he was glad one of his employees wasn't a convicted felon. Jazzy was the only person in the entire building who could legally own a gun. Ike gestured to Jazzy with his head.

"She real nice with that thing. So if I was you, I'd back my ass up to the door. Then I'll let your boy here go. Trust me, you don't wanna test her," Ike lied. He didn't know if Jazzy could hit the broadside of a barn. Right now, that didn't matter. All that mattered was if these peckerwoods believed she was a markswoman.

Dome licked his lips. No one spoke for what seemed like hours. Then Dome lowered his pipe and stuck it back in his waistband.

"Y'all back up," he said.

Ike watched as Dome and the other three bikers shuffled backward toward the door. Once the four of them were out of striking distance, he bent down and whispered in the blond man's ear.

"I'm gonna let you up, but if you even raise your eyebrows funny,

I'm gonna open you up like the first deer of hunting season, you feel me?"

"You let me up and you don't kill me, you know how this ends, right?" Grayson said. He spoke as loud as he could with the side of his mouth pressed against the Formica.

"I know you trying to save face with your boys, but if I ever see you around here again, there won't be enough left of you to put in a Ziploc bag. Word is bond. I don't sell no wolf tickets," Ike whispered. Grayson didn't respond. Ike pulled the machete away and took a step back and to his left. Grayson stood and put his hand against his neck. He bore a hole into Ike, and Ike gave it right back to him.

"You better call some of your gangster buddies, BG. Get you some silverbacks up here. Oh yeah, I seen your ink. You gonna need all them porch monkeys to back you up. We're the Rare Breed, motherfucker. We gonna burn this goddamn place to the ground and then piss on the fucking ashes. Then I'm personally taking a shit right in your bitch's goddamn mouth and make you watch," Grayson said. Ike heard Jazzy inhale sharply when the blond biker mentioned her, but she didn't flinch.

Grayson took his hand away from his neck and flung it toward the floor. Drops of blood flew from his palm and fingertips and splattered across the concrete.

"Blood for blood, nigger," he said. He put his stained hand to his lips and blew a kiss at Jazzy. Ike pointed at the door with the machete.

"You need to do more walking and less talking," Ike said. The blond biker smiled. Jazzy pulled back the hammer on her .38.

"See you soon," Grayson said.

He turned his back on Ike and Jazzy and walked out the door. His fellow club members followed him. Dome stopped and gave Ike a reproachful shake of the head before he, too, exited the store. Once he heard their bikes fire up he put down his machete. He could hear Jazzy making a wet keening sound. The gun in her hand began to tremble.

"Jazz, give me that gun," Ike said. Jazzy didn't acknowledge him, so Ike gently plucked the pistol from her hand and eased the hammer forward before shoving it in his pocket. Jazzy stood next to him with her arm still outstretched.

"Jazzy, they're gone."

"They coming back, ain't they?"

"I don't know," Ike lied.

"I think I'm gonna throw up," Jazzy said before running to the back. Ike went to the front door and locked it. He closed his eyes and put his hand against the cool metal surface to steady himself. There was a moment last night between him and Buddy Lee unrolling the rug but before they grabbed the hacksaws that he thought that might be it. He thought maybe they could grind that boy up and it would fill the festering black hole in their hearts. For an instant he thought they could just tell themselves he was the one who had killed their sons. Let that be the end of it. Let them go back to what was left of their empty lives with the knowledge they had evened the scales.

That was bullshit. He knew that now.

There was no turning back. There was no path that led anywhere except down a long road as dark as your first night in hell and paved all along the way with bad intentions. They could call what they were seeking justice, but that didn't make it true. It was unquenchable, implacable vengeance. And life, inside the graybar and out, had taught him that vengeance came with consequences.

Those bikers would be back. Maybe tonight. Maybe tomorrow. Maybe in a few days. But they would be back. They'd come roaring through town strapped and looking for a war. He needed to be ready. He didn't know how and he didn't know why, but he knew they were tied up with what had happened to Isiah and Derek. He knew it in his bones.

They'd come back looking for a war. He was going to give them a fucking massacre.

TWENTY

If there was one thing Buddy Lee had learned throughout his various stints in and out of jail, prison, county lockup, and drunk-tank holding cells, it was that you never, ever volunteered any information to a cop. It didn't matter if you were guilty or not; you didn't give them anything. They would tell you what they wanted or what they suspected you of soon enough. They were getting paid to ask questions; you didn't get paid to answer them.

He sat back against the couch, crossed his legs, and waited for LaPlata to tell him why he was here interrupting the nap Buddy Lee desperately needed.

Buddy Lee thought, *It ain't about that kid. If that was it, I'd be in bracelets by now.*

LaPlata pulled out his cell phone and scrolled through a few screens. When he found what he was searching for, he put the phone on the coffee table made from milk crates that sat between them. Buddy Lee looked at the phone. There was a picture of a bearded man with a huge black eye. His mouth was swollen, too. His lips looked like sausages. The background behind the man was the muted puke green that Buddy Lee knew so well. The picture was obviously taken in a police station.

"That is Mr. Bryce Thomason. He came down to the police station this morning and told us an interesting story. He said two old guys came in his head shop and beat the shit out of him while asking questions about the murders of their sons. Bryce also has some broken fingers. He won't be vaping with that hand for a while," LaPlata said. Buddy Lee raised his head.

"Yeah, somebody fucked that boy up good. But, ya know, he look like he got a smart goddamned mouth, so I ain't surprised. Huh, and here I was thinking you might have some news about the case," Buddy Lee said. LaPlata placed his hands on his knees.

"Let's me be real honest with you, Mr. Jenkins. Off the record. I get it. You had a rough relationship with your son because he was gay and you couldn't handle it. Now he's been killed and you can't fix things with him so you wanna fix the people who did it, because you don't think we're moving fast enough. I understand how you feel. But here's the thing. We can't have private citizens running around trying to get retribution. That's how people like Bryce here get hurt. That's how I end up having to arrest you and drag you downtown. I don't want to do that, Mr. Jenkins, but I will. People can't take the law into their own hands. That's how we get anarchy. And by the look of the bruises on your face, you've engaged in some anarchy recently."

"You really believe that, don't you?" Buddy Lee asked.

"Yes, I do."

Buddy Lee scratched at his chin. "You keep saying you understand. You got kids, Detective LaPlata?"

"I got a boy and a girl, and before you ask, yes, if someone hurt them I'd want to find the bastards and kill them slow, but I wouldn't, because I'd trust my fellow officers to find the people who did it and handle it the right way," LaPlata said.

"See that's where we are different. You saying that because it ain't happened to you, and I swear to God I hope it never does. But until you sitting on this side of the table, I'd appreciate it if you stop saying you understand. Now I'm no lawyer, but I'm thinking if you had more than the word of that boy—what you say his name was, Bryson?"

"Bryce," LaPlata said.

"Yeah, Bryce. I'm thinking if you had, say, some videos of who beat his fucking teeth in, well, you'd be arresting me right now. But you ain't because you don't. Now if you don't mind, I'm pretty damn tired and I'd like to get some sleep."

"Hey, Mr. Jenkins. I'm sincerely sorry for your loss. I don't know how it feels, but I can imagine. Because if someone hurt my kids, I'd lose my fucking mind. But let's make sure we got one thing straight. I'm giving you an out here. This is your onetime stay-out-of-jail-free card. Yeah, it's your and Mr. Randolph's word against Bryce, who is, in fact, a little shit. His two associates can't seem to remember who came in and put the hurting on him. So I'm letting this one slide. I've driven sixty miles outside of my jurisdiction to give you a warning. Next time, if there is a next time, I'm hauling you downtown, and I'll get the judge to set a bail just high enough it'll keep you in jail until we finish our investigation. We clear about that?" LaPlata asked.

"Like I said, Officer, I'm about to be dead to the world, so if you could excuse me. I've got a big night ahead of me laying here thinking about my boy and how I can't never fix things with him," Buddy Lee said. A white-hot rage flamed in his chest like a shattered hurricane lamp. This fucking cop with his crisp white shirt and his pleated pants with a crease sharp enough to slice bread wanted talk to him about loss? This pretty boy who didn't look like he would know what hard times were if they came up and spit in his goddamn face? This preppy-looking son of a bitch who probably never missed a Christmas with his family and played touch football every Thanksgiving like a goddamned Kennedy? This guy who had nice middle-class sex with his wife every other Friday night? Who never had to tell his spoiled brat of a daughter they didn't have enough money for the doll baby she wanted? Who probably lived in a nice two-story on the north side of the Cap City with his goddamned living breathing son wanted to tell him about loss? About how he couldn't fix things with Derek? Fuck him. Fuck him and his happy Norman Rockwell bullshit life. Buddy Lee was acquainted with loss in ways Det. LaPlata could never even conceive, let alone survive.

Buddy Lee ran his thumbs back and forth over the calluses on his forefingers. LaPlata stood and almost reflexively dusted off his backside.

"Stay out of this, Mr. Jenkins. My partner is headed over to Mr. Randolph's right now to tell him the same thing. Let us do our job. You can't change what happened but you can control what happens next."

You have no idea, hoss, Buddy Lee thought.

TWENTY-ONE

Ike pulled into his driveway just as the setting sun danced over the tips of the cypress trees in his backyard. He cut off his truck and went into the house. He closed the door behind him and locked it. They lived in a cul-de-sac off a side road. If someone followed him, he'd be able to see them coming, but he didn't want to make it easy for them to get inside the house. Vacuous voices chattered incessantly from the television in the living room. Mya was sitting on the couch. The smoke from her cigarette flowed up from her ashtray like a will-o'-the-wisp.

Ike hung his keys on the combo chalkboard / key rack on the wall and went to the kitchen. He heard Mya get to her feet and follow him. He grabbed the rum from the cabinet and poured himself a shot in a heavy cut-crystal glass. The rum burned all the way down to his stomach. He knew Mya would be standing near the broom closet with her arms crossed over her narrow chest. He knew the look that would be etched on her face. He started to pour himself another shot, then stopped. He put the glass in the sink and turned to face his wife. Her arms were indeed crossed over her chest as she glowered at him.

"You staying out all night now?" she asked.

"Something came up," Ike said.

"Oh, something came up? That made your phone stop working?"

"I'm sorry I didn't call."

"You're sorry. Okay. Where the hell were you? You know that

detective came by earlier looking for you. I thought he might have some news about Isiah's case, but he said he needed to talk to you personally. You got any idea what the hell that's about?"

The mention of the detective sent a shiver through his spine but it quickly dissipated. If he was looking to jam him up about the kid they'd turned into fertilizer, he would have come by the shop with a pair of handcuffs. Especially since Ike had a prior for manslaughter.

That's what they called it, anyway, Ike thought.

He gave up on the glass and took a swig of rum straight from the bottle. Mya crossed the distance between them like a gazelle. She snatched the bottle from his grip and slammed it down on the kitchen table. A few drops escaped the long neck of the bottle and splattered onto the table, then dripped off the edge.

"We ain't starting this, Ike."

"Starting what? What is it you think I'm doing?"

Mya rubbed her hands together, then held them out in front of her. As she spoke, her hands trembled.

"I don't know. I don't think you are cheating on me. We are way too old for that kind of petty shit, I hope. But you can't be running these streets drinking all night and sleeping it off at the shop because of . . ." She trailed off into a sob.

"I wasn't drinking. Not last night. And Red Hill ain't got no real streets. Just a lot of roads that don't go nowhere," Ike said in a hushed tone.

"I can't take it, Ike. I don't want to get a call about them finding your body after your truck done run off the road because you drunk. I'm barely holding on as it is. If it wasn't for Arianna, I wouldn't even get out of bed in the morning. She's the only thing that matters now, and I can't do this by myself. I can't raise her alone, Ike. I did that with Isiah and I just ain't got the strength anymore," Mya said. Tears ran down her face. Ike started to put his arms around her but she flinched. He stopped.

"I know. I know it was hard when I went away. You raised him right while I was locked up. You made him a better man than I'll ever be. But this ain't the same thing. It ain't nothing like it was before. And Arianna ain't the only thing that matters now. Don't we matter just a little bit? What we had, you and me, don't that matter to you at all?" He didn't intend to speak about them in the past tense, but the words flew out of his mouth like hornets riled from their nest. Mya didn't seem to notice.

"You know it does."

"Sometimes I can't tell," Ike said. Mya wiped her face.

"How can you say that to me? I love you, Ike. I've loved you for longer than I can remember. But our boy is dead. And I can't wrap my mind around that. I keep trying and trying and then I look at Arianna and I see so much of Isiah in her till I almost can't stand it. It hurts so bad, Ike. It's like I ain't got no room in my heart for nothing but hurt. Is that why you didn't come home? You can't stand looking at hurt anymore? Is that how it's gonna be? Like it's one night. Then a couple. Then you don't come home for weeks. Then one day you gone. Is that what this is, Ike? You testing the waters on your way out the door?" Mya said.

Ike picked up the bottle again and took a long sip. It seemed like Mya had cried so much her eyes were permanently bloodshot. Those eyes haunted him. Rimmed in red and empty as an abandoned church, they made him feel helpless. Every night her soft whimpering cries tore pieces out of his soul as they slept back-to-back in a bed that seemed to widen until it felt like they were barely in the same room. She was right. He was tired of seeing her hurt. He couldn't stand to see the pain that twisted her face into a sorrowful mask. Her pain, her sorrow, his powerlessness. He was sick of it all. He pulled out a chair and sat down at the table. He was facing the back door as Mya stood behind him.

"Last night me and Buddy Lee starting handling things," he said. It came out in one breath. One long exhalation that gathered up all the frailty and ineffectualness and misery and mourning that filled him like the stuffing in a scarecrow and scattered it into the ether.

Mya stretched out her hand in tentative increments until it touched the firm swell of his shoulder. It lay there warm and comforting like a child's favorite blanket. Like the blanket that had been wrapped around their son when they brought him home from the hospital. Ike let out a sigh. She hadn't touched him like that since Isiah . . . since they had gotten the news about Isiah.

The quiet between them changed from something hard and full of broken edges to something softer but still fragile. Ike folded his wide paw of a hand around Mya's. Over the last few months, death had carved a valley between them as deep as grief and as wide as heartbreak. Now another man's death had bridged that gap, if only for a moment.

"Good," Mya said. Her voice was hushed and conspiratorial.

"Grammy. I hungry, Grammy," a small voice said. Ike twisted himself around in the chair. Arianna stood at the threshold to the kitchen. Her braids had worked themselves loose. Her hair stood up on her head in wild corkscrews. Ike studied her small tawny face. He wasn't sure how exactly Isiah and Derek had brought this little girl into the world. He knew it involved surrogates and eggs and sperm from both of them but he wasn't sure how it all worked. All he knew was that the lawyer for Isiah and Derek's estates had said that Isiah was her biological father, but she had called both of them Daddy. He had never studied her face the way Mya had. He'd refused to. Not in a conscious way but with a seemingly instinctual avoidance. The whole thing was just something he didn't care to think about. Now he had no choice. The girl standing in front of him now had Isiah's eyes, which meant she had Ike's eyes. The slight off-center positioning of her nose was a Randolph family trait. She was lighter, of course, because her mother had been a white woman who was a friend of Isiah and Derek's, but the Randolph DNA was strong. Stronger that his inability to see past his own hang-ups. If he closed his eyes a bit, she was Isiah at two years old, holding up his arms and squealing "Up, Daddy, up!" as he waited for Ike to grab him and spin him around the room like a living carousel.

Ike turned away and stared down at the table. He felt nauseous. An avalanche of memories washed over him and buried him under the weight of all of his mistakes. So many mistakes.

"Come here, baby girl. You wanna go to McDonald's?" Mya asked. Arianna squealed in delight.

God, she sounds just like him, Ike thought.

Mya gave his shoulder a firm squeeze, then walked over to Arianna and scooped her into her arms. Ike could hear steps as she moved from the kitchen to the living room, then out the front door. Ike sipped his rum. He wouldn't tell Mya anything else. She didn't need to know about the bikers or this Tangerine they were going to try to find. Right now, all either one of them needed was this.

Ike heard Mya's car start. What that little girl needed was two people to raise her who could look her in the face without falling apart. Ike put the bottle to his lips but didn't take a drink. Instead he got up and put the bottle back in the cabinet. Buddy Lee was an alcoholic, but at the rate Ike was going, he wasn't far behind him.

Ike's phone vibrated. He took it out and checked the screen. Speak of the devil. He touched the ANSWER button.

"Hey, hoss," Buddy Lee said.

"Hey, we need to talk. Face-to-face," Ike said.

"Okay. Is it cool to meet at your shop?"

"No. Come by the house. I'll text you the address," Ike said.

Buddy Lee coughed. "Everything alright?" he asked.

"I'll tell you about it when you get here," Ike said.

He ended the call.

TWENTY-TWO

Buddy Lee parked his truck next to Ike's dually. His truck shuddered as the engine dieseled for a few seconds. Buddy Lee got out and let the truck shimmy and shake as he walked to the front door. He took a quick glimpse back at his and Ike's trucks sitting side by side. It was like seeing a pig sitting next to a princess. He raised his hand to knock on the door, but it opened before he could touch it. Ike stood in the doorway.

"We can talk in the kitchen," Ike said as he stepped aside. Buddy Lee entered the house. Ike closed and locked the door.

"Nice place," Buddy Lee said.

"It's alright," Ike said. Buddy Lee grunted.

"I got milk crates for a coffee table. This is more than alright," Buddy Lee said. Ike pulled out a chair and gestured for Buddy Lee to do the same.

"You got anything to drink around here?" Buddy Lee asked.

"I thought we said you wasn't gonna drink while we do this," Ike said. Buddy Lee ran a hand through his lank hair.

"We said I'd cut back. Trust me, I'm working on it. We alone?" Buddy Lee asked.

"Yeah. Mya took Arianna to get something to eat," Ike said. Buddy Lee nodded his head.

"I guess you wanna talk about Officer Friendly coming by," Buddy Lee said. Ike leaned forward across the table on his forearms.

"The cops came to see you?"

"Yeah. I figured that's what you was talking about on the phone. What, they didn't come by and see you?" Buddy Lee asked.

"I wasn't here."

"Well, shit, now I feel discriminated against," Buddy Lee said. Ike sat back and clucked his tongue against the roof of his mouth.

"Anyone ever tell you that you play too much?" Ike asked.

"Every day of the week and twice on Sunday. Wait, what was the thing you wanted to talk about?" Buddy Lee asked.

"We'll get to me in a minute. Tell me what the cops had to say. I know it wasn't nothing about the boys," Ike said. There was a hard edge to his voice that Buddy Lee had heard in the head shop when he was snapping the hipster's finger like a breadstick. A cold flame that burned up the oxygen in the room and dropped the temperature by five degrees.

Buddy Lee ran a hand through his hair.

"Well, I suppose the good news is it ain't got nothing to do with our friend from last night. And you right, it wasn't about the boys, either. One of them little punk-ass Smith Brothers–looking fuckers from that head shop went down to the police station on his unicycle," Buddy Lee said.

Ike cocked his head to the side. "He say he was pressing charges?" Ike asked.

"Nah. His two comrades are scared shitless. They ain't backing up his story, and the place don't have no video cameras. So we should be alright there, but Detective Egg Roll told me if he hears about us kicking any more millennial ass, he gonna put us both in a holding cell until daylight saving time is over," Buddy Lee said.

Ike frowned. "Why you call him Detective Egg Roll?"

"What? It's just a joke. Ya know, because he's Chinese," Buddy Lee said.

"I don't even think he's Chinese. I swear you white boys got a joke for everybody, but if I said your family tree ain't got no branches, you'd be ready to fight."

"Shit, nah. I got an uncle who's my cousin," Buddy Lee said. Ike rolled his eyes. "I'm joking. Everybody too damn sensitive these days."

"We ain't sensitive. Back in the day nobody could say shit or one of your uncles would've tried to hang 'em from a tree. Now I can tell you to kiss my entire ass," Ike said. Buddy Lee scratched at his chin as he considered Ike's abbreviated history lesson.

"Alright, I'll give you that. But let me ask you this: You extending that courtesy to people like Isiah and Derek, too? Could they have told you to kiss their ass?" Buddy Lee said. Ike shifted in his chair and crossed his arms. He didn't answer Buddy Lee's question.

"Be careful you don't hurt yourself falling off that high horse there, Ike," Buddy Lee said. He let out a long braying laugh that didn't stop until he started hacking. Ike got up and got a bottle of water from the fridge. He tossed it to Buddy Lee, who despite coughing like a '73 Gremlin with a bad valve, caught it deftly with one hand. Buddy Lee killed the water in two gulps and tossed the empty bottle back to Ike. Ike tossed it in the trash and sat down again. He rubbed the palms of his callused hands together before placing them flat on the table.

"Tell me what you know about this Rare Breed," Ike said.

Buddy Lee frowned. "Why the fuck you asking about them crazy motherfuckers?"

"About five of them came by the shop today. They were asking about a friend of theirs. They were packing pipes and sawed-off pool cues to jog my memory. Now, who do you think their friend was? I'll give you three guesses and the first two don't count," Ike said.

Buddy Lee let out a low long whistle.

"Shit. He's in that compost pile from last night, ain't he? Goddamn, I really could use that drink," Buddy Lee said.

"Yeah."

Buddy Lee rubbed his face before he answered Ike's question.

"They one-percenters. Got chapters all up and down the East

Coast. They mainly run guns and meth through their clubhouses and out at truck stops. I used to run with some boys that did a little business with them. Moving guns around. Handling some of their meth. They serious operators. They say you can't get a full patch unless you can prove you done some wet work for the club. They not skinheads, but they ain't big fans of people who look like you or live like Isiah and Derek. You sure it was the Breed?" Buddy Lee asked.

"I got a good look at the patch on one of them when I put a machete to his throat," Ike said. Buddy Lee leaned back in his chair until the front legs came off the floor. When all four legs were on the ground again he exhaled. It had a moist tone.

"A fucking machete. Jesus Christ. You really are crazier than an outhouse rat, ain't ya? I wish I'd been there to see it. Yeah, I used to party with some of them boys. They ain't the type to let that shit go. How you think they got a line on you, anyways?" Buddy Lee asked.

"The other one from last night must have noticed my truck. We shouldn't have parked so close to the goddamn house. That was a simp move," Ike said.

"Yeah, I didn't think about that, either. I guess we been out the game a long time."

"Too long," Ike said. Buddy Lee drummed his fingers on the table.

"From now on we use my truck. It's got four bald tires and I'm holding the door on with baling wire, but it'll get us where we need to go," Buddy Lee said.

"And where's that? What you think we should do next?" Ike asked. He had his own idea, but he wanted to see where Buddy Lee's head was at.

"Hell, if I know. I'm still trying to get my mind right. I can't for the life of me see how the Rare Breed fit into this," Buddy Lee said. He sat back in his chair. Ike turned and stared out the window over his sink. He could see the boxwoods that formed a hedgerow that separated his house from the empty mobile home next door.

It would have been nice if he could pretend that he and Isiah had planted those together in a Hallmark movie moment. Nice but a lie. The day he'd put them in, Isiah had come by to see Mya to tell her about his new job. Ike had stayed outside taking his time with the shrubs. At a certain point in their relationship, all their interactions had started ending in either arguments or evasion.

"You know how they fucking fit into this. They killed our boys. I don't know why, and right now I don't even care. One of them motherfuckers from that club stood over Isiah and Derek and blew their fucking heads off," Ike said. Saying it felt cathartic. At last there was a target in his crosshairs. A face he could put on the bogeyman that stalked Isiah in Ike's nightmares.

"Yeah. That was the first thing popped in my mind when you said they came by your place. I just . . ." Buddy Lee let the end of the sentence float between them.

"What?" Ike said.

"It just don't make no sense. If Isiah was working on a story about some guy Tangerine was seeing, what's that got to do with the Breed? Why would Derek be pissed off about that?"

"Maybe she's one of their old ladies and she saw some shit she shouldn't have seen. Maybe she was talking to Isiah about flipping on them," Ike said.

"You don't know these girls. Old ladies don't snitch. Even if they get dumped. Them MC's are a like a cult. Their Kool-Aid would make Jim Jones jealous," Buddy Lee said. Ike shifted in his chair and crossed his legs.

"You sound like you can't believe your buddies shot our kids," Ike said. Buddy Lee narrowed his eyes until they were nearly slits.

"They ain't my goddamn buddies. But I know them and I can't see them killing Derek and Isiah over a story for a gay website that maybe fifteen people have ever heard of. Plenty of magazines and newspapers and shit have done write-ups on the Breed. Hell, they got some of the headlines framed in their clubhouses. I just can't see Derek getting all bent out of shape because a biker's old lady got dumped," Buddy Lee said. Ike put his forefinger to his lip.

"What if this married guy who dumped her wasn't a part of the club?" Ike said.

"I don't follow," Buddy Lee said.

"Come on, we both knew guys from these clubs inside and on the street. They do a lot of freelancing. What if the guy who dumped her put them on her and the boys? He was married and he didn't want it to get out, so he put a greenlight on all three of them," Ike said.

"Fuck me. I never even thought about that. Goddamn liquor done pickled my brain. They definitely have taken some outside work before. Shit, they done a fair bit for Chuly," Buddy Lee said.

"One of them pulled the trigger, but somebody else gave the word," Ike said.

"Yeah, I'd say that about sums it up," Buddy Lee said. For a few moments whatever words they thought about speaking evaporated in their mouths. The ambient hums and groans of the house filled the spaces between them.

"They won't never my friends. Not really. Back when I used to go for bad, I'd fuck around with them. Hang out at their club-house. They always had a lot of women around, and I've always been a fool for a pretty smile and flexible morals. We had a lot of fun with them boys. That don't matter none now. I find the ones who put our boys down and I'll paint the inside of their clubhouse with their brains," Buddy Lee said. His watery blue eyes seemed to glow.

Ike knew what gave Buddy Lee's eyes that murderous sheen. It was the rage coursing through his veins. A poison that killed off certain parts of yourself. The parts that made you weak. It was coursing through Ike's veins, too. It was powerful but deadly. It made you determined but reckless. It gave you an edge that could turn against you and slit your own throat.

"The way I see it, there's only one way to go on this," Ike said.

"What you thinking?"

"We have to find Tangerine before the Rare Breed does. Because whoever put the paper on her put the same paper on the boys. If they find her first, they all get away. I want them, but I want the one who gave the order, too. I want to see his face," Ike said.

"I can get behind that. Find the girl, find the one who made the call," Buddy Lee said. Ike nodded and checked his watch.

"It's almost seven. Let me go change and then we head back to the city and find this bar," Ike said.

"That'll work. Shit, I should call your wife and tell her to bring me something. I'm starving," Buddy Lee said. Ike gave him a look, but Buddy Lee could've sworn there was the hint of a smile around the corners of his mouth.

"We got some leftovers from the repast in the freezer. Or some lunch meat and cheese in the fridge if you wanna make a sandwich," Ike said.

"You still got food left from the repast?" Buddy Lee asked.

"You ain't never been to a Black funeral, have you? When my granddaddy passed we ate baked ham for a month. Bread's in the box next to the microwave," Ike said. He moved past Buddy Lee and across the living room to the stairs. His shoulder brushed against Buddy Lee's. It was like a glancing blow from an anvil.

"He wound up tighter than a goddamned duck's ass," Buddy Lee mumbled. He went to the bread box and pulled out two wheat slices. He moved to the fridge and grabbed some sliced ham, sliced cheese, and a jar of mayo. As he constructed his sandwich he thought about what Ike had said about people not being afraid to tell you to fuck off these days. Derek wasn't the type to tell you to fuck off. He just cut you off like you never existed. Erase you like you were a math problem on a blackboard. The last time they had talked was when he had called Buddy Lee to tell him he and Isiah were getting married.

"So, which one of y'all gonna be the wife?" Buddy Lee had

said. He'd been sitting in his delivery truck taking a break between drops. To say that the line had gone silent was an understatement. It was more like it had ceased to be. Like God had snapped his fingers and everything on the other end of the line had winked out of existence.

"Hello? Hello? D-Man, I'm just fucking with you," Buddy Lee had said. He had heard Derek suck his teeth.

"My name is Derek. I'm never gonna be a D-Man. I'm just Derek, your gay, classically trained culinary artist of a son," Derek had said.

"Alright, alright. Damn, you really gotta drive that home, don't ya?" Buddy Lee said.

"What? That I'm gay? It's a part of who I am, Dad. Just like being allergic to cats or having green eyes," Derek had said.

"Yeah, yeah. I just don't know why you gotta rub it in my face, that's all I'm saying," Buddy Lee had yelled into the phone. He hadn't meant to yell but he couldn't help himself. There was an ugly part of him that pulsed and festered whenever Derek brought up his sexuality. It made him say things he couldn't take back in ways that couldn't be forgotten.

"Isiah asked me to invite you, but you know what? Forget it. It's going to be the happiest day of my life, but I wouldn't want to rub it in your face," Derek said.

"Hey, hey now—" But Derek had cut him off like a meat cleaver.

"I'd expect this from Mom and Gerald, but for some reason I thought you might be different. I thought you might at least pretend to be happy for me. Stupid, right?" Derek had said. His voice didn't crack, but Buddy Lee knew by the way his cadence had taken on a stilted tone he was crying.

"Just so you know, you're missing out. Arianna is going to be a beautiful flower girl," Derek had said. Then the line had gone dead. A few months later, after walking down the aisle with his husband, so was Derek.

"Oh, fuck me," Buddy Lee said. His eyes began to sting.

The familiar sound of a key being inserted into a lock broke him out of his reverie. He wiped his face with the back of his hand. He was trying to decide if he should sit down or keep standing when a slim Black woman with a crown of brown braids stepped through the doorway.

"Hello," she said. She had a fast-food bag tucked under her right arm. Her left arm was trailing behind her. A little girl with skin the color of honey was holding on to the woman's left hand.

"Uh, hey. I'm Buddy Lee. Derek's daddy."

"Yeah, I remember you from the . . ."

"When we all was down there when they, uh . . ."

"Yeah. Well, I'm Mya. And this little ball of trouble here is Arianna. I don't mean this in a rude way, but why are you in my house, Buddy Lee?" the woman asked.

"Oh, I'm . . . I was, uh . . . I was here to see Ike but he went upstairs." The little girl peeped at Buddy Lee from behind Mya's leg. Buddy Lee gave her a two-finger salute. He felt the blood rush to his face.

"How you doing, Miss Little Bit?" Buddy Lee asked.

"Arianna, can you say hi? This your granddaddy, too," Mya said. Buddy Lee heard the hollow cheeriness in her voice. Arianna hid her face in Mya's thigh.

"I met you a long time ago. Derek . . . your daddy, brought you to see me, but you probably don't remember," Buddy Lee said. Arianna hummed into Mya's leg.

"She bashful sometimes," Mya said.

"It's alright. I wouldn't want to talk to me, either," Buddy Lee said with a crooked smile.

"I'd offer you something to eat but it looks like you already made yourself at home," Mya said. Buddy Lee was suddenly aware of the sandwich in his hand.

"Oh shit. I mean shoot. Ike said it was okay," Buddy Lee said. Arianna peeped around Mya's leg at him. He winked at her and she giggled.

"It is okay. He's a guest, right?" Ike said. He was standing behind Mya. Buddy Lee hadn't noticed him come back down the
stairs. He was wearing a black T-shirt, blue jeans, and a pair of Tim-
berland boots.

"Goddamn, you quiet as a ghost," Buddy Lee said.

"Yeah, he's a guest," Mya said. Buddy Lee shifted from one foot
to the other. He waited for Ike or his wife to say something else,
but it seemed like their vocabularies had both run dry. Buddy Lee
took a bite out of his sandwich. This kind of awkwardness made him
restless.

"Me and Buddy Lee going out. I'll be back later," Ike said finally.
Ike motioned toward the door with his head. Buddy Lee slipped
past Mya.

"Excuse me, ma'am," he said. He stepped through the doorway.
Ike turned to follow him when Mya reached out and touched
his arm.

"Be careful. Don't do nothing you can't walk away from," Mya
said. Ike saw the blood-soaked tamper in his hands with bits of
skull and brains sticking to the square metal plate at the end of the
handle.

"I won't," he lied.

TWENTY-THREE

Grayson fingered the bandage against his neck while he spoke into his cell phone.

"Nah, we gonna fuck this dude up righteously. I'm talking scorched fucking earth. This boy ain't gonna know what the hell hit him. You think you and Choppa and your crew can come down, too? We need to put the Breed beatdown on this fucker," Grayson said. A series of high-toned beeps rang in his ear as Tank, the president of the Hurricane, West Virginia, chapter of the Rare Breed, yammered on about retribution, taking care of business, and Rare Breed forever, forever Rare Breed.

"Hey, Tank, let me get back to you," Grayson said. He clicked over to the incoming call.

"Yeah."

"I'm going to assume since I have not heard from you in two days you have not found the girl," the voice on the other end said. Grayson bit down on the inside of his cheek before he responded.

"No, we ain't found your side piece yet. I'm glad you called so I can tell you that's gonna have to wait. We got Breed business to take care of now. All because of you and these faggots," Grayson said.

"I thought I made myself clear the other day. Nothing is more important right now than finding Tangerine. Was there some miscommunication?"

"No, you was clear, but now I got a missing prospect and a

nigger out of Red Hill County who thinks he can hold a fucking machete to my neck and stay upright."

The voice sighed.

"Elucidate the situation more clearly for me."

"What?" Grayson said.

"Tell. Me. What. Happened." The voice pronounced each word with an overexaggerated enunciation that made Grayson's vision go stark white.

"Don't talk to me like I'm stupid. Just because I don't keep a dictionary by my nightstand don't mean I'm stupid," Grayson said.

"Tell me."

"Well, I followed your suggestion and sent a couple prospects out to the punks' house to see what they could see. When they got there apparently them boys' daddies was in the house. One of them jumped the prospects, and the other snuck up behind them and knocked them out. When the one that came back woke up his brother was gone and so was the daddies."

"Hmm."

"Yeah. Now this prospect, he saw a truck in front of the house with the name of a lawn-care business on the side of the door. You wanna know who owned the truck?" Grayson said.

"One of the fathers, I assume."

"You bet your fucking ass it did. Randolph Lawn Care. We rolled over there, but this motherfucker, he ain't no square. He got jail ink. He done some real time. We won't expecting that," Grayson said.

"Let me guess. He was able to ward off you and your brothers," the voice said.

"He got the drop on us, yeah. He don't know it yet, but that's the last time he ever gonna walk straight. We're going back and we're gonna fix him up right," Grayson said. The voice didn't speak for a long time.

"No, you're not."

"Excuse the fuck out of me? I told you, this is Breed business now. Your little honeypot is gonna have to wait. That bitch been gone bye-bye for a long time anyway," Grayson said. He picked up his mini-sledgehammer gavel and started tapping it against the table.

"No, it's still my business. Stop and think for a moment. The fathers of two dead sons are in their boys' home weeks after the funeral. Why? Did your remaining prospect note any furniture being moved out of the home? Doesn't seem like they were retrieving any family heirlooms. Then these two men, these grieving fathers, whoop your prospects' collective asses, but instead of calling the police and reporting a break-in, they disappear with a hostage in tow. Then when you and your rolling gang of miscreants confront one of these grieving gentlemen, not only does he get the drop on you, he again does not alert the police. Now tell me, what does that say to you? And before you answer, consider what you told me about one of these men. A hard man who has done hard time. What do think all this means? Better yet, tell me what you would do, being the kind of man you are, if persons unknown killed your son?" the voice asked. Grayson pulled the phone away from his ear and laid it against his forehead for a few seconds before answering the voice's question.

"First of all, I wouldn't have a gay son. Second of all, I already know this. Everything you just said, I've already thought about. That's why I'm gonna put them ten toes up. We don't need nobody poking around that thing that we took care of," Grayson said.

"How much did the prospect know about our arrangement?" the voice asked. Grayson relished the hint of fear in the voice when it asked that question.

"Don't get your panties in a bunch. He ain't know shit."

"Good. Because you know he isn't coming back, right? I know men like this. I've seen thousands of them over the years. They can't resist their true nature. If they took him out of that house, that was the last sunset he ever saw," the voice said. Grayson had figured as much himself, but hearing it from that soft-talking motherfucker made him nearly go blind with fury. He knew Andy wasn't on this side of the dirt anymore. He didn't need this arrogant asshole to explain that to him.

"Now let's extrapolate this even further. Let's assume your prospect did give them something. Maybe something about the club. Maybe they asked him about the deaths of their sons."

"Shit," Grayson whispered.

"What is it?" the voice said.

"I told them the name of the girl we was looking for," Grayson said. His neck and ears became hot as a griddle. He could almost hear the smile on the other end of the line. The poor dumb biker had fucked up, and it was up to the sophisticated, intelligent owner of a smooth urbane voice to fix the situation. Again.

"That's actually to our advantage. If they have the name and they are pursuing their own shabby mission of revenge, one just has to follow them and see where they lead us. If they have her name, they may very well find her. Of course, if you hadn't gone to the man's place of business and tried and failed to threaten him, we would have the element of surprise. Oh well. Get a few of your best men to follow this Randolph. Then when they lead you to Tangerine you can take out all your pent-up aggression on all of them at your leisure. It's the proverbial two birds with one stone. Until then, let them be. Just observe and report," the voice said. Grayson tapped the gavel harder.

"I'm gonna say something to you and I want you to listen to me good. You don't run this club. I do. You think we're your personal army. We ain't. This is how it's gonna go. We play your game for a little bit, but if it don't look like we gonna find this bitch, I'm taking care of my business. My way. No more talking. You wanna cut us loose, do it. I don't give a fuck. You can tell your daddy I said that, too. I don't wake up in the morning looking to kiss your ass," Grayson said.

"No, you don't. But you do wake up in a world where I can make one phone call to the ATF and have you behind bars for the rest of your life before my coffee is cold. I can even call in a few favors with my friends in the corrections department to make sure you spend that time being the paramour of a monstrously endowed subhuman." The voice paused. Between the beginning and the end of that pause Grayson had an image of him shoving the gavel down the throat of the owner of that sophisticated voice.

"I'll look up this Randolph's business license and get you his home address," the voice said.

"Yeah," Grayson said in a strangled groan.

"Get a couple of your guys on him. Tonight."

TWENTY-FOUR

Buddy Lee turned off Grace Street and pulled into a pay-by-the-hour parking lot. The streetlamps were covered by swarms of moths and gnats that hovered around them like living clouds. He put the truck in park and waited for it to settle. Ike was leaning against the door with his face toward the window. When the truck finally stopped rattling, Ike sat up straight and rubbed his eyes.

"You sleeping over there, hoss?" Buddy Lee asked.

"Didn't get much rest last night. I guess you got a nap today," Ike said.

"I caught a few winks," Buddy Lee said. They sat there under the streetlamps as a car drove down the street with a sound system pumping out enough bass to liquefy their insides. They heard the disjointed chatter of the denizens of the city as they wandered up and down the sidewalks and through the alleyways. Ike thought it sounded like they were underwater listening to people on the shore. He pulled the napkin out of his pocket and stared at it.

"I guess we should get to it," he said.

"What's the plan? Just go in there and start asking about some girl named Tangerine?" Buddy Lee asked.

"Yeah, but leave your knife in the truck. If LaPlata and Robbins are on our asses, we need to try and keep it quiet up in here," Ike said.

"That knife has saved my ass more times than I can count. I ain't leaving it behind. Besides, I'm not the one running around breaking people's fingers like wishbones," Buddy Lee said. Ike cut him a look but Buddy Lee ignored it.

"You ready?" Ike asked.

"When the last time you was in a club?" Buddy Lee asked.

"Michael Jackson was still alive," Ike said as he climbed out of the truck.

Garland's sat at the corner of Grace and Foushee Streets. A large picture window with a neon sign in the shape of a pair of red shoes in the corner allowed red and green lights to spill out onto the pavement. Buddy Lee stopped in front of the entrance, spit on his hands, then ran them through his hair.

"What are you doing?" Ike asked.

"You never know. I might meet a filly with low standards in here," Buddy Lee said. This time Ike did laugh. Buddy Lee smiled. The smile faltered after a few seconds.

"Let's do it," he said as he opened the door.

Garland's had a long oval-shaped bar that bisected the club right down the middle. Tables and booths filled the club on the left side of the bar. On the right were blue and red velvet love seats and beanbags. Up and down the exposed redbrick walls black-and-white pictures of Judy Garland in full *Wizard of Oz* regalia competed with color photos of Judy Garland in early twentieth-century garb from *Meet Me in St. Louis*. A large flat-screen television above the bar was playing Judy Garland singing "Over the Rainbow" on top of a techno beat. A few men were sitting at the bar. When Ike and Buddy Lee came in, two Black men sitting at the bottom of the oval snapped their heads up, appraised them, then quickly lowered their heads again. To their right, three women—two Black, one white—were squeezed into one of the love seats. Ike and Buddy Lee plopped down on a couple of stools at the end of the bar.

Ike took a quick look over each shoulder and scanned the bar. A group of clean-cut older white men sat in one of the booths with a tray of shot glasses in front of them. They raised their glasses and one of the men yelled out a toast.

"Cheers, queers!" the man said as he and his companions downed their shots. They collapsed against each other amid a chorus of laughs. Ike put his head on a swivel. Two more young white men were holding hands at one of the tables behind him. The three women in the love seat were running their hands through each other's hair.

Ike gripped the edge of the bar.

"I think this is a gay bar," he whispered.

"What?" Buddy Lee asked. He was squinting at the shelf of liquor bottles like a penitent who had just glimpsed heaven. Ike leaned over and put his mouth near Buddy Lee's ear.

"I think this is a gay bar," Ike said.

Buddy Lee spun around on his barstool. After one complete revolution he stopped and leaned toward Ike.

"Well, shit, I guess that makes sense. I ain't never been in a gay bar before. But it looks like they serve bourbon, so I guess it'll be alright," Buddy Lee said.

"Let's just ask the bartender if he knows Tangerine or the boys," Ike said. His breath was coming in short harsh bursts.

"Alright. You okay? You breathing like you running uphill backward," Buddy Lee said.

"I'm fine. Let's just do it," Ike said. Buddy Lee held up two fingers and waved at the bartender. After dropping off a pair of martinis to the two brothers at the end of the bar, he came over to Ike and Buddy Lee. He was a short Asian man with long coal-black hair that spilled over his well-defined shoulders. Ike thought his white T-shirt was three sizes too small.

"Hey, gents, what can I do ya for?" the bartender asked.

"I'll have a Coors and a shot of Jack Daniel's," Buddy Lee said.

"I just want a water," Ike said.

"Gotcha. You guys need any menus?"

"No," Ike said before Buddy Lee could respond. A few minutes later, the bartender, who told them his name was Tex, brought them their drinks.

"Anything else for you guys?" Tex asked with a smile. Buddy Lee gave Ike a curt nod as he downed his whiskey.

"Yeah. Let me ask you something. Did you know some guys named Isiah and Derek? I think they might've hung out here from time to time," Ike said. Tex's smile faltered a bit.

"Yeah, I knew them. They were good guys. They used to come out for our Blacklight Night. Derek used to make us pierogies for our monthly Paint Night. Isiah wrote an article about us for his website. They were really good guys. I can't believe what happened to them. It's bullshit, man," Tex said. Ike felt a lump rise in his throat like a whale breaching.

"Yeah, it was bullshit," Ike said.

"Were you guys friends of theirs or something?" Tex asked.

"They was our sons," Buddy Lee said. He took a long swig off of his beer.

"Aw, man. I'm sorry. I'm so sorry, dudes."

"Thanks," Ike said.

Tex pulled a white rag out of his pocket and wiped the bar down in front of Ike and Buddy Lee. One of the three women from the love seat squealed with pleasure or surprise. Or both.

"I gotta ask, what are you guys doing here? Isiah used to say . . ." Tex cut himself off.

"What did Isiah used to say?" Ike said, knowing full well what his son probably said.

"Nothing. It's nothing. I just was wondering why you guys were here, that's all."

"We trying to find somebody who might know something about what happened to them," Buddy Lee said. He killed his beer.

"Are y'all like, investigating?" Tex asked.

"We just asking questions. The cops said they wasn't getting nowhere. We just want to find out what happened to our boys, that's all. We ain't trying to cause nobody no trouble," Ike said. That was partially the truth. He didn't want to cause anyone any trouble. He just wanted to find the motherfuckers who killed his son. All of them. Every last one.

"Yeah, they came by here. I don't think it's like people don't want to help. It's like, the cops come around here and people get nervous. Lots of folks here still on the down-low. They don't want to get their names tied up in a murder case. Don't get me wrong, Richmond's a pretty good place to live if you're gay or queer or whatever, but it's still Virginia. The same people who love those statues on Monument Avenue wouldn't have a problem tying some of my customers to a fence, ya feel me?" Tex said.

"So, you're saying Isiah and Derek's friends are a bunch of chickenshits," Buddy Lee said. Tex shook his head.

"You don't get it, man. Things are better these days if you're gay, but they ain't great. You get outed and you might find out you suddenly have violated your company's rules on parking privileges, so they fire you. I mean, it's like being Black or Asian or Hispanic here in the Old Dominion. Things are better but—"

Ike let out a grunt.

"I say something wrong?" Tex asked.

"Being gay ain't nothing like being Black," Ike said. The words came out slow and deliberate. Tex furrowed his brow.

"I'm just saying we still in the South. Unless you straight and white you gotta watch your back," he said. He turned his head toward Buddy Lee.

"No offense," he said.

"None taken, I guess. I just never knew I had it so good being straight and white," Buddy Lee said. He tried to make it come out lighthearted, but the truth in the statement anchored it to the ground. Tex glanced at Ike, but whatever he expected to see was absent.

"You know anything about what happened to our boys? Did either one of them say anything about somebody threatening them or anything like that?" Ike asked.

"Neither one of them ever said anything like that," Tex said. He grabbed Buddy Lee's empty bottle and headed for the trash can under the bar.

"Hey, you know a girl named Tangerine?" Buddy Lee asked. Tex stopped.

"She used to hang around here a while back. She comes and goes, ya know."

"You ever see her with the boys?" Ike asked. Tex glared at him for a second.

"What do you mean?"

"I mean with our boys."

"Oh. No, never did. Like I said, she floats in and out. She's a party girl."

"Oh yeah? How hard do she party?" Buddy Lee asked. Now it was his turn to get a hard look from Tex.

"You'd have to ask her that," Tex said.

"I'd like to. You know where we can find her?" Buddy Lee asked.

"I just told you she floats in and out."

"Anybody around here might know her?" Ike asked.

"I guess you have to ask them," Tex said. Ike leaned forward over the bar. He stuck his chest out and cocked his head to the right.

"Hey, we got a problem?" Ike asked. Tex pushed his tongue against the inside of his cheek.

"Ya know, I have a friend who comes in here sometimes. He's a lawyer. He's about your age. He's gay, Black, and cool as fuck. You know what he told me once? He said some Black people hate gay people more than they hate racists. He told me growing up Black and gay in a small town out in the country was like being trapped between a lion and an alligator. Rednecks on one side and ho-mophobic Black folk on the other. He said the only way you don't get fucked with growing up Black and gay was if you could do hair or lead a choir. He couldn't do neither so he got out of town. I didn't really believe him. I couldn't believe it was that bad. But every day a guy like you proves him right," Tex said.

"Oh, so you think it's easier being Black than being gay? I tell you what, you go somewhere don't nobody have to know you gay unless you tell them. I'm Black everywhere. I can't hide that shit," Ike said. Tex pulled his towel out and twisted it with both hands.

"Yeah, you can't hide that you're Black. But the fact that you think I should hide who I am proves my point. Like Dr. King said: an injustice anywhere is a threat to justice everywhere," Tex said. Ike sucked his teeth and sat back onto his stool.

"You guys let me know if you want anything else," Tex said. He turned and walked to the other end of the bar.

"Damn, he dropped the Martin Luther King card on your ass. I think he won that round, Grasshopper," Buddy Lee said.

Ike didn't respond.

"I'm fucking around. I don't think he knows shit. But I bet you some of these folks do," Buddy Lee said as he gestured to the pa-trons scattered around the bar.

"Uh-huh," Ike said. He grabbed his water and chugged it down in one big gulp. He slammed his empty glass down on the bar.

Ike felt like a vise was squeezing his rib cage. The two young white men who had been holding hands were now dancing in slow languid circles with their arms draped around each other's neck. One of the brothers at the end of the bar was stroking his friend's cheek. They had made their martinis disappear like a magic trick. The three women on the love seat were playfully pulling at each other's hair.

"Think we should split up? Maybe we'll be less intimidating that way," Buddy Lee said.

"Yeah, I guess. We can work like when you in the yard trying to pick grapes," Ike said. Buddy Lee chuckled.

"I ain't heard that in a while. We used to call it 'getting pony express' up in Red Onion. I don't know why we just didn't call it gossip."

"I need to stop talking like a convict. I fall back into that shit too damn easy," Ike said.

"I still have nightmares about Red Onion. I be dreaming I'm still inside. I'm out, but I've never stopped feeling like a convict," Buddy Lee said.

"I heard Red Onion is a dungeon," Ike said.

Buddy Lee gazed lovingly at the bottle of Jack Daniel's sitting by itself like an exalted king on the glass shelf. "It is that. It'd make the devil find religion," he said. He got Tex's attention and pantomimed taking a shot. Tex dropped off his shot without a word. Buddy Lee downed it in one gulp.

"Hey, what'd I say about drinking?" Ike asked.

"I got it, okay? I'll take the girls on the couch. You wanna start on this side?" Buddy Lee said. His face became flushed as the whiskey hit the bottom of his stomach.

"Go ahead," Ike said. Buddy Lee slid off the stool and made for the love seats and beanbag section of the bar. Ike took a deep breath. He spun around on the stool and took stock of the room. He had a choice between the brothers at the end of the bar, the two men still slow-dancing, or the clean-cut older guys in the booth. Using a purely demographic equation, he decided to hit the brothers first.

"Hey, excuse me," Ike said. The larger of the two was about Ike's size with a luxuriant beard that covered most of his face. He took his attention away from his companion just long enough for Ike to see the irritation in his face.

"Yes?"

"Hey, um . . . I'm looking for this girl—"

"I think you in the wrong place," the bearded man's companion said. He was clean-shaven with a tight fade.

"Nah, it's not like that," Ike said.

"What can we do for you?" the bearded man asked. Ike could see he was going from irritated to angry. Ike forced himself to calm down and speak clearly.

"I'm looking for a girl named Tangerine. She used to hang out here sometimes. I think she a friend of my son's. I just want to talk to her."

"About what?" Fade asked.

"What?"

"What do you want to talk to her about? Are you some ex-boyfriend trying to track her down?" Fade asked.

"Huh? No, I need to talk to her about my son," Ike said.

"Is your son her ex?" Bearded Man asked.

"Look, my son is fucking dead and she might be able to help me find out who killed him. Now can we cut the shit? Do you know her or not?" Ike said. Bearded Man and Mini-Afro spun around on their stools until all he saw was the back of their heads.

"We don't know her, man," Bearded Man said. He and his companion turned their backs on him. Ike took a deep breath so violently his nose burned.

Ike felt like he was rooted to the floor. His skin was tingling all over like he had stepped on a live wire. The real estate between him and the two men seemed to fill with dangerously charged energy. They had turned their backs on him. Inside that was a sign of disrespect so egregious it might get you sent to the farm just on general principles. Ike's right hand was a fist before he realized he had curled his fingers. He stared down at it, and through a sheer force of will he made himself unfurl his fist. He had to be smart. He didn't need the cops throwing him in a deep dark hole. At least not until he finished this.

"Thanks." Ike choked the word out and walked away. The two white men slow-dancing were gone. They must have slipped out while he was interrogating the brothers. That left the guys in the booth. They were laughing over another round of shots. Ike walked over and stood next to the booth.

"Hey, how ya guys doing?" Ike asked. He tried to look friendly.

"Hey there," one of the men said. The other men stopped laughing but kept smiling.

"Hey, I'm Ike Randolph. My son was Isiah Randolph," Ike said. All the smiles faltered.

"Oh my. I'm sorry. I'm Jeff," the man closest to Ike said. He held out his hand. Ike shook it and was surprised by its firmness.

"I'm Ralph."

"I'm Sal."

"Chris."

Ike nodded to the other three men.

They don't look gay, Ike thought. As soon as the idea entered his head it seemed like he could hear Isiah's voice. How exactly did someone look gay? Did he expect them to have tattoos carved into their foreheads that declared their sexuality?

"I guess you guys knew Isiah?" Ike asked.

"He and Derek were regulars here. He did an article on my organization. Derek used to work for Chris at his restaurant," Jeff said.

"Small world, ain't it?" Ike said.

"The world is made up of a bunch of smaller worlds," Jeff said.

"What's your organization?" Ike asked.

"I run a nonprofit technical school in the East End for at-risk gay youth. We teach them industrial arts. I'm a welder by trade and a wannabe artist," Jeff said.

"You're being too modest," Ralph said. He put his hand on top of Jeff's. Ike studied the picture of Judy Garland at an anonymous cabaret club. Her deep-set eyes and come-hither pout were frozen forever in black-and-white.

"That's good. You get a lot of kids out there?" Ike asked. The four men shared a long moment of silence before Jeff spoke.

"Lots of kids end up on the streets when they come out. Not all of them, but a lot. They show up with black eyes and missing teeth. There are parents who think they can beat the gay away. Or they show up crying and terrified because their mom or dad or their pastor told them they were going to burn in hell for eternity," Jeff said. Ike studied his boots. He was one of those parents. He definitely thought he could "man up" the gay out of Isiah. Might as well tried to make him a bird and tossed him off the roof. Isiah wasn't going to ever change. He was what he was until the day he died.

"And now he's in the ground," Ike mumbled.

"I'm sorry, what?" Jeff asked.

"Um, nothing. I was just saying that's fucked up," Ike said.

"Yeah, it is," Jeff said.

"Me and Derek's dad, we were just asking around, trying to see if anyone knew anything about what happened. We're not trying to put anybody in a spot. We just wanna find out what happened to our boys," Ike said. Could these men hear the desperation in his voice? He heard it and it made him feel frail. Finding out who had killed Isiah and Derek was the life raft that he clung to in a vain attempt to keep from falling apart. It was barely working. The ragged edges of his mind might unravel at any moment, and God help whoever was around when that happened.

"I'm sorry, I don't think any of us know anything that can help. I wish we could," Jeff said.

"They were such a happy couple," Sal said.

"They had what I'm looking for," Chris said.

"You've got to stop being a ho if you want a husband," Ralph said. Chris stuck his tongue out at him and rolled his eyes.

"Ah, did any of you know a woman by the name of Tangerine?" Ike asked. Jeff's right cheek twitched.

That's a tell, Ike thought.

"I knew a girl by that name once," Jeff said. Ike thought he was choosing his words carefully. His eyes darted from left to right, and that cheek was nearly oscillating now.

"Oh yeah? Did she ever come by the school?" Ike asked.

"She used to crash there a lot," Ralph offered. Jeff moved his hand from under Ralph's, then put his hand on Ralph's forearm. A quiet gesture, but Ike read it as an admonishment.

"Tangerine didn't, uh . . . take to the industrial arts. She's a free spirit," Jeff said.

"That's one word for it," Chris said. Sal elbowed him.

"What? I'm just saying what we're all thinking," Chris said.

"She's a party girl?" Ike asked. Jeff's shoulders slumped.

"Tangerine can be a bit of a diva, that's all," Jeff said. An idea popped up in Ike's mind.

"We heard she met Derek at a big fancy party for a music guy," Ike said.

"That girl ain't never seen a scene that she didn't want to be seen at," Chris said. Jeff frowned at him but Chris didn't seem to notice, or if he did, he didn't care.

"Are you talking about Mr. Get Down's party?" Ralph asked.

"I don't know. Who's Mr. Get Down?" Ike asked.

"He's a producer. Real name is Tariq Matthews. Mainly hip-hop and trance. He lives out in the West End. Huge house with god-awful flying buttresses like something out of a James Whale movie," Ralph said. He paused, apparently hoping for a laugh.

"God, am I that old that I'm the only one who knows who James Whale is? Anyway, Tariq is a hometown hero. I taught him in the ninth grade. The year after he graduated he produced a record that went to number one in fifteen countries. Derek was in here a week before the party talking about how his company was gonna do the food for Mr. Get Down's thirtieth. God, I really am old," Ralph said. He laid his head on Jeff's shoulder.

"Is that her kind of scene?" Ike asked. Chris started to answer but Jeff cut him off.

"Here's the thing. Tangy is . . . a complicated girl. She's young and beautiful and she's finding herself. That kind of beauty and youth can get you some haters," Jeff said, staring squarely at Chris.

"Tangerine isn't even her real name," Chris said. Ralph jumped into the conversation.

"Don't be bitchy, Chris," Ralph said. Chris crossed his arms.

"Got any idea where she might be?" Ike asked.

"You think Tangy is involved with what happened to Isiah and Derek?" Jeff asked. Ike hesitated.

"Isiah was supposed to meet her here for an interview. The day before the meet, him and Derek got shot in front of that wine bar celebrating their anniversary," Ike said. Saying out loud that his boy had been shot made the sharp edges of Ike's heart grate against each other.

"Tangy's been gone since before that happened. She might be anywhere," Jeff said. As if on cue, his right cheek began to twitch. Ike gave him the hard eyes. The scary eyes. The murder eyes.

Jeff seemed to be a really nice guy. He dedicated his life to helping gay kids. He had a nice group of friends. None of that stopped him from lying to Ike's face. Jeff knew exactly where Tangerine was and how to find her. Ike could feel it in his guts.

Tangerine was the woman who sounded so afraid on that answering machine. Was she afraid because she knew Isiah had a hit on him? Did she set him up? Ike didn't know. All he really knew was that nice guy Jeff was sitting here lying to him like he was big dumb black-ass country son of a bitch. Jeff with his frosted gray tips and deliberately groomed five-o'clock shadow. Nice guy Jeff, who cared more about protecting some party girl than he cared about Ike's dead son, had a case of the city-mouse syndrome. A lot of folks that lived in Richmond liked to imagine they were smarter and more sophisticated than the people that lived in the counties. Even if most of the counties were only thirty miles past the huge illuminated RICHMOND sign that sat above the exit that took you out of the city.

Ike wondered how long it would take to get the truth out of him if he jammed his thumb into his eye and popped it like hard-boiled egg.

Jeff blinked hard. Perhaps he saw something in Ike's face that told him his eyeball was in danger of ending up on Garland's hardwood floor.

"Seriously, I don't know where she is. But . . ." Jeff said.

"But what?" Ike asked, still giving Jeff the death stare.

"If she was at that party, it probably wasn't her first time hanging out with Mr. Get Down. He might know where she is. That's all I'm saying," Jeff said. "The Man That Got Away" started pumping through Garland's sound system over a trip-hop beat. Ike relaxed.

"Thanks," he said. He turned and went back to the bar.

"Can I have another water? And let me settle up for me and my friend," Ike said. Tex came over and tossed a receipt and a pen in front of Ike. Had he really called Buddy Lee his friend? He didn't know if that was an accurate description of what they were. They'd killed a man together, so they were more than acquaintances, but he didn't think they were quite friends. Ike signed the receipt, leaving a sizable tip, and wrapped it around his debit card. A tall thin Black man stumbled up to the bar next to him. The man stroked his bushy gray goatee as he struggled to straddle the barstool.

"Hey," Gray Goatee said.

"Hey," Ike said without turning his head.

"How you doing?" Gray Goatee slurred.

"I'm alright, man," Ike said. He searched for Tex but he was taking a large drink order from a group of blue-, pink-, and green-haired androgynous white kids that had just wandered into the bar.

"All these little young bucks up in here. Too damn young, too damn crazy," Gray Goatee said. His words fell out of his mouth like marbles rolling off the edge of a table.

"Uh-huh." Ike said.

"I'm Angelo," the man with the gray goatee said. Ike didn't respond. He put his hands in his pockets and rocked back and forth on the balls of his feet.

"They fun, but what's the point? A couple hours of groaning and moaning for what? So they can just leave in the morning after pissing all over your toilet seat," Angelo said. He listed to his left before grabbing the rail on the edge of the bar and righting himself. Ike took a step to the right away from him.

"You with somebody?" Angelo asked.

"I'm just paying my tab, man," Ike said. He spoke through pursed lips, turning the sentence into one long word.

"Sure, sure, you probably with somebody. You too fine not to be," Angelo said.

"Hey Tex! Get my tab, man!" Ike yelled.

"You going? Hey wait, let me buy you a drink. Don't go yet. Let me get you a drink," Angelo said. He reached out and put his hand on Ike's forearm.

"Get your fucking hands off me, man," Ike said. The two brothers at the other end of the bar picked up their drinks and moved to the beanbags. The thunder in Ike's voice promised a storm that they wanted no part of at all. Angelo's radar didn't seem to be attuned to the changing weather.

"Hey now, don't be like that. I just want to get to know you," he slurred. He moved his hand up Ike's arm toward his coconut-sized biceps.

"I told you, get the fuck off me!" Ike snatched Angelo by the front of his shirt. The barstool went skittering across the floor as Ike slammed Angelo against the far wall. A picture of Judy Garland in a top hat and tails fell from the wall. It bounced off Ike's head but he hardly noticed. Angelo's eyes rolled around in their sockets as Ike cinched in his grip and lifted him off his feet.

"I'm sorry!" Angelo said over and over.

Ike pulled him off the wall only to slam him against it again twice as hard. Angelo tried to pry Ike's hands from around his neck, but he might as well have been trying to untie the Gordian knot.

"I told you, don't fucking touch me!" Ike yelled. He held Angelo in place with his left hand while cocking back his right. The group of emo kids that had just entered the bar pulled out their cell phones and started yelling at him as they began recording the confrontation.

Seconds before he unloaded his hammer of a right, he felt strong hands gripping his shoulders and powerful arms wrapping around his waist. Ike felt himself being pulled off balance. He let go of Angelo and pawed at his attackers.

"Fuck off of me!" Ike grunted. He felt himself being pushed

backward. He was being herded toward the door like a rampaging bull. A third set of hands had joined the fray. It was Chris.

Tex hollered at him to back off, but he might as well have been trying to soothe a swarm of hornets. Chris's face was a storm of ferocity. Were he and Angelo friends? Was he defending the man's honor? Or was he just righteously pissed? Ike had come into a place where Chris and his friends felt completely at ease and asked for their help. They had given him a glimpse into the man that Isiah had become. A good man that Ike had little hand in creating. How had he repaid their kindness? He'd jacked up a lonely drunk. Ike saw Buddy Lee running toward him out of the corner of his eye. Buddy Lee gave Chris a shove and got between him and Ike.

"What the fuck, man?" Buddy Lee cried.

Ike stopped fighting.

"I'm going, okay?! I'm going. Buddy Lee, get my debit card, man," Ike said. Tex released him. Another man, a brother in a matching white too-tight T-shirt, was holding Chris at bay as he tried to get to Buddy Lee. Tex grabbed Ike's card from behind the bar and slapped it into his hands.

"Get the hell out of here before I call the cops," he said.

"I thought you said you didn't like cops," Buddy Lee said.

"Get the fuck out!" Tex said.

"Come on, hoss, let's go before Johnny Law gets here," Buddy Lee said. He took a few steps backward before spinning on his heel and heading for the door. A few people booed as they walked by. Ike saw Jeff gazing at him from across the bar.

"I'm sorry," Ike mumbled. He knew his words wouldn't be heard over the commotion in the bar, but he still wanted to say them.

Jeff shook his head and looked away.

After forty-five minutes of silence on the interstate, Buddy Lee pulled into Ike's driveway and put the truck in park. The engine coughed and gasped as the truck idled. Ike reached for the door handle.

"What was all that about? At the bar?" Buddy Lee asked. Ike

opened the door. A warm breeze slipped past Ike into the truck. A few errant straw wrappers and empty chewing-gum sleeves stirred around Buddy Lee's feet.

"I told him don't touch me. He touched me," Ike said.

"Okay," Buddy Lee said. His voice had a light lilt at the end of the statement.

"What is that supposed to mean?" Ike asked.

"Nothing. Just I was watching you while I was talking to them ladies. Looked like he just touched your arm."

"What difference do it make? You tell somebody not to touch you, they ain't supposed to touch you. If we was inside and he did that he'd end up staring up at the lights bleeding like a stuck pig," Ike said. Buddy Lee flexed his fingers. Ike looked out the window. His shoulders slid down ever so slightly.

But we ain't inside, are we? Ike thought. The idea was his but he heard it in Isiah's voice. Buddy Lee drummed his fingers on the steering wheel.

"Did he ask you for your number?"

"Leave it alone," Ike said. Buddy Lee made a noise halfway between a laugh and a sigh.

"Alright. Did you find out anything about Tangerine before you snatched up Samuel L. Jackson, Sr.?" Buddy Lee asked. Ike shifted in his seat so he could look Buddy Lee in the face.

"Yeah. She might be hanging out with a music producer who calls himself Mr. Get Down," Ike said. Buddy Lee laughed.

"I know that ain't on his driver's license. Well, when we going to talk to Mr. Get Down?" Buddy Lee asked.

"I'll call you tomorrow. I need some sleep," Ike said.

"Okay. You sure you don't want to talk about—"

"I said I need some sleep," Ike said. He climbed out of the truck and slammed the door.

"Yeah, you need a hug and a nap, ya big baby," Buddy Lee said in a barely audible voice. He backed out of the driveway, then turned left and headed out of the cul-de-sac. He did a rolling stop at the end of the road and turned right. Humming, he turned on the radio and an old classic by Waylon Jennings came warbling out of the truck's speakers. Buddy Lee sang along as he passed an abandoned bait-and-tackle shop on Route 634. He didn't pay any attention to the old Chevrolet Caprice in the desiccated parking lot. Seconds later two heads popped up in the front seat.

"You think he saw us?" Cheddar asked.

"Nah. Too dark. Let me call Grayson," Dome said. He pulled out his cell.

"Yeah," Grayson answered.

"The white guy just dropped the Black guy off. What you want us to do now?" Dome asked.

"Stay there. See where he goes in the morning," Grayson said.

"You want us to stay here all night? It's like a little bit after eleven," Dome said.

"Did I fucking stutter? We need to find this girl. Like yesterday, and he gonna lead us right to her," Grayson said. Dome didn't respond.

"What? You got a problem with that?" Grayson said.

"Nah, but what about Andy?"

"That's all gonna get handled when we find this cunt," Grayson said. "And Dome."

"Yeah."

"Don't let him get by you or y'all gonna have to be dealt with, too," Grayson said.

He hung up the phone.

TWENTY-FIVE

ke knew he was dreaming.

It was a dream that danced at the corners of his remembrance. Isiah is standing next to him in the backyard as Ike mans the grill. It's the cookout after Isiah's graduation from college. Folks from both sides of Mya and Ike's family are there. Friends from Mya's job. A few friends Ike has made since he got out of prison. Mostly other landscapers. A few suppliers. A couple of guys from the Y. No one from his old crew, the North River Boys are in attendance. Isiah is trying to talk to Ike, but Ike isn't listening because he knows what Isiah is trying to say and he doesn't want to hear. He never wants to hear it.

Derek is there in the dream, which is a memory in technicolor. They are holding hands. Isiah is saying that Derek isn't just his friend. He tells Ike that Derek is important to him. Ike is concentrating on the burgers and hot dogs. He focuses on the red glow of the coals. The unhurried dripping of the grease from the burgers as it falls and sizzles on the charcoal. Anything to keep his mind off what his only son is saying. When he says it, Ike watches as he responds the only way he knows how to respond. No, that's not really true. He responds in the way that's easiest for him. He flips the grill. Coals fly everywhere like fiery confetti. A piece lands on Isiah's arm. It will leave a light scar that resembles a birthmark. The scene fades to black.

Then he hears a cavalcade of screams and turns to see Isiah's and Derek's heads explode in a shower of blood and bone.

Ike opened his eyes.

Narrow beams of light from the rising sun sliced through the slats on the blinds in the bedroom window. Ike sat up and touched his face with both hands. His cheeks were wet. Mya's side of the bed was empty. She must have gotten up during the night and gone to lie with Arianna. She did that from time to time now. From time to time Ike had to fight the urge to be jealous of a three-year-old. Ike swung his legs up and out of bed until his feet hit the carpet. He grabbed his phone off the nightstand and checked the time. It was ten minutes after seven. He had fallen asleep almost immediately after Buddy Lee had dropped him off around eleven. After the bar. After jacking that guy up against the wall. Isiah would have had a lot to say about that situation.

"You're just projecting your fears about your own masculinity, Dad. It's called overcompensating." He could almost hear Isiah saying it with his telltale razor-sharp sarcasm.

Ike stood. He didn't want to admit it, but Isiah would have been right. When that guy touched him, all he could see were the faces of . . .

"Stop it," Ike said out loud. His voice sounded hollow in the early morning stillness that filled the house. Ike grabbed his T-shirt off the floor and pulled it over his head. He was still wearing his jeans. He slipped down the stairs and into the kitchen. He turned on the coffee maker. While it began to rattle and hum he thought about what Nice Guy Jeff had told him last night. Mr. Get Down. Tariq. He and Buddy Lee could just go and find a house with the flying buttresses and try to bluff their way inside but Ike didn't think that was going to work. Problem was, he couldn't think of anything else that would work, either.

The coffee maker was taking its own sweet time, so Ike decided to grab the paper. The sun peeked from behind the clouds as Ike searched for it. The retired grandmother who was their paper carrier had terrible aim. Ike rooted around in the boxwood shrubs near his front door until he found the Saturday edition. When he straightened he saw Mya's car coming down the road.

A banana-yellow Caprice was following her. She turned in to their short driveway and parked. The Caprice kept on going down the road. Mya climbed out of the car holding a big bag from Hardee's. Her mouth was set in a grim line that aged her by ten years. She hurried toward the house, toward him.

"I went to get us some breakfast. I think . . . I think that car followed me to the Hardee's, then followed me back here. Ike, I think they followed me," she said. Her voice had a breathlessness that made his skin break out in gooseflesh.

"Go inside. Lock the door. Go upstairs with Arianna. Don't come down until I come get you."

"Ike, what's going on?"

"Go upstairs, boo," Ike said. Mya clutched the bag to her chest and hurried into the house. Ike went around to the back of the house. He went into his shed. Pushing past the heavy bag, he grabbed something from a hook and headed back to the front of the house.

The cul-de-sac they lived in was more like a side road. It didn't end in a circle. The gravel-covered road just stopped half a mile past his house. In addition to Ike and Mya's story-and-a-half house, Townbridge Lane had five more homes of various sizes. When he and Mya had first moved here it was considered the poor side of the county. Then some bright-eyed developer had placed cheap modular homes around them, spread some gravel on their dirt road, and rechristened it Townbridge Lane. Neighbors came and went with alarming frequency. They brought various levels of care for their front yards with them. Manicured lawns sat a few feet from front yards full of children's toys and car parts.

Ike crouched down, hiding among his shrubs. That Caprice was on its way to a dead end. They'd have to stop, turn around, and come back. Ike gripped the handle of a bush axe with both hands. The bush axe was an old, time-honored farm tool. In the days before string trimmers and brush-cutting blade attachments, the bush axe was used to clear weeds and brush from difficult-to-access areas, like a ditch bank or a rolling sloping hillside. The tool consisted of a long flat wooden handle and wide curved blade that came to a wicked point. It looked somewhat like a comma. Except a comma wasn't double edged and made out of steel.

It was entirely possible that whoever had followed Mya to and from the Hardee's was a lost traveler with a busted GPS on his or her phone. The kind that told you that you had arrived when you pulled into a cornfield. It was possible. It was also possible that the Caprice was connected to what had happened at the shop yesterday.

"This how y'all wanna do it, right?" Ike said in a low murmur.

He heard the Caprice before he saw it. When he did see it he recognized the driver. He was one of the guys who had accompanied the blond Viking he had nearly decapitated. The car was going slow enough to be sightseeing. Ike exploded from behind the shrubs like he'd been fired from a rifle. He was already swinging the bush axe as he ran. It sliced through the air in a wicked arc before slamming into the driver's side window and shattering it like a sheet of ice during a spring thaw.

"Fuck, shit!" Dome yelled. His foot slipped off the gas pedal as he tried to fold his body under the steering wheel. Cheddar reached for the .32 in his waistband, but it got hung up on the buckle on his belt. The car continued to roll even as Ike reared back with the bush axe again.

"Drive!" Cheddar roared.

"What the fuck you think I'm trying to do?" Dome howled.

Ike swung the axe again. It connected with the back window of the Caprice. There must have been an imperfection in the tempered glass, because it exploded inward, showering Dome and Cheddar with razor-sharp shards. Cheddar got his gun loose, but just as he did, Dome hit the gas. Cheddar was thrown backward and the gun went off. Dome and Cheddar both screamed as the cacophonous sound of the gun filled the car. Dome felt a bullet whiz by his head and exit through the roof. He flew down the road spitting gravel from his rear tires. Bits of glass covered him like chips of ice.

Ike watched as the Caprice reached the end of Townbridge Lane doing forty and turned right onto Townbridge Road without even attempting to slow down.

Randy Hiers, Ike's neighbor two houses down, came out onto his front step. He was wearing a wifebeater and lounge pants. Randy didn't work. He was collecting disability for a work-related injury that Ike was 90 percent sure he was faking. Randy liked to decorate his yard with Confederate flags and DON'T TREAD ON ME signs. He railed against freeloading immigrants every chance he got. Ike didn't think he recognized the irony of crusading against freeloaders while collecting disability that he didn't really need.

"What the hell is going on out here?" Randy yelled. He had the self-assurance of most mediocre men. They told themselves the world was their oyster but never realized their oyster had turned rancid a long time ago.

"Nothing you need to worry about, Randy," Ike said. He started to walk back toward his house.

"Now hold on a goddamned minute. You out here breaking some guy's windows with that . . . what is that, anyway?" he said, glancing at the bush axe. Randy shook his head like a bull and continued his righteous diatribe. "I got kids in here, Ike!" Randy said.

"You wanna see them grow up, you'll go back in your fucking house," Ike said. He didn't wait for Randy to respond. By the time he reached his front door Mya was already there waiting for him. Ike walked inside and closed and locked the door behind him.

"Ike, what the hell is going on?" Mya asked. Her face was drawn. Ike leaned the bush axe against the coatrack near the front door.

"You think you can take Arianna and stay with your sister for a few days?" Ike asked. Mya moved closer to him. Her hand hovered over his chest but didn't land.

"Ike, what is going on?" she asked again. Her tone was gentle but firm. Ike went in the kitchen and poured himself a cup of coffee. He came back in the living room. Took a long sip.

"You know how I told you me and Buddy Lee was handling what happened to Isiah?" Ike said.

"Yes," Mya said.

"This is what handling it looks like. Call your sister and see if you can stay over there for a few. Please," Ike said before taking another sip of his coffee.

TWENTY-SIX

Buddy Lee turned in to the trailer court and nearly had a heart attack. Parked in his short driveway was a gold Lexus. Standing next to the Lexus was his ex-wife. Buddy Lee parked his truck on the side of the gravel road that ran in a serpentine "S" through the trailer court.

Why in the hell is she here? Buddy Lee thought. Tremors started in his hands and worked their way up his arms. Flexing and unflexing his fingers helped slightly. He checked the rearview mirror. She was still standing by the Lexus. The breeze caught her hair and made a halo out of it around her head. Buddy Lee sucked at his teeth and got out of his truck.

Christine took a few steps toward him. Buddy Lee leaned against his tailgate. They stood there like old gunslingers. Words were usually their weapons, and their aim was deadly. The breeze died down, and Christine's hair fell back to her shoulders.

"I guess you're wondering why I'm here," she said. Buddy Lee flicked his tongue against the inside of his bottom lip.

"The thought had crossed my mind. I figured the next time I'd see you would be on Judgment Day," he said. Christine tried to smile but it fell far short of her eyes.

"Thought you didn't believe in God."

"I don't really. But who knows? Maybe I'll start going to church and hedge my bets," Buddy Lee said. Christine sniffed. The security lights in the park blinked on, and Buddy Lee saw the wet shine around Christine's eyes.

"So, what's up?" Buddy Lee said.

"Can we go inside?"

"I don't know. It's not the *Town and Country* style you're used to," Buddy Lee said.

"It's bigger than the first trailer we had," Christine said. That reference to their shared past knocked the breath out of him. After all these years he thought she'd probably had those memories scrubbed out of her mind. Made herself believe their years together were a bad dream. They certainly felt like a dream to Buddy Lee. Hazy, half-remembered visions of a person and a time he occasionally didn't believe he'd ever been or had ever existed.

"Okay, come on," Buddy Lee said. Christine followed him inside. He was sitting down on the couch when he realized he'd left his six-pack in the truck. Christine sat in the recliner.

"You want a beer? I can run back to the truck and get my six-pack," Buddy Lee said.

"No, thank you. I was thinking about what you said. I know it appears I didn't care about Derek, but I did. There were nights I stayed up all night praying for him to change. Praying to God to make me a better mother. If I was a better mother, he wouldn't have been like he was. I failed him. I failed him in so many ways," Christine said. Tears were running down her face.

"Hey, hey. You couldn't change Derek. Nobody could. You won't by yourself in that. When I was around I tried, too, but I'm of the mind nowadays he didn't need to change. I mean, if he was still here, would it really matter to you who he was laying down with at night? Because it wouldn't matter one goddamn bit to me," Buddy Lee said. He felt his throat tighten.

"I . . . I don't know. I mean he was my son. Our son. But what he was doing was wrong. I have to believe that. Because if I don't, then everything I did was a mistake," Christine said. She put her fist to her mouth and moaned.

"It was a mistake, Chrissy. We both made a lot of mistakes with him. He wasn't abhorrent. He wasn't sacrilegious. He was just Derek. That should've been enough for both of us," Buddy Lee said. He said it with a tenderness he didn't think himself capable of anymore. At least not with her.

"Gerald would disagree with you," Christine said. Buddy Lee grunted.

"I know this might be hard to believe, but the great Gerald Culpepper isn't always right," Buddy Lee said. Christine laughed. It was a harsh bark. Buddy Lee scratched his chin.

"What?"

"You know the one thing I always liked about you? No matter what, you were real. There's no phoniness with you, Buddy Lee. What you see is what you get. Even if what I got drove me crazy sometimes," Christine said. Buddy Lee felt his face warming.

"If I could've faked it sometimes, maybe we would've made it," Buddy Lee said with a smile. Christine didn't give him one in return.

"I just left a party at my house where I'm fairly certain there is a woman my husband is screwing two times a month. It's the kind of party I used to dream about attending when I was a little girl. Fancy silverware. Real plates. Not a Styrofoam cup in sight. Two live bands. The best food. The best liquor money can buy. Not that rotgut my daddy used to drink." She shifted in her chair.

"I was standing next to one of the richest men in Virginia while he told a nasty joke about why Black men have such big dicks, as a Black woman served me another glass of prosecco. Gerald's dad laughed at that joke so hard he started choking. All these rich sons of bitches at my house to celebrate the great Gerald Culpepper announcing that he's going to give up his judgeship to run for governor. He says it's because he wants to help people." Christine's voice began to quaver.

"And all I could think about was that none of these people here gave a damn about my son. My baby. Laying in his grave.

Including me. So I left. I came to talk to the one person who knows how it feels. Even if we hated each other, we loved Derek. Didn't we?" Christine asked.

Before Buddy Lee could answer, Christine began to howl. Great trumpeting cries that shook the trailer. She slipped out of the recliner and onto his floor. Her white capris picking up brown smudges from Buddy Lee's carpet.

"If I hadn't abandoned him, maybe he'd still be alive! You were right. It's all my fault," Christine sobbed. Buddy Lee thought she sounded like an animal caught in a snare. It made his skin crawl. A part of him, the part that still cared for her—hell, loved her—told him to go to her. It told him to put his arms around her, take in her scent, and tell her that wasn't true. That it wasn't her fault. That the only person responsible for what happened to their son was the bastard that pulled the trigger.

He didn't move.

Because the other part of him, the part that knew the part that loved her was a nostalgic fool, believed she needed to feel this. She needed to have this pain touch her in places her money and status couldn't shield. She'd turned her back on their son. He'd been dismissive and cruel. They both needed to own that shit.

"You didn't kill him, Christine," Buddy Lee said finally. Christine's cries were ebbing. The howls becoming fainter and fainter. She hugged her knees to her chin. Buddy Lee went to the kitchen and grabbed a couple of paper towels. He folded them and gave them to Christine. She wiped her eyes and her nose.

"Oh God, I'm just a mess, Buddy Lee. You know he called me a couple of weeks before it happened? I ignored the call. I couldn't get into it with him about Gerald and his politics and the gay-rights agenda. I just didn't want to deal with all that." She sighed. "Huh, who are we kidding? I never wanted to deal with it. I didn't know it would be the last time I'd get a chance to talk to him. Ah, Jesus," Christine said.

"Nobody ever knows the last time is gonna be the last time

until it's too late. You ain't alone in that. That's what makes living so damn terrible sometimes," Buddy Lee said. Christine looked up at him.

"Have the police been in touch with you? Have they made any progress at all?" she asked.

"They been in touch. Don't know how much progress they done made," Buddy Lee said.

Christine nodded. "You know, I think about what I would do if I could confront them. The person who did it. Guess that'll never happen. They got my boy's blood on their hands and I'll never get to see them pay," Christine said. She began to wail again. Buddy Lee stood near her. He looked down and watched as her body trembled and rocked. He watched as his hand eased toward her head. At the last moment he pulled it back and put it in his pocket. Instead he plopped down beside her.

"Me and Ike, Derek's husband's daddy, we been kinda poking around this thing," Buddy Lee said. He didn't lean in close or put his arm around her. He simply said it while staring straight ahead.

"'Poking around'? What does that mean?" Christine asked, sniffling.

Buddy Lee nodded. "Trying to see if we can shake some shit loose. We gonna be talking to this music fella soon. Gonna see if knows where this girl is that might be able to tell us what started all this shit," Buddy Lee said.

Christine raised her head. "That's all you're doing, right? Looking into it? You're not trying to hurt anybody, right?"

Buddy Lee shook his head. He was remarkably good at lying to her. "Nah. All we doing is trying to get to the truth."

"I don't want anyone else to die," Christine said.

"They won't," Buddy Lee said. He thought, *Unless they the ones that killed the boys.*

"I know you, Buddy. That temper of yours. You've never been able to control it," Christine said.

"I never put my hands on you. Never."

"No, you didn't. But you broke my uncle's jaw."

"He called me a piece of white trash, then he spit on me. What was I supposed to do? Give him a deep-tissue massage and burn incense?" Buddy Lee asked. Christine laughed. This one was different. It was like honey on his soul.

"You always could make me laugh. So, when you going to talk to this—what did you call him? A music fella?" Christine asked.

"Made you laugh. Made you cry, too. You and Derek," Buddy Lee said. He puffed up his cheeks and took a long breath. "We're probably gonna go talk to him tomorrow. I think Ike needs a break today. We been running kinda hard."

Buddy Lee thought, *We been running around breaking people's fingers and tipping over fake cakes, then we ended up grinding a boy into manure, then we got in a fight at a gay club. Shit, Ike needed a break? Truth is, we're both old and we're both tired as hell. I need a break just as much as he does.*

He clucked his tongue against his teeth.

"Look, what I said the other day at the grave, I didn't mean it."

"Yeah, you did. One thing about you, Buddy Lee Jenkins, you ain't got no problem calling people out on their bullshit," Christine said, slipping into her Red Hill County accent. Now it was Buddy Lee's turn to laugh.

"They let you use them kinda words up on Monument Avenue?" Buddy Lee asked. Christine pushed herself up off the floor. She wiped off her backside, and Buddy Lee watched as her hands moved over her firm buttocks.

"I don't live on Monument Avenue. We moved out to King William three years ago. Garden Acres. We're pretty much by ourselves out there, so nobody cares what I say," Christine said. She wiped her eyes again before balling up the paper towel and putting it in her pocket.

"I guess I should get going," Christine said. Buddy Lee nodded.

"Why'd you really come out here? I didn't think you even remembered where I lived," Buddy Lee said.

"The last time I was in Red Hill was rather memorable," Christine said.

"Derek ran away from home and hitchhiked all the way down I-64 to here. If I'm correct, I think your husband threatened to put me so far down in a cell I'd have to get on a stepladder to kiss the devil's ass," Buddy Lee said.

"That was after you headbutted him, Buddy Lee."

"He has a big head. It's an easy target. Anyway, I didn't like the way he was putting his hands on Derek. Or how you didn't say nothing about it," Buddy Lee said. Whatever magic spell had been cast between them broke so cleanly Buddy Lee thought he could see the fractures in the air between them.

"I need to go," Christine said.

"You never answered the question."

"I suppose I wanted you to convince me I wasn't as bad a mother as I thought I was." Christine said. She opened the door, and Buddy Lee could hear the crickets singing to their loves in the distance. Christine paused in the doorway.

"You really think you're going to find out who did this?" Christine asked. Buddy Lee stared up at her. He didn't see the high-society icon of the upper-crust establishment of Virginia. He saw that girl with the cornflower-blue eyes he'd first met at that field party so long ago.

"I'm dedicating the rest of my shitty life to it," Buddy Lee said.

"That sounds like something you would say," Christine said. She stepped out into the night and closed the door behind her. Buddy Lee began to sing:

> *"And soon they'll carry him away.*
> *He stopped loving her today."*

Buddy Lee's voice cracked as he sang the old George Jones classic. He sang it low and soft, but the words still felt sharp and full of spikes.

TWENTY-SEVEN

Ike got up at seven on Monday morning. The house was quieter than usual. Mya and Arianna were staying with Mya's sister for the time being. He grabbed his phone and called Jazzy.

"Hello?"

"Jazz, it's me."

The sleepiness in her voice evaporated.

"Hey. What's . . . what's up?"

"I was wondering were you up to coming in today? We can get the guys and hit some of the jobs we called off on Friday and Saturday," Ike said. The phone line was silent.

"Jazz?"

"I don't know if I'm ready to come back," she said.

"That's cool. I'll just go in and get the guys out on some of the small jobs, and when you're ready—"

"I don't know if I'm ever gonna be ready to come back," Jazzy said. Ike put the phone against his forehead.

"Ike, you hear me?" Jazzy asked. Ike put the phone back to his ear.

"Yeah. I hear ya, Jazz."

"I love working for you, but it's like Marcus says. Who knows when those guys might show up again?" Jazzy said.

"I get it, Jazz. I'm sorry I put you through that," Ike said.

"I'll send Marcus by tomorrow to get my stuff off my desk, if that's okay," Jazzy said.

"Alright," Ike said.

"Are you mad?" Jazzy asked.

"What? No. No, I understand, Jazz. I should never have brought that shit to our door."

"What do you mean you brought to our door? What's going on, Ike?" Jazzy asked.

"Nothing you have to worry about, Jazzy," Ike said. It came out with harshness he didn't intend. "I mean, it's nothing to get concerned about. It's all good." Jazzy didn't speak for what seemed like minutes.

"Whatever is going on, don't let it tear down everything you've built. You're better than that. You're better than those funky-ass bikers," Jazzy said. He heard the hitch in her speech and he figured she was a few seconds from crying.

"I won't, Jazz. You tell Marcus he better treat you right or I'm coming to see him," Ike said.

"Oh, boss, he's fine. I guess I better get up. I need to go look for a new job," Jazzy said. Ike chewed at his bottom lip. Jazzy had been with him since she'd graduated from high school five years ago. He had not only come to depend on her but he had grown to like her. If he squinted real hard and prayed to God, Allah, and Krishna, he could sometimes do the books on the computer. Jazzy knew the system backward and forward. It would take time to train a new person on the computer. It would take even longer to train them to be compatible with his particular circadian rhythms.

"Hey, if you ever change your mind, the door is always open," Ike said. A lump was doing its level best to form in his throat.

"I hear you. Hey, Ike, be careful, okay?"

"I'm as careful as a long-tail cat in a room full of rocking chairs," Ike said.

"I think that's the first joke I've ever heard you tell. Well, the first funny one, that is. I guess I better go," Jazzy said.

"Okay. Bye.

"Bye," Jazzy said. She ended the call. Ike tapped his phone against his forehead. Jazzy wasn't exactly like a daughter to Ike but she was damn close.

"Goddammit," he said. He got up and put on a pot of coffee. He didn't even feel like going to the shop now. He'd just take another personal day and go in early tomorrow since he'd be writing up the work orders and working accounts payable and receivable.

An hour later, as he was on his third cup of coffee, there was a knock at the door.

Ike put his cup down and went to the closet in the hallway that led to the stairs. He grabbed the piece of rebar he'd hidden there the other night after his run-in with the Caprice. The fourteen-inch piece of iron was only an inch around, but it was as heavy as a hammer. Ike went to the door and peered through the diamond-shaped window.

"Aw, hell," he said. He opened the door. Buddy Lee stepped into the house with a Hardee's bag.

"Glad I caught you before you went to work. I brought biscuits," he said.

"You should call first," Ike said. Buddy Lee gave the rebar a quick once-over.

"Damn, you really must hate Jehovah's Witnesses," Buddy Lee said. Ike thought he must be getting used to Buddy Lee's attempts at humor. He didn't even roll his eyes this time.

"Had some visitors Saturday," Ike said. Buddy Lee stopped in his tracks as Ike closed the door.

"Breed?"

"Yeah. Two guys in a big yellow banana boat followed Mya home," Ike said.

"Did they see you?" Buddy Lee asked.

"Yeah. I busted out their windows with a bush axe," Ike said. Buddy Lee slumped against the wall as Ike shut the door.

"Didn't you tell me you pulled a machete on them the other day?" Buddy Lee asked.

"Yeah."

Buddy Lee pushed off the wall and went into the kitchen. He sat down at the table and Ike joined him.

"You got a thing for sharp objects, huh? Jesus. I'm surprised this house is still standing," Buddy Lee said. He pulled one of the biscuits out of the bag and put it on the table in front of Ike. Ike grabbed it and took a bite. He spoke as he chewed.

"I sent Mya and the girl to stay with her sister for a while. Until this is over," he said.

"That's good. That little girl don't need to be mixed up in none of this. How did your wife take it? Leaving her house and all," Buddy Lee said.

"She won't say it but I think she wants us to make it right. Whatever that means. You know, seeing them at the shop was one thing. Seeing them at my fucking house was another. It ain't like it wasn't real before that. I mean, I guess it was like if anything went down it was on me. But seeing them on my road . . ." Ike let the sentence fade away.

"You got something else to lose," Buddy Lee said.

"Yeah."

"If you want out, I get it. I ain't gonna think less of you," Buddy Lee said.

Ike shook his head. "We in too deep now, homie. The only way out is through."

Buddy Lee chuckled. "My mama used to say that."

"I used to hear my granddad say it. Him and my grandmama raised me. At least they tried to. I gave them some early gray hairs," Ike said.

"My mama told me when she was pregnant she prayed for a boy. Then once I was born she prayed for discernment," Buddy Lee said with a rueful smile. Ike thought there was a lot of hurt behind that smile, but he wasn't the one to pull it out of Buddy Lee.

"Say, you think you gonna need more than that piece of rebar around here? Because my half brother Chet can get us some pieces."

Ike frowned. "I can get a gun if I need to. This is Virginia. They damn near sell them at Seven-Eleven."

"Hey, Ike, no offense, but the Rare Breed ain't a social club. You gonna need more than farm tools if they decide to come back and light this house up," Buddy said.

"Do you get a commission or something?" Ike asked.

"Alright, alright, it was just a suggestion. I guess the next time they come by you can throw a pitchfork at them. Anyway, how we gonna get to this producer fella? If he's as big-time as you say, I don't reckon we can walk up to his front door," Buddy Lee said.

"I googled him last night. Can't find his address nowhere. Looked up articles on the newspaper website. It just says he resides in the Richmond Metro area."

"Shit," Buddy Lee said.

"Yeah," Ike said. Buddy Lee tapped his foot. The sound reverberated across the kitchen.

"Wait a minute. Didn't that boy at the cake shop say they had done a job for the producer?" Ike asked.

"Yeah. I'm figuring that's where Derek met Tangerine," Buddy Lee said.

"Okay. So, they would have the address, right?" Ike asked.

"Yeah, but they ain't gonna hand it over to us. We went in there breaking cakes and shit," Buddy Lee said.

"That was all you," Ike said. Buddy Lee snickered.

"Whatever, point being we ain't high on their list of friends these days," Buddy Lee said.

"We don't have to be. I got an idea," Ike said. He pulled out his cell phone and called Essential Events Bakery. The phone only rang twice before a pleasant-sounding woman answered it.

"Essential Events, Carrie speaking. How may I make your day wonderful?" she said.

Ike deepened his voice and stretched out his enunciation. Mya called it his "talking to rich white people voice." He used it when he had to arrange a bid on a huge, ostentatious estate or condominium down by the river.

"Hello, I'm Jason Krueger and I'm an associate of Tariq Matthews. You may know him better as Mr. Get Down? Well, a few months ago your firm handled a party for us at Mr. Matthews's home, and he was so impressed he'd like to hire you again for an upcoming event. However, he is very pressed for time and he would like to discuss the menu with one of your associates. Today, if that's at all possible," Ike said.

Buddy Lee covered his mouth with his forearm and stifled a laugh.

"Oh my, today? We are really swamped. Could we possibly do it tomorrow? I'd be more than willing to drive out there myself," Carrie said. Ike took a deep breath and let out a long and hopefully frustrated sounding sigh.

"Tomorrow is fine, I suppose. Could you make it around one? And do you still have the address?" Ike said. Ike could hear the hollow sound of plastic keys clicking.

"Yes, we do," Carrie said.

"Could you read it back to me, please? I want to make sure you have it correct," Ike said.

"Of course: 2359 Lafayette Lane, Richmond, Virginia, correct?" Carrie asked.

"You got it," Ike said. He hit end.

"That was almost too easy," Buddy Lee said.

"The hard part comes next. Trying to get to him," Ike said.

"What's our play if this don't work?" Buddy Lee asked.

"I got another idea but it's some DEFCON-5 type shit. Let's try this first," Ike said.

Ten minutes later they were in Buddy Lee's truck heading down the highway.

TWENTY-EIGHT

B uddy Lee turned down Lafayette Lane and eased to a stop. There was a guardhouse in the middle of a two-lane driveway that led into a larger subdivision. Actually, "subdivision" was a bit of a misnomer. Buddy Lee could see beyond the guardhouse there were only six houses visible. Each one had a back- and front yard the size of half a football field.

"Flying buttresses," Ike said.

"What?" Buddy Lee said.

"The third house on the left. The big-ass one. It's got flying buttresses."

"What the fuck are flying buttresses?" Buddy Lee asked.

"Don't worry about it. Here comes the guard," Ike said. A large burly Black man was shuffling toward the truck with a clipboard in one hand and walkie-talkie in the other. Ike thought one of the worst things you could give a man was a clipboard. He'd been at the mercy of men with clipboards. They could keep you out of a gated community or put you on a bus to prison. Give a man a clipboard and watch his true nature come out. The guard knocked on Buddy Lee's window. Buddy Lee cranked it down.

"Hello, sir, who are you here to see today?" the guard said. Buddy Lee gave him his best good-ol'-boy smile.

"Yes, sir, we are here to talk with Mr. Matthews. We are . . . here to pick up some furniture he's donating to the DAV," Buddy Lee said.

"What's your name, sir?"

"Buddy Lee Jenkins." The guard checked his clipboard.

"I'm sorry, sir, I don't see that name listed here," the guard said.

"Call him and tell him we want to talk to him about Tangerine and we ain't leaving until we do," Ike said. The guard parted his lips, then thought better of it. Instead he spoke into his walkie. After some static tinged back and forth, the guard pointed to the third house on the right.

"Mr. Mathews says come on down," the guard said.

Ike spied a silver BMW in the rearview mirror, driven by a woman with the most severe I-want-to-speak-with-the-manager haircut he'd ever seen. She zipped by them doing at least thirty miles per hour, like she had some dalmatians in the trunk that she needed to make into a coat.

"Thank you, hoss," Buddy Lee said. As he drove past the guardhouse the burly man waved.

"I'm surprised that worked," Buddy Lee said.

"Talking about Tangerine got his attention," Ike said.

"Yeah, he bit on that like a big mouth bass," Buddy Lee said. A cough racked his body and forced him to lean on the steering wheel with his hand over his mouth.

"Hey, you okay?" Ike asked.

Buddy Lee nodded as he coughed again. He leaned back and rooted around in his drink holder for a napkin. He wiped his hand, then his mouth.

Ike noticed a pinkish sputum on the napkin. He could lie all he wanted, but Ike knew Buddy Lee was far from okay.

"Gotta quit smoking," Buddy Lee said.

"I ain't notice you smoking," Ike said.

"Shit, maybe I should start," Buddy Lee said.

They drove down the sinuous road that wound through the community. Ike noticed each of the homes had a low boundary wall made out of brick or exposed river stone and bifurcated by a black wrought-iron gate. Each lawn was manicured within an inch of its life. Red maples were planted in the middle of the road at regular twenty-foot intervals. Buddy Lee turned down the driveway of the third house and stopped at the gate. Ike heard an insectile buzzer sound, and the black gates opened like butterfly wings. They went through the gates, and Ike felt a trickle of ice water slip down his back as the gates closed. The sound of the lock engaging gave him flashbacks.

Buddy Lee followed the exposed aggregate roadway until his truck was in the far right curve of the circular driveway. A chopped-and-dropped Mercedes-Benz SUV was parked at the bottom of a set of massive steps that led up to the front door of the mansion. Buddy Lee put the car in park and killed the engine.

Four walking appliances in black blazers came down the steps of the mansion with the flying buttresses, accompanied by a short dark-skinned brother with elaborately braided cornrows. He wore a bright-lime-green tracksuit and a gold Afro-pick pendant on a long chain. Ike thought the pendant weighed more than the man wearing it.

Buddy Lee and Ike climbed out of the truck and stood side by side in front of the quintet. Ike thought they looked like they had all been transported from the set of an unimaginative rap video.

"Pat 'em down," the brother with the cornrows said.

Ike and Buddy Lee raised their arms. Getting frisked was an acceptable indignity if this got them closer to finding Tangerine. One of the behemoths patted them both down. He pulled Buddy Lee's knife out of his pocket.

"That's for apple coring," Buddy Lee said. The man, who was obviously a part of Tariq's security detail, held the knife up to his face.

"This thing's a goddamn antique," he said before pocketing it.

"That knife belonged to my grandfather. I'll thank you to put it back in my hand," Buddy Lee said.

"You'll get it back before you leave," the bodyguard said.

No one spoke for what felt like minutes. Ike decided to jump in the deep end.

"Do you know a girl named Tangerine? We're trying to find her. She might know who killed our sons," Ike said. The man in the tracksuit, who Ike assumed was Tariq, didn't seem to register his question. He pulled a small joint out of his pocket and stuck it in his mouth. The security guard closest to him lit it for him with a gold cigarette lighter. Tariq took a long drag, held it, and let the smoke flow out his nostrils. Buddy Lee jumped into the conversation.

"We ain't looking to jam her up. We just want to know what happened," Buddy Lee said. Tariq still kept his cards close to the vest.

"Look, somebody stood over my son and pumped two bullets in his head. I just want to find out who did it, and I . . . we . . . think Tangerine can help."

Nothing.

"Do you speak English?" Buddy Lee said. He didn't try to hide his frustration. Tariq took another long puff on the joint. He plucked it from his lips and used it as a pointer as he talked.

"Here's the deal, Salt and Pepper. You gonna stop trying to find Tangerine. You gonna go back home and leave this the fuck alone. You gonna leave Tangy alone. This is a onetime, nonnegotiable offer. You are gonna accept the terms of this agreement, or I'm gonna have my fellas here fold you up, put you in an envelope, and mail you back to wherever the fuck you came from," Tariq said.

Buddy Lee caught Ike's eye. Ike stared back. After a few seconds he turned his attention back to Tariq.

"I told you we don't want to hurt her. We just wanna talk," Ike said. He pronounced each word with a measured caution. The four security guards had taken positions at his eleven, one, five, and eight o'clock. The air around them was charged like a thunderstorm was approaching. Tariq was still standing near the stone-carved front steps.

"You don't listen too well, do you, fam?" Tariq said. He made a shooting gesture with his joint.

"Well, shit," Buddy Lee whispered.

The guards advanced on them. Two for Buddy Lee, two for Ike. The pair that locked on Ike came at him with short, precise movements. Their punches were specific and targeted and full of bad intentions. Ike took a kidney shot from one of the bodyguards, a light-skinned brother with a flattop, which nearly made his legs buckle. Ike trapped the man's right arm with his left and jammed his thumb into the man's Adam's apple.

The light-skinned man stumbled backward grabbing his throat, just as his partner, a brother with a mini-Afro, clocked Ike on the side of the head with a fist roughly the size of a Smithfield ham. Ike tried to tuck his chin into his chest but he still got the brunt of the blow. As he tried to steady himself, Mini-Afro executed a spinning heel kick that should have violated the laws of physics for a man his size.

It caught Ike in the solar plexus, and he felt a spasm ripple through his midsection like he'd been tased. He fell back against the truck. Light-Skinned had recovered somewhat and was advancing on him from the left. Acting purely on instinct honed from hundreds of throwdowns, inside and on the street, Ike grabbed the passenger door, opened it with deft fingers, and slammed it into Light-Skinned. The bottom of the door caught him in the shin, and he immediately dropped to one knee like he was about to propose.

Mini-Afro caught Ike in the chin with a two-piece combo. Black stars twinkled in front of Ike's eyes. Grunting, he launched himself at Mini-Afro. They collided like a pair of mountain goats. Ike hooked the other man's leg with his own as he executed a tangled pirouette. They fell to the ground in a twisted conflagration of arms and legs and fists. Light-Skinned was back to his feet, and this time he was holding a collapsible baton.

Ike ended up on top of Mini-Afro. Ike hit him with a right cross, then a right elbow strike. Mini-Afro's nose flattened against his face like a jellyfish. Blood flowed unfettered from both his nostrils and into his mouth. Ike doubled up on him. Two fast brutal punches that closed the man's left eye like a curtain. Then Ike's world exploded in a nuclear flash of white light and searing pain so intense he thought he was going to vomit.

Light-Skinned reared back and struck him in the back with the baton again. Ike sloughed off Mini-Afro like an old coat. Light-Skinned stepped on his partner's kneecap in his haste to get to Ike. Ike saw the big man bearing down on him with a long black baton. It resembled the ones favored by the corrections officers in Coldwater.

Ike was flat on his back. He could feel the heat from the asphalt through his T-shirt. The pain in his neck was like a pair of pliers pinching his second and third vertebrae.

Light-Skinned was almost on top of him. Instead of kicking up at the man's face, which is what Light-Skinned was probably expecting, Ike kicked at the side of his knee with everything he had left.

He didn't hear the crack he was hoping for, but he did hear a pitiful baying howl. Light-Skinned fell against the side of the truck. The baton dropped from his hand as he tried to grab on to the truck to keep himself from falling to the ground.

Ike got to his feet. In one swift motion he kicked Mini-Afro in the kidney and then headbutted Light-Skinned above the left eye. The move hurt him almost as much as it did Light-Skinned, but it served its purpose. Light-Skinned slid down the quarter panel of Buddy Lee's truck. His face left a red streak on the rusted metal. Ike moved to help Buddy Lee but stopped in his tracks when he saw the gun.

Buddy Lee was getting his ass kicked.

It wasn't a complete shock, in all honesty. The moment he saw the two monsters run at him with the grace of gazelles, he knew he was in for a beating. Men that big shouldn't be able to move that fast, and when they could, it meant they were well-trained and skilled. Which meant he was going to get his ass handed to him.

Buddy Lee decided to go out swinging. It was the only way he knew.

The first monster that approached him had a mustache so full it was a like a cat had taken up residence on his upper lip. The other grizzly bear was so cockeyed Buddy Lee figured he could see around a corner without turning his damn head.

Buddy Lee went at them like a windmill on legs. He swung on Cockeyed while he kicked at Cat Stache. He caught Cockeyed just below the left eye. Buddy Lee felt his foot connect with Cat Stache's right knee. He might as well have been throwing beans at a tank. Cockeyed slammed him in the stomach and doubled him over. Cat Stache grabbed Buddy Lee's arms and made him stand upright. Cockeyed started peppering him with lefts and rights like it was his new favorite hobby. Buddy Lee knew that he was going to be pissing blood for a week. Cockeyed grabbed him by the chin and forced him to look at him.

"You gonna learn today, old man," Cockeye said.

I'm a quick study, you son of a bitch, Buddy Lee thought. In an effort to demoralize Buddy Lee, Cockeyed had gotten within striking distance of Buddy Lee's right foot. Buddy Lee kicked the man as hard as he could, right in the nuts.

Cockeyed's legs slammed shut at the knees as he bent over and cupped his balls. The shock of seeing his partner fall to the ground unnerved Cat Stache to such an extent he eased his grip on Buddy Lee's arms. Buddy Lee took the opportunity to ram the back of his head into Cat Stache's mouth. He thought he could feel the man's lips flatten against his teeth. Buddy Lee spun around and gave Cat Stache a left hook right behind his right ear. The man fell against the hood of the truck.

That was when he saw the gun.

It was a huge semiautomatic in a shoulder rig that dangled against Cat Stache's right side. Buddy Lee had always had fast hands. His daddy had taught him how to lift wallets and watches before he taught him to ride a bike. All the bodyguards were probably packing, but they had taken Ike and Buddy Lee lightly. They saw a couple of old geezers who were in need of an attitude adjustment. They probably figured they could handle the two of them without even wrinkling their coats.

Everyone makes mistakes, Buddy Lee thought.

He slipped his hand inside Cat Stache's blazer and relieved him of his gun. Buddy Lee spun on Cockeyed and Tariq and Cat Stache, who was now Red Stache because of all the blood coming out of his mouth.

"Back your raggedy asses up!" Buddy Lee said. He moved toward the driver's side of his truck while keeping his eye on Tariq and his private army. Ike moved toward the passenger's side. He stood behind the open door, half in and half out of the truck. Mini-Afro was back up and he had his gun in his hand, pointing it at Buddy Lee.

"Drop the fucking gun!" Mini-Afro yelled.

"Suck my crooked red dick, Barry White. I ain't dropping shit," Buddy Lee said. His chest was on fire, but he used every ounce of his will to push the pain aside.

"We just wanted to talk," Ike said. Buddy Lee had moved all the way to the driver's side of the truck.

Tariq's guards gathered around their employer like a phalanx. He spoke from behind the safety of their broad shoulders. Smiling, he took a long toke on his joint. Ike realized he was enjoying this.

"Give it up, fam. You ain't about this life. Tangerine is off-limits to you. Drop that gun, gramps, before you really get hurt," Tariq said.

"Why don't you come out from behind your boys and we'll see who's about that life and who's still sucking on their mama's titty," Buddy Lee said. Tariq's smile faltered.

"I live in a real nice neighborhood with some real nice white people. You probably got about two minutes to get out of here before the cops show up. They look out for us high-rolling taxpayers," Tariq said.

"You talk to Tangerine, you tell her we need to talk to her. Our boys tried to help her and they got killed. She owes us that," Ike said.

"Toss him my knife," Buddy Lee said. Cockeyed, who had taken the knife off of Buddy Lee, blanched.

"Put the gun down and you get your knife," he said. Buddy Lee aimed at his forehead.

"I know your boy got a bead on me, but hear me when I tell you this: there'll be two of us dead if you don't hand over that knife," Buddy Lee said. There was a flatness to his voice that Ike had never heard. He realized Buddy Lee was fully prepared to die over that jackknife. The bodyguard must have realized it, too, because he pulled it out his pocket and tossed it to Ike. Ike in turn threw it on the seat.

"I'm keeping your gun," Buddy Lee said.

They both climbed in the truck. Buddy Lee fired it up and mashed the pedal to the floor. The security guard missed getting run over by a frog's hair.

TWENTY-NINE

Buddy Lee had hopped on the interstate and taken them out of Richmond. He took the first exit after they had cleared the city limits and pulled into a gas station. He'd barely shut off the truck when he opened the door and vomited. It looked like a child had spilled a can of red-and-green finger paint on the ground.

"I think that fella turned my liver sideways," he said when he was done. Ike wound down the window and checked his face in the side mirror. There was blood on his face. His chin was swelling like a puffer fish's. He touched the back of his head. The baton had reopened the wound the kid had given him with the chair.

"Yeah, they fucked us up pretty good," Ike said.

"Tried," Buddy Lee said.

"What?"

"I said they tried to fuck us up pretty good."

"You need to check the mirror," Ike said. Buddy Lee lay back against the bench seat.

"I'm not saying we didn't take no licks, but we still here, ain't we? A lot of people we used to run with are gone. Now, I ain't much on religion, but like you said: Everybody got a skill. A thing they put on earth for. Maybe this is why we still around. To finish this," Buddy Lee said lying back against the headrest.

Ike wasn't sure if he was hyping up himself or Ike. But he had to admit Buddy Lee had a point. They both went quiet as their bodies registered the pain that was sure to get worse as day gave way to night.

"That knife means a lot to you, doesn't it?" Ike asked, finally breaking the silence. Buddy Lee pulled the jackknife out of his pocket. He held it in front of his face and stared at it for a long time before he spoke.

"It belonged to my daddy," Buddy Lee said. He didn't offer any other explanation than those five words. Ike didn't need one. The knife had belonged to Buddy Lee's father. That explained it all.

Ike changed the subject.

"He knows where she is. He wouldn't have gone through all this if he didn't," he said. Buddy Lee wheezed, coughed, then spit out his window.

"Yeah, but he ain't likely to tell us now. You think we could take him when he leaves his house? Get him out in the boonies and make him tell?" Buddy Lee said. Ike used a crumpled napkin to wipe the blood from his knuckles.

"I know a guy might be able to help us get to him again," Ike said.

"Well, shit, I wish you had said that before I got my ribs rearranged," Buddy Lee said.

"We didn't part on the best of terms. It's a long story but he owes me. I think it's about time I collect."

"You wanna go now?" Buddy Lee asked.

"Ain't no time like the present," Ike said.

"Can you drive? I think if I hiccup too hard I'm gonna pass out," Buddy Lee said.

Ike got back on the interstate, then took the Chesterfield exit. Chesterfield County was a huge municipality that encompassed several small towns within its borders and enormous swaths of wilderness that remained essentially unchanged since before Captain John Smith had told his first lie about his adventures in the New World.

Ike drove along rolling back roads lined by ditches deep enough to dive in and do the backstroke. Finally, he came to a shopping center that sat in the middle of a field on a lonely spit of land near Route 360. A cornfield bordered the strip mall to the north, and several abandoned shipping containers and trailers to the south. Ike remembered when he first got out, there had been a fleet repair shop near the strip mall. The place had been a huge sheet-metal monstrosity that bore more than a passing resemblance to his shop. Now even the bones of that building were gone. Scattered to the four winds or the nearest salvage yard.

Ike pulled into the parking lot of the strip mall and parked the truck.

"Stay in here," Ike said.

"Shit, you ain't gotta tell me twice," Buddy Lee said. He reached into the cup holder and retrieved his knife. He held it out toward Ike.

"What I'm supposed to do with that?"

"Stick people with the sharp end."

"I ain't gonna need that," Ike said.

"Look, you said there was a long story to this shit. In my experience that usually means shit didn't end all copacetic. You don't need to go walking in there naked. So it's either this or the gun," Buddy Lee said. Ike's eyes settled on the knife. Maybe he should take it. How long had it been since he'd talked to Lance? Ten years? A lot of things can change in that time. People forget their debts. Their loyalties change and shift like smoke. The knife would be protection. The gun would be an act of aggression.

Ike grabbed the knife and put it in his front pocket.

"I'll be right back," Ike said.

"Ain't like I was gonna run a marathon. Just don't lose it," Buddy Lee said. Ike gave him a look.

"You ain't gotta worry about that," Ike said,

Ike heard the robotic ding of a doorbell as he entered the barbershop. There were five chairs with five different men and boys of various ages in them. The shop smelled of cleaning chemicals, machine oil, and air fresheners that reminded him of cheap cologne. The far-left wall was a bank of mirrors. The far-right wall had posters of Michael Jordan dunking, Mike Tyson boxing, and a chart of various hairstyles along with the prices for said hairstyles. A fifty-inch flat screen dominated the rest of the wall. The Wizards were playing the Celtics as subtitles crawled across the bottom. A slice of late-nineties R&B was raining down from a couple of speakers in the ceiling.

"Be with you in a minute, chief," said one of the barbers, an older man with white sideburns but coal-black hair on top. The cacophony of buzzing coming from the various trimmers sounded like lazy hornets flying around the clients' heads.

"I'm looking for Slice. He here?" Ike asked. The older man stopped and gave Ike a long once-over.

"Who's asking?" the older barber asked. Ike hesitated.

"Riot. Riot Randolph," he said.

The clippers in the old barber's hand started to tremble. He snuck a glance toward the back of the building. A pair of blue velvet curtains hung over an opening there.

"Hang on," the old man said. He flicked a button on the side of the clippers and sat them on the shelf behind him. A cell phone appeared in his hand. Ike watched as the man's thumbs flew over the screen. Seconds ticked by and then the older man looked up at Ike.

"Take a seat," he said.

"You gonna finish or you want me to come back?" the older barber's client asked. The rest of the guys in the shop burst out laughing.

"Slow your roll, young buck, or my Parkinson's might kick in," the older barber said.

"You ain't got no Parkinson's, Maurice," the client said.

"But that's what I'll tell people when they ask why I chopped your head up, though. I'm just a confused old man," Maurice said, adding comical withered intonation to his voice at the end of his statement. Another burst of laughter filled the shop. Ike sat in the last chair in a row of chairs bolted to the floor and to each other. Ike felt a hair tickle his throat. He coughed and grimaced. The muscles in his chest felt like they were wound tight as a fishing reel. Every breath made him wince. The pain in his body was getting close to matching the pain in his soul.

"Look at this shit. Man, I don't know why they got this stuff on the TV," a large man in the third chair getting his beard dyed said. He pointed at the flat screen, bringing his hand from under the smock covering his upper body. Ike followed the man's finger and saw a commercial for a show about a drag-show competition.

"You know why it's on. White folks love seeing Black men in dresses. It's a whole thing about feminizing us, making us weak," the barber dyeing his beard said.

"It's a C-O-N-spiracy, huh, Tyrone?" a young light-skinned brother working on a client's lineup said.

"Oh, you don't think they want our 'women'—quote, unquote— independent and our men weak and gay? That's how they keep us in line. It ain't paranoia if it's true, Lavell," Tyrone said. Lavell laughed.

"Now you sound like one of them super-woke brothers on You-Tube in the kufu hat," Lavell said.

"Look, I don't care if they gay and shit, but why they gotta be all over the place with it? They getting out of pocket with that shit," the man getting his beard dyed said.

"How they rubbing it in your face, Craig? They breaking in your house and putting lipstick on you in your sleep?" Lavell asked with a chuckle.

"You know you sounding real suspect, Lavell. You got some spar-kly high heels under your bed?" Craig asked.

"Yeah, they yo momma's," Lavell said. Maurice brayed at that remark.

"For real, though, them boys up there, they the result of the government splitting up Black families. Made welfare more attainable than living on one income. Made women think they didn't need no king in they life. That's how you get niggas in wigs and makeup prancing around like goddamn Tinkerbells," Craig said.

"I don't think that's how it works, man," Lavell said. Craig snorted.

"Let my boys come home talking about that gay shit. They gone be living in a cardboard box down by the river. Nah, bump that, I'm a beat that shit out of them. Any man let his son grow up gay, he done failed. It's like Chris Rock say, your only job is to keep your daughter off the pole and keep a dick out your son's mouth," Craig pontificated.

"I've watched a bunch of his HBO specials, and he ain't never say that last part. And why you thinking about a dick in your son's mouth? You need therapy, Craig," Lavell said.

"Forget you, Lavell, that's why I get Tyrone to cut my hair," Craig said. One more round of laughter filled the shop as the conversation moved on to the Wizards' chances or lack thereof against the Celtics.

Ike gripped the sides of his chair. A dull ache worked its way up from his hands to his forearms. He realized the chairs in the barbershop were similar to the chairs he'd seen in the police station. Ike used to like coming to the barbershop, before he started losing his hair and took to shaving his own head. The agile banter, the casual camaraderie, the give-and-take of friendly insults and jabs—it was all a part of the character and culture of the barbershop. Many times he thought of it as the last place you didn't have to apologize for being a Black man.

This conversation showed him that there was another side to the barbershop. A side he'd always known was there but had dismissed. It could be a place of circular logic, where obtuse thinking was confirmed and reinforced by a pervasive groupthink. Yeah, you had some brothers like Lavell going against the tide, but for the most part everybody got in fucking line. Did they really think boys were gay because you weren't a good father? He might not have been there for Isiah the way he wanted to, but even he knew that didn't make his son gay. He didn't pretend to understand Isiah's life, but he understood that much.

Six months ago, you would've been laughing right along with them, though. Before they put a bullet in Isiah's head. Before they killed your boy, Isiah thought.

"You alright, chief?" Maurice asked. He eyed Ike warily.

"What?" Ike said.

"You breaking my armrest there, chief," Maurice said. Ike released the armrests and saw he had nearly pulled the hard-molded plastic off the iron frame. A brother with a clean-shaven head the size of a basketball leaned through the curtains. His skin was the color of obsidian.

"Come on back," he said. It sounded like bricks in a washing machine. Ike got up and went through the curtains. He entered a storeroom set up to be an office, and a luxurious one at that. A large ornate wooden desk with a leather-bound chair under it. The floor covered in deep-pile brown carpet. A glass-top coffee table sat in front of a plush leather recliner. A tray with three half-gallon bottles of gin, bourbon, and rum sat on the right side of the recliner. In the recliner was a trim Black man in a pair of black dress pants and a gray T-shirt under a silk black button-up long-sleeved shirt. Tightly coiled dreadlocks fell down to the middle of his back.

The clean-shaven man stepped in front of Ike.

"You carrying?" he said.

"Just a knife in my pocket for work," Ike said. The clean-shaven man patted Ike down with hands the size of car batteries. He pulled the knife out of his pocket.

"Get it back when you leave," the man said. He went to the corner of the office and leaned against the wall.

I've heard that before, Ike thought.

"Been a long time, Ike. Thought you didn't go by Riot no more,"

Slice said. He spoke with a soft lisp and a hint of southeastern Virginia rolling around in the back of his throat. When Ike had gone inside Slice was a skinny seventeen-year-old kid taking over the North River Boys for his brother Luther. Now he was Lancelot Walsh aka Slice aka the Man in the Cap City. After Luther got hit they'd all retreated back to Red Hill. Slice had been in a bad place. The whole crew had been in a bad place. Romello Sykes and the Rolling 80s had killed Luther in retaliation for a scrap they'd gotten into at a house party in the middle of no-fucking-where. It wasn't even business. Just some personal dick-swinging bullshit. The North River Boys had gone running back home to Red Hill with their collective tails between their legs. Romello had snatched off their masks and revealed them to be the wannabe gangsters they really were.

Ike, no, Riot couldn't let that shit go. Fuck Romello and fuck the Rolling 80s. He hadn't been a wannabe. He'd found Romello. He'd dealt with Romello. Then the state of Virginia had dealt with him. They were the ones who put him in prison, but Ike had been the one who'd taken away his wife's husband and his son's father.

"I needed to get your attention. How you been, Slice?" Ike asked. Slice bore down on him with his coal-black eyes like chips of hematite. He was drinking dark brown rum out of a cut-crystal glass.

"What you doing here, Ike? I thought you won't 'bout this life no more? Last I heard you was cutting rich people's grass, giving the La Raza a run for they money," Slice said.

"I was. I mean I am. I need a favor."

"What kind of favor could somebody like you want from somebody like me? You want me to take care of whoever beat yo ass? Oh yeah, you done got walloped, bruh," Slice said. Ike set his jaw and pushed his tongue into his cheek.

"I need a meet with a homeboy I think is one of your clients. I need it today," Ike said. Slice smiled. It was like watching an icicle form.

"What you know about my business, Ike?" Slice said.

"I know you run shit from Cap City to Red Hill and up to DC. I know you move weight and guns up the Iron Corridor. I know you own Club Roja. Nice touch. You name it for Red Hill? And I think I know you can set this meetup because this motherfucker is the type that would either buy big weight or want to tag along with some real ballers. And you the realest baller I know," Ike said. Slice sipped his drink.

"You keeping tabs on me, Ike?" he asked. The question itself was fairly innocuous, but the subtext was as menacing as a tiger sitting in your back seat. Ike had known dangerous men all of his life. There were several John Does buried in a pauper's grave that would say Ike was a dangerous man. They radiated a dark energy that was fueled by the fusion of determination, will, and the not-so-subtle ability to not give a fuck. Slice was one of the most dangerous men Ike knew. He'd earned his nickname from his penchant for slicing off fingers and tongues. Not those of his enemies, but those of his enemy's brothers and sisters, wives and children.

"Not like that, Slice. I just be hearing stuff. I'm out the game, but the game don't want to leave me alone," Ike said. Ike could feel a mad tension in the room wash over him and swallow him whole. Slice stared at him over the edge of his cup. Craig had spoken about kings. Ike didn't want to be a king. A king never sleeps. He ends up like Slice. Staring at everyone and anticipating how they might try to come for his crown.

"And who is the motherfucker you want to meet?" Slice said. He drew the word "motherfucker" out until it sounded like it had seven syllables.

Ike crossed his arms.

"Mr. Get Down," Ike said. Slice's eyes crinkled. He chortled.

"You want to talk to Tariq? My business partner? Oh yeah, I've got a piece of his catalog. He's an investor in a few of my clubs. I put some money in that Brown Island Jam he put on last year. That runt has fattened my pockets a lot over the years, and I gotta be honest with you, Ike, it don't seem like you wanna sit down and break bread with this nigga. I don't think I'm gonna be able to help you out, homie. I can't have you messing with my bag," Slice said.

Ike felt the spit dry up in his mouth. He'd been afraid of this. Time makes loyalty thin. People shed it like snakeskin.

"Oh, because he your business partner?"

"I know what you about to say," Slice said.

"I know you do. Cuz I was more than your business partner. I was your boy. I was Luther's boy. I've never asked you for nothing. Not even when I went inside. You the one told me you was gonna make sure I was straight in there. You the one told me I had nothing to worry about. You the one said Mya and Isiah wouldn't have to lift a finger. You said they was family. Then you sent her three hundred dollars. Once. I put in work and what did I get for it? Four niggas trying to punk me and a wife who had to work three jobs to take care of our son while I was on some old thug-life shit," Ike said. It dawned on him that he was yelling. The monster in the corner pushed off the wall but Slice held up his hand.

"Shit was complicated, Ike. Ain't none of us know Romello's cousin was hooked up with the East Coast Crips. We didn't know they was running things in Coldwater. You went inside and we was fighting for our lives out here. Shit got real fucking hectic. Did I fuck up with Mya and Isiah? Yeah, and that's on me. But let's be real. Ain't nobody put a gun to your head and made you go find Romello and beat him to death in the middle of the street. That's on you," Slice said.

Ike took a step forward.

"Yeah that's on me. I killed that motherfucker with my bare hands in front of his mama and his girl. I went to prison for seven years and left my family. I own that. But I did it for your brother. I did it for the North River Boys. I did it for you. I did it because nobody else would. I cared more about my clique than I did my woman and my son. I gotta own that, too. But I know if things had been the other way around and I had been the one to get my head blown off in a trick's bed that was running with the Rolling 80s, your brother would have done the same thing for me. That's what Luther was about. You saying things got complicated. But you won the war. You retired the Rolling 80s. Moved your mama and your whole crew out the trailer park and up into Carytown. When y'all was popping bottles and making it rain, I was shanking motherfuckers. When you was fucking strippers and video models, I was listening to that revolutionary bullshit from the Black God Coalition so I'd have somebody to watch my back. When you was drinking Cristal I was drinking toilet wine. I got out and I never came looking for you. I let it go that you had my wife wiping people's asses and had my son wearing hand-me-downs. I made a promise to them that I would not be the person I used to be. But now I'm here and I'm asking . . . nah, I'm telling you: you owe me. You owe my wife. I'd say you owe my son but he's dead. And you protecting the one person that might be able to help me find out who did it." Ike paused. "What you think Luther would say right now?"

Slice stood up and walked over to where Ike was standing. Ike towered over him but Slice didn't seem to notice. Ike dropped his hands to his sides and spread his feet. He made a mental note of where the monster in the room was standing in relation to him and Slice. He tensed his shoulders and waited for Slice to make a move.

"He might have been your friend but he was my brother. I know what you did for us. For him. But you ain't gonna stand there and rub it in my fucking face," Slice said.

"I'm not. I'm just stating the facts. I've never asked y'all for nothing. Ever. But this one thing . . . Lance, he knows where this girl is that knows who killed my boy. They shot him six times. Lit him and his friend up. Then they stood over them and put two right in they face. I couldn't even recognize my son. I didn't know who he was. My son, Lance," Ike said. Was he crying? He didn't know and he didn't care. He was tired of hiding how much it hurt to lose Isiah. If Slice and his behemoth wanted to call him a bitch, let them. Trying to hold all this agony and grief inside was like wrestling a bag of pythons. The grief was choking the life out of him.

Slice turned his gaze to the wall.

"You ain't planning on putting paws on Tariq are you?" he asked. Ike blinked his eyes hard.

"No. He knows this girl named Tangerine. I think she knows who killed Isiah and Derek," Ike said. He paused. He'd called Derek Isiah's friend. That was wrong. He was his husband. He was Isiah's husband. Ike tried to say it but his mouth just didn't seem to be able to form the words.

"Tangerine." Slice chuckled.

"You know her?" Ike asked.

"Nah, but with a name like that, I bet she wear clear heels," Slice said.

"I just want to talk to her. Tariq can make that happen," Ike said.

"Let me ask you this. If she tell you what you wanna know, then what?" Slice asked. He seemed genuinely curious.

"What you mean 'then what'?" Ike said.

"I just don't see you being 'bout it like that, Ike," Slice said. Ike stepped closer to Slice, crowding his personal space.

"Then you done forgot who the fuck I am," Ike said. Slice turned his gaze back to Ike and smiled.

"There he is. There's the one-man Riot," Slice said. He turned his back to Ike.

"Come back in an hour. I'll have Tariq here," Slice said.

"Thank you," Ike said.

Slice walked over to his recliner and sat down. "Don't thank me. We even now, Ike," he said. Ike picked up the implied threat. He turned to leave. Slice's man handed him back the knife.

"You know, I used to be jealous of you and Luther. He used to act like you was more his brother than I was. When you put that 187 on Romello, it made me hate you a little bit," Slice said.

"You never had to be jealous of me. Luther told me to always look out for you," Ike said. Slice laughed. It was a hollow sound.

"That made it even worse, Ike."

Ike went through the velvet curtains and headed for the front door of the barbershop. He was almost out the door when he stopped and walked over to the chair where Craig was sitting. Tyrone had finished dyeing Craig's beard, and now they were just shooting the shit about who was the best rapper alive.

"And don't say that white boy Eminem," Craig said.

"Man, you crazy. Em a beast," Tyrone said.

"He alright," Craig said.

"You need hearing aids," Tyrone said.

Ike went and stood in front of Craig. The other man scowled at him.

"Can I help you?" Craig said. Ike cocked his head to the side and looked down at him. He knew he should probably let it go but he couldn't. He wished someone had said to him what he was about to say to Craig.

"If I snuck in your house one night and slit your son's throat, I guarantee the last thing you would be worrying about was if he was gay or not," Ike said.

"The fuck you say to me?" Craig said.

"You heard me. You just don't wanna listen," Ike said. Craig started to rise out of his chair.

"You get up out that chair, they gonna be picking pieces of you out the walls for a week. Trust me, you don't want none of this," Ike said. Craig started to respond, but Ike gave him his back and walked out of the barbershop.

Buddy Lee sat up straight when Ike got in the truck. His head had finally stopped spinning.

"What's the word?" he asked. Ike pulled Buddy Lee's knife out of his pocket and handed it back to him. He started the truck and backed out of their parking spot.

"We gotta wait an hour. They gonna bring Tariq over here," Ike said.

"You think I got time to get a trim? Do they cut white-boy hair in there?" he asked. Ike ignored him.

"Hey, you alright?" Buddy Lee asked.

"Not even close," Ike said.

"Place around here we can get a drink while we wait?" Buddy Lee asked. He expected Ike to cut his eyes at him again, but the big man surprised him.

"Yeah, I could use one, too," Ike said.

THIRTY

They ended up at a squat cinder-block building that sat on the side of Beach Road near what was left of the old Swift Creek Bridge. A sign that sat on spindly metal legs with an exaggerated arrow pointing at the building let passersby know the Swift Creek Lounge was open for business. Even though it was just a little after two, the gravel parking lot was half full. Ike parked Buddy Lee's truck and the two of them walked up to the door.

"For a guy who said he ain't been out on the town in a decade, you sure had this place memorized," Buddy Lee said,

"Places like this never close. It was here before either one of us was born, and it'll be here long after we're gone," Ike said. The interior of the building was cast in blue-tinged shadows illuminated by the neon Coors sign hanging over the cash register. A quorum was posted up at the end of the chipped and scarred bar, loudly debating the merits of Mopar engines versus Hemis. An old jukebox sat near a pair of battered pool tables. A litany of down-home blues songs poured out of the jukebox one after another. A barroom DJ had programmed the Swift Creek Lounge soundtrack for the next hour or so. First up was "Born Under a Bad Sign" by Albert King.

Ike and Buddy Lee sat on a pair of stools near the door. Buddy Lee winced as he raised his hand to get the bartender's attention. A slim sister in a black tank top and jeans came on over and smiled at the two of them.

"What can I get ya fellas?"

"Two shots of Henny," Ike said.

"You got it, sugar," the bartender said. She slipped away to get their drinks.

"What's Henny? I mean I'm gonna drink it, but I'm just curious," Buddy Lee said.

"You ain't never heard of Hennessy?" Ike asked.

"I mean, I've heard of it, I just didn't know it had a nickname. I guess it's a . . ." Buddy Lee said. He stopped and studied the bottles behind the bar.

"It's what? A Black thing?" Ike asked. Buddy Lee sucked at his teeth.

"You know, I bet you thinking, *He keeps saying he ain't racist but he sure saying some racist shit,*" Buddy Lee said. The bartender dropped off their drinks. Ike grabbed his shot glass.

"I've learned to always be ready to be disappointed by white people. Doesn't always happen, but when it does, it don't shock me anymore. You ain't the worst I've had to deal with," Ike said. Buddy Lee ran his finger around the rim of his glass.

"I ain't trying make no excuses, but when you grow up around people—your aunts and uncles, your grandparents, your brothers and sisters, your friends—all of them saying things that you don't even think about being wrong or right, you don't put that title on yourself. Like you remember when they used to play *The Ten Commandants* on television every Easter? And there's this part where this boy tells his granddaddy to look at the Nubians? My granddaddy on my mama's side would always make this joke about them not being Nubians, they just, well, you know what he said. And I used to laugh at that joke because it was my granddaddy saying it. I never thought, I never had to think how somebody like you would feel about that joke. Then when I got older I stopped thinking about it, because if that joke was fucked up, then what did that say about my granddaddy? What did that say about me that I laughed at it?" Buddy Lee said.

Ike downed his shot. The cognac burned in a comforting, familiar way. For a moment he was twenty-one again.

"That you ignorant as hell," Ike said.

"Yeah, well, I guess that's a pretty good assessment," Buddy Lee said.

"It's easier to keep your head in the sand than it is to try and see things from somebody else's point of view. There's a reason why they say ignorance is bliss," Ike said.

"So you do think I'm racist," Buddy Lee said.

"I think maybe for the first time in your life you're seeing what the world looks like for people that don't look like you. I mean you still ignorant as hell, but you learning. But then, so am I. We both learning. We both done said and did shit that we wish we could take back. I think if you figure out at one point in your life you was a terrible person, you can start getting better. Start treating people better. Like as long as you wouldn't laugh at that joke now, I think you on the right road. Same as if the next time I get offered a drink I don't go the hell off and just walk away, instead of jacking somebody up because they had the nerve to think I was in a gay bar to meet somebody," Ike said. He held his shot glass up and motioned for the bartender.

Buddy Lee downed his shot, too. He gasped as he sat the glass down on the bar.

"Goddamn that shit will take the paint off a ball hitch. I guess you're right. Feels like we waited pretty late in the day to start learning shit," Buddy Lee said. The bartender brought them two more shots.

"Day ain't over yet," Ike said.

Ike drove them back to the barbershop. The parking lot was virtually deserted. There was a black Jaguar parked near the barbershop. The only other vehicle in the parking lot was Buddy Lee's truck. Ike shut off the truck.

"Look like everyone went home early," Buddy Lee said.

"Slice probably sent everybody home. Mr. Get Down is hometown royalty. Fools would be all up in his grill asking for autographs and shit," Ike said.

"He can shut down the whole strip mall?" Buddy Lee asked.

"He owns the strip mall," Ike said.

When they entered the barbershop Tariq was sitting in the last chair near the curtains. He had his hand in his lap like he was sitting for an old daguerreotype photo. His eyes were shining and bestial. Slice was sitting in a metal folding chair near the entrance to the adjoining restaurant. His bodyguard was standing behind Tariq as if he were about to give him a trim.

"You got fifteen minutes," Slice said. Ike took a step toward Tariq.

"You can't touch him. Ask your questions," Slice said. Ike stepped back. Buddy Lee scratched his chin.

"We know you know where Tangerine is. Like we said, we ain't trying to hurt her. We just need to talk to her," Buddy Lee said. Tariq's chest rose and fell in rapid succession.

"We can't touch you now. But you have to leave eventually," Ike said. Tariq flinched.

"I'm with Slice. You heard what he said," Tariq said. His previous formidability was gone. He sounded like a kid asserting his allegiance to the biggest bully on the playground. Ike nodded at Buddy Lee.

"His son is dead. Mine, too. Do you really think I give a fuck who you with? You tell us where Tangerine is and you never have to wonder if that noise outside your window is me coming for you with a pair of pliers and an ice pick," Ike said. Tariq considered his hands as if this were the first time he'd ever noticed them. If Slice was perturbed by the threat, he was keeping his feelings to himself as he scrolled through his phone.

"Look, we trying to help her. Because the people who killed our boys are still looking for her, and they ain't gonna stop. Wherever she went, it ain't fucking far enough," Buddy Lee said.

"I told her to just stay with me, but she said she didn't want to pull me into it. Said she was gonna go where no one would ever think to look for her. Go to where the ghosts are," Tariq said. The swagger of Mr. Get Down was all gone. All that was left behind was heartbreak.

"Where's that?" Buddy Lee asked. Tariq raised his head.

"She said the people chasing her were killers," Tariq said.

"So are we," Ike said. Tariq leaned his head back.

"Look, what happened this morning. I was trying to protect Tangy, ya know?" Tariq said.

"You tell us where she is and all is forgiven," Ike said. Buddy Lee snorted. Ike shot him a look. Buddy Lee shrugged. He was getting used to Ike's looks. Tariq slumped in the chair.

"She told me I talked a good game but I was just a shook one. That I was a social media gangster. And she was right. Mr. Get Down is just a nerd from Huguenot High School who learned how to work a drum machine and a keyboard. Y'all the real thing," Tariq said. Ike didn't respond.

"Cousin, you ain't got no idea. Now where this girl at?" Buddy Lee said. Tariq put his face in his hands.

"If you find her, take care of her, okay? Promise that."

"We got her," Ike said. Tariq nodded.

"She went home. Back to Adam's Road. Back to Bowling Green," Tariq said.

"What's her real name? I know Tangerine ain't on her driver's license," Buddy Lee said.

"I don't know. All I ever knew was Tangerine," Tariq said. His face shuddered like he had bitten into a lemon.

"You lying. You know her name. You done come this far; don't hold back now," Buddy Lee said.

"Pliers and ice picks," Ike said. Tariq's eyes went from bestial to haunted.

"Uh . . . I . . . shit. Her name really is Tangerine. Tangerine Fredrickson. Are we cool now?" Tariq pleaded. Ike rolled his shoulders. They were still sore.

"We good," Ike said.

"If it was up to me I'd feed you your hand until you shit fingers, but I guess we good," Buddy Lee said. Ike shook his head.

"Let's go," Ike said. They turned and headed for the door.

"We even now. Remember that. All debts are paid," Slice said. Ike stopped and glanced over his shoulder. Slice was still scrolling through his phone.

"Sure," Ike said.

"Bowling Green is about an hour away if we take 301," Buddy Lee said once they had gotten back in the truck.

"Yeah. You think he was telling the truth?" Ike said.

"I kinda believe he was. He got one of the worst tells I ever seen in my life. I hope he don't play poker. Besides, he scared shitless of your friend. He ain't lying," Buddy Lee said.

Ike started the truck. "He ain't my friend, and he should be terrified of him."

"See, that wasn't so bad. Riot must have put the fear of God in you the way you was going on," Slice said.

"Those guys, they not gonna hurt her, are they? They not gonna hurt me, either, right? I mean we partners. They know that," Tariq asked. Slice raised his head from his phone.

"Devonte, take this baby back to its crib." Devonte grabbed Tariq by the arm and half carried him, half dragged him out of the barbershop. Slice touched the home screen on his phone. His call was answered on the second ring.

"You calling to pick up them MAC-10s?" Grayson asked.

"My mans told you they too hot right now. Can't move those things nowhere," Slice said.

"Then to what do I owe the pleasure?" Grayson said. Slice waited a beat before answering.

"Remember about a month ago when you was sweating everybody and they mama about a girl named Tangerine?" Slice said. Grayson breathed deeply but didn't speak.

"Oh, I got your attention now, Sons of Anarchy?" Slice said.

"You got my interest. You tell me something I can use, you'll get my attention," Grayson said. Slice laughed.

"First, let's lay down what this piece of information is worth," Slice said.

"How much blood I gotta lose to get this info?" Grayson asked.

"Not enough for you to miss it. I'm looking to diversify one of my revenue streams," Slice said.

"Aw, shit," Grayson said.

"What's that about?" Slice asked.

"Nothing, you just sound like somebody I know. Get to the point," Grayson said.

"You got a connect to a good cooker for ice. I want to get me a meet with him. I may be willing to take a few kilos off his hands," Slice said.

"I hope to God you on a burner," Grayson said.

"I have a phone for every day of the week. Now, can you set it up?" Slice asked.

"I can, but I can't make no promises. That boy twitchy," Grayson said.

"I can handle twitchy. A bag full of hundreds can do wonders for your anxiety."

"Alright. What you got?"

"Damn, you rush your lady like this? Shit," Slice said.

"You got something or not, man?" Grayson said.

"Yeah, I got something for you. I heard from a little birdie that she staying out near a place called Adam's Road in Bowling Green. If you leave right now, you might beat the two dudes looking for her," Slice said.

"Two dudes? Was one of them a big-ass hoss of a Black dude?" Grayson said.

"Yeah, you know him?"

"Me and him got unfinished business. Adam's Road, right?" Grayson said.

"Yeah. Let's make that meet happen next week," Slice said.

"Yeah, I gotcha on that. Hey, the Black, he a friend of yours? Cuz he gonna get that work," Grayson said.

Slice let a few seconds tick by. "Nah. Do what you gotta do."

THIRTY-ONE

Ike pulled out of the parking lot and headed for the old Route 207 that would take them to the Powhite Parkway that cut through Richmond, then to 301.

Buddy Lee lay his head against the window as they rode through the rolling hills of Route 301. Acres of lush farmland that were dotted with miles of white fencing interrupted here and there by homes older than Ike and Buddy Lee combined. Where the land hadn't been claimed for grazing or growing, dogwoods competed with pine trees and maples for the attentions of their mutual lover, the sun.

Buddy Lee flicked on the radio, and Merle Haggard's rumbling baritone came warbling through the speakers singing "Mama Tried."

"Mama tried but Daddy didn't give a damn," Buddy Lee said.

"I thought you said your daddy taught you all that travelers' shit. Tells and all that," Ike said. Buddy Lee closed his eyes.

"He did. He was also a nasty drunk who like to smack my mama around if the macaroni and cheese was too dry. He came and went so often he was like a friend who looked you up when he was in town. He had a bunch of outside children. Chet is one of them. So was Deak. I got a half Indian sister in Mattaponi. Shit, I always said I wasn't gonna be like him if I had kids. Well, I kept that promise. I was worse," Buddy Lee said.

"My mama and daddy died when I was nine. Hit a slick patch

on Route17 and went flying off the side of the Coleman Bridge. Me and my sister moved in with my daddy's parents. I put my grandparents through hell, and all they ever did was try and love me. I was so angry. I used to walk around waiting for an excuse to go off. Angry at God for taking my parents, angry at my parents for dying, angry at my grandparents for trying to pretend everything was gonna be alright. I was so messed up. Fell in with Luther and his crew. He let me use all that anger. Pointed me at a target like a gun and let me go off," Ike said. He passed a truck pulling a horse trailer.

"I love Isiah, I really do, but there are days I think I shouldn't have had a son. I was too messed up in the head to be a good father," Ike said.

"I think if you loved him and did the best you could, you was a good daddy. That's what I tell myself anyway," Buddy Lee said.

"You really believe that?" Ike asked.

"Most days I do."

"I got so mad when he came out," Ike said. He eased the truck through a sharp curve that took them past a couple of horses lazily grazing in an expansive pasture.

"You didn't know before? I caught Derek kissing another boy, but I knew way before that," Buddy Lee said.

"I knew. I think deep down inside I always knew but I didn't want to accept it. I couldn't accept it. I couldn't wrap my mind around it, ya know? Like what did that mean? It was like he'd told me he was an alien. Shit just seemed unnatural to me," Ike said.

"But you still loved him. You never stopped loving him, right?" Buddy Lee asked. Seconds went by before Ike answered.

"I tried to stop loving him. For a while I couldn't even look at him. All I could see was him doing shit with some guy. I'm sorry. Derek wasn't some guy."

"Nah, it's okay. I mean, I get what you saying, but I never wanted to stop loving Derek. I just wanted him to be normal. I guess it took me a long time to get it."

"Get what?"

"Get that what's normal ain't up to me. That it don't fucking matter who he wanted to wake up next to as long as he was waking up," Buddy Lee said. Ike drummed his fingers against the steering wheel.

"I went up for manslaughter. My homie got taken out, so I went and found the boy who gave the go-ahead and I beat him to death in his mama's backyard. Stomped that boy right into the ground. I thought I was standing up for my crew. But they didn't stand up for me. I got inside and found out I was on my fucking own. So when four brothers tried to jump me and make me their cell-block bitch, I had to get on with a new crew," Ike said. He flexed his hand.

"I did some foul-ass shit to get this tat. But I needed the backup. The boy I killed was hooked up with the East Side Crips. That's why I joined the Black Gods. I was scared. A lot of what I did back then was because I was scared. But all those things I had to do fucked me up in the head," Ike said.

"I saw things inside, too. I get what you saying. In there you can't be soft or they knock out your front teeth and make you put your hair in pigtails and sell you for a box of smokes. But everything about prison is all the way fucked up, man. People ain't supposed to live like that," Buddy Lee said.

"I never could shake it, ya know? It's like it made me look at everything through convict eyes. He came out the day he and Derek graduated from college. We had a cookout at the house. Had a lot of people over there. My sister Sylvia was there with her husband. People from work. I was at the grill burning it up, ya know? And he brought Derek over. I remember he took his hand. And I pretended like I didn't see it, and Isiah starts saying 'Dad, I have to tell you something,' and I just keep flipping them goddamn burgers because I know what he is gonna say and I don't want to hear, and he says 'Dad, Derek isn't just my friend. He's my boyfriend. Dad, I'm gay. I'm gay and I love him,'" Ike said. He took a deep breath.

"I fucking lost it. I went crazy. I flipped the grill over. Food and charcoal went everywhere. A piece of charcoal landed on Isiah's arm, burned him pretty bad. I said . . . I said some terrible shit. To him and Derek. Mya was crying and yelling at me. People was staring at me like I was an animal. I was mad as hell. Embarrassed. I went inside and slammed the door so hard the glass broke," Ike said.

"And all I kept thinking was why did he have to tell me? Why that day? Why couldn't he have kept that to himself? I didn't need to know that shit, right? I kept making it all about me. Took me years to understand he told me because even though we didn't get along, he wanted me to know he was happy. He wanted to share that with me, and I fucked it up. I let him down," Ike said. The lump in his throat felt like he had swallowed a brick. Buddy Lee cleared his throat.

"Neither one of us was Howard Cunningham. And still the boys made something of themselves. They were good to their friends, good to each other, good to that little girl. Even with daddies like us they grew up to be good men. No matter how many times we let them down, they came out alright," Buddy Lee said.

Ike shook his head. "We gonna find Tangerine. We gonna find who did this. We're done letting them down."

Forty-five minutes later they passed a large black wooden sign with bright-green letters that spelled out BOWLING GREEN. The truck began to lose, then gain, power. Ike put the pedal to the floor. The engine whined like a newborn.

"We need some gas," Buddy Lee said. Ike saw a gas station with two pumps up ahead on the right. He pulled in and rolled up to the pump just as the engine died.

"The gas hand says you have a quarter tank left," Ike said.

"What can I tell ya? Shit don't work like it used to. That goes for the truck and the owner," Buddy Lee said. He got out and stretched his arms to the sky. His back snapped, crackled, and popped like a bowl of Rice Krispies.

"I'll get the gas if you pump it. I need a beer," Buddy Lee said.

"Hey, get me one, too," Ike said. Buddy Lee raised his eyebrow. "Been a long day."

Buddy Lee limped across the parking lot and entered the store. He grabbed a Busch tallboy can for himself and got Ike a Budweiser. He sat the beer on the counter.

"Let me get, uh, twenty-five on pump seven," Buddy Lee said. The clerk, an older white woman with a mop of unruly gray hair, bagged his beer and rang up the gas.

"$29.48," she said. Buddy Lee figured she must have been smoking since she was a fetus. He handed her two twenties.

"You from around here?" Buddy Lee asked.

"Been here thirteen years. Moved down from DC with my ex-husband. He was a horseman. Worked on the farm where Secretariat was born," she said.

"No shit?" Buddy Lee said.

"Yeah, he was better with horses than he was with marriage," the clerk said.

"Say, you don't know a girl name of Tangerine Fredrickson do you?" Buddy Lee asked. The clerk curled her lips like she had bitten into an apple and seen half a worm.

"You a friend?" she said.

"Nah, it's kind of a funny story. I found her purse with her license and stuff in it, but I'm not from around here and for the life me I can't find this address. You know whereabouts she lives? Maybe give me a landmark or something? Her ID says Adam's Road but my GPS acting like it got Tourette's," Buddy Lee said with a smile. The clerk didn't smile back.

"Lunette Fredrickson lives out near the water tower on Adam's Road. The sign got shot down last year and the county ain't replaced it yet."

"Lunette, huh? She related to Tangerine, I guess?" Buddy Lee asked.

"Yeah," the clerk said. The sour expression on her face deepened.

"Okay, well, thank you," Buddy Lee said. He took his change and headed for the door. He snuck a glance at the clerk on his way out.

You better hope the wind don't change or your face is gonna stay like that, Buddy Lee thought. He walked out to the truck. Cars and trucks zipped by on the two-lane highway that ran past the gas station. Ike was already pumping the gas. Buddy Lee got in and put Ike's beer in the drink holder before cracking open his own.

"Thanks," Ike said. He grabbed the beer and killed most of it in one gulp.

"I think we should be looking for a road next to the water tower. Adam's Road," Buddy Lee said.

"How you know that?" Ike asked.

"I had a talk with the clerk inside. She gave some info on a Lunette Fredrickson, who is related to Tangerine."

"Now what? We go down Adam's Road and stop at every house and ask them if they know Tangerine?" Ike asked.

"You got a better idea?" Buddy Lee said. Ike shrugged.

"You the one that knocks. This is MAGA country," Ike said.

In the end it only took two houses. At the first house no one answered. At the second one, a trailer with a wooden ramp, a young white guy with a Confederate-flag tattoo on his chest directed them to the last house on Adam's Road. They drove past a sign that alerted them they were approaching the end of state maintenance. On the left side of the road was a mailbox at the beginning of a long dirt lane. The name FREDRICKSON was written on the mailbox in small stick-on letters.

"This is it, I guess," Ike said. Buddy Lee bit at his thumbnail.

"You know, you was right."

"About what?" Ike said.

"I don't think those people would have talked to you the way they did to me," Buddy Lee said. The Confederate-flag tattoo unfurled in his mind.

"I guess you woke now," Ike said. Buddy Lee saw him smirk out the corner of his eye. He turned down the lane and navigated the potholes that dotted the road like they were driving over a slice of Swiss cheese. Buddy Lee peered out the window as they passed the magnolia trees that lined the driveway. The craggy road ended in a barren front yard and a ramshackle two-story house with a decaying porch that wrapped around most of the first floor. An expansive meadow overgrown with kudzu and honeysuckle that seemed to go on for acres made up the backyard. A four-door sedan with four different-colored doors sat near the bottom step of the porch. Ike pulled up next to the sedan on the passenger side near the far right side of the porch and killed the engine.

"Here we are," Ike said.

"How you wanna play this?" Buddy Lee asked.

"Play it straight. Tell her what's up. Ask who was the guy and if he knew about Isiah and Derek," Ike said.

"How hard are we leaning on her?" Buddy Lee asked.

"She's a woman. I'm not leaning on her at all. You ain't, either," Ike said.

"Okay, but if she stonewalls us, I got some girl cousins we can call," Buddy Lee said. He grabbed the gun and tucked it in his waistband near the small of his back.

"I don't think we gonna need that," Ike said.

"Better to have it and not need it than need it and not have it," Buddy Lee said.

They climbed out of the truck and made their way to the front door of the house. They both stopped after a couple of steps.

A young woman had stepped out onto the porch. Midnight-black hair fell down to the small of her back. Her skin was nearly the color of burnished bronze. Under any other circumstances Buddy Lee would have found her ravishing. Her big brown doe eyes peeked out at them under flowing lashes.

The shotgun she was pointing at them cast a shadow that dimmed her loveliness.

"Yeah, she's a defenseless damsel in goddamn distress," Buddy Lee said.

THIRTY-TWO

"Hey easy now, sis, we just wanna talk," Buddy Lee said.

"Whatever you selling we ain't buying. Whatever you wanna talk about we ain't listening," the woman said.

"Are you Tangerine?" Ike asked. She swung the barrel of the shotgun in his direction. Ike noticed she had the stock cradled in the crook of her arm and was holding the pump with the opposite hand. But her finger wasn't in the trigger guard. Ike studied her. The tremble of her full lips. The wild rapid movement of her eyes. They darted side to side like weasels trapped in a cage. She was scared. She was nervous. She was gorgeous. She was a lot of things, but a killer wasn't one of them. He knew what a killer looked like. He saw one in the mirror every day.

"Who I am doesn't matter, papi. Now you and discount Sam Elliott get back in your truck and get out of here," Tangerine said.

"That's the second time I've been compared to that ol' boy in a less-than-flattering way. I think my feelings starting to get hurt," Buddy Lee said.

"Oh gee, I'm sorry. Maybe you should leave and seek therapy," Tangerine said.

"Isiah was kind to you. Derek wanted to help you. Isiah was my son. Derek was his. They died because of what you told them. Our sons are dead because of you. The least you can do is talk to us," Ike said.

Tangerine flinched. Ike thought she was batting her eyelashes at him until he saw the dark lines of mascara start to trickle down her cheeks. Ike was sick to death of tears. His own, Mya's. Isiah was the star in their universe. When he had died that star had collapsed in on itself creating a black hole. That black hole swallowed every ounce of joy they had ever felt. All because this girl on the porch had a secret lover who was willing to kill to stay a secret. She hadn't pulled the trigger but she was damn sure involved. Let her weep until she cried blood.

"I didn't mean for any of that to happen," Tangerine said. The streaks on her face gave her a Lone Ranger mask.

"Then put down the seed-sower and talk to us, girl," Buddy Lee said. Tangerine bit her bottom lip. Ike watched the barrel of the shotgun lower in minute increments. The wind stirred, engulfing them in the scent of magnolias.

"Come on inside," Tangerine said.

"I'll feel better when that scattergun ain't in her hands," Buddy Lee whispered.

"If she was gonna shoot us she would have done it already," Ike said.

"Oh well, that's good," Buddy Lee said.

They stepped up on the porch and entered the house. The scent of whiskey permeated the foyer and the front room. A saggy sofa sat in the middle of the front room. Grainy images flickered across an ancient floor-model television that sat near the couch at an angle. A dining table stuck halfway out of a kitchen and into the living room. Tangerine placed the shotgun on the table.

"Terry, who is that?"

A tall white woman came from the back of the house. She was wearing a floral print housedress and flip-flops. Her doughy face was partially hidden by lank blond curls that spilled to her chin.

"Tangerine, Ma. My name is Tangerine, and it's nobody. Go lay down," Tangerine said. Ma acknowledged Ike but her eyes lingered on Buddy Lee.

"No, no, we have guests. Invite your friends in. I'll make some drinks," Ma said.

"You must be Lunette. I like the way you think," Buddy Lee said. He gave her a wink. Lunette giggled.

"Ma, they ain't gonna be here that long," Tangerine said.

"Well, they can at least stay for one drink," Lunette said. With the matter settled, she turned and headed back into the rear of the house. Buddy Lee heard her moving around in the kitchen. He could see that the hallway had a cut-through that led to the kitchen.

"Sit," Tangerine said. Ike and Buddy Lee went into the front room. In addition to the sofa there was a recliner and an ottoman. Ike and Buddy Lee sat on the sofa and Tangerine sat in the chair. Ike took in the rest of the room. There was a woodstove in the far corner. Framed pictures were scattered over the weathered walls at haphazard intervals. Ike saw a younger version of Lunette and a diminutive brown-skinned man in some of them. In others there was an older Lunette, with a few more miles on her face and a bright-eyed little boy with a mixture of her and the brown-skinned brother's features. As the people in the photos aged, the distance between them increased. The brown-skinned brother was conspicuous by his absence in most of the later pictures.

"I told Isiah I had changed my mind. I didn't want to do the interview anymore. So how do you know what happened to them has anything to do with me?" Tangerine said.

"Because the people at my boy's job heard him say the fella you was fucking was a two-faced son of a bitch. Then him and his husband end up dead with their brains all over the sidewalk," Buddy Lee said. Tangerine flinched at the vitriol in Buddy Lee's words.

"I told them it was dangerous. I told them, but Derek was mad and Isiah was determined. They didn't understand what they were dealing with at all. That's not my fault. If you think I wanted them to die you can take me up on my first offer and get the fuck out of here," Tangerine said. Ike jumped into the fray.

"Look, all we want from you is the name of the guy you were seeing. Who is he? We'll take care of the rest," he said.

"I'm not telling you that. I shouldn't have told Derek and Isiah. I should have just let it go when he broke things off. His life is complicated. I knew that when I met him. Look, I was drunk and I was venting at the party. I was all up in my feelings. That was a mistake," Tangerine said.

"Telling Derek about your boyfriend?" Ike said.

"Yeah. That too," Tangerine said. Ike could see the resemblance to her mother, but she had more in common with the boy in the pictures.

"If you don't want to tell us, tell the cops," Buddy Lee said. Ike turned and faced him. He couldn't have been more shocked if Buddy Lee had grown a second head on his shoulder.

"I want to find the people who did this and I don't care how it gets done. If you don't want to tell us, tell the fucking cops," Buddy Lee said.

"I'm sorry but I can't be a part of this," Tangerine said.

"A part of this? You are *this*. It's all about you. You killed my son and his . . . husband, but all you care about is saving your own ass," Ike said.

"Listen, babyboy, I don't know if you noticed, but the only person who cares about my ass is me. Don't come in here laying your bag at my feet. You hollering about how much you care about your dead gay sons because you treated them like shit when they were alive," Tangerine said. She pushed a lock of hair out of her face. Ike shot up off the couch. His fists were clenched tight.

"You don't know shit about me and my son," Ike said.

"Oh, I don't? I bet you tell people how much you loved him, but you only loved parts of him. Not all of him. Not everything. Now you want me to risk my life to make you feel better about yourselves. That ain't my job, booboo," Tangerine said. Ike took a step toward her. She looked up at him and smiled.

"I know you. I've always known men like you. You strut around like Billy Badass, but you lie to people about your son and his 'room-mate,'" Tangerine said as she made the sign for air quotes. Ike felt his fists unfurl. The accuracy of her statement made his head hurt. It was like she had been peeping in his window for the last ten years.

"We know we ain't shit. You ain't gotta tell us. We do enough of that to ourselves every day. But that don't mean our boys should rot in the ground while your boyfriend gets to skip all across God's green earth because you're too chickenshit to come forward. I know you know he's looking for you. He got some badass biker boys try-ing to hunt you down. He wants them to take the top of your head off. Now if we found you, how long you think it's gonna take before they do, too? You come with us and you tell the cops, they can pro-tect you," Buddy Lee said.

"No, they can't. Everything that's going on, it's not him. He's tied into a situation that he can't control. The people he answers to are the ones behind this. Rich-ass wannabe movers and shakers who control everyone and everything in their orbit. He's as much a vic-tim in all this as—"

"If you say Isiah and Derek, we are going to have a fucking prob-lem," Ike said. Tangerine licked her lips.

"He once told me they wanted him to be a lion and a lion doesn't feel guilty for eating a sheep. They've abused him all his life and they don't care how broken he is. You have no idea what kind of shit you're dealing with," Tangerine said. Her hazel eyes seemed to glow.

"You don't really believe that horseshit, do you? He is trying to kill your ass and mount it on his wall," Buddy Lee said.

"I'm telling you, you don't know him. You don't know what he's going through. This is way bigger than you think," Tangerine said.

"He killed my son. I know all I need to know except his name," Ike said.

"Drinks! I hope you like Cuba libres," Lunette said. She had four glasses on a plastic tray. She sat the tray on the ottoman and started handing out the rum-and-coke concoctions.

"Thank you, ma'am," Buddy Lee said.

"My name's Lunette, not ma'am. You can call me Sugar if you want, though." She winked at Buddy Lee, who killed his drink in two gulps. Ike held his in an iron grip as he focused on Tangerine. Tangerine took a sip. This time she did bat her eyes at him.

"You thinking about hitting me, aren't you? That your kink?" she asked.

"No. I'm thinking I wish my son hadn't tried to help you, but that was the kind of man he was. He would help anybody. Even someone who didn't give a damn about him," Ike said.

"Trying to guilt me ain't a good look, babyboy," Tangerine said. Ike thought she meant for it to sound hard, but it came out flat.

"I'm not trying to guilt you. I'm stating facts."

Tangerine opened her mouth to respond, but then the sound of a car door slamming came from the front yard. Ike stood. The skin on the back of his neck prickled like a ghost was tickling him. He locked eyes with Buddy Lee.

"I haven't had these many guests since before your daddy left," Lunette said. She sashayed toward the door. The ice cubes in her glass clinked like castanets.

"Ma, what are you doing? I told you we gotta be careful," Tangerine said. She popped up and grabbed Lunette by the arm.

"I'm gonna see who it is," she slurred. Ike wondered how much rum she'd put in her drink. He sat his glass down on the ottoman.

"Wait. Let me take a look," Ike said. He went to the window on the left side of the doorjamb. Peering through the filthy pane of glass he saw a blue minivan. It had parked on the other side of the sedan to the far left of their truck. It was accompanied by three motorcycles. The motorcycles had parked in the gap between the van and the sedan.

Six men were walking toward the house. They all had on baseball caps pulled low and they were all holding guns.

"Get down!" Ike yelled. Lunette broke free from Tangerine's grasp and walked toward Buddy Lee.

"What is he talking about, handsome?" she asked with a smile as she swirled her drink.

Gunfire erupted from outside. The interior of the house became a hellscape of shattered glass, wood splinters, and fragmented Sheetrock. Lunette's body did a shuddering box step as bullets tore through her chest and belly. Her floral housedress was drenched in blood, turning the daisies on it to roses. Tangerine launched herself at her mother even as Buddy Lee reached out for her and tried to pull her down. Ike was on his stomach and pulling himself along the floor. Lunette's body folded in on itself and crumpled. Her glass slipped from her hand and rolled along the uneven wood floor.

Footsteps pounded on the porch as Ike reached the dining room table. The front door burst open from one swift kick. just as Ike reached up and grabbed the stock of the shotgun. He pumped a round and aimed at the man in the doorway.

Cheddar paused. He hadn't expected to be staring down the barrel of a 12-gauge. Ike aimed at the general area of his head and pulled the trigger. Half of Cheddar's face evaporated in a red mist of flesh, bone, and brain matter. His baseball cap flew off what was left of his head and fluttered to the floor as his body fell half in, half out the front door. Ike pumped the shotgun again, expelling the spent shell and sliding another one in the chamber. The second man on the porch jumped sideways as Ike aimed at his chest. Ike pulled the trigger and the shotgun roared again even as the third scurried back to the van. The buckshot caught Gremlin where his thigh became a part of his abdomen, blasting him off the porch. When he hit the ground, his large and small intestines began to unspool like a ribbon of saltwater taffy soaked in merlot.

Ike pumped the shotgun again. The spent shell was expelled again but this time it wasn't replaced.

"Buddy, shoot!" Ike yelled.

Buddy Lee popped his head up over the back of the sofa where he had landed with Tangerine under him. He pulled the gun from his waistband and took aim at the four men who were moving toward the house in a crouch. He was a terrible shot. He thought he winged one while the other three ran for cover.

Ike scurried across to the dead man in the doorway and grabbed the gun in his hand. It was a submachine gun. Either a MAC-10 or Uzi, he wasn't sure. Ike aimed at the van and the sedan and unloaded.

"Fuck, fuck, fuck!" Grayson screamed as bullets pinged off the sedan. Chunks of metal and fiberglass sprayed his face and eyes. He screamed again and this time it was a wordless howl of unmitigated fury. He leaned the machine gun around the front bumper and fired blind. Dome took a position next to Grayson.

"My gun jammed!" he howled. Grayson ignored him.

"Oh God. Oh God, my guts. My fucking guts!" Gremlin moaned.

Ike leaned back in the doorway as another burst from the third man's gun ripped through the air. Ike returned fire until he heard the dry click of an empty magazine. Moving on pure instinct he reached in the dead man's pockets and found another clip. It had been years since he'd handled a gun, but his hands didn't seem to notice. They popped out the clip and replaced it with ferocious alacrity. He fired off a quick burst just as Grayson peeped around the front bumper of the sedan.

"Go for the truck!" Ike shouted. He tossed Buddy Lee the keys. Buddy Lee snatched the keys out of the air with his free hand. He dragged a howling and crying Tangerine through the kitchen and out the back door. Ike fired off another burst at the sedan.

"Fuck this!" Grayson spat out. He stood up and leaned across the hood of the sedan. He swept the barrel back and forth across the porch laying down a line of fire that plucked at the house like the claws of a demon. The expelled shells danced across the hood and rolled off the edge onto the ground.

Ike scooted under the window, stood, and fired out of the fractured lower pane. Grayson disappeared behind the trunk of the sedan. Ike kept firing in the general vicinity of the sedan, the van, and the bikes until he heard the engine of Buddy Lee's truck fire up and roar like a tornado.

Grayson replaced his clip, moved to the rear of the van, and fired at the house again. He didn't hear the truck start up, but saw it back up, then spin around so that the back window was facing him. He aimed at the truck and fired. The back window shattered, but then he received a rain of bullets from the house that forced him to hit the deck.

One of his other brothers, Gage, was crawling toward him holding his thigh. He didn't see the last member of their hit squad, Kelso. He and Gremlin and Cheddar had ridden their bikes. Dome, Gage, and Kelso had taken the van. He'd figured six Rare Breed with guns was more than enough for a nigger, a shitkicker, and a slut.

He was getting real sick of being wrong.

Buddy Lee pulled Tangerine down as he floored the truck. Shards rained over the nape of his neck and down his back.

"Shit, goddammit!" Buddy Lee said as he wheeled the truck in a wide arc, then backed up to the front of the house at an angle. He heard a scream like a horse being gelded as he ran over the legs of the man in the yard, crushing them beneath the weight of his Chevy.

Ike came running out of the house firing the machine gun as he leapt in the truck bed. Buddy Lee hit the gas as Ike fired at the two men who had scuttled behind the blue minivan. Buddy Lee slammed into the sedan, sending it crashing into the first two bikes. The conservation of momentum sent the second bike plowing into the third. Buddy Lee kept the hammer down, turned left, and headed down the lane.

Ike let off one last blast from the submachine gun, spraying the rear of the van. The glass in the rear door exploded along with the rear driver's side tire. Grayson and Dome had kept moving around the van as the truck shot by like a cannonball until they ended up crouched down like a pair of turtles near the front bumper.

Grayson jumped up in time to see the truck turn left and take off down the highway. Grayson wiped his eyes with the back of his hand. Sweat, blood, and bits of metal stuck to the hairs on his forearm. His ears rang with a high-pitched metallic whine. Dome rose and stood beside Grayson. Kelso crawled from under the sedan.

Grayson stopped staring down the lane and took in the scene swirling around him. Three of his brothers were down. Cheddar was dead. Gremlin was right on his heels. Gage was bleeding out all over the red clay that covered the yard.

"Dome, they got me in my leg, Dome. I'm bleeding a lot. God it hurts, I'm bleeding a lot, Dome," Gage rasped.

"My guts, man. I can see my guts," Gremlin said. His words were so light the wind nearly snatched them away. Dome and Grayson walked over to their mortally injured brother. Most of the lower half of his stomach was gone or slipping through his hands like a greased eel. He was lying in a pool of blood and shit large enough to soak in like a hot tub.

His legs looked like breadsticks made by a blind baker. If Gremlin made it, which judging by all the blood he was currently swimming in was highly unlikely, he'd probably have to use one of those shit bags for the rest of his life. He'd never ride again. Grayson knew he wouldn't want to live that way.

"We can't leave him like this," Grayson said. He pointed his gun at Gremlin's face. Dome turned his face to the setting sun. The shrill treble of a chorus of crickets filled the air.

"See you on the other side, brother," Grayson said.

He fired a volley of bullets into Gremlin's face. The staccato burst sounded like someone had dropped a thousand nails on a metal desk. Grayson put the machine gun on the ground near Gremlin's body. He went over to the demolished bikes. He tried to pick up his bike, but the ape hangers were bent in all the wrong places. The gas tank was leaking. One of the cams had a huge dent. A huge gash zigzagged across the leather seat. The front wheel was caved in on itself. It was a like a child's first attempt at writing a capital "D."

Grayson laid the bike back down.

"Alright, then," Grayson said. He knew in his gut that Andy was dead. The idea that two old bastards who should be sitting on the couch draining tallboys had gotten the drop on a prospect was far-fetched but not impossible. As he took in the carnage laid out before him, he realized he'd made two mistakes.

He'd taken these men lightly, and he'd been holding back. The first mistake was his fault. He would never forget nor forgive himself. The second mistake belonged to a rich boy who had never gotten dirty or bloody or been in a fight. Yeah, he'd paid them, but that didn't even matter anymore. This had become more than business a long time ago. Now it was more than personal. It was about honor. If he couldn't handle these two, then he didn't deserve to be the president. He didn't deserve to wear the goddamn patch. Might as well take it off and throw it in the fucking trash.

This was crazy. All of it.

Cheddar dead.

Gremlin dead.

Gage probably bleeding out.

Not to mention what had happened at the Black's shop. Grayson rubbed his face.

His hand lingered on the scar that bisected his cheek. There was going to be no more holding back. No more half measures. All that was done.

"Dome, you got a spare in this thing?" Grayson asked.

"Yeah, I mean I think so. It's my wife's van; I don't drive it much," Dome said.

"What we gonna do with the bikes? We can't just leave them," Kelso said. Grayson pulled out his knife and went to each bike. He used the tip of the knife to unscrew the mounting bolts on the license plates. He pocketed all three license plates. The cops might check the VINs, but they could always report the bikes as stolen.

"You two get the cuts off of Cheddar and Gremlin. Then change the tire. Load up Gage so we can get the fuck out of here. We in the middle of bumfuck, but you never know what nosy-ass neighbor might have called Johnny Law. When we get back to the clubhouse I'm calling a war party. We gonna drop hell at this motherfucker's front door," Grayson said. Dome and Kelso fidgeted in place, shooting worried glances at each other.

Grayson went back over to Gremlin's body and picked up his gun. He glared at Dome and Kelso with such baleful intensity that he gave himself a headache.

"Did I fucking stutter?" Grayson asked.

THIRTY-THREE

"**P**ull over!" Ike hollered from the truck bed. Buddy Lee didn't seem to have heard him. The truck shimmied and shook as he flew down the single-lane blacktop. Ike could see the needle on the speedometer was ticking past ninety.

"Buddy Lee, pull over so I can get in!" Ike said, using the full force of his voice. He saw Buddy Lee's watery blue eyes in the rearview mirror. The whine of the engine eased and the truck coasted to the shoulder of the road. Ike hopped out and jumped in the cab. He'd barely shut the door before Buddy Lee took off, tires spinning and gravel shooting up into the air.

Ike felt something warm and moist against the small of his back. He leaned forward, and as he did, Tangerine slumped over into his lap. He grabbed her by her narrow shoulders and sat her up.

"Fuck," Ike whispered.

Tangerine's entire right side was bathed in red. A bullet hole the size of a dime in the crook of her elbow was vomiting blood at an alarming rate.

"What, somebody behind us?" Buddy Lee said. His eyes scanned the rearview and side mirrors. Ike took off his shirt and his belt. He wrapped the shirt around Tangerine's arm, then cinched it tight with his belt. A huge dark wet spot radiated out from Tangerine and stretched across the truck's bench seat.

"She's hit," Ike said.

"What? Fuck shit goddammit to hell! Is she dead?" Buddy Lee

asked. Ike put his finger against the side of her neck. He felt a pulse flickering like the frantic wings of a bumblebee.

"She ain't dead but she might be in shock," Ike said. He pulled his cell phone out of his pocket. He dialed Mya's number. His fingers left muddy splotches on the touch screen.

"What's your address?" Ike asked as the phone rang.

"Huh, what?" Buddy Lee said.

"We need to get her looked at and we can't go back to my house. They don't know where you live. What's your address?" Ike said.

"Oh, 2354 East End Road," Buddy Lee said.

Mya picked up on the fourth ring.

"Ike?"

"Meet us at 2354 East End Road. Bring your first-aid kit. We'll be there in thirty minutes," Ike said.

"Are you hurt?" Mya said. Ike winced. There was something broken in her that was just starting to heal. He heard it rip wide open with that question.

"Not me. Not Buddy Lee. But we need your help," Ike said.

"Alright," she said. She hung up before he could say any more.

"Shouldn't we take her to the hospital?" Buddy Lee asked.

"Doctors gotta report all gunshot wounds to the cops. There's three dead bodies back there. You wanna explain that to the police?" Ike asked.

"What if she dies, Ike? She's the only one who knows who this son of a bitch is," Buddy Lee said.

"Buddy, we could both get hemmed up for this shit," Ike said. Buddy Lee bit the corner of his bottom lip.

"But if she tells the cops—"

"Did you hear what she said? This guy sounds connected. He might have the cops in his back pocket," Ike said.

"Can't be all of them," Buddy Lee said. He took a sharp curve at sixty miles per hour, then kicked the truck back up to eighty. A groan escaped Tangerine's lips. Ike leaned her head back to make sure she could breathe.

"We can't win. . . . We can't," Tangerine whispered.

"Stay with me, girl!" Ike yelled. He put his arm around her and let her lay against his bare chest.

"Buddy Lee, listen to me. We go to a hospital we gonna have a lot of questions to answer," Ike said.

"You told me you was willing to do anything to get the people who killed the boys. Did you mean it? Because I did. If I gotta go back inside for this bastard to get caught, then I'm gonna be getting a new orange jumpsuit and some slippers. Now how about you?" Buddy Lee asked. Ike closed his eyes so tight he thought his eyelids might pop off his face.

"She said him and his people was rich, right? That means he gets rich-man justice. We'll be inside, the boys will still be dead, and he'll get a fancy lawyer to make everything go away. He'll probably still kill Tangerine for shit and giggles. Buddy Lee, we can't fix this if we doing twenty-five to life," Ike said. Buddy Lee took his eyes off the road for an instant and looked at Ike.

"Did we get that girl's mama killed, Ike? How did them peckerwoods find us? Did they follow us? Cuz if they did, they was mighty slick about it. Ain't like you can sneak up on a body if you on a Harley," Buddy Lee said. Tangerine mumbled again.

"No . . . win . . . we can't. . . ."

Ike smoothed down her hair. Her skin was clammy to the touch.

"The only person who knew where we were going was Slice," Ike said. That statement didn't need any more explanation. Buddy Lee struck the steering wheel with the palm of his hand.

"That cocksucker! But why? Didn't you say you took care of the boy that killed his brother? Why would he double-cross you like that?" Buddy Lee asked.

"I don't know. I think the thing about Luther might be a part of it. Deep down inside he's pissed at himself because he didn't handle it, and pissed at me because I did. Still don't explain how him and the Rare Breed know each other. I didn't think they ran in the same circles, but Slice has his fingers in a lot of pies, I guess. We gonna have to circle back to that another time, though," Ike said. Tangerine mumbled something else, but it was so insubstantial Ike couldn't catch it.

"We in over our head, ain't we, Ike," Buddy Lee said. It wasn't a question.

Ike smoothed Tangerine's hair again. "It don't matter. We gotta finish it."

They pulled up to the trailer so hard and fast Buddy Lee had to stand up on the brake. The truck slid across the gravel and came within five inches of Mya's car, which was parked a half a step away from Buddy Lee's front door. Ike was out and running to the house with Tangerine in his arms before Buddy Lee had shut off the engine. Mya hopped out of her car with a diaper bag over her shoulder and Arianna in her arms. Buddy Lee killed the engine and climbed out of the truck with his keys in his hand.

"Open the door for Ike, I'll get Little Bit," Buddy Lee said. Mya traded him Arianna for the keys and went to his door. As he walked back to his truck with Arianna, Buddy Lee heard a gentle *tap, tap, tap* sound. He squatted down to his haunches with the little girl in his arms. She giggled as he groaned. There was a thin but steady stream of oil leaking from the undercarriage.

I know I rode you hard, girl. Just hold out a little bit longer, Buddy Lee thought. He straightened and went to the rear of his truck. He used one hand to drop the tailgate. He sat down and balanced Arianna in his lap. She pawed at the scruff on his chin.

"I sure do need a shave, don't I? Grandpa looking like a werewolf," Buddy Lee said.

"Why don't me and you stay out here for a minute? You wanna sing a song? You know 'I Saw the Light'? Hank Senior used to sing that one. My mama loved that song. She sang to us once when she was trying to keep us occupied cuz our lights was off and my daddy had run off with the money for the bill. See, I can tell you all this because you ain't gonna remember it. Hell, you might not even re-member me," Buddy Lee said.

"Take her to the kitchen," Mya said. Ike swung a right and carried Tangerine into Buddy Lee's tiny kitchen. It was more like a kitch-enette. Buddy Lee had an old, yellow chrome-and-Formica table. Ike swept the few dishes onto the floor with Tangerine's feet and lay her prone form across the tabletop. Mya unloaded the diaper bag. Ike saw a bottle of alcohol, bandages, sutures, and rubber gloves.

"Go on outside. I'm gonna try to make this as sterile as possible."

"You sure?" Ike said.

"Isaac, you're just gonna get in the way," she said. Using his Christian name was Mya-speak for "I'm not asking."

Ike went outside and closed the door behind him. He saw Buddy Lee and Arianna singing on the tailgate. The little girl was giggling, and Buddy Lee made exaggerated faces as he sang a tune Ike didn't recognize. It sounded vaguely religious. Buddy Lee had a powerful, melodious voice that rose and fell in all the right places. Ike couldn't carry a tune even if it was in a bucket.

Ike didn't want to intrude so he sat on Buddy Lee's cinder-block steps. Barely a minute later Buddy Lee picked up Arianna and joined him on the step. He sat Arianna on the ground. She imme-diately picked up a rock and threw it into the air.

"She reminds me of Derek. He'd find a stick and play by himself until the cows came home," Buddy Lee said. Ike hugged himself, squeezing his own shoulders. Twilight was rapidly approaching and the temperature was dropping just as quickly.

"Isiah would make up stories about some elves that lived in a tree in the backyard. It was a whole saga with wars and marriages and shit," Ike said.

"You think she gonna make it? Tangerine, I mean," Buddy Lee said.

"She'll make it. Question is, will she tell us who the guy is?" Ike

said. Arianna plopped down on her butt and banged two rocks together.

"She really done convinced herself he loves her. Like she don't
believe he had nothing to do with all this," Buddy Lee said.

"You love a person enough and you'll make excuses for almost
anything. I saw guys on death row get requests for conjugal visits
from women on the outside," Ike said.

"Yeah, but them women crazy," Buddy Lee said.

"Love is a kind of crazy," Ike said. Buddy Lee toed the gravel
with the tip of his boot. He had no witty rejoinder in the chamber
for that one.

"Buddy Lee Jenkins, who the hell let you watch their child?"
Margo asked. Buddy Lee and Ike stood up as she came around the
corner of Buddy Lee's truck.

"First off, I'm an excellent babysitter. Second, this ain't just any
little child, this my granddaughter, Arianna," Buddy Lee said. He
scooped Arianna up off the ground.

"If you such a good babysitter, why you letting her sit on the
ground? Jesus H. Christ," Margo said.

"Little Bit, can you say hi to the mean lady?" Buddy Lee said.
Margo slapped him on the arm.

"Don't pay him no mind, cutie pie. Ain't you just about the prettiest little thing I've ever seen in my life," Margo said. She ruffled
Arianna's hair.

"And who is this here tall drink of water with a phobia against
shirts?" Margo said. Ike instinctively crossed his arms. Margo
smirked and winked at him.

"I'm Ike. I'm Arianna's uh . . . grandfather, too," Ike said. Margo
nodded.

"Well, nice to meet you, Ike. Piece of advice, don't let Buddy
Lee let your granddaughter sit on the naked ground. My son got
trichinosis like that. Well, I'm off to bingo. Y'all keep your eye on
this little beauty. She here when I get back I just might have to steal
her," Margo said.

"Alright, have fun," Buddy Lee said.

"I'd ask you to come with me but I'm afraid you'd be like your friend here and lose your shirt," Margo said. She disappeared around the corner of her trailer. A few seconds later they heard her Volkswagen Bug start up and take off out of the trailer court. Ike thought the Bug's engine sounded like an outboard motor.

"You and her friends?" Ike said. He raised his right eyebrow.

"She's my neighbor. She's a good woman. Not big on taking any shit," Buddy Lee said.

"She like you."

"What? No. We just neighbors," Buddy Lee said.

"You think what you want, but I bet if you had taken her up on her offer, you'd be playing bingo right about now," Ike said.

"Friends can go to bingo," Buddy Lee said. Ike noticed his ears were turning a soft shade of crimson.

"Did you like the lady, Little Bit? I'm a little afraid of her," Buddy Lee said. He bugged his eyes out and blew air between his lips. Arianna let out a high-pitched squeal.

Ike lowered his head and silently traced the fissures in the cinder blocks between his legs.

Look at what you're missing. What you missed with her daddy, a voice in his head whispered. The worst thing was he knew the reason why he wouldn't allow himself to get closer to her. For the first time since she had come to live with them, it made him ashamed. Ike wondered, *How many chances does a man get to make the right decision before fate decides he doesn't deserve another bite at the apple?*

Mya stuck her head out the door.

"We need to talk," she said. Ike and Buddy Lee and Arianna entered the trailer.

"She'll make it," Mya said. She was standing next to Buddy Lee's table. Tangerine was lying on her side with her back toward them.

"She lost a lot of blood, but that wound in her arm is an in and out. I can't be sure without an X-ray, but it doesn't look like it shattered any of her bones. She might have some nerve damage, though. She wasn't in shock. She just fainted. She going to need a place to rest, and somebody is going to have change that bandage and clean it. Now, do y'all wanna tell me who she is and how she got that hole in her arm?" Mya asked.

"She's the girl Isiah and Derek were trying to help. We think her boyfriend was in this shit that got the boys killed. We went to talk to her about going to the cops," Ike said. He thought, *Or telling us who her boyfriend was so we can cut his fucking head off.*

Buddy Lee picked up the explanation.

"Some boys found us and shot up her house. They shot her mama, too. We think they the same sons of bitches that killed the boys," Buddy Lee said. Mya put her hands to her mouth and closed her eyes.

"Did she tell you anything?" Mya mumbled from behind her clasped hands. Ike shook his head. Mya pulled her hands away from her face.

"This poor child. We have to get her someplace safe where she can heal," Mya said.

"I think I know somebody," Ike said.

"Are they . . . an ally?" Mya asked.

"A what?" Ike said.

"An ally. Isiah told me . . ." She paused. "Isiah told me that was what you called someone who was LGBTQ-friendly," Mya said.

"Let me guess, she secretly a lesbian?" Buddy Lee said. Mya looked over her shoulder at Tangerine's prone form.

"Wrong letter," Mya whispered. Ike frowned.

"What are you talking about, puddin?" Ike said. He hadn't used that term of endearment in so long it surprised him. By the way Mya's eyebrows arched, it surprised her, too. She rubbed her hands on her pants.

"Your friend is a transgender woman. Wherever you take her they need to be an ally. You don't need to take her to somebody that's gonna kick her out in the street if they find out," Mya said.

Ike sat down on the arm of Buddy Lee's sofa. Buddy Lee put Arianna down. She ran to Mya and grabbed her grandmother's leg.

"Wait, so she's a he?" Buddy Lee asked in a low tone.

"No. She is a she who has not had gender-reassignment surgery yet," Mya said. Buddy Lee sat next to Ike on the couch and dropped his head. He ran his hands through his hair.

"And I thought this day couldn't get any crazier," he said.

"You called her a she. But she still has a . . ." Ike said. He let the statement hang in the air.

"She is presenting as a woman. She seems to be living as a woman. So she is a woman," Mya said.

"They teach you all about that at the hospital?" Buddy Lee asked.

"Some of it, yeah. Most of it is just being respectful of people and accepting them for who they are," Mya said. Ike felt her gaze boring a hole in him like she was wielding an earth auger. No one spoke for a moment. Mya scooped up Arianna and let her lay her head on her shoulder.

"She pretty," Arianna said.

"Hmm?" Mya said.

"She pretty," Arianna said. Mya turned and saw Tangerine giving Arianna a weak wave. Arianna waved back.

"I guess we should go back to my sister's," Mya said.

"No. Not yet," Ike said.

"What you mean 'not yet'? You the one told us to leave," Mya said.

"Yeah, I know. Now I'm thinking I don't want you on the road alone. I'm gonna take Tangerine to a place she'll be safe. Y'all stay here and wait for me until I get back. Then I can drive you to your sister's and Buddy Lee can follow us," Ike said.

"Where you taking her?" Buddy Lee said.

"No place you need to know about. If you don't know, you can't tell," Ike said.

"I wouldn't tell, Ike," Buddy Lee said. He sounded affronted.

"I know you wouldn't want to, but if them boys catch you, they gonna push hard. This way you can't," Ike said. Buddy Lee went to scratch at his chin and stopped.

"That's why her friend so hot to put her in the ground," Buddy Lee said.

"It ain't just about him having a girlfriend who knows some shit about him. It's about who she is," Ike said.

"You think Tariq knows, too? That why he put his boys on us like that?" Buddy Lee said.

"Makes sense. Hardcore hip-hop producer don't want nobody to know he on the down-low," Ike said.

"I'm not gay," a weak voice said from the kitchen. Ike and Buddy Lee shared a look that was becoming their shorthand. Ike stood and went into the kitchen. Tangerine was sitting on the edge of the table. Mya had fashioned her a sling out of one of Buddy Lee's bedsheets. Her hair was stuck to her face. She had a beach towel with the words ATLANTIC CITY silk-screened on it wrapped around her like a toga.

"You're not?" Buddy Lee said.

"No, I'm not, Gomer Pyle," Tangerine said.

"I'm so confused," Buddy Lee said. He leaned back against the couch. Ike went and stood in front of Tangerine.

"We gotta get you somewhere safe," Ike said.

"I was somewhere safe. I was safe and my mama was alive," she said.

"They were gonna find you eventually," Ike said.

"You don't fucking know that," Tangerine said.

"Yes, I do. Because your boy, whoever he is, he don't want nobody to ever find out he was with somebody who was . . ." Ike stopped himself. He was still making bad decisions. Still saying the wrong things.

"Say it. I've heard it before. Somebody like me. Even my mama used to call me a fucking freak. She wouldn't call me Tangerine. Said she named me after my daddy. That was his name and I should be proud to have it, and now she's dead and she'll never be able to call me by my real name," Tangerine said. She began to weep. Great racking sobs that made Ike's chest hurt. He went to her, and before he knew what he was doing, he tried to put his arms around her. She pushed him away. Ike stepped back with his arms awkwardly open.

"Tell us his name, sis. Let us put an end to this thing," Buddy Lee said.

"You don't fucking get it. We loved each other. He's not in control of this. I'm not saying he's not involved, but he's not the one doing this," Tangerine said. Her cheeks glistened as her tears soaked her face.

"Tell us," Buddy Lee said as gently as could.

"He killed our sons. He sent people to kill you. They took your mama from you. Tell us, Tangerine," Ike said. He put his hand on her shoulder, but in his mind he was touching Isiah. She wasn't his son. But he felt like through her he could glean an inkling of the pain and misery and sense of unfairness that he could never experience, that people who lived under an umbrella made of a panoply of letters knew intimately. How many times had Isiah cried the way Tangerine was crying right now? Wept until he found the strength to live as he was meant to live. As a man who was so much more than who he slept with? Who had a father who refused to see him as anything more than a disappointment?

"You still love him, don't you?" Ike asked. Tangerine didn't answer his question.

"I just want this all to go away," she said.

"It ain't going nowhere, girl," Buddy Lee said, but Ike held up his hand.

"Let's get you some clothes. We gonna take you somewhere you can be safe, okay?" Ike said.

He let her go and gestured with his head for Buddy Lee and Mya to follow him. They all stepped back outside.

"You think you got a couple of spare shirts and a pair of pants me and her can borrow?" Ike asked. Buddy Lee nodded.

"I don't know about you, but my shirts should fit her. Jeans, too.

You gonna look like you wearing your baby brother's clothes if you put one of my shirts on," Buddy Lee said.

"I've got a couple of my T-shirts in the back seat," Mya said.

"That's good, puddin," Ike said.

"She gotta tell us Ike. Preferably sooner than later," Buddy Lee said in a hushed tone.

"Her mama got killed right in front of her. A dude she loves is trying to kill her. She can't tell us nothing right now. Let's get her someplace safe. Give her some time," Ike said.

"We need that name, Ike," Buddy Lee said.

"And she needs to come to terms with the fact a man she was in love with punched her mama's ticket," Ike said.

"Alright. You take her to a henhouse the foxes can't find. I'll stay here with Mya and Little Bit. But the clock is ticking. I ain't gotta tell you that," Buddy Lee said.

"These men that killed her mama, are they the same people that followed me the other day?" Mya asked. Ike sighed.

"Yeah."

"If you find this boyfriend, are you going to kill him?" Mya asked. Buddy Lee moved away from the three of them and inspected his undercarriage again.

"Yes," Ike said. Mya rocked side to side gently as Arianna played with her braids.

"Good. Here, hold her for a minute. I might have some sweatpants in the back seat, too," she said, handing Arianna to Ike. He swallowed hard and took her in his powerful hands. Arianna reached up and pulled on his chin.

"You couldn't have left her with Anna?" Ike asked. Mya stopped and leaned against the trunk.

"Anna's out. Nobody at the house but us. Couldn't leave her there alone. Trust me, I didn't want to bring her here for this," Mya said before she disappeared in the back seat. When she reappeared she had a shirt and a pair of yoga pants. As she walked past him Ike grabbed her hand.

"I'm sorry about all this. I'm sorry about everything," Ike said. Mya gripped his hand.

"Just get them," she said before going in the trailer. When she came back Tangerine was with her. She had on the shirt and the pants. Both appeared two sizes too big. Tangerine swayed softly but she didn't seem in danger of passing out again.

"Can I get that shirt?" Ike asked. Buddy Lee hitched up his jeans and headed into the trailer. They could hear the shuffling of doors and the slamming of dresser drawers. A few minutes later he came to the door and tossed Ike a flannel shirt.

"Belonged to my brother Deak. He stayed with me for a while a few years ago. He's about your size."

Ike slipped on the shirt. It was tight in the arms but it would do.

"I'll take the truck. Y'all sit tight and wait till I come back," Ike said.

"Ike, that truck is full of blood and the back window is blown out. And it's leaking oil like a racehorse pissing. She's my baby but I don't know how much longer she's for this world," Buddy Lee said.

"I don't want to leave y'all stranded without a car seat and with a truck that might seize up while you got Arianna with you, on the off chance you have to leave. And if you did have to leave, I don't want her riding around in the night air. Trying to be a good babysitter, like your friend said," Ike said.

"We ain't babysitting. We're her grandparents. You could take the car and take her with you," Mya said.

"She likes to stay with you. I think she is scared of me sometimes," Ike said.

"I think it's the other way around, but whatever. How long you gonna be?" Mya asked.

"Fifteen minutes each way," Ike said.

"Go on then. The quicker you leave the faster you'll be back," Mya said.

"Give me the heater and you keep the street sweeper," Buddy Lee said.

"No! No guns around my granddaughter," Mya said.

"Mya, we have people looking for us. Those people have guns," Ike said.

"That's why you need to get going and bring your ass back. We'll be here. Go," Mya said. Ike looked at Buddy Lee. Buddy Lee shrugged his shoulders. He was not stepping between a man and his wife. Better to step between a hungry wolf and a rabid dog.

"Mya, I'm leaving the gun with Buddy Lee. I trust him," Ike said. He went to the truck and grabbed the MAC-10. When he handed it to Buddy Lee they locked eyes. Buddy Lee nodded.

"This all we got. That .45 is empty. You pulled on that thing until it went click. Give me the keys," Ike said.

"There's a spare under the visor. I'll keep my regular ones so I can lock the door," Buddy Lee said.

"Let's go, Tangerine," Ike said. Ike got in the truck. Tangerine got in the passenger side.

"Bye, pretty lady!" Arianna said. Tangerine smiled and waved at Arianna.

"Bye, sugar button," she said.

"Hurry back now. Don't pick up no stray hookers or wooden nickels," Buddy Lee said.

"Watch your mouth," Mya said.

"Sorry, ma'am," Buddy Lee said.

"Thirty minutes," Ike said. He started the truck and backed out of Buddy Lee's truncated driveway.

As the taillights receded down the road, Buddy Lee, Mya, and Arianna went back inside the trailer.

Buddy Lee gripped the MAC-10 with one hand and locked the door with the other.

THIRTY-FOUR

Ike dialed Jazzy's number as he headed for the northern end of Red Hill County. She picked up after three rings.

"Hey, Ike, what's up?" Jazzy said.

"Jazz, I need a favor." Ike said. Jazzy must've picked up something in his tone because instead of "sure" or "no problem" she said:

"What is it?"

"I got a friend who needs a place to crash for a few days. She's been hurt and she got a bandage that she gonna need help changing. I know you was a CNA before you came on with us at the shop," Ike said. Ike thought he heard the line hum, but he knew that was his imagination. Cell phones didn't have landlines that could hum.

"Ike, I was a CNA for three weeks. Lord, I don't know. I gotta ask Marcus."

"I'll give you two extra weeks on your last check," Ike said.

"Two extra weeks? Really?"

"Really," Ike said. Jazzy sucked her teeth.

"That got to do with them biker boys from the other day?" Jazzy asked. Ike almost lied.

"Yes, but you'll be alright. No one knows where you live and no one is following me." Ike said. He was doing his best to make sure that wasn't a lie. He took the long way down back roads that made it hard for someone to hide a tail.

"I don't know, Ike," Jazzy said.

"Three weeks. Three extra weeks. Please, Jazzy. She needs help. If you don't want to do it for me, do it for Isiah," Ike said.

"Them biker boys got something to do with what happened to Zay?" Jazzy asked.

"Yeah. I'm pretty sure they did," Ike said. More silence. It floated between them, deep and oppressive. Finally Jazzy spoke again.

"Okay. Bring her over. How long you say she need to be here?"

"Just a couple days. Thank you, Jazzy," Ike said.

"I'm gonna have to buy Marcus two new PlayStation games with my check to keep him from running his mouth," Jazzy said.

"See you in a bit," Ike said. He hung up.

"You didn't tell her," Tangerine said.

"I don't think it's my place to tell her anything," Ike said.

"You sure my mama is dead?" Tangerine asked. The question almost made Ike run off the road. He chose his next words carefully.

"I don't know. Everything was happening so fast. But I don't think she made it," Ike said, his voice hoarse. Tangerine leaned her head on the window. Cool air filled the cab of the truck through the shattered rear window. Tangerine's hair danced and cavorted around her head like dark fairies.

"She only let me come home after I gave her half the money Tariq had fronted me. Twenty-five hundred dollars, and she still kept calling me by my dead name," Tangerine said.

"Did you tell her you was running for your life?" Ike asked.

"Yeah. That's why she didn't take all of it," Tangerine said.

"What's a dead name?" Ike asked. Tangerine drew her legs up under her thighs.

"The name I was born with, not the name I chose," Tangerine said.

"The pictures on the wall. Are they . . . ?"

"That was before. Before I found myself," Tangerine said.

"Oh. Okay," Ike said.

"My daddy was half Black, half Mexican. All man, like my mama used to say. He caught me wearing my mama's high heels one time.

He punched me in my chest so hard I spit blood for three days. He made me walk in high heels the rest of the weekend. Around and around our house until my feet bled. Bleeding from my mouth, bleeding from my feet. Hurting all over. That was when I really knew," Tangerine said.

"Knew what?" Ike asked.

"That they got it wrong when I was born. That I was always a girl. It was the people around me that wouldn't accept it. All that shit he did to me and all I could think about was one day I'd find some heels that fit. Soon as I could, I got out of Bowling Green and headed for Richmond. Got into doing makeup and hair for people. That's how I met Tariq. Did the makeup for a couple of his videos. We started hanging out and he started letting me tag along to parties. After a while the parties got fancier and fancier until one night we was at some ball for the city and I met Him there. Capital H. From the start it was different with Him. Like Tariq, he knew, but he never seemed like he could accept that he liked me. We'd do stuff, like not even sex stuff, just going out to the club, and then later he'd get high. Hurt himself, slap me around, then apologize. When I met Him, he went old-school and slipped me his number on a piece of paper. We got down a couple of times before I told him. I was so scared. You never know how a guy is gonna react. He didn't care. That was the thing he always said. 'I don't care about what's between your legs, just what's in your heart.'" Tangerine took a breath.

"I've been the fucktoy before. This felt different. It was different. Oh, shit, I don't know why I'm telling you all this. Maybe because I'll probably be dead in a week and it don't matter," Tangerine said.

"That's not gonna happen," Ike said.

"Oh, you don't think so?"

"No, I don't," Ike said.

"And why is that?"

"Because once you tell me who it is, I'm gonna kill him. I'm gonna take my time and I'm gonna make it hurt. And I think you know I'm telling the truth, and I think that's why you won't tell me. Because you keep telling yourself you still love him," Ike said. Tangerine didn't say a word. She squeezed herself into a tight ball and put her chin on her knees. The truck hit a bump and she winced as her arm bumped against the door. She put her good hand to her face and trembled all over.

"I keep trying to tell you, you don't understand. He cares about me. He can't be who he really is. His family won't let him. It's complicated. He's married. His family has this public persona that they'll do anything to protect. You could never understand this. No one judges you because of who you love," Tangerine said.

Ike gripped the steering wheel tight as a vise.

"I don't know how many times I have to say this to you. He had my boy killed. Buddy Lee's boy, too. He sent people to kill you and they killed your mama. That *is* who is he is. You think he loves you. I get that. But a man don't hide what he loves. And he sure as hell don't let a son of a bitch try to put her six feet under," he said. Tangerine dug around in the pocket of the yoga pants.

"You hid from loving Isiah," Tangerine said. Ike sucked at his teeth.

"I hid it from him. Not from anybody else. I gotta own that. I learning how to own it," Ike said.

Tangerine licked her lips.

"Here, look at this. Read this and tell me he doesn't care," she said as she scrolled through her phone. When she found what she was looking for, she handed Ike the phone. She had pulled up a text message. The number she had been texting was saved in her phone as "W." Ike flicked his eyes down at the phone as he scanned the black single-lane road that unspooled in front of him like an oil slick.

There is no one that understands me
The way you do. When we are together
I can be my full self. No masks. And yes
The sex is amazin

Ike handed her back her phone.

"Let me ask you a question. He talks real nice, but has he ever taken you anywhere besides a motel? Has he ever even taken you to the motel, or do you have to meet him there? Do you even have a picture together?" Ike asked.

Tangerine was quiet.

"That's what I thought. I ain't gonna pretend to know how hard this is for you, but you gotta know there is only one way this ends. It's either him or us. All us," Ike said. He turned down Crab Thicket Road. Jazzy's trailer was the last one on the left.

"Us? We're an 'us' now? You didn't want nothing to do with your own son, but now I'm supposed to believe I'm a part of the team?" Tangerine said. The words shot out of her mouth like shrapnel.

"You on the team because I can't let what happened to Isiah and Derek happen to anybody else. I ain't gonna lie and say I get you, because I don't. I can't even pretend I know what it must be like to be . . . you. But if all this has taught me one thing, it's that it ain't about me and what I get. It's about letting people be who they are. And being who you are shouldn't be a goddamn death sentence," Ike said.

"I think about Isiah and Derek a lot. If I had just kept my fucking mouth shut they would still be alive. Now my mama is dead, too. I can't do this anymore," Tangerine said as Ike passed a field full of hay bales being loaded on a flatbed truck. The sun was setting quick, and the men in the field were moving fast to beat old Sol before he vanished behind the horizon. The sky was full of ambers and magentas that ran together like melted wax.

Ike pulled into a long driveway covered in crushed oyster shells that was lined on both sides by a throng of blackberry thickets and wild daylilies, their orange petals standing out in sharp contrast to the verdant green leaves of the blackberry bushes. At the end of the driveway was a white double-wide with red shutters. Jazzy's car was the only one in the front yard. Ike pulled alongside it and cut the engine.

"I'm sorry," Ike said.

"Don't say that. Don't say that because you trying to butter me up," Tangerine said.

"No, I mean . . . I know you didn't mean for any of this to happen. But it did and now this is where we at. A man once told me we can't change the past but we can decide what happens next. That's where you at right now," Ike said. He got out of the truck.

"Come on. Let me introduce you to Jazzy."

"You sure she ain't gonna mind having me here?" Tangerine said. She was still in the truck.

"I'm thinking she'll be okay with it. She ain't a dinosaur like me. And her and Isiah were good friends in school. She knew he was . . . gay a long time before I did, and she never turned her back on him," Ike said.

"I told you, I'm not gay," Tangerine said.

"Jazzy is as close as we gonna get to an ally in Red Hill County," Ike said. Tangerine took her good hand away from her face. She used it to open the door. She followed Ike over the stepping stones to the front door of the double-wide.

Buddy Lee used the neck of the bottle of beer he was drinking to move the curtain of his living room window aside. The sun was dipping lower than a ballroom dancer. The tribe of country critters began to chant their nightly prayers. Frogs, crickets, and mockingbirds all sang songs of praise to their various gods.

A cough seized his chest like the pincers of a blue crab. Dots danced in front of his face as he tried to force the sputum and phlegm out of his rotting lungs. A strong hand slapped his back. Buddy Lee put his hand against his mouth and caught what his lungs had tried to hoard.

"Thank you. Got a bit of a bug in my throat," Buddy Lee said. He didn't want to wipe the blood and spit on his pants, but he also didn't want Mya to see it. Her smooth, impassive face appraised him with the cool detachment of a woman who had heard her share of death rattles.

"Cancer? Or emphysema?" she asked.

"Can I have a tissue?" Buddy Lee asked. Mya went to the kitchen and came back with a paper towel. Buddy Lee wiped his hand, then balled it up and put it his pocket.

"Just a bug in my throat," Buddy Lee said. Mya put her hands on her hips. She seemed ready to call him a liar. Instead she shook her head reproachfully and sat down on the couch with Arianna. Buddy Lee peered out the window again.

Come on, Ike, Buddy Lee thought.

Jazzy waved to Ike as he backed out of the driveway. They'd given Tangerine a sleeping pill and put her in the back bedroom. Tangerine had been nervous about Marcus coming home and kicking her out, but Jazzy had assured her it would be fine.

"Girl, as long as he got his *Call of Duty* and a bag of potato chips, he don't give a damn what's going on. He probably won't even notice you here," Jazzy had said. Once they had put Tangerine in the bed, Ike had questioned how confident she was in that assertion.

"I don't know. He can be weird. I guess them three extra weeks will make him feel better about it," Jazzy had said.

Ike shifted the truck from reverse to drive and took off down the road. He had the truck up to sixty miles per hour as he crested around a soft curve.

"SHIT!"

The word echoed in the cramped confines of the truck as Ike buried the brake pedal into the floor.

The flatbed that had been in the field was now in the middle of the road on its side. Hay stretched across the roadway from ditch to ditch like someone had just shaved a giant. Ike saw some men moving around the truck. A few were standing with their hands in their pockets and their heads bowed. That was the universal sign language for having fucked up in a royal way. Ike put the truck in park. He hopped out and walked over to one of the men with his hands in his pockets.

"Hey," Ike said. The man didn't acknowledge him.

"Hey, man, what's going on here?" Ike asked.

"What it look like, Cochise?" the man said.

"You gonna want to take some of that bass out of your voice, son," Ike said. The man, a young white guy with sandy-brown hair under a dirty trucker cap, gave Ike his full attention. He was taller than Ike by half a foot but he took a step back. His subconscious warned his body to protect itself.

"The truck driver overcorrected on the turn. He swear he wasn't on his phone, but we all know he lying," Trucker Cap said.

"How long we looking at?" Ike asked. Trucker Cap gave the question some thought.

"You looking at an hour at least, hoss. We gotta get the hay up and flip the truck over and probably get a tow," he said. As soon as the words were out of his mouth he took another step back. A dark cloud rolled over Ike's face like a thunderstorm coming in off the bay.

"Alright," Ike said. He pulled out his cell phone. Mya's phone went to voicemail. Ike cursed and dialed her again. It went straight to voicemail again. He called Buddy Lee. Straight to voicemail.

"Fuck," Ike said. Crab Thicket Road was a dead end, just like Townbridge Road. The ditches on each side of the road were too deep for him to drive through and go around the overturned truck and all the spilled hay.

He called Buddy Lee again.

"Answer the goddamn phone," Ike said. It went to voicemail again. Ike slapped the roof of the truck. He called Mya again.

It went to voicemail.

"Ain't much of a signal out here. We had to use the radio to call the wrecker," Trucker Cap said.

Ike slammed his fist against the hood.

He hit it again.

And again.

And again.

THIRTY-FIVE

Ten minutes.

It was only ten minutes after Ike and Tangerine left that Mya got the phone call. Buddy Lee had drunk the last of his beer and was making Arianna a grilled-cheese sandwich when Mya's phone began chirping.

"Is that Ike?" Buddy Lee asked. Mya pulled her phone out of her pocket and checked it.

"No, it's our neighbor. MaryAnne," Mya said. She put the phone to her ear.

"Hello?"

"Hey, Mya, it's Randy, MaryAnne's husband? Your house is on fire," Randy said.

"What?!" Mya screamed.

"Yeah, I already called the fire department but I wanted to let you know because—"

Mya hung up on him. She jumped up off the couch and picked up Arianna.

"Hey, what's wrong?" Buddy Lee said. He put Arianna's sandwich on a paper plate and brought it into his living room.

"The house is on fire. I gotta go," Mya said. She started for the door.

Buddy Lee dropped the plate on his ersatz coffee table and stepped in front of Mya.

"Hey, hold on now. What do you mean your house is on fire?"

"My neighbor's husband just told me our house is on fire. He's called the fire department but I gotta go!" Mya said. Buddy Lee put his hand on her shoulder.

"Mya, you can't go over there," Buddy Lee said.

"The fuck I can't," Mya said. She shrugged off his hand.

"Listen to me. This is bait in a trap and you about to be the rabbit that takes it," Buddy Lee said.

"Buddy Lee, I ain't got time to stand here and trade Uncle Remus proverbs with you. My house is on fire. I have to go. Now get out of my way."

"Mya. Stop and think. There are some boys out there who want to see me and Ike's head on a stick. We took off with a girl they trying to fill full of lead like she a storage locker for bullets. These boys know where Ike lives. Now, I ain't a smart man, but even I can see the odds of your house catching fire the same day we had a run in with these boys. Sis, them odds on the south side of zero," Buddy Lee said.

"His baby shoes are there. A lock of his hair from his first haircut is there. There's a poem he wrote me in second grade. You don't understand. It's all I got left of him. I can't lose him all over again. I can't," Mya said. Her face was twisted into a half frown, half snarl that was moments away from becoming a vale of tears.

"Sis, I don't think there's nobody within a hundred miles that understands like I do. But if your house is on fire right now, ain't nothing gonna be left by the time you get there," Buddy Lee said.

"I'm sorry. I didn't mean it like that. But I gotta try," Mya said.

Buddy Lee rubbed his face, then put his hands on his hips.

"Alright, let's go. But call Ike and let him know we're leaving," Buddy Lee said.

"I'll call him on the way," Mya said.

They'd tried to call Ike three times. Two times it went straight to voicemail. The last time it didn't even get that far. Buddy Lee knew there were parts of Red Hill that had spotty service. Then there were parts where you'd be better off sending a message by Pony Express than trying to make a phone call. That knowledge didn't help calm his nerves. Splitting up had felt like a mistake. He *knew* going to the house was a mistake. But Mya didn't give him much choice. He couldn't make her stay, and there was no way he was going to let her go alone.

He didn't have many mementos of Derek. The only one he really had was the picture in his wallet, and he couldn't imagine how'd he react if that suddenly went up in flames. When the people you love are gone, it's the things they've touched that keep them alive in your mind. A picture, a shirt, a poem, a pair of baby shoes. They become anchors that help you keep their memory from drifting away.

Mya turned onto Route 34 doing thirty-five. The first left would be Townbridge Road. The sky was full of stars that twinkled like cast-aside diamonds. Buddy Lee felt his stomach fall to his knees.

Mya turned onto Townbridge.

"Wait," Buddy Lee said.

"What?" Mya said.

"Where's the smoke? Where's the flames? Where's the god-blessed fire department?" he said. Mya eased her foot off the gas and stopped the car.

"Oh no," Mya said.

The chrome spokes on the wheels of the fifteen motorcycles idling in front of her house shimmered in the glare of her headlights. The engines sounded like a pack of wolves snarling just before they set out for the hunt.

"Back up," Buddy Lee said.

Mya didn't move.

"BACK UP!" Buddy Lee screamed. Arianna began to cry. Mya put the car in reverse and hit the gas. The four cylinders under her hood sounded like a rusty hinge. Buddy Lee grabbed the machine gun from between his legs. He clicked off the safety and lay the gun in his lap.

"I did what you said. You can let me go now, right?" Randy said. He was in front of his house on his knees. Grayson had the barrel of a .357 pressed against the nape of his neck.

"Yeah, but you're a fucking rat. Who does that shit to their neighbor?" Grayson said. He cracked Randy on the back of the head with the butt of his gun. He watched as the chick put the car in reverse and started backing up.

"LIGHT IT UP!" he roared. A few brothers set fire to the rags that draped the necks of the glass bottles they were holding. They tossed them through the windows of Ike and Mya's house. The rest of the brothers took off after the small maroon sedan.

Mya ran off the road, took out a mailbox, then corrected herself and got back on the gravel. The headlights of the motorcycles advanced on them like a swarm of fireflies. Mya rocketed past the stop sign at the end of the road, slammed on the brakes, and put the car in drive.

Buddy Lee saw a new set of lights bearing down on them from the driver's side.

"Fucking hell!" he said, just before Dome crashed into them with a late-model royal-blue Bronco like a wrecking ball. The car flipped over once, then twice before resting on its side, where it balanced precariously for a moment until gravity claimed what was hers and it ended up upside down on the roof. The bikes surrounded the car like a crowd watching a busker.

Buddy Lee's mouth was full of blood. The bitter coppery taste was making him gag. He coughed and tried to spit. The blood splattered across his face. A few of his back teeth felt untethered from their sockets. His body was a live wire of agony. Pain sparked up and down every nerve, every synapse. He spit again, and this time a couple of his blocky back teeth came flying out and landed on the headliner.

Where was the gun? Where was it? Shit. He had to move. If he could get out of the car he could get their attention. They'd come after him and leave Mya and Arianna alone. He had to move. He was upside down but he had to move. Buddy Lee wasn't much on seat belts but Mya had insisted he wear one when they had gotten in the car. It might have saved his life, but now it was a noose slowly strangling him as he hung upside down like a butchered buck. He reached for the clasp. His fingers felt confused. He tried to unlatch the seat belt but his digits didn't want to cooperate.

He heard the sound of heavy footsteps on gravel, then the screech of metal against metal as the passenger door was forced open.

Grayson dropped down to his haunches.

"You must be the other daddy. Y'all like Ebony and Ivory," Grayson said.

"I could've been . . . your . . . daddy but the line was too long," Buddy Lee said.

Grayson smiled. He held his .357 by the barrel and smashed Buddy Lee in the side of the face. Buddy Lee felt something in his cheek give way. Pain coursed through his whole head like a runaway train. Grayson put the business end of the gun against Buddy Lee's stomach.

"Where's Tangerine?"

"I don't fucking know. Ike took her away from here. You ain't never gonna find her," Buddy Lee said.

Grayson moved the barrel from Buddy Lee's stomach to his mouth. He pushed it down his throat until the trigger guard was nearly touching his nose.

"Tell me where she is and I won't shoot this half-breed in the back seat that's crying her fucking head off," Grayson said.

Buddy Lee started flailing his arms and squirming against his seat belt.

"You keep your fucking hands off her! You fucking cocksuckers leave that girl alone." It came out like a garbled gibberish, but Grayson knew what he was trying to say.

"She mean something to you, huh? Who is she? Is she the Black's daughter? Wait . . . don't tell me. The two pansies had a baby. How the fuck does anybody let them have a kid? Jesus, what is this world coming to?" Grayson said. Grayson took the gun out of Buddy Lee's mouth.

"Tell me where Tangerine is or I start using her for target practice."

"I don't know! He took her and he didn't tell us where he was going. She's just a baby. Leave her the fuck alone. You wanna kill somebody, kill me. Come on, do it, shit for brains. DO IT!" Buddy Lee screamed. Grayson stood.

"Dome. Get that brat out of the car. See if that bitch has a cell phone, too," Grayson said.

He dropped back down to eye level with Buddy Lee.

"I think you're telling the truth. That would've been smart, him not letting you know, and he strikes me as one of the smart ones. And don't worry, I'm gonna give you what you want. It gonna be sooner rather than later. I'd do it right now but you're lucky. I need you to deliver a message, and it looks like this bitch done broke her neck," Grayson said.

"No, Nanny! Ganpa!" Arianna cried. Buddy Lee heard the door screech as Dome pried it open. Then there was the clink of buckles being unlatched. That sound broke him in places he thought were already shattered.

"Alright. We are gonna take this mongrel with us. Maybe that'll motivate you to find Tangerine," Grayson said.

"Arianna ain't got nothing to do with this. Let her go. LET HER GO!" Buddy Lee howled.

Grayson laughed.

"This is Arianna? So, that's who he was calling out for. I'm fig-uring the white one was yours, right? Yeah, right before I shot him in the face he said her name. I wondered why he'd be calling out for a girl. I thought it was his mama. Lots of people call for their mama," Grayson said. The blood from the wound on his cheek was dripping into Buddy Lee's eyes. He blinked hard as he strained his neck to look up at the big blond biker.

"You will. Before me and you is done I promise you, you will," Buddy Lee said.

"Bring us the girl, Ivory. We'll be in touch," Grayson said. Buddy Lee watched as his boots walked away from the car. A few seconds later he heard the bikes tearing their way down the road, the thun-derous rumble of their engines becoming faint echoes at they dis-appeared into the night.

THIRTY-SIX

ke stormed past the receptionist at the emergency department desk and pushed through the heavy vinyl doors.

"Sir, you can't just go back there!" she said as he did exactly that. Ike went straight to the nurse's station. A young Latinx woman in light-blue scrubs got up and came from behind the desk as he approached.

"Ike, she's in surgery," the woman said.

"Surgery for what, Silvia?" Ike asked.

"She has a ruptured spleen, a perforated intestine, a punctured lung, and there was a fracture in her skull," Silvia said. Ike swayed on his feet. He put his hand on the desk and let his head hang low.

"Ike, Dr. Prithak is one of the best thoracic surgeons in the entire state. Mya's one of us. She's been here for ten years. She's like everybody's mom. We got her, Ike. Believe me. Just go back out to the waiting room, and I'll come get you when she's out," Sylvia said. Ike's heart was beating so hard his ears were ringing.

"What about Arianna? Where's Arianna? Where's Buddy Lee?" Ike asked. Once the road was finally cleared, Ike had driven like a bat out of hell over to the trailer court. He'd alternately continued to call Mya and Buddy Lee as he chewed up the road. When he pulled up to Buddy Lee's trailer and saw that Mya's car was gone, he'd experienced a terror so complete it felt like he was about to have an out-of-body episode. That terror had been replaced with despair moments after he answered the call from the hospital where his wife worked.

"I think I can answer your questions," a deputy said. Ike straightened and faced the man. He was a wiry specimen. The brown-and-tan uniform of the Red Hill Sheriff's Department clung to his sharp, angular physique.

"What happened?"

"Let's go over here and talk, Ike," the deputy said. Ike didn't recognize him, but everyone in Red Hill knew Ike. They either remembered the criminal he used to be or they were familiar with the man he'd become. Such was the curse of a small town. Ike followed the deputy through the vinyl doors and down the hall to the chapel. Red Hill General's chapel was a shabby thing made up of two short pews, a picture of a Gregg Allman Jesus, and a couple of fake stained-glass windows. Ike stood near the pew as the deputy stopped just inside the door frame.

"I'm Deputy Hogge. I'm so sorry about all this, but we have some things we need to clear up," he said.

"What. Happened?"

Deputy Hogge's shoulder stiffened. "Just stay calm, Mr. Randolph, I'm gonna tell you."

"I can't stay calm because no one will tell me a goddamn thing. So can the next words out of your mouth be how my wife and my granddaughter and our friend ended up in the hospital?" Ike said. His brain registered that he had called Arianna his granddaughter and Buddy Lee his friend, but he couldn't ruminate on that now.

"Sir, I'm trying to tell you, but you need to calm yourself. Now, what did the hospital tell you when they called?" Deputy Hogge asked.

"You already know what they said. There'd been an accident. My wife and her passenger Buddy Lee Jenkins had been injured. They didn't tell me about Arianna and they didn't tell me what happened. This is as calm as I'm gonna get," Ike said.

"This wasn't an accident, Mr. Randolph. A person or persons unknown intentionally ran into your wife's car. They set fire to your home, assaulted your neighbor and . . ." Deputy Hogge paused. Ike's chest tightened.

"They took your granddaughter. They kidnapped her," Deputy Hogge said. The ground beneath Ike's feet vanished. He collapsed in the pew. Deputy Hogge sat next to him.

"I talked to your friend but he wasn't much help. Now, please don't take this the wrong way, but is there anyone you can think of that has a problem with you? You know, anybody from back in the day?" Deputy Hogge asked.

"Leave me alone," Ike said.

"Ike, we are gonna do everything to find that little girl and the people who did this, but I need you to be honest with me. Stealing a child and burning down a house are personal attacks. Extremely personal. You know who did this. Tell me so we can get her back before it's too late," Deputy Hogge said.

"I don't know anything," Ike said. That wasn't a complete lie. His life was a roundabout spinning out of control. Isiah was dead. Mya was fighting for her life on an operating-room table. Arianna was gone. Their house was a pile of cinders. He didn't know how to stop the chaos he and Buddy Lee had unleashed. He didn't know how to protect the people he loved. He didn't know anything anymore.

"Are you sure about that?"

"Just go, man. Please, just go," Ike said.

Deputy Hogge stood and adjusted his uniform.

"If you change your mind, you know how to reach us. And if you don't change your mind, you might wanna get ready for another funeral," Deputy Hogge said.

Buddy Lee could feel eyes on him. It made the hairs on his arms stand at attention. He opened his own eyes and saw Ike standing at the foot of his bed.

"What the fuck happened?" Ike said. Buddy Lee scratched at his chin, then flinched. The wound on his cheek made his whole face tender.

"Your neighbor called and told Mya the house was on fire. She was dead set on going over there. When we got there the Breed was waiting for us. House wasn't even on fire then. They did that while we trying to get away. They came at us on the bikes, then a son of bitch driving a Bronco ran into us from the side. Ike, they took Arianna. They snatched that little girl right up. They took Mya's phone, too. Said they'd be in touch. They wanna trade Tangerine for Arianna," Buddy Lee said.

"No, they don't. They want us to bring Tangerine to them so they can kill us all," Ike said.

"Did she tell you anything about this guy?" Buddy Lee asked. Ike shook his head.

"Nope. She still can't believe he the one doing all this. She even showed me a text message from him. That fucker talks slick as fish grease. She's hooked," Ike said.

"I don't suppose she had his name on the text, did she?" Buddy Lee asked.

"She got him saved in her phone as 'W.' I don't know if that's the first letter of his first name or the first letter of his last name or what," Ike said. He grabbed a chair that had been placed against the wall and sat down next to Buddy Lee's bed.

"What did they say about Mya?" Buddy Lee asked.

"She got a lot going on. She in surgery right now."

"Goddamn it. Goddamn it to hell," Buddy Lee said. Ike heard voices in various degrees of distress drift up and down the hallway outside of Buddy Lee's room. They joined the beeps and whistles of numerous monitors and machines to create an ambient mechanical soundtrack to Ike's and Buddy Lee's thoughts.

"I'm sorry, Ike," Buddy Lee said. Ike didn't say anything.

"I shouldn't have let her go. I should have stopped her, but she wanted to save what she could. I should have gone over there by myself. I should have done anything but let her go out that door," Buddy Lee said.

"Yeah, you should have. And we should have left it alone. Let the cops handle it, whatever that ended up looking like. But we didn't and now here we are," Ike said.

"We gotta get her back, Ike. Whatever it takes, we gotta get her back," Buddy Lee said.

"I'm not giving them Tangerine. And I'm not going to let them hurt Arianna. They killed our boys. They killed Tangerine's mama. They tried to kill my wife. They burned down my fucking house. I'm not letting them take one more goddamn thing," Ike said.

"I wish I had never got you into this," Buddy Lee whispered. Ike scooted his chair up closer to Buddy Lee's bed.

"You didn't twist my arm," Ike said.

Buddy Lee swallowed hard. "What if I did, though?"

Ike cocked his head to the side. "What are you talking about?"

Buddy Lee put his hand over his face. He fingers brushed against the stitches on his cheek. The blood-pressure monitor began to beep erratically.

"Would you have gotten on with this if that tombstone hadn't gotten smashed?" Buddy Lee asked. Ike leaned forward. His eyes narrowed to slits. Buddy Lee saw the gears in his head locking in place.

"You?" Ike said. Buddy Lee could barely hear the single syllable.

"You wasn't gonna be down for it, and I couldn't do it by myself. I'd asked my brother Chet and he blew me off. Look, it made me sick. I swear it made me sick to my stomach, but I knew you wouldn't help unless . . ." Buddy Lee said. Ike was up and out of the chair in a matter of seconds. His powerful hands locked around Buddy Lee's neck and lifted him up out of the bed, ripping his IV line out of the port on the back of his hand. The blood pressure monitor fell over like a rotted tree.

"YOU! Arianna might be dead. Mya is at death's door. Tangerine's mama is dead! All because of you! You did this!" Ike said. Spittle flew from his lips and rained down on Buddy Lee's face.

"We . . . have . . . to . . . finish . . . it . . . for . . . the . . . boys," Buddy Lee croaked. Each word cost him precious gulps of air as Ike throttled the life out of him. Buddy Lee could feel the bones in his neck being ground to powder. Ike bared his teeth. He let Buddy Lee fall back in the bed.

"You motherfucker. You guilted me into doing this, you piece of shit," Ike said.

"I know. It's all my fault. But we're in it now," Buddy Lee said.

"For a minute I thought you wasn't so bad. I trusted you. But it's just like I said: you wanted the scary-ass Black dude to do all the hard work for you," Ike said.

"I wanted the only man in the world who knew what I was going through to help me make it right," Buddy Lee said, rubbing his neck.

"Guess neither one of us is a good judge of character," Ike said. He headed for the door.

"Ike—"

"Don't say a goddamn thing. Not one word. I need to go and see if my wife made it out of surgery. If she did, I have to figure out how to tell her her grandbaby is gone. Then I gotta figure out how to get that baby back without turning over Tangerine. I gotta do all this by myself because your ass went and cracked our son's tombstone, you stupid fucker," Ike said.

Buddy Lee watched as Ike stalked out of his room.

Buddy Lee coughed. The act caused his ears to pop. He'd been alone before—that was nothing new. Nights spent out in his car or truck after tying one on so hard he knew he couldn't drive. Days after being released from the graybar hotel, hitching his way back home because he had no one waiting for him on the other side. Long evenings sitting in his trailer staring at flickering electric shadows on the idiot box as he swallowed beer after beer trying to forget the tender kisses of his first love or the laughter of his only son. Buddy Lee closed his eyes.

This felt different. This felt permanent.

It was an hour later when his phone rang. Not his cell phone but the phone in the room. Buddy Lee stretched his arm over the railing and grabbed the handset.

"Hello?"

"Buddy," Christine said.

"What do you want?" Buddy Lee asked.

"I was calling to check on you. I saw the news," Christine said.

"Red Hill made the news? That's a first," Buddy Lee said.

"It's not every day kidnappers take a little girl and burn down her grandparents' house. Are you okay?" Christine said.

"We're her grandparents, too, Christine," Buddy Lee snapped.

"I know that, okay? This is all so much after what happened to Derek. I don't want anything to happen to her. I don't want anything to happen to anyone," Christine said. Her sadness was palatable. It made Buddy Lee wince.

"Hey, look, I'm sorry. Like you said, this is a lot," Buddy Lee said.

"Do you think this has anything to do with what you told me the other day?" Christine asked. Buddy Lee didn't answer.

"Okay. I'm going to ask you again: How are you?" Christine said.

"Don't do that."

"Do what?"

"Care about me. It's easier when we hate each other," Buddy Lee said.

"I never hated you, Buddy Lee. You got on every one of my nerves, but I never hated you," Christine said.

"Gerald don't mind you yapping with your ex-husband? Or is he listening in on the line?" Buddy Lee said.

"Ha. Gerald Winthrop Culpepper doesn't have time to stalk my calls. He's too busy working on his campaign," Christine said.

Buddy Lee sat straight up in his bed. A nurse came in the room but he waved her away.

"Say what now?" Buddy Lee asked.

"Gerald is gearing up to run for governor. I told you that the other day. His daddy been pushing for this since he lost his own bid for the governor's mansion."

"No, not that part. Say his name again. His whole name," Buddy Lee said.

"What? Why?"

"Just do it."

"Gerald Winthrop Culpepper. He was named after his great-grandfather. Are you okay?" Christine asked.

"I'm fine," Buddy Lee said. Pieces were falling into place in his head like a giant game of Tetris. It all made sense now. Why Derek was so pissed about Tangerine's boyfriend. What had he called him? A hypocrite and an asshole. Christine had said Derek had called her before he got killed. She had ignored it, but Derek wasn't the type to take no for an answer. He probably went over there to see her. Ran into Gerald. Told him about himself.

"Motherfucker," Buddy Lee said.

"What did you call me?" Christine asked.

Buddy Lee knew why Tangerine had him saved in her phone under "W." Now it made sense how they met. Gerald Culpepper and Christine were always in the paper at this or that high-society get-together. When Tangerine had mumbled "We can't win," she wasn't saying they couldn't make it. She was saying "Wynn."

Short for Winthrop.

"What's the name of that place you moved to in King William County?" Buddy Lee asked.

"Garden Acres. Buddy Lee, what's wrong?" Christine asked.

"Nothing."

He put the handset back in the cradle. He got out of bed and went over to the teak cabinet in the corner. His clothes were in a clear plastic bag on the second shelf. By the time he had his boots on, the nurse he had waved away had returned.

"Mr. Jenkins, you need to get back into bed. The doctor wants you under observation for the next twenty-four hours," she said.

"Darling, I'm walking out that door in the next ten seconds. If you need to tell the doctor I left against medical advice, well, I reckon that's okay. But I'm not staying here one more minute," Buddy Lee said. The nurse threw up her hands and grabbed his chart off the foot of the bed.

It took him a while to find his truck. Ike had parked it way out in the far end of the lot. Buddy Lee grabbed his key ring, unlocked the door, climbed in the truck. He flipped open the glove box. The big semiautomatic was in there. He checked the clip. It was empty. So was the chamber. Ike had been riding around empty-handed. The MAC-10 was in Mya's car sitting in some good ol' boys' salvage yard. That was alright. He started the truck.

The engine clanged and shook as the truck struggled to idle. Buddy Lee reached behind the bench seat. He moved his hand carefully over the broken glass that had fallen in the gap.

When he found what he was looking for, he closed his hand around it and pulled it from behind the seat. It was an old wooden baseball bat with nails driven into it at regular intervals. His former co-worker Chuck called it a homemade mace. A lot of folks still paid in cash when he made his deliveries. He could have gotten a gun, but if he got pulled over by the DOT, he'd lose his job, go to jail, and his boss would probably have to pay a fine. This peacemaker seemed like a good alternative. He'd only had to use it twice. Usually pulling it was enough of a deterrent.

A baseball bat with nails. A tamper. A .45. It occurred to Buddy Lee that anything could be a weapon if you were dedicated enough. Even love. Especially love.

Buddy Lee pulled out of the parking lot and merged into traffic.

He started to sing. It was a song his grandmother would sing at every funeral for a member of the Jenkins clan. When her time came they sang it at hers.

"O, death . . . O, death, Won't you spare me over 'til another year," Buddy Lee crooned as he rode down the highway.

THIRTY-SEVEN

Garden Acres was indeed in the middle of nowhere. The GPS had gotten him within ten miles of the planned community. From there, it was looking for real-estate signs that advertised lots for sale, which led him to a wide side road with a blacktop so smooth it looked like it was poured fresh every night. Buddy Lee had the gas pedal to the floor. His truck was barely hitting fifty. The motor cried out for mercy, but that particular emotion was in short supply tonight.

Buddy Lee turned onto Garden Acres Drive. A cloud of gray-and-black smoke billowed from his duals. The road was lined by pink rhododendrons and had a concrete gutter that ran alongside the road. Buddy Lee passed house after house that cost more than he had ever made, legally or illegally. Intricately landscaped lawns would have given Ike and his crew a run for their money, bisected by long paved driveways. Many of those driveways had brick columns with a mailbox built into its center. A few had gates. Most of them had attached two-car garages. There was stunning sense of conformity throughout the neighborhood. Like here was a standard architectural design that denoted affluence.

Buddy Lee brought the truck to a halt. Christine was one of those who parked her car in front of the garage instead of inside it. Buddy Lee thought Gerald probably had a work vehicle and a fun-time vehicle. No room for Christine's gold Lexus.

Buddy Lee turned onto the driveway. He revved the engine a few times.

"One more time, ol' girl. Give me all you got one more time," he murmured.

Buddy Lee hit the gas. His truck, a used rambling wreck that he paid fifteen hundred dollars for six years ago, roared to life even as oil shot out of the exhaust pipe. Buddy Lee raced up the driveway. By the time he flew past Christine's car and careened through the garage door he was doing forty-five. He smashed into a candy-apple-red Corvette parked next to a black BMW.

Buddy Lee undid his seat belt and climbed out of the truck. Beautiful brass carriage lights ignited on both sides of the front door, a wooden, barn door–style piece of art with wrought-iron corbels running across its face. It sat at the top of seven wide brick steps. Buddy Lee climbed those steps, gripped the Louisville Slugger with both hands, and smashed the nearest brass light to smithereens. He heard footsteps racing around inside the two-story mansion.

"Gerald! Come on down, you fucking cocksucker! Come on down you murdering son of a bitch!" Buddy Lee screeched. Two small terra-cotta lions sat on each side of the front door next to a glazed clay planter. Buddy Lee obliterated each lion and planter with a couple of swings from his bat. Plaster chips flew up and landed in his lank hair.

"You were fucking that girl, Gerald. You were fucking her and Derek found out!" Buddy Lee bellowed. He hopped down off the steps. A picture window to the left of the door felt the fury of his bat. It took two hard swings, but the window eventually broke into a million pieces.

"Buddy Lee! Stop this!" Christine shrieked. She was standing on the other side of a cloth-covered chaise that sat in front of the former picture window. Buddy Lee pointed at her with the bat.

"He killed our son, Christine. He killed Derek. HE KILLED HIM!" Buddy Lee bellowed.

Christine put her hands to her mouth. "What are you saying?"

"Derek found out he was cheating on you with this girl named Tangerine. Come on down, Gerald. Or should I call you Wynn? That's what she called you, right, you son of a bitch!" Buddy Lee said.

"Gerald, who is—"

Gerald's voice cut her off midsentence. It echoed through the house with the unmistakable tinniness that came from a speaker.

"The police have been called, Buddy," Gerald said.

"Come out here, Gerald. I'm gonna bash your fucking brains in, but not before I make you say my boy's name. Get out of your panic room and come on out here, boy," Buddy Lee said.

"Buddy Lee, the police will be here any minute," Christine said.

"You think they can get here before I shove this bat down Gerald's throat? Come on out, boy. Face me. Face the father of the man you killed. You got the stones for that? Or do you get the Breed to do all the work for you?" Buddy Lee said. Gerald spoke again. Buddy Lee could hear the smirk through the speakers.

"This isn't a B movie starring Warren Oates, Buddy Lee. I suggest you put that bat down and get on the ground. Right now, you're just looking at felony destruction of property and trespassing. Don't add attempted murder to the list," Gerald said.

"I ain't attempting anything, bitch. You ain't coming out, I'm coming in," he said. He went back to his truck. He tried starting it. The engine sputtered but didn't catch. He tried again.

"Last time, ol' girl," he thought. The truck turned over but just barely. Buddy Lee backed up and disentangled himself from the garage door. He slipped the gear shift into drive.

Gerald came out of the darkness with his cell phone in his hand. He stood behind Christine as she stared out the hole that used to be their window.

"Did he leave?"

"No. Who is Tangerine?" Christine asked with eerie calm.

"Oh my God," Gerald said. He grabbed Christine by the arm and snatched her away from the picture window just as Buddy Lee's truck came careening into their living room. The bricks around the window cracked, shifted, and fell to the ground like a meth head's teeth. The chaise crumpled under the weight of Buddy Lee's truck. The front wheels spun across the wood floor leaving black streaks of rubber in their wake. Buddy Lee fell out of the truck with the baseball bat in his hand. Using it as a cane, he climbed to his feet.

"I'm coming, you fucker. I'm gonna see what your insides look like," Buddy Lee said. Gerald dragged Christine through the batwing doors that separated their kitchen from the dining room. Buddy Lee followed them, digging holes in the Sheetrock with his bat as he stalked them. He knocked one of the batwing doors off its mounts with one swing. Gerald stood behind Christine. He had a butcher knife in his hand.

"You ever killed a man, Gerald? Up close and personal like? Not over the phone. Felt his blood splatter on your face? Heard the last rattle of his breath in his throat? Smelled the shit in his pants when his bowels let go? I have. So believe me when I tell you that knife ain't gonna slow me down one fucking bit," Buddy Lee said.

"Please, Buddy Lee, stop," Christine said.

"HE KILLED OUR BOY!" Buddy Lee roared. He swung the bat in a whistling half circle and took out the coffee maker sitting on the granite countertop than ran the length of the far-left wall.

"Say his name, Gerald!" Buddy Lee yelled. He slammed the bat against a juicer that had evaded his first attack.

"Say it! DEREK WAYNE JENKINS!" Buddy Lee shouted.

"Drop the bat!" an authoritative voice said behind him. Buddy Lee froze.

"Drop it!"

Buddy Lee glanced back over his shoulder. Two deputies were standing behind him with their hands on their guns. Buddy Lee dropped the bat. It clattered against the Italian marble that covered the floor.

"Thank God for white privilege," Buddy Lee said under his breath.

He launched himself at Christine and Gerald. Gerald pushed his wife at Buddy Lee. Buddy Lee swatted her aside and grabbed the butcher knife in Gerald's hand by the blade with his right hand. He punched Gerald in the face with his left. The second his knuckles connected with that lantern-sized jaw was the happiest moment Buddy Lee had experienced in months. Even as strong arms snaked around his body, he kept hitting Gerald. He wrenched the knife from his hand and let it fall to the floor. Blood flowed from his sliced palm and rained down on the tile. When he was out of arm's reach Buddy Lee kicked at Gerald's face. The deputies struggled to get him down to the ground.

"He killed my boy! He killed my boy! My boy! My boy!" Buddy Lee screamed until his words ran together and became an unintelligible song of sorrow.

Buddy Lee leaned back against the cold cinder blocks that lined the holding cell. They had bandaged his hand and tossed him in the tank an hour ago. It was a weekend so there were a lot of drunks sharing the twenty-by-twenty space with him—a few raggedy-faced boys who were in the throes of opioid addiction and one quiet fella that seemed primed to burst into tears at any minute.

It was like the good ol' days all over again. He probably wouldn't get bail, or if he did, it would be so high he'd have to climb on a table to pay it. He was looking at least a couple of felonies. Add to that his past convictions, he could be looking at real time.

He'd failed. Failed Derek. Failed Isiah. Failed Ike. Failed Mya. Failed Arianna. He was what he had always been. A fuckup.

"Jenkins." A deputy with a face made for radio said. Buddy Lee squinted at him.

"Yeah."

"Get up. Somebody wants to talk," the deputy said. Buddy Lee didn't move. Who the hell wanted to talk to him?

"Who is it?" he asked.

"Get your ass up, or do we have to come and put you in the chair?" The deputy asked. The "chair" was a four-way restraint device for unruly prisoners. Buddy Lee had been in the chair once. He didn't seek another ride on that particular conveyance. He stood up and faced the wall. Two deputies joined Hatchet Face. They handcuffed him before leading him out of the cell. They led him down an antiseptic white hallway lit by a series of flickering fluorescent lights. They came to a room marked LAWYER with black letters on a gold background. Hatchet Face opened the door, and the deputies guided him into the cool narrow room. Strong hands pushed him down into a chair. They uncuffed his right hand and looped the empty cuff to a ring on the underside of the table.

"Who wants to talk to me?" Buddy Lee asked. The deputies didn't respond. They slipped out without closing the door.

"We need to have a conversation, Mr. Jenkins," Gerald said as he walked into the room.

THIRTY-EIGHT

B uddy Lee tried to jump up out of his chair, but the handcuff caught him short. He sat back down as Gerald closed the door behind him. He walked to the other side of the metal table and pulled the chair back just far enough to stay out of Buddy Lee's reach.

"It has always bewildered me why these tables are bolted to the floor but the chairs aren't. This room is supposed to be where defendants meet their attorneys. If you are that angry at your advocate that you would hit him or her with a table, you probably are guilty as sin," Gerald said. He smiled at Buddy Lee. A purplish welt had sprung up on Gerald's chin. Another one was located just above his eye.

"You killed my boy," Buddy Lee said. He instinctively wrenched his handcuffed arm.

"Buddy, you need to listen to me."

"You killed my son," Buddy Lee seethed. Gerald shook his head. To an observer it would have appeared to be an empathetic gesture.

"Buddy, we have to approach this like adults," Gerald said.

"I'm gonna cut your dick off and make you eat it," Buddy Lee said. Gerald leaned forward and put his hands on his knees. He wasn't smiling.

"This room doesn't have any recording or video equipment, so we can speak frankly. My associates have the girl. Your granddaughter. You know where Tangerine is. They will contact you when you get out of here and arrange the details of the trade. You and Mr. Randolph will bring Tangerine to a location of our choosing. You will do as you're told or I'll have my associates chop that girl into bite-size pieces," Gerald said.

"You hurt that little girl and there won't be a hole deep enough for you to hide in. I promise you that, hoss," Buddy Lee spat.

"Oh, Buddy Lee, you're so melodramatic. Don't you see I hold all the cards here? I have the little girl. I'm a judge. You tried to murder me in my own house." Gerald ran his finger over the wounds on his face. "If I wanted, I could make a call and have your bail set to six figures. You will do what trash like you was made to do. Follow instructions."

"That scar from that headbutt healed up real good didn't it?" Buddy Lee said. Gerald laughed.

"Always the hypermasculine hard man, hmm, Buddy? Tell me, in your whole life what has that ever gotten you but misery?" Gerald asked. He seemed genuinely interested in Buddy Lee's answer. Buddy Lee sat back in the chair and traced his forefinger over the wiry stubble over his chin.

"You're right. There's been times I've been miserable. Times where all I wanted to do was lay down and die. If I added them up, those times would beat the good times two to one, no doubt about that," Buddy Lee said. Gerald opened his mouth to speak, but Buddy Lee held that forefinger up and waggled it side to side.

"But good times or bad, I ain't never lied about who I was. I ain't never pretended to be anything but a hell-raising, whiskey-drinking, hard-loving redneck son of a bitch. Most nights I sleep like a baby. I ain't ashamed of who I am. I'd like to think my boy picked that up from me. How about you, Winthrop? How you feel about yourself coming home to Chrissy after spending all night bumping uglies with Tangerine? What do the man in the mirror think about the man who always running his mouth about people he called deviants and disgusting? Who talks about it ain't Adam and Steve, it's Adam and Eve and all that happy shit, when the whole time he was lighting it up with the T in LGBTQ? Which one of us you think sleeps better . . . hoss?" Buddy Lee asked. He leaned forward. Gerald smiled but a vein in his forehead throbbed. Buddy Lee laughed. He leaned his head back and chortled to the rafters.

"Oh, you didn't know we knew about that? Hey, no judgment here. I'm what you call an ally," Buddy Lee said. Gerald stopped smiling.

"I'm going to tell the magistrate I'm not pressing charges because I know you are so distraught over your dead pervert of a son. You will go to Ike and the two of you will bring me Tangerine. Do this and the little girl will be returned to you unharmed. However, if you don't follow your directions to the letter, I can assure you Arianna will die a most horrible death," Gerald said. He stood and headed for the door. When he turned the knob Buddy Lee spoke. He didn't shout and he didn't yell.

"One day sooner than you think the last thing you gonna hear is your heart going still. And the last thing you ever gonna see is me or Ike standing over you holding it in our hands. Remember I told you that," Buddy Lee said. Gerald chuckled. The echo bounced around the room.

"My associates will be in touch," Gerald said. He left the room.

"Sooner than you think," Buddy Lee said softly.

THIRTY-NINE

Ike dropped a few coins into the vending machine to get a soda. He watched the spiral spring spin and drop the soda can into the bin. He reached in and grabbed it. He wished the machine had cans of beer or, better yet, a bottle of whiskey. Mya had come out of surgery but she was still unconscious. The doctor said because of the swelling on her brain she might wake up in a few hours or she might wake up in a few weeks. The hospital staff had offered him a recliner to sleep in beside her bed. He would have slept on the floor. Tomorrow he'd have to see what was left of their house. What was left of their life. Perform all the adult tasks that came with material tragedies. Call the insurance company, get a police report from a sheriff that knew he was holding something back. All the mind-numbing minutiae that kept the world moving even after you've lost everything.

His cell phone chirped.

He picked it up and saw it was Buddy Lee. He hit END.

The phone rang again.

He hit END again.

The phone rang again. This time he answered it.

"Call here again and I'll kill you," Ike said.

"It was Gerald Culpepper," Buddy Lee said.

"What? Who is that?" Ike said.

"Derek's stepfather. He's who Tangerine was fucking. He's

a judge and he got the Rare Breed in his pocket," Buddy Lee said.

Ike moved to the molded plastic chair in the waiting room and sat down with his drink.

"Ike?" Buddy Lee said.

"How'd you find this out? Why should I believe you?" Ike said.

"You said Tangerine had her man saved in her phone under 'W,' right? Gerald's middle name is Winthrop. That's when it hit me. Why Derek would be so upset about some fella dumping Tangerine. Why it pissed him off so bad. Then I talked to his mama, and she said a couple of weeks before the boys got shot Derek had tried to reach out to her," Buddy Lee said.

"But he got hold of his stepdaddy instead," Ike said.

"And he probably threatened Gerald. Ol' Winthrop is one of them rah-rah all-American types. Women need to be barefoot and pregnant, Black people need to know their place, and anybody that ain't T-square straight is the devil," Buddy Lee said.

"He wouldn't want the world to know he was messing around on his wife. Especially with Tangerine," Ike said.

"Yeah. He's the one behind all this, Ike. The Rare Breed might've pulled the trigger but he pulled the goddamn strings. He wants me and you to bring him Tangerine in exchange for Arianna. He's gearing up for a run for governor and he can't have all this hanging out there," Buddy Lee said.

"And when did he tell you this?" Ike asked.

"Right after I drove my truck through his house and tried to brain him with a baseball bat full of nails," Buddy Lee said.

"Let me guess: he ain't pressing charges," Ike said.

"No. He wants all three of us. They gonna call you any minute now. Look, I know you're pissed at me, and I don't blame you one bit. If I could change everything, I would. But if we don't work together on this, none of us are gonna make it," Buddy Lee said.

"Mya just got out of surgery," Ike said.

Buddy Lee sucked at his teeth. "What the docs say?"

"She could wake up in a couple of hours. Or she could wake in a few days or a few weeks," Ike said.

"I don't know what to say, Ike," Buddy Lee said. Ike caught his reflection in the snack machine. The slouch of his shoulders. The defeated tilt of his head like he was carrying an invisible mill-stone around his neck. His son gone. His granddaughter taken. His wife halfway between this world and the next. His home re-duced to a pile of cinders. All because of one man. A man who thought the rules didn't apply to him. A man who thought he couldn't be touched.

"Where are you?" Ike asked.

"I'm standing outside the King William County jail. Actually I've walked down the road a piece," Buddy Lee said.

"I gotta get one of my guys to bring me the smaller work truck. Hang tight. I'll be there in about an hour," Ike said.

"Hey, I don't want you to leave Mya if you don't want to," Buddy Lee said.

"She would tell me go and get our granddaughter back, so that's what I'm gonna do. Give me an hour."

Ike pulled up to the sidewalk in front of the jail. Buddy Lee loped over to the car. He climbed in and closed the door. Ike made a U-turn and headed back to Red Hill.

They drove in silence for a few minutes for before Buddy Lee started rambling.

"I meant what I said that day in your shop. I can't live in a world where Gerald Culpepper gets to breathe and our boys are in the ground. But . . . I shouldn't have done what I did. I'm sorry."

"You doing that might have pushed me toward the edge, but I was the one that made the leap," Ike said.

They turned onto Route 33, leaving King William behind. The

headlights illuminated a green road sign that said Red Hill was twenty miles away.

"They haven't called you yet?" Buddy Lee asked.

"Not yet. They probably trying to find a good place to bury us all. We know too much about where this Gerald likes to stick his dick," Ike said.

"Yeah. We gotta figure out a way to flip this around them. Get Arianna back without turning over Tangerine."

"I've been thinking about that. When it looked like I was doing this alone, I came up with an idea," Ike said. Buddy Lee raised an eyebrow.

"We back on?" Buddy Lee asked.

"This is a mess but you didn't make it by yourself," Ike said.

"Okay. What's the play?" Buddy Lee asked.

"Ya know they got something we want and we got something they want. We need something they want more than Tangerine," Ike said.

"Like what? We gonna steal one of their bikes?" Buddy Lee asked.

"No. My first thought was to find out where one of them lives and scoop up one of their old ladies," Ike said.

"Goddamn, son. They must clank when you walk," Buddy Lee said.

"What?"

"Your brass balls. But I gotta admit, I like it. They wouldn't be expecting it," Buddy Lee said.

"Yeah. But now we know who the real head of the snake is, I'm thinking we need somebody closer to the throne," Ike said. He took his eyes off the road and stared at Buddy Lee for what seemed like a full minute.

"Oh. I see where you going with this, but I'll tell you what, I don't think Gerald cares all that much about Christine. He can't if he was doing what he was doing with Tangy," Buddy Lee said.

"That how you really feel or are you getting soft on me?" Ike asked.

"If we telling the truth and shaming the devil, I still am sweet on her in a way. But the only thing Gerald Culpepper loves is power and . . ." Buddy Lee said. He stopped and put his finger to his lips.

"And what? I ain't telepathic," Ike said.

"One time Derek told me the only bad thing he ever heard his mama say about Gerald was that he could be a daddy's boy," Buddy Lee said.

"He loves power but he loves his daddy more," Ike said.

"Yessir. Derek told me how Gerald and his daddy was as thick as thieves and tight as a pair of pantyhose. Gatsby Culpepper is an asshole just like his son. Derek told me Gatsby wouldn't let him call him Granddaddy. Talking about how Derek wasn't a true Culpepper so he didn't get that honor," Buddy Lee said.

"You know, you told me you and Derek didn't get along, but it sure seem like y'all did a lot of talking," Ike said. Buddy Lee grunted.

"That was only when he was mad at his mama. You know how that is. I ate that shit up, but then he would try to tell me about Isiah and, well, I wasn't too receptive to that," Buddy Lee said.

"Yeah. I didn't, uh . . . I didn't listen to Isiah when he would talk about how happy he was with Derek. I mean, I didn't wanna listen," Ike said.

"Maybe we can be better grandfathers than we was fathers," Buddy Lee said.

"You know where this Gatsby lives? They haven't called yet, but when they do we won't have much time to make a move," Ike said.

"Can we google it?" Buddy Lee asked.

"Probably. You can google anything these days."

"That's what they tell me," Buddy Lee said. They drove on in silence for a mile or two.

"Did you really drive your truck through his house?" Ike said.

"Yeah, but I fucked up and took a left at the sink," Buddy Lee said. Ike and Buddy Lee stared at each other at the same time.

Buddy Lee started laughing.

Ike just shook his head.

Ike was right.

When they got back to Buddy Lee's trailer, Ike pulled up Gatsby Culpepper's address on a free Google search. The site he used advised him that for $29.99 he could get Gatsby's criminal record, too.

"This says he lives just outside of Richmond in Charles City County," Ike said. He checked his watch.

"It's almost eleven. I say we go now."

Buddy Lee leaned his chair back on two legs before letting it rest on all four again. He rubbed his face with his left hand. The wound on his right hand was pulsating under its bandage. He took a sip from a mason jar that had a nebulous form floating near the bottom. Once upon a time it had been a half of a peach. He'd found the jar in his closet hidden behind his winter clothes. Like a squirrel and his nuts, Buddy Lee sometimes forgot where he kept his emergency rations.

"Last I heard he was living alone. I don't know if he has a dog. I don't know what kind of security system he might have or how many guns he might be packing. I kinda feel like we should at least do a dry run and see what he working with," Buddy Lee said. He handed Ike the jar. Ike took a sip and handed it back to Buddy Lee. Buddy Lee took it, tipped the mason jar up, and savored the burn of the corn liquor in his chest.

"I don't care what he's got. I don't care who lives with him. I don't care about his dog. We going in there and we taking him out. Anybody or anything try and stop us, we taking them out, too," Ike said.

"Duly noted, but I've been ruminating on something," Buddy Lee said.

"What's that?"

"My daddy used to say, 'Work smarter, not harder,'" Buddy Lee said. Ike put his phone in his pocket and crossed his arms.

"I'm listening."

"Let's say we go up here and try to grab ol' Gatsby and the shit gets hectic. Then we get locked up and them Breed boys call us while we're sitting in the stir. What if instead of going up in there like a bull in a china shop we get him to come on out and walk himself right into our arms," Buddy Lee said.

"And how you think we gonna get him to do that?" Ike asked.

"Well, Gatsby's an old man. And there ain't nothing an old man likes more than a pretty young thing. And we just happen to have a pretty young thing on our team," Buddy Lee said.

"You talking about Tangerine? She don't even believe this bastard is out to kill her. How we gonna convince her to help us snatch his daddy?"

"Simple. We tell her the truth," Buddy Lee said.

FORTY

Jazzy met them at the door.

"How's Mya?" she asked.

"Stable. We need to talk to your guest. Send her outside," Ike said. He went back to his truck and leaned against the grille. Buddy Lee stood next to him with his hands in his pockets. The moon was a sliver of white in the night sky. A thin blanket of mist rolled across the fields that bordered Jazzy's driveway on either side.

Tangerine took her time coming down the steps. She stood in the yard just out of their reach. She had on a pair of lounge pants with white kittens on a black background. Her hair was piled on top of her head in a loose bun.

"You see the news?" Ike asked. She nodded.

"Gerald wants us to trade you for Arianna," Buddy Lee said. Tangerine snapped her head in his direction.

"Yeah, we know. The Honorable Gerald Winthrop Culpepper is the fella who dumped you and got this whole greasy ball of shit rolling. He's the one that had Derek and Isiah killed, and he's the one who got your mama killed, and he's trying to kill you like it's his new favorite hobby," Buddy Lee said.

"How did you—"

"We might not look like much, but between the two of us we got a half-decent brain. 'W' is short for Wynn. Winthrop is Gerald's middle name. Gerald is Derek's stepdaddy," Buddy Lee said.

"That's why Derek was so upset. That's why Isiah was going to run the story," Ike said.

"It ain't his family, Tangy. It ain't his wife. It's him. He's the one making the moves. He's the one who told his boys to kidnap a little girl," Buddy Lee said.

"They'd as soon kill her as look at her," Ike said.

Tangerine shook her head violently. Her long black hair fell around her shoulders.

"Well, what do you want me to say? That I'm a dumbass? That I was an idiot for thinking he actually had feelings for me? Congratulations, you was right! I'm just another in a long line of stupid-ass sidechicks!" Tangerine said. She sat on the bottom step. Ike pushed himself off the truck and approached her.

"We didn't come here to run you down or make you feel bad. Gerald ain't the person you told yourself he was. That's a hard lesson, but it ain't nothing to be ashamed of, Tangerine. We all learn that lesson or we teach it to somebody. But now that you know, you can't hide from this no more," Ike said.

"We not gonna turn you over to them. That ain't even on the table," Buddy Lee said.

"Winthrop said he gonna send Arianna back in chunks if we don't," Ike said.

"We not gonna let that happen, but we need your help, sis," Buddy Lee said. Tangerine wiped her eyes with the back of her hand.

"He never cared about me at all, did he?" she said.

"He don't care about nobody but himself, sis," Buddy Lee said.

"He killed my mom," Tangerine cried. Her body trembled as she wept. Ike sat on the step and put his hand on her shoulder.

"Help us make it right. Help us make him pay."

Tangerine navigated Ike's truck down the single-lane side road that led to Gatsby Culpepper's estate. The long branches of oak and maple trees encroached on the road from both sides. Tangerine came out of a soft curve and saw a sign that hung from the arm of a seven-foot-tall post that said NORTH POINT. The post sat at the end of an exposed aggregate driveway that stretched into the darkness for about two hundred yards. She turned in to the driveway and parked the truck off to the side near a shallow ditch. She killed the lights and shut off the engine. The Chevy was Ike's errand truck. He used it to shuttle supplies between jobs when they got backed up or encountered a problem. He'd taken off the magnetic door signs that identified the truck as a part of his fleet.

Turn it on, Tangy, Tangerine thought. She checked her makeup in the rearview mirror. Her war paint was flawless, as usual. She popped the hood and got out of the truck. She went around to the front and raised the hood, then made a show of looking at the engine in case Mr. Gatsby Culpepper was peeping at her through his bedroom window. Throwing up her hands in exasperation, she walked up the gentle rise to the front door.

The dulcet tones of "Moonlight Sonata" echoed through the house as Tangerine pushed the doorbell. House? Calling this place a house was like calling the Taj Mahal a crypt. Technically accurate but wholly incorrect. North Point was a three-story English Tudor monstrosity that spilled over a half-acre meticulously landscaped lot surrounded by a throng of ancient oaks, maples, and dogwoods. Lights flicked on in the second story, then the first story. A large black door that was more like the drawbridge of a castle opened abruptly. She hadn't heard any footsteps approaching or the mutterings of a poor soul roused from his slumber at one o'clock in the morning.

"Can I help you?" the man standing in the door asked. He was a few inches taller than Tangerine. He had a shock of snow-white hair parted on the left side and swept back from his forehead. He was wearing a light-green golf shirt and tan khakis. He was standing in a foyer that was as big as her first apartment; it led to a great room with sprawling vaulted ceilings. Tangerine barely noticed. Her eyes focused on the gun in his left hand. It was a huge Dirty Harry–style pistol with a long barrel that was laying against the man's hip.

"I said, can I help you?" Gatsby asked. Tangerine froze. She tried to force her mouth to make words, but all she could do was look down at that cannon the old man was holding.

"Miss?" Gatsby asked. Tangerine snapped her head up and gazed into the old man's eyes. They were green with impossibly huge pupils. She swallowed hard. They were not the kindly eyes of a good Samaritan.

"Um, my car broke down and my cell phone is dead. I was wondering if you could come take a look at it. Maybe it needs a jump or something. I know it's late but I'm not mechanically inclined," she said. Gatsby gave her the once-over. Tangerine smiled at him. Gatsby smiled back. Even though she was a foot away she could smell whiskey on his breath.

"And what do I get in return?" Gatsby said. Tangerine suddenly felt a lot better about what was going to happen to this old man. Gatsby laughed lightly.

"Just a joke, dearie. Let's go take a look at it," Gatsby said. He closed the door behind him and followed her to the bottom of his driveway.

"How'd you find yourself out this way, dearie?" Gatsby asked. He still had the gun in his hand.

"Was leaving a friend's house and my truck just died."

"If you were my friend you'd be spending the night," Gatsby said. Tangerine fought down a rising tide of nausea as she took her place at the front of the truck. Gatsby leaned under the hood. He lay the gun on the fender.

"Here sugar, hold my phone. There's a little flashlight doohickey on there," Gatsby said.

"I got it," Tangerine said. She brushed her knee against the gun. It tumbled off the fender and landed on the ground.

"Damn it, darling, be careful; that's a loaded pistol," Gatsby said. He bent over to retrieve his gun.

Ike and Buddy Lee emerged from the darkness at opposite ends of the truck. They were wearing matching blue bandannas and black knit winter caps. Buddy Lee kicked the six-shooter out of Gatsby's reach. The older man rose up to his full height.

"What the hell is this?" he asked. His tone made it clear he was a man who always expected his questions to be answered.

Ike struck Gatsby behind the left ear with his right fist. The old man fell to the ground like he'd been hit with a hammer.

"That was smooth, knocking that gun on the ground," Buddy Lee said as he picked up the .44.

"Can we just get him in the truck and get the hell out of here?" Tangerine asked.

They tied his hands and feet with zip ties and covered his mouth with duct tape before throwing him in the truck bed and covering him with a heavy tarp. Ike got behind the wheel, Tangerine moved to the middle, and Buddy Lee got in the passenger seat. As they left North Point in the rearview mirror, Buddy Lee clucked his tongue.

"What?"

"I'm wondering if he had video cameras," Buddy Lee said.

"We got on masks," Ike said.

"I don't," Tangerine said.

"You see that house? If he has a camera system, it's probably one of them fancy ones that's hooked to his smartphone. We'll just make him erase it," Ike said.

"How you gonna make him erase it?" Tangerine asked. Ike glanced at her.

The question died in the air between them.

By the time they pulled up to Buddy Lee's it was a little after two. Ike backed up to the door and put the truck in park. When he killed the engine Buddy Lee hopped out and opened his door.

"Tell me if you see anybody looking," Ike said when he joined him at the tailgate.

"Aye, aye, captain," Buddy Lee said.

Ike moved the tarp and gripped Gatsby by his golf shirt. He pulled the man out of the bed and into Buddy Lee's trailer in one smooth movement, even as the older man twisted and bucked. Ike tossed him on the floor in front of Buddy Lee's sofa. Gatsby groaned behind his tape. Buddy Lee toed the duct tape on Gatsby's mouth.

"Shit, there really are a thousand uses for this stuff," Buddy Lee said.

"Yeah. I've used it to stop a leak on a lawn sprinkler," Ike said.

"No shit?"

"No shit," Ike said. Buddy Lee blew air over his lips. He bent over Gatsby. He patted his pockets until he found the old man's phone.

"I figure between the two of us we can dope out how to erase this thing. After that, what's our next move?" Buddy Lee said.

"I'll take Tangerine back. Then we wait for them to call and tell us where they want to do the exchange. They gonna have all kinds of demands. Now we got something Gerald wants more than he wants Tangerine. Now it's time for us to make a few demands of our own," Ike said.

"What if they don't go for it?" Buddy Lee asked.

"Gerald will go for it. Every good son wants to save his daddy," Ike said.

Ike pulled into Jazzy's driveway and stopped the truck. Tangerine was resting her chin on the back of her hand. Ike put the truck in park.

"It don't look like he had a camera system. There won't no app on his phone or nothing. At least not one me and Buddy Lee could find," Ike said.

"No offense, but you two are not really the most tech-savvy guys on the planet. But you aren't really worried about him ever going to the cops, are you?" Tangerine asked. Ike didn't answer.

"That's what I thought. You know, I only helped you so we could get Arianna back. I don't want to think about anything else that might happen," Tangerine said.

"Then don't," Ike said.

"How do you do it? Kill people and keep going like nothing happened. Like at the house. You stepped over my mama and blew those guys away like it was something you did every day. And it don't seem to bother you at all. I feel so guilty about my mama, about Isiah and Derek, I can't eat. I can't sleep. I jump at every noise. I cry for no reason. Not you and Buddy Lee. You two just keep moving forward like sharks. I don't know how you do it," Tangerine said.

"People like Isiah and Derek and your mama didn't deserve to die the way they did. And the people that killed them don't deserve to live. I can't speak for Buddy Lee, but that's what keeps me going," Ike said.

"Revenge?" Tangerine asked. Ike smiled ruefully.

"No, hate. Folks like to talk about revenge like it's a righteous thing but it's just hate in a nicer suit," Ike said.

FORTY-ONE

D ome was a big believer in karma. You do foul shit; foul shit comes back to you tenfold. Dome couldn't think of anything much fouler than kidnapping a little girl.

When they had gotten back to the clubhouse, he'd been tasked with watching the curly headed cherub. He wasn't sure how he'd drawn that straw, but he didn't want somebody like Too Much watching her. He'd probably offer her a sip of his Jack Daniel's. Dome tapped the remote and flipped through a hundred different channels while the girl slept on a makeshift cot he had constructed out of blankets and a piece of plywood. They were on the back porch that he and Cheddar and Gremlin had converted into an extra room. Up front the rest of his brothers were whooping and hollering. They were all hyped up about setting a house on fire and running a woman off the road. All Dome could think about was how Gremlin and Cheddar were lying out in the middle of that girl's front yard. He wondered if the buzzards were circling over them yet? Were their mouths full of maggots?

Dome changed the channel again.

Grayson scrolled through the phone they'd taken off the bitch when they'd grabbed the crumb snatcher. The time in the corner said 4:45 A.M. It was time to call the Fathers of the Year. An early morning call would catch them all disoriented and scared to death for the rug rat. Grayson stopped on the listing for "Ike" in the phone and pressed send.

He answered on the second ring.

"Hello?"

"Hey, nigger. I told you blood for blood. Or a little runt for a slut. Here's how it's gonna go—"

"I want to talk to the man in charge," Ike said. Grayson almost guffawed.

"You making demands on me, Sambo? I am the man in charge, boy," Grayson said.

"No, you just the messenger. Gerald Culpepper is the man in charge, and I want to talk to him," Ike said. Grayson squeezed the phone. Gerald and his stupid ass. He should've never talked to his wife's ex-husband, but he wanted to play Bond villain and rub salt in the wound. He got off on that shit.

"You deal with me. I'm the big dick in this deal and you about to get fucked unless you do exactly what I tell you. Or do you want me to start sending you pieces of that little half-breed?" Grayson asked.

"You do that and I'll start sending you pieces of Gatsby Culpepper," Ike said. Grayson had been slouching in his president's chair. Now he sat up ramrod straight.

"What the fuck are you talking about?" Grayson asked. Ike didn't respond. Instead Grayson heard someone moaning in the background. Not a fun, good-time, ball-juggling moan, either. This was an agonized sound.

"Gerald, is that you, son?" Gatsby said.

"What the fuck?" Grayson asked. Ike came back on the line.

"Now *I'm* gonna tell *you* how it's gonna go. You call Gerald and tell him we got his daddy. Then you call us back and we'll tell you where we gonna meet. We'll bring Old Man Culpepper and you bring Arianna."

"That's not the fucking deal, you—"

"You gonna need to start watching your mouth or I'm gonna pull one of Papa Gatsby's teeth out and make a ring out of it. Oh, and hear me when I tell you this, son: don't even think about riding back out to Red Hill. If I even hear a motorcycle on television, I might get nervous. I get nervous, I'll put two in Old Man Culpepper's head before you can say Smith and Wesson. I told you I don't sell no wolf tickets," Ike said.

The line went dead.

Grayson pulled the phone away from his face and stared at it. He wanted to toss it across the room. Stomp on it until he heard the satisfying crunch of plastic under his boot. He sat it on the table. It wasn't a phone anymore. It was the physical manifestation of this whole godforsaken shitstorm. The neat black rectangle was a window into the parallel universe he now inhabited. A place where two old ex-cons kept outflanking him at every turn.

Grayson got up and grabbed a toolbox off a shelf in the back of the garage. He rummaged around until he found a short stubby carpenter's pencil. He pulled a receipt out of his pocket from Hardee's. He went back to the table and jotted down Ike's number. He folded the receipt and put it back in his pocket. He grabbed the phone and walked outside. A few of his brothers were milling around in the yard. A few were leaning against their rides with some bunnies on their laps. Grayson put the phone on the ground. He took a step, pulled his .357 from the small of his back, and pumped all six bullets into the phone. He roared as he pulled the trigger until the gun went *click*.

Then he went back inside and called Gerald.

Ike poured some moonshine into his coffee.

He could hear Buddy Lee pestering Gatsby with questions. The old man's mouth was re-taped so he couldn't answer any of Buddy Lee's queries.

"You remember when Derek graduated from college and none of y'all showed up? He told me about that. I was in jail, so I had an excuse, but you? You was retired. I mean, I know he was your step-grandson, but damn, you couldn't skip a tee time to see him walk that aisle? I gotta tell you, Gatsby. That's pretty unchivalrous for a southern gentleman," Buddy Lee said. Gatsby mumbled. Ike figured it was a combination of all the curse words in his repertoire.

Ike's phone rang.

Ike touched the screen and held it up to his ear.

"Listen to me, you goddamn savage: my father has nothing to do with what's going on. You let him go, and I mean right goddamn now, and maybe, just maybe I won't have Grayson slit that mongrel's throat," Gerald said.

"I'm getting sick of telling you boys about your mouth," Ike said. He snapped his fingers. Buddy Lee grabbed Gatsby and pulled him into a sitting position. Ike came into the living room.

"Don't you worry about my mouth. Worry about that little girl," Gerald said.

"Hey, son? You hurt one hair on her head and I'll make sure your daddy dies screaming," Ike said.

"I want to talk to him," Gerald said.

"You get five seconds," Ike said. Buddy Lee ripped the tape off Gatsby's mouth. Ike held the phone to his face.

"Gerald!" Gatsby said. Ike pulled the phone back and Buddy Lee slapped the tape back over his mouth.

"He's alive. Arianna better be, too, or you're gonna have to bury your daddy in a coffee can," Ike said.

"You bring him and Tangerine to—" Gerald tried to say but Ike cut him off.

"No. No Tangerine. Just your daddy and Arianna. That's how it works. We'll call you back in one hour," Ike said. He hung up the phone.

"You pushing them hard. What if they hurt her?" Buddy Lee asked. Ike put his phone in his pocket.

"They won't. We got to his daddy. Right now, they know we willing to do anything. They hurt that girl, they don't know what we'll do next. Now we gotta find a place to meet them. And we gonna need guns. Lots of guns," Ike said. Buddy Lee sucked his teeth.

"I think we can kill both them birds with one stone. But we gotta go talk to some folks. What we gonna do with him?" Buddy Lee asked.

"We'll chain him to the sink in the bathroom," Ike said.

"You came up with that quick," Buddy Lee said.

"This ain't my first rodeo."

"I know, mine neither. You got a talent for it, though," Buddy Lee said.

"Unfortunately," Ike said.

"Turn here," Buddy Lee said. The rising sun bounced light off the metal sign attached to the chain-link fence. The sign said MORGAN'S MARINA in big bold black letters against a white background. Ike drove through the open gate and pulled up to a narrow building with board-on-batten siding. Beyond the building a long salt-treated dock extended into the Chesapeake Bay. On each side of the pier were about a dozen slips with boats and yachts of various sizes and levels of ostentatiousness. Ike put the car in park.

"Alright. Now it's your turn to stay in the car," Buddy Lee said.

"You gonna be alright in there by yourself?" Ike asked.

"He might be a gunrunner and crazy right-wing militia maniac, but he's still my half brother. I'll probably be alright," Buddy Lee said. He climbed out of the truck and headed for the office of the marina. A sleigh bell clanged as he entered the building. A couple of good ol' boys were paying for some bait at the counter. Chet rang them up, glanced at Buddy Lee, then handed them their change. The men nodded at Buddy Lee in an almost unconscious gesture of southern hospitality. When the men left, he and Chet were alone.

"You should know better than to bring somebody like that to my shop," Chet said. He gestured to the parking lot. Ike was standing next to the truck talking on his cell phone.

"Oh, I forgot you don't like Virgos," Buddy Lee said. Chet grunted.

"What you want, Buddy?" he asked. Chet was tall and rangy like Buddy Lee, but he had a thick mop of white hair and wisp of a beard to match. A LIVE FREE OR DIE tattoo undulated on his bicep as he flexed his arm. His gray T-shirt already had sweat patches under the arms. It was only 8:30.

"I need a favor," Buddy Lee said. Chet came from behind the counter. They were only a foot apart.

"I told you the last time you came out here I'm fresh out of favors for you. You know how much trouble you and Deak got me into? Chuly sent Skunk Mitchell up to talk to me about it. *The* Skunk Mitchell. They thought I was a snitch because you and Deak couldn't keep it under sixty. That deal cost me a shitload of money and many a sleepless night, but you want a favor," Chet said.

"It cost me five years. It would have killed Deak if he had gone inside. But since you brought it up, didn't the state drop them weapons charges against you after me and Deak got pinched? Huh, ain't that a coincidence?" Buddy Lee said. Chet glowered at him, but Buddy Lee hit him with his ten-kilowatt smile.

"Don't worry, I never mentioned that to anybody. I mean who would believe it, anyway? Wouldn't no man worth a damn drop a dime on his own brothers to save his own worthless hide, right? We're all blood. Might be rotten blood but it's blood all the same. But that's water under the bridge now, ain't it, hoss?" Buddy Lee said.

Chet pulled a container of Skoal out of his back pocket and put a chunk in his cheek.

"Ain't nothing I can do for you, Buddy," Chet said. Buddy Lee fingered a bright orange-and-red lure hanging from a carousel near the cash register. It became a poor man's kaleidoscope as it spun.

"You wanna be mad at me because Skunk made you shit your pants, that's fine. I can take that. You wanna be pissed I cost you a payday, I'll take that, too, although I have my suspicions about that.

What I can't take, what I can't abide is you turning your back on Derek. He was my son. He was your nephew. Some dirty no-count sons of bitches shot him down like a dog. Here I am circling in on the cowards that done it, and all I need is the keys to that place you got down in Mathews. All I need is a place to work, and you saying you can't do that for me? Then don't do it for me. Do it for Derek. Do it for him," Buddy Lee said. Chet walked back to the counter and pulled a Styrofoam cup from a shelf under the counter. He spit a huge dollop of dark liquid in it.

"Your son. The fa—" Chet didn't get to finish the epithet because in one smooth motion Buddy Lee jumped forward, opened his knife, closed the distance between them, and put the blade to his neck.

"No. Not that word. Not anymore. Not about my boy. I used it enough myself when he was alive. That word is dead for me now," Buddy Lee said.

"You put a knife to my throat, Buddy Lee, you better play the fiddle with that son of a bitch. Come into my house and put a knife to my throat and bring a spook with you? You ain't shit," Chet said. Buddy Lee saw his own eyes in his brother's. The corrosive rot of the rage they had both inherited from their father.

"You talk all that shit about being a patriot and a warrior, but when I came to you about finding the people who did Derek, you acted like I had asked you to rope the goddamn wind. He was your nephew but you couldn't be bothered. I tell you what, that *man* out there done rolled with me harder and deeper than you ever have. He's the brother I should have had. But you can fix that now. You can help make all this right. So you can either hand me them keys or I bleed you and take 'em. But I promise you one way or the other I'm leaving here with 'em." Chet bared his brown teeth like a rat. Buddy Lee pressed the knife deeper into the taut flesh of Chet's throat.

"We gonna settle up later, brother," Chet said. He shook a key chain with two keys attached to it. It had appeared in his hand as if by magic. Buddy Lee plucked the keys from his grip. He backed away from him while still pointing the knife at him. The handle of the door pressed into his Buddy Lee's back. He closed the knife and put in his back pocket.

"I'm gonna fuck you up, Buddy. You better watch your goddamn back," Chet said.

"Life beat you to it, brother, but you more than welcome to try and take your turn," Buddy Lee said.

Buddy Lee climbed in the truck. Ike got in and started the engine.

"You alright?" Ike asked. Buddy Lee shoved the keys in his pocket.

"I was thinking about how the good die young," Buddy Lee said.

"I guess that's why we're still here," Ike said as he put the truck in gear.

"Let's go check this place out. Get the lay of the land, so to speak. I've been there once but it was a long time ago. I wanna see the dance floor before we cut a rug."

ke turned right off Route 14 onto Route 198. He'd had a few jobs out in Mathews County over the years but not many. Most of the people out this way worked their own yards.

"Stay on this until we hit Tabernacle Road. Gonna take a left onto that," Buddy Lee said.

Tabernacle Road was the first hard-surface left turn after you drove through the town of Mathews. Past the grocery store and the post office and the library. Past a Civil War statue two steps from the courthouse building. Ike took that left and followed Tabernacle until Buddy Lee told him to turn right onto a long dusty logging road.

The road wound down through a dense canopy of pine trees until it came to a gravel road bisected by a horse gate. Ike stopped the truck and Buddy Lee hopped out with the keys. He unlocked the gate and Ike drove through it. Buddy Lee hopped back in the car and they continued down the gravel road. At the end it opened into a spacious meadow. To their left was a narrow barn-red rectangular steel building with one roll-up door in the center of the rectangle. There was a window to the right of the roll-up door. The building itself was nearly a hundred feet long. To their right were several tactical targets arranged on a shooting course. Most of the targets were paper silhouettes over plywood. A few of them were cartoonish images of Black and Hispanic men.

"Your brother is a real asshole," Ike said when he saw them.

"Yeah. I won't argue with you on that one," Buddy Lee said. Ike parked the truck. They got out and walked up to the main building.

Buddy Lee unlocked the door and Ike followed him inside. A bunkhouse table sat to the right of the door. A few chairs were scattered around the table. Bits of random bric-a-brac were dotted throughout the space. A couple of fishing rods. A stuffed deer's head lying on its side. A DON'T TREAD ON ME flag that must have fallen off the wall. To their left the cavernous structure was filled with twenty or so wooden crates, hard plastic totes, and a few gunny sacks.

Buddy Lee wandered over to the crates. He pulled the lid off one and whistled.

"Goddamn. You could stop a rhino hopped up on meth with this son of a bitch," Buddy Lee said. He pulled a fully automatic shotgun with a revolving cylinder out of the box.

"You got shells to go along with that?" Ike asked.

"He got more shells than a shark got teeth in this other box," Buddy Lee said as he pulled the lid off another crate.

"Those street sweepers ain't legal in the States," Ike said. Buddy Lee waved his hand over the crates and boxes.

"None of this is legal, Ike. Them militia boys he run with don't cotton to any laws except the Second Amendment."

"I know that. I'm just thinking about whether or not the ATF got your brother under surveillance. Gonna be some fireworks here tonight," Ike said.

"If the Feds were onto him, this place wouldn't be here. I don't think we need to worry about drawing no attention tonight, neither. We so far in the woods we'd have to go back five miles the other way to find the boondocks," Buddy Lee said.

"If you say so," Ike said.

Buddy Lee continued exploring the crates. The sheer depth and breadth of the amount of machine guns, rifles, pistols, and—God save us—land mines was mind-boggling.

We might need every bit of this, Buddy Lee thought. He opened a crate against the wall.

"Well, shit. Ike, come here," Buddy Lee said. Ike came over and stared in the crate.

"That's what I think it is?" Ike said.

"Yep. I suppose if you got loose lips like Chet you best be paranoid and have a backup plan," Buddy Lee said. Ike peered in the crate, then at the door of the bunkhouse, then back in the crate.

"You know it don't matter how many guns we got here, it's just two of us. Maybe we need our own backup plan," Ike said.

"What's going on in that big ol' cranium of yours?" Buddy Lee said.

"I'm thinking we gonna need more bang for our buck. Come on, let's get back to Red Hill. We need to go by the shop. I got an idea," Ike said.

"What, we gonna challenge them to a duel with shovels?" Buddy Lee asked.

"Not exactly," Ike said.

By the time they'd gone to the shop, gotten what they needed, then gone back to the compound and put it in place, then gone back to Buddy Lee's, it was a little after one. Buddy Lee could hear a solid thumping sound coming from his trailer.

"If I gave a damn about this trailer, I'd be upset, 'cause it sound like that ol' boy in there kicking like a mule," Buddy Lee said. Ike followed Buddy Lee into his house.

Buddy Lee went down the hall to his bathroom. He poked his head inside.

"If you don't stop kicking that wall, I'm gonna come in there and I'm gonna break your fucking legs," Buddy Lee said. His statement caught Gatsby in mid-kick. The older man put his foot down flat on the floor.

"That's better," Buddy Lee said. He went back to the living room. Ike was on the sofa, so he melted into his easy chair.

"We got some time. You wanna go check on Mya?" Buddy Lee asked.

"I called the hospital while you was talking to your brother. No change," Ike said. Buddy Lee took a deep breath.

"She gonna be alright, Ike."

"I don't know if any of us are ever gonna be alright ever again," Ike said. He pulled out his phone and sent a text message to Gerald:

> 3493 Tabernacle Road.
> Mathews Va.
> 8pm

He put the phone away.

"All I know is, no matter what happens tonight, we putting them boys in the ground. All of them," Ike said.

"Ike," Buddy Lee said.

"Yeah?"

"I wish we had met at the wedding. I wish both of us had been there."

"My grandmother used to say if wishes were horses, beggars would ride. But I hear what you saying. I wish we had, too," Ike said.

"Well, I'm gonna get some sleep. We had a long day. I'd say we committed at least fifteen felonies," Buddy Lee said.

A few minutes later Ike heard him snoring. Ike laid his head back on the sofa but he didn't close his eyes. He knew if he slept, Isiah would be waiting for him in his dreams.

Or his nightmares.

FORTY-THREE

Margo was just about to sit down and settle in for the *Jeopardy!* Tournament of Champions when someone started banging on her door.

"God bless it," she murmured as she went to the door. When she opened it Buddy Lee was standing on her front step.

"Jesus, you look worse than the last time I saw you. Are you getting any sleep at all?" Margo asked.

"Anyone ever tell you that you have a way with words?" Buddy Lee said.

"It's a gift. What's up? You get a new truck? About time, if you ask me," Margo said. Buddy Lee moved stray strands of hair out of his face. For an instant Margo thought she saw a glimpse of the bright-eyed handsome country boy he used to be once upon a time.

"No, that's my partner's truck. Hey, I wanted to tell you, you're a good neighbor. You check on me and make sure I'm not turning into a pickle inside a bottle of Jameson. I think you're probably the only person on earth who cares about what happens to me," Buddy Lee said.

"Well, that's nice of you, but why you talking like you about to lead the Charge of the Light Brigade?" Margo asked. Buddy Lee put his foot on her top step and leaned forward.

"I ain't never had very many female friends. I've known a lot of women, but I can't say many of them was what you'd call friends.

I think you're my first, Margo." He stopped. She watched him set his jaw before he continued.

"You're a good woman and a good friend. Take care of yourself," Buddy Lee said.

"Buddy Lee, what's going on?" Margo asked. He flashed a crooked grin.

"Giving you your flowers while you're still alive, sugar," he said. He stepped back and gave her a two-finger salute. She watched him lope over to his partner's truck and climb in the passenger's side. A cloud of dust followed them as they tore out of the trailer park.

"Come on, Gatsby. Last stop, everybody off," Buddy Lee said. He helped Ike drag the old man out of the truck bed and into the bunkhouse. They tied him to a metal folding chair with another pair of zip ties. The chair was sitting next to a fifty-five-gallon metal drum. At the base of the drum was a box with some wires and a flat circular wheel inside.

"Alright, I'm gonna move the truck. Keep an eye on him," Ike said.

"I'll try not to kill him," Buddy Lee said. Gatsby's eyes went wide.

"Oh, calm down, I'm just fucking with you." He turned back to Ike. "Remember, if you go past the other entrance, go down to the post office and turn around. Be quick. There's not supposed to be another road back here. Chet used to complain about the county charging him more taxes the more egress points he had or something. We don't want to draw no attention," Buddy Lee said.

"Long as that other gate ain't locked, we should be okay," Ike said.

Ike moved the truck to the head of the other road, then made his way back to the compound through a footpath that took him pass a corrugated metal outhouse. The past few nights had been cool, as the last vestiges of winter refused to cede their kingdom to the spring. Tonight, the air was unseasonably sultry. By the time he made it back to the bunkhouse he was coated in a thin sheen of sweat.

Buddy Lee was sitting on the bench that ran along the back wall of the structure. He was holding an AR-15 with an extended mag. Ike grabbed an automatic shotgun out of the crate and loaded it with high-velocity shells. He sat down at the table that was situated near the center of the building. He checked his watch. It was 7:30 P.M.

"You think there's anything after this? After we die, I mean?" Buddy Lee asked.

"You worrying about your soul, Buddy Lee?" Ike said. He was cradling the shotgun like a newborn.

Buddy Lee cleared his throat.

"I mean, if there is, I'm pretty sure where I'm headed. I've made peace with that, I reckon. I just wonder, I mean, do you think we'll see the boys? Like, if we don't make it out of this, you think we'll pass them on our way down south?" Buddy Lee said. Ike peered out the window. The sun had set but a half-moon had clocked in for the night shift.

"I hope not," Ike said.

"You hope not? Man, the only thing that keeps me holding on to any of that shit my pastor used to scream about while he was juggling them old copperheads they kept in the back of the church is the notion I might see my boy again. Get a chance to tell him all the things I should have before they took him from me," Buddy Lee said.

"The only thing I'd want to say to Isiah is that I'm sorry. And I couldn't say it enough even if I had forever to say it. I couldn't say it enough," Ike said. His voice trailed off to a whisper.

In the distance they both heard the roar and thunder of motorcycle engines. Wordlessly they both got up from their seats. Buddy Lee cut the zip ties that secured Gatsby to the folding chair. He also cut the ones around his ankles.

"Get up," Ike said. He grabbed Gatsby by the arm and walked to the roll-up door.

Ike pushed a button on the wall next to the door and it began to rise. He gripped his shotgun tight and stood shoulder to shoulder with Gatsby. Buddy Lee did the same on the other side. He checked his watch. It was 7:45.

"They tried to get the jump on us," Buddy Lee said.

"It's like that story. The wolf gets to the turnip patch at six in the morning. The rabbit been there and gone," Ike said.

"We the rabbits, in that story, right?" Buddy Lee said.

"Yeah, but we gonna eat them like we're the wolves," Ike said.

A phalanx of motorcycles poured into the meadow. They pulled in front of the tactical course and faced the building. Ike counted twenty-five by the time the Cadillac SRX pulled in behind them. The blond Viking was riding a chopped hog with ape hangers and a high sissy bar in the back. There was a green sack covering the sissy bar. The blond biker popped his kickstand and got off his bike. The green sack was attached to his saddle bags with bungee cords. He released the cords and removed the green sack. Arianna was in a car seat that was strapped to the sissy by about five miles of rope.

Ike almost shot him right then and there.

The air shimmered with the heat from the collected engines revving and growling. Gerald climbed out of the Cadillac. He was wearing a white button-down shirt open at the throat and loose-fitting khakis. He strode over to stand in front of the Viking. Gerald put his hands on his hips and jutted out his chin. Buddy Lee gripped his rifle. He knew when a prick was preening. He was trying to use some bullshit psychological manipulation. Maybe he thought if he didn't act like he was scared shitless it would make it so.

"You okay, Pop?" Gerald yelled. Gatsby shook his head.

"What have you done to him?" Gerald said.

"He's fine. He got to see how the other half lives, is all. Other than that, he's alright. Now cut the girl loose," Buddy Lee said. Sweat was working its way across his brow like a lazy caterpillar. The night had enveloped them all.

"You know the story of Alexander the Great and the island of Tyre?" Gerald said.

"You giving a fucking history lesson . . . now?" Buddy Lee asked. Gerald smiled.

Ike said, "Tyre was supposed to be impenetrable, but Alexander took it after six months. The point was that he had more determination than any other general. Now, can we get on with it?"

Gerald stopped smiling.

"You ain't the only one who can read a fucking book, Winthrop," Ike said.

"Send my father over," Gerald said.

"Cut the girl loose and send her over," Buddy Lee said.

"Grayson," Gerald said. Grayson unbuckled Arianna from her car seat. He lowered her to the ground. The wind came up and tossed her curls around her head.

"Hey, Little Bit!" Buddy Lee said.

"Come on over, booboo," Ike said. Arianna took a step toward them. Grayson's hand shot out and wrapped around her wrist. Arianna squealed. The sound set Buddy Lee's teeth on edge.

"Let. Her. Go," Ike said.

"Grayson, I have this under control," Gerald said.

"Bullshit. You ain't got nothing under control. These bastards have your daddy, and you just letting them get their little mongrel back? Fuck that. Same time, shitkicker."

"Same time. We send them at the same time," Buddy Lee said. He nudged Gatsby. The old man took a few tentative steps. Grayson released Arianna's arm.

"Run," Grayson said.

Arianna held her left hand against her ear. She took a few steps, then stopped.

"Come on, Little Bit. Come on over," Buddy Lee said. Arianna began to cry.

"Oh no, Little Bit, don't cry. Just come on, baby girl," Buddy Lee said. Gatsby was halfway across the yard.

"Arianna. Come on, baby girl. Come to . . . come to Grand-daddy," Ike said. Arianna took a halting step.

"That's right, baby, come on to Granddaddy," Ike said. Arianna took off running. Her chubby legs pistoning up and down in short choppy bursts of movement. She ran past Gatsby as he stumbled toward Gerald.

"Come on, Pop, let's get you out of here," Gerald said. He held out his arms for his father.

The rest of the club had dismounted their bikes. Guns appeared in their hands like a quick-cut editing technique. Ike got down on one knee and held out his arms to Arianna while balancing his shotgun against his shoulder.

"Yeah, sugar, that's it. Come on to Granddaddy," Ike said.

Grayson moved to his right. He pulled his .357 from his waist-band. He wanted to get up close and personal with these fuckers.

Arianna leapt into Ike's waiting embrace. He gripped her tight with one arm and grabbed the shotgun with the other before fall-ing back into the bunkhouse.

Gerald smiled at his father. The old man pulled the duct tape away from his mouth with a determined snap of his wrists.

"Gerald, what the hell have you gotten yourself mixed up in this time?" Gatsby roared.

Gunfire erupted as Buddy Lee dropped the roll-up door. Bul-lets exploded through the metal siding and ripped dime-sized holes through the roll-up door. Buddy Lee went to one of the windows and began returning fire with the AR-15. He strafed the entire meadow from left to right. The bikers scattered like roaches. A few hid behind the backstops of the tactical targets. A few more flipped one of the picnic tables and used that as cover as they returned fire. The majority of them retreated into the brush that surrounded the meadow and began returning fire from the shadows.

Ike opened the crate near the back wall of the bunkhouse and lowered Arianna into it. A burning sensation erupted in his left bicep like he'd been touched by a hot poker. Ike flopped to the floor and crawled over to the window opposite Buddy Lee.

The automatic shotgun bucked hard as he unloaded on the darkness. The rear parking lights of the SRX cast a red glow across the meadow as the car began to lurch forward. Ike saw a group of bikers trying to make a run for the far side of the compound. They danced and jumped like religious zealots in the throes of ecstasy as the slugs from the shotgun ripped into them.

No, you don't, you motherfucker. You don't get to leave the party early, darling, Buddy Lee thought. He emptied a fusillade of bullets into the SRX. The SRX's fiberglass body was no match for the AR-15's power. Each bullet punched quarter-sized holes in the vehicle from the engine to the hatchback. The car careened off the side of the road and down a slight embankment until it crashed into the wide trunk of an oak tree.

Buddy Lee popped out his empty clip and slammed another one home. Ike likewise had to reload. The bikers took this opportunity to advance on the bunkhouse. They peppered the steel building with an endless tempest of gunfire as they pushed forward.

Ike wiped his eyes and his hand came away mottled in red. Chunks of concrete and slivers of metal sheeting were raining down on them. Ike and Buddy Lee may have had the more powerful weapons, but the Rare Breed had the numbers. Buddy Lee dropped to the floor, held his rifle aloft, and fired blindly through the nearest window. Ike fired one last barrage before tossing the automatic shotgun aside. He knew he had taken out a few of the Breed but not enough. Not nearly enough.

He crawled across the floor on his belly until he reached the fifty-five-gallon drum. As Buddy Lee continued to shoot blindly, Ike set the "timer." The timer was in actuality a cannibalized CD player and a simple circuit attached to an old ignition switch. The ignition switch was taped to the underside of the lid of the drum.

Ike had come up with the idea as soon as he'd seen what was in that special crate near the back wall. It was their way out. It was what was going to allow them to pay the debt they owed their boys. A debt that was about to be paid in blood.

Ike had known they needed something powerful on their side against Gerald and his boys. Something that would level the playing field. Something made with the ammonium nitrate–rich fertilizer Ike had in dozens of bags back at his warehouse. A landscaper might not have guns, but he had a lot more than shovels. Neither one of them had much experience, but Google had helped them once again.

The huge drum was nearly full of fertilizer and gasoline. When the timer went off it would send a charge through the circuit to the ignition switch. The ignition wires had been peeled back just enough to make room for a spark. A simple but deadly effective bomb.

"Let's go!" Ike said. He disappeared inside the crate near the back wall. Buddy Lee let off one last salvo, then made a dash for the crate. He shimmied down the aluminum ladder and followed Ike, with Arianna in his arms, into the tunnel that ran under the bunkhouse.

Grayson emptied his .357 into the building, dropped the empty shells, then reloaded. He only had two more speedloaders left. That was twelve shots. Dome hit the building with a blast from his MAC-11. Grayson heard a few more shots from his brothers. He peered from around the backstop at the building. It resembled a block of Swiss cheese. Inside, a fluorescent light fixture hung from the ceiling by a thin wire. It swung lazily back and forth creating a strobe-light effect through the window. Grayson fired three more shots at the window.

There was no return fire.

"Goddamn it, I think we got their asses!" Grayson thought. He stood up straight.

Nothing. Not a peep from the outbuilding.

"We got 'em. WE GOT 'EM!" Grayson roared. He smacked Dome on the back.

"Go drag 'em out. We gonna make an example of these fuckers," Grayson said. Dome stood up but hesitated a moment. He really didn't want to see that little girl's dead body.

"Don't make me have to tell you again," Grayson said. Dome forced his legs to move. The rest of the members of the club that weren't dead or injured followed him as he stalked toward the building.

Dome kicked open the front door that was to the left of the roll-up door.

When the orange flash filled his entire field of vision, one word appeared in his mind seconds before he was vaporized.

Karma, Dome thought.

Then everything went black.

Ike almost cried out for joy when his hands found the cool metal rungs of the ladder that sat at the bottom of the faux privy. He pulled himself and Arianna up one rung at a time until they emerged inside the outhouse. Ike pushed the door open and took great deep breaths as he and Arianna stepped out into the sweltering night. Buddy Lee followed them covered in soot and coughing up a lung. Arianna was sobbing uncontrollably.

"It's okay, baby girl. We gotcha," Ike murmured as he held her tight.

"Jesus H. Christ, you'd think Chet would have put a better ventilation system in that tunnel. It's got everything else but an easy chair down there," Buddy Lee said.

"I'm gonna take her to the truck. She's scared," Ike said.

"I'm gonna stay here and see if I can catch me a breath. When you get back we'll go on down there and see about our friends," Buddy Lee said. He started coughing again.

"Be right back," Ike said.

"I'll be here," Buddy Lee said as Ike and Arianna made their way up the path.

Ike strapped Arianna in the passenger's seat. He pulled up a game on his cell phone that involved flying pieces of fruit and put the phone in Arianna's lap.

"Grandpop gotta go check on something, okay?" he said. Arianna ignored him as she moved her tiny fingers across the phone's screen.

Ike and Buddy Lee walked back along the path to the compound in silence. Ike could smell the results of their handiwork on the breeze. A witch's brew of immolated flesh and a harsh chemical scent halfway between chlorine and alcohol.

"Fucking hell," Buddy Lee said when they reached the compound. More accurately, when they reached the place where the compound had once stood. A flickering ring of flames one hundred feet in diameter encircled the former militia headquarters. The steel outbuilding was gone. The concrete footing that it had sat upon was cracked in the middle and scorched from end to end. The tactical shooting range had been obliterated. Piles of burning hay from the target backstops littered the ground in all directions.

The motorcycles that had been parked in diagonal lines with military precision were formless clumps of metal more akin to amoebas than machines. Here and there were recognizable parts. A handlebar, a foot peg, a front wheel, but for the most part the bikes had been reduced to twisted amalgamations of leather, steel, iron, and chrome. Their owners had suffered a similar fate.

Ike carried Gatsby's pistol. Buddy Lee had his knife and the AR-15 slung over his chest on a strap. They moved through the bodies ready to finish what they had started, but Ike soon came to realize that wouldn't be necessary. The Breed was done. The ones who hadn't been torn asunder by the initial explosion had found their insides liquefied by the subsequent shock wave.

Bodies and body parts were strewn across the clearing like party streamers. Buddy Lee glanced up at a pine tree near the tactical course. There were two arms in the tree. They were both left-handed. Buddy Lee shook his head.

"I think this chapter of the Rare Breed done got closed down permanently," Buddy Lee said.

Ike was about to respond when they heard a pitiful whimpering coming from the direction of the SRX. Ike and Buddy Lee looked at each other, then walked over to the vehicle. All the windows had been shattered from the force of the blast. Ike peered inside the car.

Gatsby was lying over on his side. Blood was dripping from his ear. His lower torso and lap were soaked in red. Ike could smell the pungent odor of shit wafting up from the inside of the car. Ike reached his hand inside the window and put his fingers to the older man's neck. There was no pulse.

Buddy Lee opened the driver's side door.

Gerald Winthrop Culpepper fell to the ground like a sack of wet laundry. He was moaning and whimpering from a place deep in his broad chest. His khakis were so soaked in blood they appeared burgundy. Gerald pulled himself along the ground through the detritus that covered the forest floor. Buddy Lee pushed aside a clutch of brambles as he followed behind Gerald. Ike came up alongside them. Buddy Lee put his foot in the middle of the Gerald's back and stopped his forward progress.

"Where you going, hoss?" Buddy Lee asked conversationally. Ike came around the back of the car. He had the .44 down by his side. Buddy Lee grabbed Gerald by his shoulders and flipped him over.

"Please don't," Gerald rasped.

"Don't what?" Ike said.

"Please don't kill me. I'm sorry. I'm so sorry," Gerald said. His broad face was slick with sweat. All around them the gentle crackling of the flames filled the night, drowning out the natural sounds of the forest.

"Everybody sorry when they get caught," Buddy Lee said.

"Please, I'm sick. I'm a sick man," Gerald said.

"Oh, you sick? Why, because you liked being with Tangerine?" Ike asked.

"Yes! I need help!" Gerald gasped. Ike leaned forward and stared in the man's bloodshot eyes.

"You think my son was sick? Or his son? Or Tangerine? You think they deserve to die because you can't deal with who you are?" Ike asked. Gerald said nothing. Ike straightened himself.

"The funny thing is, if my boy was here, he'd feel sorry for you. If his son was here he'd probably forgive you," Ike said. Buddy Lee opened his knife. It clicked as he locked the blade in place.

"But they ain't here, are they?" Buddy Lee asked.

"No, they ain't," Ike said.

Ike and Buddy Lee threaded their way through the woods as they took the path back to the truck. They didn't speak because there wasn't anything left to say. Ike felt like he could sleep for a hundred years. His mind and body both felt as if they had been wrung dry. For the first time in a long time Buddy Lee didn't want a drink. He didn't want anything to dull this moment. Not one damn thing.

They came up on to the private road where the truck was parked.

The passenger door was wide open.

"Arianna?" Ike said.

"Little Bit!" Buddy Lee said. His heart hammered against his ribs. What if they'd done all this and then Arianna got lost in the fucking woods?

"She right here," a gravelly voice said.

Grayson was standing in front of the truck. He had Arianna cradled in his left arm. His right hand was holding the .357. The barrel was pressed against her temple.

"Drop the guns," Grayson said. His face was slathered in blood and dirt. Saliva spilled from his mouth in long silvery strands. The light from the half-moon made him look like the ghost of a true Viking—a phantom covered in face paint who'd escaped from Valhalla intent on spreading terror across the land of the living.

"Let her go," Ike said.

"Fuck you. Drop the guns and toss me the keys."

"The keys? Hoss, you don't look like you could drive a fucking nail," Buddy Lee said.

"I'm so fucking sick of you. Of both of you. Drop the guns. Toss the keys. Now. Or I'm gonna blow this little bitch's head off," Grayson said. His breath was coming in sharp bursts that made him grimace.

Nothing was said for a few painfully long moments.

"Ike, do what he says. It's what my daddy would do." Buddy Lee said. Ike stared at him.

Buddy Lee nodded.

"Yeah, boy, do what I say," Grayson said.

Ike dropped the gun. Buddy Lee slipped off the rifle and laid it on the ground. Ike made a big show of digging around in his pockets for the keys. While Grayson focused on Ike, Buddy Lee slipped his knife out of his back pocket and palmed it as he stood up. As Ike rummaged around in his pocket Buddy Lee quietly opened the blade with his thumb.

"Okay, here's the keys," Ike said holding them up in front of his face.

"Toss them at my feet. Be careful. I'm feeling woozy. You don't want me to slip and pull this trigger by accident," Grayson said.

Ike tossed the keys. They landed just a few inches shy of Grayson's boots. Grayson went down to one knee. He pawed at the ground with his left hand while keeping Arianna in the crook of his elbow. He gripped the keys and straightened himself. He took the gun from Arianna's head and pointed it at Buddy Lee.

"I wish this was the piece I did your boys with," Grayson said.

"Let her go!" Ike roared. Grayson's eyes flicked toward him.

Buddy Lee launched the knife at Grayson with a vicious underhanded throw. The blade impaled itself in his neck with a wet sucking sound. Grayson pulled the trigger of his gun in a wild, rapid succession of shots. Arianna tumbled from his arms. Ike surged forward, dropped to his knees, and caught Arianna and pulled her to his chest. He rolled to his side and kept his body between her and the gunfire.

Grayson staggered around in drunken concentric circles. The .357 slipped from his hand. Blood as slick and whispery as mercury poured from the wound in his neck. In his desperation and fear he pulled the knife free. This just hastened his demise, as the blood now poured forth like a geyser. He pitched forward and landed facefirst in the dirt even as blood still bubbled from his neck.

Ike got up with Arianna in his arms. She wasn't crying. She wasn't making any sound at all. Ike thought that was almost worse than her cries. There was no need to check on the biker to make sure he was dead. The blood trail that followed him was all the proof Ike needed.

Instead he went to Buddy Lee. He was sitting on the ground leaning his head against the truck. He had his hands pressed against his abdomen. Ike placed Arianna on the hood. He went down to his knees and put his arm around Buddy Lee's thin shoulders.

"Get up. We gotta get you to a hospital," Ike said.

"I . . . don't . . . think . . . that's . . . gonna . . . cut . . . it . . . , hoss," Buddy Lee said. He moved his hands. His gray shirt was so wet with blood it looked black in the moonlight.

"Shut up and let's go," Ike said. He started to rise and Buddy Lee grabbed his arm. His palm was cold and clammy. His hand was covered in his own blood.

"I . . . ain't . . . gonna . . . make . . . to . . . the . . . victory . . . party," Buddy Lee said.

Ike went back down to one knee. Buddy Lee's breathing was becoming shallower and shallower.

"Stay . . . with . . . me," Buddy Lee said. Ike shifted his weight until he was sitting next to Buddy Lee. He put his arm around the man and felt the brittleness just under his skin. It was like hugging a baby bird.

"It's cancer, ain't it? All the coughing and shit," Ike said. Buddy Lee nodded, his head moving at a snail's pace.

"You . . . think . . . I'll . . . see . . . the . . . boys?" Buddy Lee asked. Ike had to strain to hear him. He bit his bottom lip so hard it nearly bled.

"I hope so," Ike said.

"Me too," Buddy Lee said.

Then he slumped against Ike's chest. His head lolled to the side and he was still. Ike wrapped his arm around him and pulled him close. He sat that way until Arianna spoke.

"Him tired?" she asked. Ike wiped his face. He carefully lay Buddy Lee on his side.

"Yeah, but he gonna rest now," Ike said.

FORTY-FOUR

"Ike, somebody wants to talk to you."

Ike looked up from his invoices.

"Alright, Tangy. Give me a minute," he said. He got up from his desk and walked out front. The crew was already out for the day. Right now it was just him and Tangy at the office. She'd been on for two weeks and was catching on quick as a hiccup. Jazzy stopped by every now and then to check up on them, but Tangy was doing just fine.

"As soon as I get on my feet I'm gone," Tangy had said. Ike had told her he didn't blame her but he still hoped she would change her mind.

Det. LaPlata was waiting for him in the lobby.

"Detective LaPlata," Ike said.

"Mr. Randolph, do you have a moment to talk?"

"Sure," Ike said. He reached under the counter and grabbed a bottle of water from the cooler he stored there.

"The funeral for Mr. Jenkins was nice," Det. LaPlata said.

"Yeah," Ike said.

"I was glad to see your wife and your granddaughter there. Mrs. Culpepper, too. She took it pretty hard, didn't she? I don't think my ex-wife would cry that hard over me," LaPlata said.

Ike didn't say a word.

"It's incredible. No one knows who burned down your house,

kidnapped your granddaughter, and tried to kill your wife and Mr. Jenkins, but apparently they had a change of heart and dropped Arianna off at your office. Simply amazing," LaPlata said. Ike sipped his water.

"Miracles happen every day," Ike said.

"Mr. Randolph, can we cut the shit? We both know it was the Rare Breed that kidnapped your granddaughter and tried to kill your wife and Buddy Lee and burned your house down. We both know you and Buddy Lee went on the warpath all across the state culminating in a scene out of the goddamn *Wild Bunch* at a compound owned by a dummy corporation with ties to the Sons of Freedom, who just happen to have ties to the late Mr. Jenkins's brother. A murder scene where a whole bunch of bikers and a former state senator and a sitting judge were found dead," LaPlata said. Ike put his water bottle on the counter.

"I did see something on the news about that. They were saying that judge had a relationship with them bikers? I think they were saying the bikers had been bribing him for a while? Channel Twelve was saying my son and his husband's name was coming up in the investigation. You think this judge had something to do with what happen to my son? To Buddy Lee's son?" Ike asked. LaPlata gave him a long hard look.

"Well, it doesn't really matter now does it, Mr. Randolph? You can't prosecute a dead man," LaPlata said.

"Guess not," Ike said. LaPlata moved up to the counter and leaned on it with both hands.

"You don't really think anybody believes Buddy Lee Jenkins killed all those bikers and the Culpeppers by himself, do you? That he just happened to figure out how to construct a fertilizer bomb with a ninth-grade education?" LaPlata asked. Ike crossed his arms, careful not to touch the wound on his left arm.

"Why are you here, Mr. LaPlata?" Ike asked.

"Detective LaPlata, Mr. Randolph. And I'm here because there's an awful lot of people missing or dead around you. A lot of them deserved it but some of them didn't. I don't think there are very many people who are gonna shed a tear because Slice Walsh hasn't been seen in weeks. And even the members of his club thought Grayson Camardie was a piece of shit. But I also don't think Lunette Fredrickson deserved to have her guts sprayed all across her living room floor. Frankly, there are so many jurisdictions involved, it'll never get settled. I couldn't even get authorization to pull your cell phone records. Most everybody who counts is content to lay it all on Buddy Lee and make this whole thing go away," LaPlata said.

"But not you," Ike said.

"No, not me. Too many questions are still floating around unanswered. No, I can't let it go, because men like you are dangerous, Mr. Randolph. Today it was avenging your son. Tomorrow it'll be some guy who flips you the bird. I'm here because I want you to know I'll be watching you," LaPlata said. Ike finished his water and tossed the bottle in the trash.

"You can watch all you want. But next time you come by my place of business you should probably bring a warrant, or I might start thinking you're harassing me," Ike said. LaPlata gave him the cop's eyes, but Ike wouldn't drop his gaze.

"I haven't started to harass you yet, Mr. Randolph," LaPlata said.

The chime on the door rang.

"Detective LaPlata," Mya said. She was holding a huge bag of food from Sander's. They'd cut her braids during surgery so she was rocking a pixie cut. Arianna came bounding through the door. She darted past LaPlata and headed straight for Ike. She tugged on his pants leg as he ruffled her hair.

"Hello, Mrs. Randolph," LaPlata said.

"Let me walk you out, Detective," Ike said. LaPlata nodded to Mya. Arianna waved goodbye to him. LaPlata waved back before he turned and headed for the exit. Ike followed him.

"There's my Little Bit!" Tangerine said. LaPlata heard Arianna giggle.

LaPlata stepped through the door but then he stopped and faced Ike.

"Was it worth it, Riot?" he asked. Ike smiled.

"That's not my name. And as far as it being worth it, you'd have to ask Buddy Lee that. But I think if he was still here he'd say . . ." Ike lowered his voice:

"'I could kill them all a thousand times and it wouldn't even come close to being enough. But it would always be worth it,'" Ike said, but it was Riot who bored his way into LaPlata's soul with his flat dead eyes.

LaPlata took a step backward.

"Goodbye, Detective," Ike said.

He closed the door.

ke parked his truck and grabbed the brown paper bag sitting in the passenger seat. He got out and began threading his way through the headstones that filled the cemetery like it was a forest of granite.

He came over a slight hill and saw Margo on her hands and knees at Buddy Lee's grave. She was planting red, white, and blue petunias.

"Hey," Ike said. Margo looked up and gave him a half smile.

"Don't criticize my work, Mr. Landscaping Man," Margo said. She stood and wiped her hands on her jeans. Humming, she gathered the empty plastic tray that had held the petunias. She put a small plastic trowel in her back pocket.

"I ain't got nothing to say. Looks good to me," Ike said.

"I figure he could do with some sprucing up. God knows he never did anything with that damn trailer," Margo said.

"I think he'd like it."

"Ha! He'd make some smart-ass comment about the colors. Call me Captain America or some other foolishness," Margo said.

"Yeah, he probably would," Ike said. Margo wiped her eyes with the back of her hands.

"Lord have mercy. He could be an aggravating cuss, but I sure do miss his ass," Margo said. Ike took a breath, sucked his teeth, then spoke.

"Yeah. Me too."

"Well, I'll let y'all have some privacy," Margo said.

"You don't have to go," Ike said.

"Yeah, I do. I'll be bawling like a baby in a minute, and I think neither one of us wanna see that. Look, I know you can't say it, but I gotta ask. He went out fighting, didn't he?" Margo said. Ike gave her a long unblinking look. She studied his eyes, saw the answer to her question, and nodded her head.

"Okay. Okay," she said. She turned and hurried down the hill. Ike stared after her for few moments before he faced the grave. The black granite headstone said BUDDY LEE instead of William. When the state medical examiner had released his body Buddy Lee's sister had reached out to Ike about paying for the funeral. He'd said he would but with two conditions. They had to bury him next to the boys, and the headstone had to say Buddy Lee.

She'd gladly accepted his conditions since it meant she didn't have to pay for anything.

Ike pulled a can of beer and small bottle of liquor out of the paper bag. He opened the beer and took a long sip. It was crisp and cold as the first morning of winter. He poured the remainder of the can on the grave. He made sure he didn't get any on the petunias.

"Hey, man. I think I'm gonna invite Margo to Arianna's birthday party next week. She could probably use the company. Hell, we all could. Tangerine says she is gonna come up with a special hairdo for Mya and Arianna for the party. Them three done got thick as thieves. Insurance man says they gonna start on the house next week. We still staying in that hotel. It's pretty fancy. Like you would say, 'it's like shitting in high cotton.'" Ike blinked his eyes.

"Arianna is smart as a damn whip. Tangy got her counting to fifteen. Mya's got her studying flash cards with animals on them. She can even tell a dog from a wolf. I've been trying to show her how to fight, but Mya keeps saying she's only three. We play this game where she punches the palms of my hands. She loves it. In a couple years we'll move up to mitts. Might even get another heavy bag one day."

Ike felt a lump rise in his throat but he forced it down.

"She's growing like a weed, man. Anyway, I'm gonna talk to the boys for a minute, okay? I know you ain't really a fan of Hennessy," Ike said.

He sat the empty beer can on Buddy Lee's headstone. He unscrewed the cap on the bottle and took a long swig. It burned going down but settled in his stomach with comfortable warmness that made his upper body tingle. He poured a little bit of the cognac on Isiah's and Derek's graves.

"I love you, Isiah. I know it didn't always seem like that. I know I didn't always act like it, but I love you so goddamn much. We tell Arianna about you and Derek all the time. We show her the pictures that made it through the fire. We tell her how she's loved by so many people. Me, her grandmothers. Her Aunt Tangerine. Her two guardian angels." Ike got down on one knee and took another sip of the cognac.

"She won't ever have to wonder if the people who are supposed to love her no matter what actually do. I promise you that. She won't ever have to go through what you went through. What I put you through," Ike said.

He touched the new headstone. Ran his fingers over the engraving of Isiah's name, then Derek's.

"You know how you used to say love was love? I didn't get it. I didn't want to get it, I guess. But I understand now. And I'm so goddamn sorry it took all of this, but I really do get it now. A good father, a good man, loves the people that love his children. I wasn't a good father. I'm not a good man. But I'm gonna try to be a good grandfather," Ike said. He rose to his feet.

"I'm gonna try real hard," Ike said.

The tears came again. They poured from his eyes and ran over his cheeks. Flowed down to the stubble on his chin.

This time they didn't feel so much like razorblades. They felt like the long-awaited answer to a mournful prayer for rain.

ACKNOWLEDGMENTS

A novel is always a collaborative effort. The words are mine but the polishing and molding of the story bears the fingerprints of many hands.

I'd like to thank Josh Getzler, my agent and the biggest champion of my writing. Thank you for believing in me and my stories. Fate threw us together and I couldn't be happier about it.

Thank you to Christine Kopprasch and the entire team at Flatiron Books. I continue to learn from you even as I attempt to teach you as many Southern colloquialisms as possible.

I'd like to thank my friends and fellow writers Nikki Dolson, P. J. Vernon, Chad Williamson, and Jerry Bloomfield for reading early versions of this book. Your candor and support meant more than I could ever say.

And as always, thank you, Kim.

You know why.

You've always known.

ABOUT THE AUTHOR

S. A. Cosby is an Anthony Award–winning writer from southeastern Virginia. He is also the bestselling author of *Blacktop Wasteland,* a *New York Times* Notable Book, which won an L.A. Times Book Prize and was named as a Best Book of the Year by NPR, the *South Florida SunSentinel,* and *The Guardian*, among others.